THE
GODD
CHIP

BOOK 1

THE UNITY OF FOUR

K. PATRICK DONOGHUE

Published by Leaping Leopard Enterprises, LLC

This book is a work of fiction. All the characters, incidents and dialogue are drawn from the author's imagination or are used fictitiously. Any resemblance to actual locations, events or persons, living or dead, is entirely coincidental.

Published by Leaping Leopard Enterprises, LLC
www.leapingleopard.com

First edition: August 2020

Cover art and design by Asha Hossain Design, LLC and K. Patrick Donoghue

DEDICATION

To my darling wife Bryson,
for your continued love, support and encouragement

CONTENTS

(Contents listing continues onto the next page)

CONTENTS

(Contents listing continued from previous page)

ACKNOWLEDGMENTS

received a great deal of support in crafting *The GODD Chip* and I would like to acknowledge the special people who helped me.

To developmental editor Dustin Portia, thank you for your challenges and suggestions. Your feedback improved the quality of the story.

To my copyeditors, Annie Jenkinson and Roxana Coumans, thank you for your thorough and timely scrubbing of the draft manuscript. Your attention to detail was much appreciated.

To the cadre of readers who reviewed the prerelease draft of *The GODD Chip*, including Lisa Weinberg, Paulette Jones, Terry Grindstaff and Giles Ziolkowski, thank you for your comments, suggestions and edits. They helped me apply a final layer of polish on the story.

To my cover designer Asha Hossain, thank you for turning my original design concept into an eye-catching cover.

And to cap off the acknowledgments, I would like to thank my web designers, James Lee and Kevin Maines, for continually improving my author website as I add more titles.

NOTES TO READERS

Greetings, friends, fans and new readers! Thank you in advance for choosing to read *The GODD Chip*, book 1 in my new medical thriller series, the Unity of Four.

As you prepare begin reading, I would like to draw your attention to the five appendices at the back of *The GODD Chip*. They provide valuable background context for the story setting and define important terms used in the book.

While much of this background information is sprinkled throughout the story, I believe it would be to your advantage to immerse yourself in the background "lore" before diving too deeply into the book.

For example, this story takes place in the year 2137, almost seventy years after an era known as the Genetic Revolution. One of the appendices provides an overview of the Genetic Revolution and its aftermath. That same appendix defines an important term used throughout the book — *gutation* (a mutation of a "designed" gene).

As another example, most of the action in *The GODD Chip* takes place in three of six countries formed after the United States dissolved its fifty-state union in the early 22nd century: New Atlantia, Carapach and the Hawaiian Islands. One of the appendices briefly describes each of the six new countries and discusses what led to the breakup of the USA, Canada and many of the world's larger nations.

There is an appendix that outlines the worldwide caste system that arose after the Genetic Revolution, another that provides background about the GODD chip — the gene therapy at the center of the story, and finally an appendix devoted to describing the humanoid androids prevalent throughout the book.

Whether or not you decide to read the appendices before beginning the story, just know they are there in the event you find yourself puzzled by a term or a certain aspect of the story. Also, please note that each appendix is footnoted in the early chapters of the book when important terms or "lore" aspects are first mentioned.

With that counsel provided, I hope you enjoy the futuristic tale told in *The GODD Chip*, and I thank you for your interest in my story!

NIGHT OF THE JAKALIS

Gutant refugee village
Limahuli, Kauai, the Hawaiian Islands
June 2137

As the rain shower began to pelt the village, Natti sharpened her gaze on the swaying fronds outside the bedroom window. "Recheck all the locks…doors *and* shutters."

From behind, she heard the sounds of Kaleo, Avana and RJ testing the bolts and latches protecting the small cottage. Grasping a spear in one hand, the fifteen-year-old Natti felt for the knife strapped to her hip with the other.

Somewhere out there was a horde of jakalis readying to attack. Masked by darkness and the falling rain, the human mutants would soon creep from the jungle surrounding the village. Natti was sure of it. She could feel their presence. She could smell them. *Keep your wits about you, girl. Stay focused.*

A thump from above signaled the beginning of the assault. Natti tightened her grip on her weapons. "Kaleo, one's on the roof."

"I heard. I'm ready."

While jakalis were not stupid, they were slow learners and prone to repeating mistakes. Case in point: the roof attack on Natti's cottage never worked, but it was a regular tactic of theirs anyway. One of them would climb the side of the house and drop smoking chunks of wood down the vents to force Natti and her housemates out of the home. Other jakalis would lie in wait in the jungle brush and attack everyone who came out.

But the vents in Natti's home had been sealed long before she was assigned to the cottage, as were the vents in all the other cottages ringing the village commons.

Natti frowned when she heard two more thumps on the ceiling. She peered through the slit of the steel shutter barring the window. "How are they getting on the roof? I don't see any of them out my window."

"I don't know," said ten-year-old RJ from the bedroom across the hall. "I don't see any, either."

"I see them. Look up. They're dropping down from the trees," Avana said.

Natti craned her neck to look up at the palm trees at the edge of the clearing. Several jakalis were shimmying up the trunks. *Now, that's a new one*, thought Natti. *I'll bet they'll try to light the roof on fire again. Good luck with that.* Even if they managed to start a fire in the pouring rain, the roof panels were made of sheet metal.

The sound of their grunts and snarls sickened Natti, reminding her of the months of brutality she had endured as their prisoner until Chief Akela and his Makoas rescued her and offered her sanctuary in the village.

A blow on the front door shook Natti back to the present.

"They're trying a ramrod again," said Kaleo.

"How many of them?" Natti asked.

"Only two, but they've got a huge log. Looks like one of the pilings from the pier."

Natti adjusted her position to gaze up at the roofs of the cottages closest to hers. Similar onslaughts were underway at all of the ones she could see. *Where are the Makoas? What are they waiting for?*

As she turned away from the window, Natti heard a woman scream for help. As more panicked pleas echoed through the rain, Natti returned to the shutter slit and searched for the woman, but the shrill voice was soon swallowed under a crescendo of snarls from the jakalis.

All of a sudden, the thumping on the roof ceased, as did the pounding at the front door. A flash of movement crossed in front of Natti's field of vision. Jakalis began to pour through gaps in the underbrush, all racing to participate in the kill.

More screams cut through the hiss of the pounding rain, these ones from children. Natti recognized the ploy immediately. The jakalis were inflicting pain on their unfortunate victims, trying to rouse those locked in their homes to mount a rescue. Natti wanted so badly to cover her ears but doing so risked falling prey to a second wave. *There must be a hundred or more jakalis out there.*

"I see laser beams! Here come the Makoas!" Avana said.

Resting her head on the cold steel of the shutter, Natti whispered, "Praise the four gods."

The sounds outside began to change. The screams of the children faded beneath howls from the jakalis. Natti closed her eyes and prayed for another Makoa victory.

CHAPTER 1

BITTER CHOICES

National Gene Center
Minneapolis, Lakelands Province, New Atlantia

D r. Takoda Wells watched Billy Hearns run around the room with the model airplane clutched in his hand. The ten-year-old mimicked the sound of jet engines and swooped the plane in arcing paths through the air. He looked healthy and happy, as a boy his age should.

But Billy's outward appearance was deceptive. The child's DNA was breaking down. He was yet another victim of the *Genetic Revolution**, the failed era of genetic manipulation that had already claimed more than a billion lives.

Like millions of other parents in the 2070s and 2080s, predecessors in Billy's ancestry had "designed" many of the physical and mental traits of their children by replacing undesired genes in their embryos with genes that produced preferable traits. It was a practice that had allowed parents to craft their visions of "perfect" children. If they'd only known what was to come.

The glow of the practice and the promising new age quickly turned into a nightmare, creating a genetic catastrophe whose ripple effects multiplied and worsened with each subsequent generation of children.

The cause of the nightmare? A slew of self-replicating, synthetic proteins developed to create designer genes turned out to be flawed, creating

---

* For more background on the Genetic Revolution, turn to Appendix A: The Genetic Revolution on page 321 *gutations*, or gene-replacement mutations. Many of these gutations were passed from one generation to the next and further mutated into new forms over time.

As single entities, most gutations were benign, but when several combined, as in Billy's case, the effects could be lethal…not just to the child cursed with the gene-replacement mutations, but to others as well.

That was why the laws of *New Atlantia** mandated Billy Hearns had to be euthanized now, before he progressed any further into puberty. He could not be allowed to mature sexually, for if he fathered a child, his gutations could pass to his offspring.

Worse, if he was allowed to live, even if he was forcibly sterilized, his gutations would turn him into an insane, rage-filled monster — a jakali — by the time he turned fifteen or sixteen. Thereafter, he would maim, defile and kill with abandon until he eventually succumbed to the breakdown of his DNA or his reign of terror was cut short by a bullet or laser beam.

In the view of the ruling *castes*** of New Atlantia, it was better to nip the problem in the bud before it arose, no matter how cruel it seemed to euthanize an innocent child.

Takoda did not share that view. Neither did his colleague and friend, Dr. Yon Fujita. Particularly when it applied to Billy. For Takoda and Yon knew things about Billy's DNA the New Atlantians did not, something that might save Billy from his ancestral fate, something that might also save the lives of millions of other children.

If only Billy's mother would cooperate before it was too late.

Takoda was still watching Billy play when Yon entered the observation booth. As soon as he saw his Japanese colleague's expression, he knew the meeting with Sarah Hearns had not gone well. Still, he felt compelled to ask, "How did it go?"

---

* New Atlantia is one of the six nations that formed as a result of the dissolution of the United States of America in 2101. For more details about the six nations, turn to Appendix B: The Realignment of North America on page 323.

** For information about the caste system of the 22nd century, turn to Appendix C: Castes of the 22nd Century on page 326

Yon shoved her hands in her lab coat pockets. "As awful as you'd expect. No parent reacts well when they hear their child has to be put to death."

Truer words had never been spoken. Takoda thought of his daughter and how crushed he had been when he received the news of her Jakali Syndrome diagnosis two years prior. As his anger began to stir, he pushed aside the memory and focused on Yon. "Do you think she'll finally cooperate?"

"I don't know, Tak. I really thought she would open up this time, but she was too angry to listen to me. Hopefully, she'll cool off before they leave."

Gazing back at Billy through the two-way mirror, Takoda said, "We can't put that kid to sleep, Yon. He could help us change everything."

"Not without Sarah's help, he can't. Alone, Billy's DNA isn't enough. You know that."

"Yeah, I know." Takoda held up crossed fingers. "Here's hoping you can find a way to get through to her, *fast*."

"Amen to that."

Cracking open the consultation room door, Yon peeked in. Sarah Hearns was slumped over the table picking at her fingernails. Beside her, there was a pile of used tissues. Yon inhaled deeply and walked into the room. The red-faced, teary-eyed Sarah looked up briefly and then returned to fidgeting with her nails.

"Where's Billy? I want to go home now," Sarah said.

Yon took a seat next to Sarah. "I know. But we need to talk about options for Billy before you go."

"*Options?* You just told me he has to be put to sleep. He has no options. Not anymore."

"Beacon can help, Sarah, if you'll let us. We can give Billy a chance to live."

"I'm not giving you my son."

"But, Sarah, if you don't, he'll die."

With a defiant glare, Sarah said, "Better to die now than become a Beacon lab rat, or rot away in some godforsaken gutant colony."

"We don't treat anyone we rescue like that, Sarah. Not gutant children, not refugee families, not didgee conscripts. Billy will have a fulfilling life for as long as we can manage his condition."

Sarah's glare sharpened. "You don't care about Billy. All you care about is the damn chip."

Yon resisted the urge to debate with the grieving mother. "The chip is important to us, Sarah. I won't deny it. But Billy is just as important. Give us the chance to prove it."

"Why do you care about the chip so much? It didn't work."

On that point, Sarah was wrong. The *GODD chip** implanted in Billy *had* worked...at least, for a while. The smart-proteins injected along with the banned device had healed some of his early gutations. But, for some reason unknown to Yon, the chip had been removed before his latest gutations emerged, leading Sarah to believe the treatment had failed. Yon had tried to pry the reason for the removal from Sarah on several occasions but the mother would not tell her.

Sarah had also refused to tell Yon who had treated Billy with the chip and proteins. Given the treatment was illegal, Yon understood why Sarah had been tight-lipped about it initially, but Yon had hoped Sarah would have softened her stance by now.

After all, Yon or Takoda could have alerted New Atlantia's genetic crimes division when Takoda first spotted the GODD chip proteins in Billy's repaired DNA over a year ago. That would have meant instant euthanization for Billy and the execution of Sarah and her husband Rodrick.

By keeping their knowledge of Billy's altered DNA a secret, Yon and Takoda had gambled that Sarah would take them into her confidence, but she had resisted their every attempt to discuss the chip. Even now, with her son's life in the balance, Sarah still resisted. Takoda's earlier com-

---

* For a more expansive description of the GODD chip, turn to Appendix D: The GODD Chip on page 328.

ment flowed through Yon's mind. *Here's hoping you find a way to get through to her, fast.* Yon took a deep breath and made another plea.

"We think it did work, Sarah. The proteins injected with the chip are still active, and the repairs they made are still intact. That's why you must tell us who treated Billy, so we can talk to them about why they took the chip out and see if it's possible to reimplant it. Putting the chip back in might add years to Billy's life and resolve more of his gutations. And if that happened, what we'd learn could help millions of other kids. But to do all of that, we also need Billy. We need to watch him mature, see how the chip and proteins interact with his gutations."

During Yon's entreaty, Sarah's defiance seemed to wane. The scowl on her face faded and she relaxed her stiff posture. As tears began to trickle down her cheek, Sarah reached for a new tissue. "You really think you can help Billy?"

"With your help, I'm sure of it."

Between sniffles, Sarah asked, "If I agreed to help you, how would you do it? How would you get Billy, me and the girls out of New Atlantia?"

That's an excellent question, thought Yon. If Sarah had agreed to the rescue a year ago, it would have been a much easier task. There would have been plenty of time for Beacon to wait for the right conditions to smuggle the family out of the country. But now that Billy had been designated for euthanization, it would be especially tricky.

"It depends on how much lead time you can give us, Sarah. By law, you have up to ninety days to schedule Billy's procedure. If you're willing to push it back that far, it will give Beacon more time to put a plan in place."

"Impossible. Rodrick won't have it. We've talked about the possibility of euthanization many times over the last two years, ever since Billy's first gutation, and Rodrick's been adamant — he isn't in favor of dragging things out. He'll want the minimum waiting period."

Yon's stomach cramped. The minimum waiting period was one week. "Sarah, we need more time than that. Can't you talk to him? I know it's tough to have a euthanization hanging over the family's head for ninety days, but every extra day we get to plan, the better the chances of success."

Sarah shrugged. "I can try, but he's an Evvie Guild member through and through. Very rigid in his views. Very by the book about everything to do with gutant laws. He feels the same way about sterilizing me and the girls. Minimum waiting period. Get it done and move on."

As Yon watched Sarah begin to weep, her stomach cramps intensified. The bitter choices faced by parents in Sarah's and Rodrick's situation ate at Yon. There was no right answer as to what waiting period was best for families. More often than not, regardless of the period chosen, Jakali Syndrome diagnoses destroyed families.

Suddenly, Yon felt selfish for prodding Sarah to reopen the painful discussion with her husband. And she realized that if the discussion went poorly, Sarah might shut down any further talk of a rescue. With her finally showing some receptivity, Yon didn't want to risk losing her cooperation. "On second thought, don't talk to him, Sarah. We'll figure out a rescue plan. Give me twenty-four hours to work out the details with my colleagues and I'll get back to you with the plan. Just keep an open mind until then. Okay?"

The sobbing mother nodded. Yon rose from her seat and wrapped her arms around Sarah. As she held her tight, Yon's mind raced. *How in the world are we going to pull this off?*

CHAPTER 2

TIP-OFF

Warehouse District
Bloomington, Lakelands Province, New Atlantia

Under the dim light by the warehouse door, Major Damon Spiers waited for the overdue tipster.

"Any sign of our songbird, yet?"

Damon's question was directed to his deputy, Sergeant Cassidy Willow, an *android** who was back at headquarters operating the drone providing surveillance of the warehouse complex.

"No, sir. The access road is clear."

After adjusting the fit of his earbud radio, Damon checked the time on his holoband. The wrist-worn device displayed 2:43 a.m. "All right. I'll give him another fifteen minutes, then I'm out of here."

"Copy that."

Leaning against the building's corrugated wall, Damon wondered whether the informant had developed second thoughts about coming forward. The man had clearly been nervous in their earlier phone call. His voice had trembled and he'd repeatedly stuttered as he told Damon he had important information about the Beacon underground network.

Damon hated the network's name as much as he despised their mission. No matter how virtuous they claimed to be in their anonymous proclamations, they were nothing but criminals, human traffickers who posed a serious threat to New Atlantia's security.

---

* For more information about androids that appear in this story, turn to Appendix E: Androids in the 22nd Century on page 331.

For four years, Damon and his Beacon task force had failed to infiltrate the network or apprehend any of their members. They had come close to nabbing some of the agitators on several occasions, but each time, the Beacon rats had managed to escape. Their elusiveness was maddening to Damon.

And he was not alone in his frustration. None of his peers in the other New Atlantian provinces had foiled Beacon smuggling ops, either. Still, Damon felt inordinate pressure to crack the network. The survival of New Atlantia depended on maintaining the integrity of the country's borders and the longer Beacon continued to brazenly smuggle their "rescues" into neighboring Carapach through Damon's province, the greater the likelihood they would destabilize the country.

As he fumed about that possibility, Cassidy radioed with an alert. "Major, I have eyes on a cruiser headed your way. I am releasing a nano now."

"Copy that. Let me know as soon as you have the guy ID'd."

Nanos were one of the most useful devices in the New Atlantia Security Force arsenal of surveillance devices. To the casual observer, the miniature drones looked and behaved like flying insects but, in actuality, they were sensor-laden machines that provided excellent close-up reconnaissance that was often difficult to acquire with higher-flying drones and stationary security cameras.

Cassidy would guide the nano to within feet of the informant and collect facial recognition data and other biometric information. The minidrone would also scan the vehicle's registration chip, image fingerprints present on the vehicle and snip samples of the tipster's hair for later DNA analysis. By the time the man greeted Damon, the data provided by the nano would allow Cassidy to access the informant's full NASF profile.

As the sound of the approaching car grew louder, Damon stepped back under the glow of the warehouse's security lights. While there was no one else in the vicinity, he wanted to make sure the tipster was able to easily identify him and verify he was alone. The man had been adamant he wanted to meet somewhere discreet and wanted Damon to come alone.

After suggesting the warehouse for the rendezvous, Damon had said, *"I can't guarantee there won't be other people around. The warehouse is in*

*a commercial district, but if some folks are milling about, none of them will
be NASF.*"

"*If there are other people, how will I pick you out?*" the informant had
asked.

"*Just look for the tall black man with long white hair.*"

When the car appeared from around the corner of the building, it
turned toward Damon and shined its headlight bar on him. From the
curve of the oblong light, Damon could tell the vehicle was the recently
released Hutech RiverForge cruiser, a damn expensive tri-surface automobile. Capable of propelling on wheels, via maglev or by hydrojets, the
RiverForge was in high demand in Damon's province given the abun-
dance of lakes, streams and rivers throughout the region. The four-door
vehicle was also highly sought after for its quad-driver system which allowed the car to be driven by a human, android, the auto's self-driving
navigation system or by New Atlantia's satellite traffic management network. *The man must be an evvie*, thought Damon. Few people from the
lower castes could afford such a vehicle.

As the RiverForge slowed to a stop a short distance from Damon, the
headlight bar turned off and the vehicle's blacked-out window tint was
deactivated, providing Damon his first glimpse of the tipster seated in
the rear compartment. He was definitely an evvie. The genetic superhumans were easy to identify, even when inside a car.

Damon whispered, "You got him yet, Cass?"

"Working on it. Positive ID on face rec, waiting for confirmation on
fingerprints."

The gull-wing rear door opened and the man stepped out. He was at
least six-foot-five, a few inches taller than Damon. Elegantly dressed in a
suit and tie, the athletic, brown-haired Anglo waited for the door to close
before turning toward Damon. As he started to walk, Cassidy recited a
brief bio through Damon's earbud.

"His name is Rodrick Hearns. Evvie caste. Age sixty-four. Lives in a
suburb of Chicago. No criminal record. Married to a blenda-caste named
Sarah, maiden name Upshaw. She's thirty-two. Three kids. One boy. Two
girls. One of them, the boy, just failed his third DNA test. He's been designated for euthanization. Diagnosis is pre-Jakali Syndrome. Procedure

is scheduled for next Monday. Sterilization of the daughters and mother are set for the following day."

This should be interesting, thought Damon. *I'm glad I stuck around.*

"Maj. Spiers, I presume," said Rodrick.

"Yes, that's right. And who might you be?"

"I should think you would know that by now. Glider drone hovering above. Nano buzzing around us." Rodrick said. "But, just in case your computers are slow, my name is Rodrick Hearns."

Ah, the RiverForge is outfitted with surveillance detection, thought Damon. It was an illegal module for most New Atlantians, but not for Evvie Guild members. Rodrick was obviously an important man…one who neither stuttered nor appeared jumpy.

Damon shook the man's hand and said, "Kind of far from home, aren't you, sir? Minneapolis is a long way from Chicago, even using maglev the whole way."

"Yes, it is."

"It was clever of you to use a stand-in to call me. Was it an android or a friend of yours?"

"My apologies for the deception, Major, but it was important to protect my identity for as long as possible."

"Oh, and why is that?"

"Again, I would think that would be obvious to you by now. Whoever is on the other end of the drone feeds, communicating with you through your ear-comms, should have filled you in by now."

"Be that as it may, Mr. Hearns, I'd like to hear it from you directly."

Rodrick sighed. "It's rather difficult to say the words."

The reaction was common among evvies in Damon's experience. Most of them viewed themselves as perfect in every way. Admitting deficiencies of any kind did not come easy.

"I just discovered my wife has been in contact with Beacon. In fact, I think they have been in contact with her for quite some time. Ever since our son's second jakali gutation was detected."

Damon nodded. Grooming was a common tactic used by Beacon operatives given how much New Atlantian parents worried about the outcomes of their children's DNA tests. What better time to begin recruiting than after a second failed test, particularly when jakali-related gutations were involved?

For New Atlantia had a strict three-strike law. If a child exhibited three or more jakali gutations by the age of ten, two penalties were enforced; the child was euthanized and the remaining family members were sterilized…except for evvies and didgees, of course. Given the absence of any gutations in their DNA ancestry, evvies and didgees were exempt from the law's sterilization requirements.

Though the law was considered draconian compared to jakali management policies in many other countries, New Atlantia's approach assured eventual cleansing of the dreaded condition from the nation's population and Damon supported it. Beacon, on the other hand, viewed the law as abhorrent. They advocated more compassionate policies and often found willing listeners among parents whose children were at risk of developing JS…and apparently, Rodrick's wife was among those willing to listen.

"I take it your wife hasn't reported the contact to NASF," said Damon.

"That would be a correct assumption."

"Failure to report contact with Beacon is a serious crime, Mr. Hearns. Conspiring with them is even worse. You and your wife could be executed."

"I understand that, Major. It's why I'm reporting it now."

"What was the nature of the contact? What did Beacon want? Or, if your wife sought them out, what did she want?"

Damon could guess the answer already, but it was important to capture Rodrick alleging the crime. The nano's video recording would ultimately be needed to garner arrest warrants.

"Withdraw your drones and I'll tell you."

The look on Rodrick's face was as tense as the tone of his answer.

So, that's the game, thought Damon. *Rodrick isn't interested in ratting his wife out, having her arrested. Makes sense. He's an evvie. He doesn't want the publicity. It's bad enough the man decided to marry a blenda, so why further risk his social standing over a public trial and his wife's execution, or face accusations of participating in a Beacon scheme, himself? No, he's looking for a hush-hush deal.*

"I can't do that, sir. Not without some indication as to the nature of the contact."

"Major, there's a reason I sought you out instead of going to my local NASF precinct. You're the man responsible for cracking down on Beacon in this province. I'd like to help you do that but I want assurances in return."

"What kind of assurances?"

"Withdraw your drones."

The man had already admitted enough to throw him *and* his wife in jail but playing hardball to force a confession would likely result in a protracted legal battle with the Evvie Guild. In the interim, any chance of "cracking down" on Beacon would be lost. As soon as Beacon became aware of the arrests, and Damon knew they would find out, whatever scheme they had in the works would be dismantled.

Most likely, that scheme involved smuggling the children out of the country. While it was perfectly legal for a family to leave New Atlantia *before* receiving a jakali diagnosis, once the diagnosis was made, the jakali management law kicked into effect. That meant the Hearns boy had to be euthanized, no ifs, ands or buts. And it meant sterilization was required for his sisters and mother. If *any* family member tried to leave the country without complying with the law at this point, they would be subject to immediate execution.

This was when Beacon was the most devilish in Damon's opinion. They convinced people like Rodrick's wife that it was inhumane to kill a ten-year-old who would not transform into a murderous jakali for another five to seven years. Better to wait until violent symptoms developed and then try to manage the symptoms with medications for as long as possible.

If the underground terrorists could not convince grieving parents to smuggle out their pre-jakali child, then they focused on circumventing the sterilization of the remaining family members. It was a barbaric practice, Beacon told parents. Especially for the other children in the family. After all, they were not the ones diagnosed with JS, and they might never incur the same gutations as their diagnosed sibling. Better to smuggle them out and protect their rights to procreate.

However, this sales pitch ignored the fact that *all* children in the family were products of their parents' DNA, meaning that even if some of the children didn't contract JS, they could pass on their parents' replacement-gene mutations to their offspring. Sterilizing all family members was the only way to ensure no dangerous gutations could be passed on.

If Beacon had made either of these smuggling pitches to Rodrick's wife, Damon reasoned it might be worth cutting a deal to learn more. Damon and his NASF team might learn enough to intercede and catch the Beacon devils in the act. Damon touched his earbud and spoke to Cassidy. "Deactivate surveillance. Withdraw the drones. I'll call you if I need you."

"Copy, Major. Signing off."

Damon heard a tone in his earbud, signaling communications had been terminated. He removed the radio, showed it to Rodrick and then slid it into his pants pocket. "Okay, Mr. Hearns. You have five minutes. Make 'em count."

Rodrick turned toward his RiverForge and spoke a coded command. Turning back to face Damon, he said, "I've activated a jamming signal, just in case your colleague put the drones in stealth mode instead of deactivating them."

You are one cautious evvie, thought Damon. *And a smart one.*

"Now that we're truly alone," Rodrick continued, "let's talk assurances. First, I want *full* immunity for me, my wife and my girls. No jail time. No executions."

"Immunity from what, Mr. Hearns?"

"Beacon has offered to smuggle my wife and daughters out of the country before their sterilizations."

"I see. How much are they asking for?"

In true Robin Hood fashion, Beacon's fees for smuggling varied depending on the caste of those smuggled. The higher one's caste, the more one paid, and vice versa. Given Rodrick's status as an evvie, Damon suspected the proposed fee was astronomical.

"They've not asked for any money. They want a different form of payment."

"Such as?"

"They want my son."

For a moment, Damon thought his ears were playing tricks on him. "Excuse me? They want what?"

"My son."

"What the hell for?"

"I have no idea. It's macabre."

Damon frowned and lowered his head. *What would Beacon want with a gutant destined to become a jakali?* He knew the Beacon rats were bleeding hearts, but a pre-jakali? A kid designated for euthanization? He looked back up at Rodrick. "Are you *sure* about that, sir? Are you sure you didn't misunderstand? I mean, it's not uncommon for Beacon to offer to smuggle out pre-Jakalis along with the rest of the family, but I've never heard of them wanting a JS kid as payment."

"If you doubt my word, I can play you a recording of my wife discussing the offer with her parents."

"Recording?"

"Yes. You see, my wife has been acting strangely lately, so I've been keeping close tabs on her...um...activities."

Nothing says love like surveilling your wife, thought Damon. "Tell me more about the offer."

"Do we have agreement on the assurances?"

"Tell me what else you know. If I like what I hear, I'm open to a deal."

Rodrick slid his hands into the pockets of his slacks. "I'm afraid I don't have much more to offer, Major. My wife didn't get into specifics on the call. I'm sure she didn't want to put her parents in a bad spot, make them accessories, she just wanted someone to talk to about the situation. She's obviously conflicted. Regardless of whether she accepts Beacon's offer or not, she loses her son."

Damon nodded. "I'm sure it's a hard time for her...and for you. I've been there myself. I know first-hand what a jakali diagnosis can do to a family."

"Oh?"

"Yeah, my only boy was put to sleep almost two years ago. Wife couldn't deal with his death, the stigma. Committed suicide. End of family."

After a short spell of silence, Rodrick said, "I don't know what to say, Major…other than, I'm sorry."

"Yeah. Me too." Damon momentarily choked up. Clearing his throat, he said, "Anyway, it's a raw deal for any family to go through, so I get why your wife is conflicted. It's also what pisses me off about Beacon, preying upon vulnerable families, taking advantage of tragedy to further their own goals. It makes me sick to my stomach."

"I feel the same way. They're wicked. It's why I reached out to you. I want you to stop them before they destroy my family."

"Understood," Damon said. "I take it your wife hasn't talked to you about any of this?"

"No. She knows how I feel about upholding New Atlantia's genetic purity laws and how I feel about Beacon."

"And you haven't confronted her?"

Rodrick shook his head. "I considered it, but the hard truth is — I don't think I could stop her from following through without turning her in. We don't have the best relationship as it is. But I still love her, Major, and I love my kids. If there was anything I could do to prevent my son from turning into a jakali mongrel, I'd do it in a heartbeat. But there's no cure, there's no stopping the mutations from happening. Putting him to sleep now, as gut-wrenching as it will be, is the most merciful thing we can do for him."

Damon thought of his own son. Rodrick's assessment was sad but true.

"Did your wife tell her parents how they plan to smuggle her and the children out?"

"No."

"Do you know when Beacon plans to pull this off?"

"No, but it obviously has to happen before next Monday. That's when Billy, my son, is scheduled to be put to sleep."

Damon felt a sudden need to reconnect with Cassidy. If Rodrick had no insight into the timing, it meant the plot might occur at any time. Full-scale surveillance was needed immediately. As he pulled his earbud radio from his pocket, he said, "Where is your family now, Mr. Hearns? I mean like, right now, this instant."

"At home, but not to worry, Major. I have a house full of androids with instructions to prevent anyone from leaving or entering until I return. Besides, at this hour, they're all asleep anyway."

Famous last words, thought Damon. "I hear you, sir, but I can't take the risk. Beacon is as slippery as any criminal organization on the planet."

As Damon wedged the comms device into his ear, Rodrick said, "Before you call anyone, Major, do we have a deal?"

Damon stroked his stubbled chin. Although Rodrick's insight into Beacon's plan was paper-thin, his claim that the network was demanding the boy as payment was alarming. If true, it portended a new escalation in Beacon's agitations — an escalation with sickening implications. Damon had no choice but to cut a deal with Rodrick. He needed as much cooperation as he could get from the evvie to snare the Beacon operatives involved in the plot *before* they tried to smuggle the family out.

"All right, Mr. Hearns. I'll agree to your assurances provided you give me your full cooperation. That means surveillance inside and outside your home, access to all electronic communications and private data for you and your wife, plus any other assistance I may require."

Rodrick extended his hand. "You will have my unqualified cooperation. Just make sure you catch the scumbags before they get their hands on my family, Major. That's what's most important to me."

"Deal." Damon shook Rodrick's hand. "Now, if you'll excuse me, I need to kick my team into gear on this pronto. I'll be in touch later today."

CHAPTER 3

HARSH LESSONS

Gutant refugee village
Limahuli, Kauai, the Hawaiian Islands

A rap on the door stirred Natti awake. Curled on a mattress on the floor, she squinted through half-open eyes and saw glints of sunlight emanating from beneath the bedroom door.

RJ's angelic voice beckoned her to wake up. "Natti, oh Natti. Chief Akela is here. He wants to talk with you. Natti… can you hear me? Are you awake?"

"Yes, I'm awake. Tell him I'll be out in a minute."

Lowering her head back to the mattress, she clutched her blanket around her body and thanked the four gods for another sunrise. Natti, like many other citizens of the world, was a devotee of *Unity*, a religion with Taoist roots that arose during the worst days of the Genetic Revolution. The four gods at the core of the religion were representations of the Taoist principles of compassion, harmony, the inevitability of change and trust in the flow of all things.

With her prayer complete, she pushed aside the blanket and crawled onto the floor. With the assistance of a nearby chair, Natti dragged herself to a standing position and limped to the bathroom.

Once there, she grabbed the robe hanging on the back of the door and put it on. As she tied the terrycloth belt into a knot, she gazed up at the mirror above the sink. It was a painful but necessary ritual, one that helped Natti "keep it real," as they used to say in olden times.

The face that looked back at her was scarred and dotted with large reddish blemishes. Along with her nearly bald head, she looked like a chew-toy doll ravaged by a dog. She smiled, revealing the gap where her upper front teeth had once been before jakalis had knocked them out. "Hello, you gorgeous gutant. Ready for another day in paradise?"

She winked at her reflection and donned a baseball cap embroidered with the logo of a long-forgotten farm equipment company. As she left the bathroom and made her way toward the bedroom door, Natti winced with each step. It took a while each day for her reconstructed leg to limber up. Looking down at the leg's disfigured toes, she praised the four gods again. If not for the kindness of the island people, she would have lost the leg altogether...and probably her life. She owed them everything.

In turn, Natti did her part to contribute back to the village community, spending her days tending the needs of others. It was exhausting but Natti didn't mind. As a member of the village, she was protected from jakalis and the sportsmen from other lands who hunted gutants for kicks. In return, she gladly served as a mechanic, nurse and stand-in mom to RJ and Avana. Given the village had endured another jakali attack the night before, Natti suspected her mechanical skills were the impetus behind Akela's morning visit.

When she opened the door, Natti found the great Hawaiian chieftain sitting on the floor, RJ perched on one of his crossed knees. Akela was helping the gutant boy tie his shoes. Still too young to display any deformities or aberrant behaviors, the fair-haired, freckled RJ looked like he ought to be running about on a playground. Instead, he had multiple jobs like the rest of those who found refuge in the village.

"Aloha, Natti," said Akela.

Akela scooted RJ off his knee and stood. Natti returned the greeting and approached him. Placing her hands on his shoulders, she leaned forward and touched her forehead and nose to his. After the traditional Hawaiian embrace, she said, "Let me guess. Some Makoas need fixing up."

"Your intuition belies your young age, Natti. Several of our Makoas were damaged in last night's attack. It seems the jakalis are becoming more proficient in the damage they inflict."

Natti found it funny to hear Akela refer to her as young. Given everything she had been through since she was outed as a pre-jakali and banished to the islands by her father, Natti considered herself old in body and soul...even though she was still in her mid-teens.

"All right. I'll go see what I can do." Turning to RJ, Natti said, "Where are Kaleo and Avana?"

"Helping with the clean-up from last night," RJ said.

"Did they bring you anything to eat before they left?"

The young boy shook his head.

"Are you hungry?"

RJ nodded. Natti reached out her hand. "Come on, we'll get you something to eat on the way to the garage." She turned to Akela. "Is that okay with you?"

"Of course, but take the back way to the dining hall."

"Gotcha," Natti said.

Although it was impossible to spare the youngsters in the village from all the sights and sounds of the jakali attacks, Akela and the other elders in the village did their best to avoid exposing the youngest of the children to traumatic situations wherever possible. Natti knew it would be hard enough for RJ to cope with the loss of more friends from last night's attack, and he didn't need to walk through the latest scene of carnage until it was cleaned up.

After filling a sack with fruit, bread and milk in the village dining hall, Natti and RJ climbed the red clay path to an old automobile garage that sat on the top of a hill overlooking the village. About halfway up, Natti turned to look at the ocean. The shimmering, royal-blue water was as beautiful as ever.

As a child, long before she was abandoned, Natti had dreamed of visiting such a tropical paradise. It had been an impossible dream, for travel beyond the continent had been outlawed thirty years before Natti was born, but that had not stopped Natti from cherishing scenes she had seen on holovids; people sunbathing, playing in the surf, watching stunning sunsets. It had looked fun, carefree and exotic. Little did she know at that time that such paradises had already started to become colonies for gutants and feeding grounds for jakalis.

Oh, how she hated the term gutant. The name was almost as demeaning as the identi-chip embedded in her neck and the scars left when the doctors neutered her. Was it not bad enough that she bore the physical manifestations of her gutations? Did they really have to go the extra mile to "brand" her physically and socially?

I'm not even responsible for the gutations!

"Ow!" RJ said. "Let go! You're hurting my hand."

Stirred from her thoughts by RJ's plea, Natti looked down to see her trembling hand squeezing RJ's wrist. She let go immediately and knelt. "Oh, RJ, I'm so sorry. Is your hand okay?"

The boy rubbed his wrist and nodded. "Why did you do that?"

"I…I…got angry. Not at you. Other stuff. I forgot I was holding your hand."

"Jakalis?" RJ asked.

"What?"

"Were you thinking about jakalis? Is that what made you angry? They make me angry."

"They make me angry too," she said, stroking RJ's hair.

"Are they ever going to go away, Natti?"

The hopeful eyes accompanying RJ's question saddened Natti. She desperately wanted to say yes. She smiled and hugged him. "I pray for it every day."

When they arrived at the garage, Bali was the first to greet them. The Makoa-class android smiled and said, "What's shaking, guys?"

With long, braided black hair, tanned skin and a penchant for walking around bare-chested and barefoot, Bali looked like many of the human Hawaiians who ran the refugee village…except for the fact Bali was eight feet tall, as were all of the Makoas that protected the village. Beneath their eerily human exoskin, however, Makoas were military-grade fighting machines.

From what Natti had been told, for a time after Old America dissolved, Makoas had been the androids of choice for many of the world's armies. But once countries started dumping their unwanted gutants and jakalis on the islands, the Hawaiians had stopped exporting Makoas, partly to protest the dumping and partly to defend themselves against the burgeoning number of jakalis. Eventually, the loss of exports led to a shutdown in new production of Makoas, meaning the village had to make do with their current inventory of androids and spare parts.

"Hey there, Bali," said Natti. "Akela sent me to patch you guys up."

"And I'm here to make sure she does stuff right," said RJ.

Natti turned to RJ. "I thought you were here to eat."

"I can do both at once."

He smiled, took the bag of provisions from Natti and walked inside the garage.

The still-smiling Bali gestured to Natti to follow him. "Last night wasn't too bad. We did some of the component swap-outs ourselves, but there are still some delicate repairs needed."

"Uh-huh," said Natti. Makoas had a way of making the horrific sound benign, and Bali's appraisal was no exception. As Natti wound her way around the scattered limbs piled on the cement floor, she looked toward the recharging docks lining the wall to her right. Of the ten docks, all but two were occupied by standing Makoas. On the opposing wall, there were another ten docks, of which seven were currently in use. Most of the androids looked battered. "Geez, Bali, if this is your idea of *not too bad*, I'm not sure I want to see what you consider bad."

"Hey, look at the bright side, Natti. We didn't lose any Makoas last night, just some limbs. That's something, right? We all still have our brain cores and the limbs are repairable. All in all, I'd say I provided a fair assessment."

"What about your weapons?"

"Meh…a few scratches and dents. No biggie."

"Yeah, right." Natti immediately formed a vision of twisted barrels and shattered targeting consoles. Turning the bill of her ball cap around to the back of her head, Natti proceeded toward the water hose spigot near the garage entrance.

The grossest part of repairing the Makoas and their weapons was the noxious oily slick oozed by jakalis. It was somewhere between the odor of rotting food and the sickly smell of dead animals. During her captivity by the beasts, Natti had become nose blind to the stench, but after she was freed and her sense of smell readapted to the pleasant aromas of the lush Kauaian surroundings, her sensitivity to jakali odors returned. It was a good thing too. In the jungle, they were easier to detect by smell than by sight.

After washing down the pile of limbs, Natti went to work, swapping out joint components, reconnecting hydraulic lines and electronic sensor modules, reattaching the limbs and testing the functionality of her repairs. As she toiled at her workbench, a comment Akela had made earlier bubbled up in her mind. He had said the jakalis were becoming more proficient in their attacks, and Natti could see what he meant.

The severed Makoa limbs were not haphazardly ripped off as they had been in the past. Whether a foot, leg, arm or hand, the jakalis appeared to have developed a clear strategy. They now made clean incisions into the Makoas' skin at the joints. Once the joint innards were exposed, they went after the hydraulic lines and electronic wiring. Clean cuts, once again, rather than the frenzied-looking tears of old. The only damage Natti observed that showed the application of brute force was the rending of the ends of the metal limbs that once connected to joints. Natti called Bali over and asked, "How are they doing this? All these straight cuts."

"They're working in teams now. A bunch of them swarm, get one of us down on the ground. Then, some of them concentrate on a limb and immobilize it while another one of them starts cutting with makeshift knives, or knives they've taken from us. When the deed's done, they swarm again and rip off the limb."

Natti frowned. "How can they hold one of you down? You're strong enough to knock a dozen of them away with one swoop of your arm."

"They sacrifice a lot of their kind to do it. For every one of our limbs they get, we get thirty, forty jakalis. It's very inefficient, but they don't appear concerned with their losses."

Unnoticed by Natti, RJ had come up beside her. He said, "Have they tried to take your guns?"

Bali nodded. "Yeah, not just our laser pistols. They go after our rifles, laser long-guns and our knives. Most of the damaged weapons over there were broken by Makoas. Better to make them inoperable than let the jakalis get hold of them."

Natti stared at the pile of gnarled weapons. *A jakali with a laser pistol. What a terrifying thought.* She didn't see how these new coordinated behaviors were possible. From her time as their captive, she had never seen them work together when on a rampage. Male or female, it was every jakali for themselves. They were too filled with fury and lust to cooperate. The only times Natti observed them demonstrating teamwork was after they'd finished satisfying their sexual desires and their hunger to kill. It was as if they got high from their savagery. Only then had Natti seen glimpses of their humanity…tending to each other's wounds, sharing the leftovers from a kill, setting the defenses of the caves where they slept. But it had never lasted for long.

As memories of their abuse began to flow into her consciousness, Natti turned from the weapon pile and went outside to take in some fresh air. RJ followed her out and said, "Are you okay, Natti? You look angry again."

She put her arm around him. "You sure know how to read me, don't you?"

RJ shrugged. "Sometimes. Mostly when you're mad."

"I get mad a lot I guess, huh?"

"Yeah, but it's okay. There's lots to be angry about."

"There's lots to be happy about too." Natti smiled and mussed his hair. "Come on, help me fix up the guns and then let's get out of here. You still have homework to do."

Later that afternoon, Natti felt her anger rising again as she watched RJ turn to look out the window for the umpteenth time instead of focusing on the book in front of him.

"You won't find the answer outside," she said. "Now, come on, answer the question. When did the Genetic Revolution begin?"

RJ turned to look at her. "Does it matter?"

"Of course it does."

"Why?"

"Because we have to make sure future generations know the past. It will help them avoid the same mistakes in the future."

"Sez who?"

"Sez me. Now, answer the question or your butt's on kitchen duty all weekend."

RJ sat up straight. "Hey, that's not fair."

"Life's not fair, buddy. The sooner you realize that the better. Now, when did the Genetic Revolution begin?"

Natti suppressed a laugh as the boy's face turned red. Finally, with a dramatic flop of his arms against the table, RJ answered. "I don't remember. Somewhere around 2070."

The answer was close enough for Natti. "Okay, and when did the first really bad gutation occur?"

RJ's sigh was thick with irritation. "For cripes sake, who cares, Natti? It was like *fifty, sixty* years ago. Long before I was born, or *you*."

"That's not an answer, RJ. If you want to move on to the next level, you have to complete this level first. That means nailing your history facts."

"Look, I know it was the necro outbreak, okay? A skin gutation that made it possible to spread flesh-eating bacteria to other people. I know necro broke out in multiple countries and killed millions and millions of people around the world. Who cares what year it started?"

RJ's point was hard to argue. Knowing the relevant facts seemed more important to Natti than the date the gutation began. RJ knew the name of the gutation and the nature of the disease. But the teaching guide required her to enter a date for RJ's answer. Given that he had the approximate date range right, she penciled in the answer on her grading sheet. 2082, fifty-five years ago.

Moving onto the next battery of questions, Natti asked, "Define gutation."

She looked up to see RJ peering out the window again. No doubt he could hear the sounds of other children playing in the village square.

"RJ, pay attention. Define gutation."

With his gaze still locked on the window, he said, "Messed-up genes."

"Be more specific. What you described is a *mu*tation. What makes a *gu*tation different from a mutation?"

The boy turned to look at her. "Geez, Natti. You think I don't know? I am a gutant. You're one too. So are most of the children in the village."

"Then it should be an easy question to answer, right?"

RJ sat back and folded his arms across his chest. "Gutants are freaks. Kids like us whose great grandparents fooled around with their babies' DNA. They replaced genes they didn't like with ones they did. But they fooled around too much, and the genes they changed began to break. That's what gutations are…broken replacement genes."

His answer was not a textbook description of gutations, but it was close enough for Natti. "Good. Now, when do gutations begin to appear in a person?"

"When kids start to turn into adults."

"Right. And why is that?"

"Because that's when the hormones that change us from kids into adults start messing up our DNA."

"Very good, RJ. You said that very well."

"Now, how is a gutant different than a jakali?"

"Jakalis have a whole bunch of gutations instead of just a couple."

RJ's answer was partially correct but not completely accurate. Jakali Syndrome occurred in teens with *twelve specific* gutations, not just *a whole bunch*. And the average gutant typically had more than a couple of gutations.

Gutants might develop benign conditions, like permanently losing all their body hair as teens, or breaking out in reddish splotches like Natti, or other skin maladies that never went away. Further along the spectrum of severity, they might stop growing or begin to demonstrate learning impairments. Or they might develop early-onset cancers, arthritis or other chronic conditions. Their immunity to certain diseases might falter, and so on. The list of possible gutations was limited only by the number of synthetic replacement genes in a child's DNA.

RJ's answer missed another key point. Until all twelve of the specific gutations of a jakali occurred, kids diagnosed as pre-jakalis were technically considered gutants.

"You can do better than that, RJ. That's a sloppy answer."

"Come on, Natti. Give me a break." RJ asked. "I want to go outside and play. It will be dark soon. Can't we stop now?"

Natti looked at the long shadow of the window panes stretching across the floor. She was inclined to continue the quiz but realized RJ had spent the morning working in the garage and then studying with her for most of the afternoon and it was clear his attention span was waning. "Yeah, I guess that's all right. We can finish up tomorrow."

As RJ bolted out of his seat and ran for the cottage door, Natti called after him. "Just make sure you come home before the sunset bell. You hear me?"

"Yes, ma'am!"

He slammed the door on his way out, leaving Natti to clean up. As she limped across the living room to pick up his books and stow his school supplies, Natti listened to the chatter and laughter of the children outside. Closing her eyes, she sat down on the sofa and soaked in the happy sounds.

Natti smiled as she recalled playing in the schoolyard with her friends. Back then, she had loved to play on the swings most of all. She remembered the rush of wind through her hair and the thrill of soaring high into the air.

Reaching up, she stroked the bubbled skin on her mostly bald head and sighed. *How long has it been since I was on a swing? Two years? Three? I'm pretty sure there wasn't a swing set in the internment camp or quarantine center. So, it had to have been before I was sent away.* She slid her hand down and touched the puffy scars on her face. *It seems so long ago.*

After uttering another sigh, Natti opened her eyes and pushed off the sofa. *Stop torturing yourself, girl. There's nothing you can do about it. What's done is done. Now, get moving, it's gonna rain tonight. I can feel it in my leg.* As she rubbed the mangled limb, she finished her thought. *And that means everything has to be buttoned up before the jakalis attack.*

Somewhere in the Nahanni Mountains
The Northlands (Old Canada)

Caelan Horn aimed his binoculars at the cave entrance and watched his hunting androids sneak closer to the opening. Satisfied with their progress, he zoomed out and panned the field glasses to the left. On the ridgeline, his snipers were in position, ready to fire upon any living creature the hunt-droids flushed out. When it came to jakalis, Caelan never took chances.

Many compared them to zombies of old holovids, but jakalis were not sloth-like nor did they stagger around in a half-conscious haze. Despite their physical maladies, jakalis were quick, strong and agile, especially when on a rampage. They were also hyper-alert, their black eyes constantly scanning their environment for prey. And they were vicious, relentless attackers — both the males *and* the females.

But Caelan could understand the connection people made between jakalis and zombies when just considering their physical appearance. Gaunt and hunched over, jakali bodies were coated with a slick of oil that oozed from their pores. Beneath the oil, their skin was mottled with dark-colored blemishes and scaly to the touch. Many were bald or in the process of losing their hair.

Constant muscle spasms wracked their bodies and contorted their facial expressions, the latter preventing them from producing sounds beyond grunts and snarls. Whether those sounds were shouts of anger, cries of pain or both, Caelan didn't know. He only knew jakalis grunted and snarled a lot.

He had been hunting the trail of this particular jakali pack for three days, ever since he'd been hired to recover villagers snatched by jakalis during a raid on an Alaskon fishing village near the border with the Northlands. At first, it had been easy to follow the jakalis, as their trail had been marked by the blood of their prey.

Then, as the human devils moved into the mountains, the bodies of their victims — some complete, others torn into parts during their fits of rage — began to appear at intervals. If not for nightfall, Caelan and his hunting squad would have closed in on them the previous day, but there was no way he would have risked taking on jakalis at night. During the daytime, they were easy to spot at a distance but, at night, only their heat signatures gave them away. And those signatures were hard to detect in the rocky terrain of the mountains.

Unfortunately, that decision had allowed the jakalis to skitter into the mountains where their trail had become harder to follow, especially after the jakalis had tossed away the remains of their last unwanted Alaskons.

Thankfully, their oily slicks had a pungent, nauseating odor. Everything they touched reeked of it, from the branches they brushed up against, to the ground they stepped on and the rocks they climbed. If there had only been one or two of them, the mountain winds would have cleaned the air of their stench overnight, but nature couldn't mask their odor so quickly when they traveled in larger groups.

"Steady, lads," Caelan whispered, "wait until Devo gives us a count."

It was silly talking to robots in this way, but sometimes Caelan forgot his Makoas were machines. Decades of investment into technology to "humanize" androids had made them nearly indistinguishable from living, breathing homo sapiens.

No one was interested in machines following them around everywhere, but if the androids looked, sounded, felt and acted like real humans, well, then it made their omnipresence in twenty-second-century society less creepy.

Out here in the wilderness, however, creepy or not, androids like Caelan's Makoas were an absolute necessity. The upper reaches of the Northlands had become the latest dumping ground for jakalis cast out of Alaskon, Pacifica and Carapach, and no man, not even an experienced bounty hunter like Caelan, was capable of taking on packs of jakalis alone.

He felt a vibration from his earbud radio. A message from Elvis, Caelan's lead hunter-android, played in his ear. "All in position. Requesting permission to insert Devo."

"Permission granted."

Even with binoculars, Caelan would not have been able to see Devo. But that was a good thing. Amid the legions of real flies and other insects that infested the jakalis' cave, the nano drone would go unnoticed.

With its camera and surveillance sensors, Devo would zoom into the cave and provide Caelan and his contingent of Makoas with a video and data feed of the cave layout and its occupants. Lowering his computer goggles into place, Caelan said a quick prayer and girded for the scene Devo would relay.

In Caelan's experience, the inside of a jakali cave was more disgusting than the worst gutant internment camp. The floor was typically slimy, strewn with debris and excrement and speckled with the blood of their victims. For jakalis always kept a few live humans with them, just in case the urge to beat, defile or kill flared up while the jakalis rested. In a pinch, they were even known to eat them.

Caelan's goggle screen switched to night vision as Devo flew into the cave. Amid the black background, he saw swirls of small green lights flitting about. As he had expected, the cave was infested with flying insects.

Devo moved deeper into the opening, and Caelan spotted six sleeping jakalis sprawled across the floor. He grimaced when he saw the jakalis had hollowed out a pit near the back wall. In it, there were at least two Alaskons, possibly three. They were huddled so close together, it was difficult to confirm their number.

"Elvis," Caelan said, "we need Devo to get us a better look at the Alaskons in the pit...close in for facial recognition."

When it came time to flush out the jakalis, Caelan wanted to make sure they did not shoot at the Alaskons. Given their likely condition, they would look very similar to the jakalis — coated in blood and jakali oil, their hair matted and little to no clothing covering their bodies. The Alaskons would also be just as frightened as the jakalis by the bright lights and echoing booms of Caelan's flash grenades, and they would spill out of the cave with the same panic as the jakalis.

"Facial recon data acquired," replied Elvis.

"Good. Keep Devo close to the Alaskons, just in case." Caelan removed his goggles and blinked several times to adjust his eyes to sunlight. Pressing his hand against his earbud, he said, "It's your show from here, Elvis. Make us proud, lad."

Caelan picked up the binoculars and trained them on the cave opening. There was no audible chatter between the Makoas in his earbud to tell him when the raid would begin; his androids communicated with each other through radio signals.

He saw a blur of motion cross the black maw of the cave before a blinding flash of light blocked his view of the hillside. The accompanying boom of the grenade followed two seconds later. From his ridgeline perch two hundred yards away, Caelan saw a second flash and then smoke began to pour out of the cave accompanied by the high-pitched screeches of the roused jakalis. To his right, Caelan heard the sizzle of a laser blast, and on his left the crack of rifle fire. The smoke was too thick for Caelan to see whether the shots hit their intended targets, but the croaking wails of jakalis confirmed some had landed.

Lowering the binoculars, Caelan reached for his long-laser. In the time it took him to activate and bring the weapon to bear, several more shots and blasts echoed in the small canyon. As the smoke began to dissipate, Caelan saw the legs of a shape darting back and forth on the ledge outside the cave. He aimed his laser-sight at the shape and pressed the guidance tracker. The weapon tugged his arms to the left to follow the legs' frantic dash in that direction.

The laser vibrated when the target was locked. Caelan edged his finger toward the trigger. But then the figure fell to the ground, curled into a ball and covered its head. Then he saw Elvis race into view, snatch up the figure and speed away.

A shriek pierced through the sounds of chaos. Caelan heard a commotion to his right and turned to see Prince, his best sniper, leaping over the ridge. Raising his laser-sight back to his eye, Caelan followed the line of the streaking Prince and spotted a jakali clutching a writhing Alaskon girl against his chest as he scampered down the hillside. When the jakali noticed Prince racing toward him, he stopped and gripped the girl by the neck with both hands. The girl began to flail her arms and legs. Caelan returned his finger to the trigger, locked onto one of the jakali's legs, and fired.

The beast crumpled to the ground, releasing the girl. Prince appeared again through the laser-sight, this time standing directly above the jakali. He dispatched it with a blade through its chest and then scooped up the girl.

Just that quickly, the battle was over. The jakali pack was wiped out and the Alaskons rescued.

Later, as his androids torched the jakali carcasses and detonated the cave, Caelan tended to the rescued Alaskons — two teenaged girls and one similarly aged boy. Their vacant expressions reflected the horrors they had endured.

He bathed them in the icy river, bandaged their visible wounds, dressed them in fresh clothes and layered blankets around their shoulders. Caelan offered them food as well, but the catatonic teens seemed not to hear him. They just stared into the distance, clutching the blankets against their shivering bodies.

Caelan had his doubts about whether the teens would ever recover from their ordeal. He felt the same about the village from which they had been taken. The terror wreaked by the jakalis would become part of all of them, as indelible as the gutated DNA that turned the once-humans into animals.

CHAPTER 4

SIZING THE ENEMY

NASF Province Headquarters
Minneapolis, Lakelands Province, New Atlantia

The briefing room was packed. Damon Spiers locked eyes with each member of his task force as he finished his introduction. "Bottom line…we haven't had an opportunity as good as this in over a year. We have to make sure we take advantage of it. That means catching Beacon in the act and capturing as many of them as we can. Understood?"

As his team members nodded, Damon called on Cassidy Willow to take over the briefing. "Sergeant. Recap the plan."

The blond, Steel-class android pushed up from her seat and headed for the lectern as Damon stepped away. In the center of the briefing table was a holonode. At present, it displayed hovering images of the Hearns family. As soon as Cassidy reached the podium, the display switched to the title page of a presentation that read, *Operation Clamp*.

"You've all received the briefing packs so I only plan to touch on the highlights," Cassidy said. "To begin, as you all know, Billy Hearns is scheduled to be euthanized in approximately forty-eight hours and Beacon still has not attempted to kidnap him, his mother or his sisters. Based on new information passed to us by Rodrick Hearns this morning, we now believe Beacon plans to stage the kidnapping in two separate operations, one targeting Billy, the other focused on the mother and the girls.

"According to Mr. Hearns, Mrs. Hearns has announced she will not accompany her husband to the Minneapolis Gene Center for Billy's euthanization. Instead, she intends to spend Monday evening with her daughters at a church near the family home in suburban Chicago, where they plan to hold a private candlelight vigil for Billy. As you can see on the map on the next screen, that church is a few blocks from Lake Michigan, the most likely escape route to smuggle the Hearns females out of New Atlantia."

One of the officers across the table from Damon raised a hand. "Excuse me, Sgt. Willow. Why is the boy being euthanized in Minneapolis instead of the Chicago GC?"

"Chicago had a rogue-virus scare late last week," Cassidy said. "The center is shut down until the Department of Health certifies the facility is germ-free."

"I see…that's rather convenient, isn't it?" replied the officer.

"We're on the same page, Fenner," said Damon. "The rogue scare was likely a Beacon hoax, part of their smuggling plan. They want that boy in Minneapolis. It's so close to our border with Carapach, they can get him out of New Atlantia much faster and with less risk than if they traveled up Lake Michigan and backtracked across Wisconsin or fled into the Northlands."

Another hand went up. "But, sir, following that logic, why wouldn't Beacon want the whole family together in Minneapolis? Splitting their operation increases their risks."

Cassidy answered before Damon could speak. "Yes, but it also complicates our ability to disrupt their plans."

"That's right," said Damon. "Whether Beacon knows we're aware of their plans or not, they want to make it tough for *anyone* to intervene, particularly the Billy Hearns part of the operation. And make no mistake about it, people. He's the prize they are after. In fact, it wouldn't shock me to find out the Chicago part of the operation is bogus, a hoax to draw attention away from Minneapolis."

"Why is that, Major?" posed a third officer. "I mean, what's so special about the kid?"

"Good question, Schwartz. The genetic crimes division has just finished analyzing his DNA profile. Turns out Billy is pretty unique. Cassidy, continue. Educate them."

"Yes, sir." Cassidy looked around the room as she spoke. "As you all know, Jakali Syndrome results from the gutation of twelve specific genes. But not all twelve gutations happen at one time, nor do they occur in the same order in all children. JS can arise from 1.3 million different combinations of the twelve gutations. However, ninety-two percent of jakalis arise from just seventy-eight of those combinations. Even though Billy has only developed four of the twelve JS gutations thus far, the order in which his specific gutations have occurred already makes him an extreme outlier."

"Okay, so he's an outlier. Why's that such a big deal?" Schwartz asked.

"Unknown at this point, but GCD considers it significant," said Cassidy.

For a brief stretch, the room was quiet. Then, Schwartz posed another question. "How'd Beacon find out about the kid's DNA?"

"I'll take this one, Cass." Damon turned toward Schwartz. "We don't know that…yet. We've long suspected Beacon has access to the New Atlantian Gene Registry, but we can't find their backdoor into the databank. We also believe they have people embedded in our gene centers and DNA labs even though GCD conducts thorough background checks on every new hire in those facilities."

Fenner's hand went up. "Major, there's something else I don't get. Why go through all the hassle of smuggling him out of the country? If the kid's DNA is what they're after, why doesn't Beacon just sample his blood and tissues?"

"GCD has some theories as to why they want the boy, not just his DNA, but they're speculative at this point and they don't make a difference to the job we have to do. Capiche?"

"Uh…yeah. I mean, yes, sir."

"Major?" It was Schwartz again.

Damon sighed. "What is it this time, Sergeant?"

There was a smattering of snickers in the room. Schwartz' face turned red.

"Sorry, Major, I don't mean to be a thorn in your side. I was just wondering why we don't take Mrs. Hearns into custody and let GCD interrogate her? Matter of fact, wouldn't it be a good idea to lock up the boy too? Somewhere where Beacon can't get to him? You know, quarantine him until GCD sorts out Beacon's motive for wanting the kid."

Those options had indeed been debated at the highest levels of the Lakelands province, but, in the end, the leadership had agreed with Damon. The greatest strategic intelligence would come from Beacon operatives captured during the kidnap attempts, not from Mrs. Hearns. The underground network was not prone to sharing its strategic objectives with outsiders, therefore Mrs. Hearns would have little strategic insight to offer. Besides, after the plot was foiled, GCD could interrogate her all they wanted.

For the same reason, Damon had argued against taking Billy into custody. As soon as Beacon discovered either the mother or the boy was under wraps, they would cancel the kidnap attempts, leaving NASF with nothing.

The only objection to Damon's conclusion had come from the Prefect Munoz, the man who governed the Lakelands province. *"But, Maj. Spiers, is it prudent to use the child as bait without knowing why Beacon wants him? What if the worst should happen and Beacon is successful?"*

Damon had expected the objection and had been prepared with an answer. *"Billy won't live long enough to help Beacon, even if they find a way to get past us. We will be embedding a tracking device in his body. If our plan to trap them starts going sideways, we will signal the device to electrocute Billy. He'll die within seconds."*

With that response lingering in his mind, Damon leveled his gaze at Schwartz. "We considered a lot of options, Schwartz. But at the end of the day, the plan we've put together gives us the best chance of success. Now, enough questions." Damon stood. "You all have your assignment packs. Study them and be ready to roll within the hour. I want everyone in position at least twenty-four hours *before* Mr. Hearns leaves for Minneapolis with Billy. If we get any new information, or there's a change in plans, Cassidy will put out the word. Got it?"

A chorus of "yes, sir" echoed in the room.

"Good. Dismissed."

Takoda Wells' residence
Wolf Lake, East Dakota, Carapach

Takoda rolled off Ellie and settled on the bed next to her. Drenched in sweat and breathing heavily, he stared at the ceiling as endorphins bathed his brain. Ellie slid over and tenderly kissed his cheek, his shoulder and chest.

"Feel better now?" she asked.

"Much better," he said.

He smiled at Ellie and smoothed the raven strands of her hair over her shoulders. The android always seemed to know when his mind was troubled. And with Billy's euthanization just two days away, Takoda had gone to bed consumed with apprehension about the impending rescue attempt. Now, though, he felt relaxed.

"Good. Try to sleep," Ellie said, laying her head against his chest.

Closing his eyes, Takoda stroked her back until he drifted off.

When he awoke several hours later, sunlight was streaming into the room through the sheer curtains. Takoda turned away from the glare and discovered the bed next to him was empty. Looking past the rumpled sheets and pillows, he saw the alarm clock. It was after nine.

Takoda cursed and bolted up. Ellie had turned the alarm off. He was four steps out of the bed before he remembered it was Saturday. With a sigh of relief, he turned around and retrieved his boxers from the floor next to the bed.

After pulling them on, he went to the window and pushed back the sheers. It looked to be a glorious day, not a cloud in the sky and a light breeze rippling through the trees. If he recalled correctly, the temperature was expected to climb into the seventies, perfect weather to spend the day fly fishing in the stream and napping on his hammock under the shade of trees. Both would be welcome respites from the rescue preparations.

With a yawn, Takoda stretched his arms above his head and padded out of the room. He was a little startled when he reached the kitchen and saw Akecheta sitting at the breakfast table instead of Ellie. Then he recalled he had promised to teach Ake the finer points of fly fishing this weekend.

Takoda considered himself fortunate to have both Ake and Ellie as android companions. Beyond their pre-programmed skills, they brought lively presences to his otherwise empty home. And though they were different class androids with different constructions and functionalities — Ake was a Makoa-class, Ellie was an Athena-class — Takoda had customized their external features to make them look like part of the same family. And he took pride in his Sioux Indian family.

"Morning, big fella, where's Ellie?" Takoda asked.

"She went into town for groceries," said Akecheta. Takoda watched the android's eyelids flicker, a sign that he was communicating with his counterpart, Ellie. "She says she will be back in approximately twenty-seven minutes unless you want her to get you breakfast on the way."

"No, that's okay. Tell her I'll slap together something here."

"Yes, sir." Akecheta pointed to the beverage dispenser on the counter. "There is fresh coffee and Ellie suggests you consider protein cakes for breakfast."

"Does she now?" Takoda walked to the pantry to evaluate alternative options. "Any messages overnight?"

"Only one. A holosnap from Dr. Fujita. Do you want me to play it now?"

"No, that's okay. I'll look at it in my office."

After toasting a bagel to go along with his coffee, Takoda left Akecheta in the kitchen and headed for his office. On the way, he passed through the living room and paused to say good morning to his wife and daughter. Their smiling faces stared back at him from the table full of picture frames.

Placing his breakfast aside, he knelt before the table and murmured a brief prayer. When he finished, he took hold of his favorite photo of them and touched their faces. "May the four gods continue to watch over you, my loves."

He remained there a little while longer, recalling the memories associated with each picture on the table. As painful as it was to revisit happier times, the trip down memory lane brought a smile to Takoda's face. He had been blessed to have them in his life. The sentiment of the picture frame in his hands reflected his feelings perfectly. *Gone too soon. Cherished always.*

The words echoed in his mind as he replaced the photo in its honored place in front of the others. The ritual completed, Takoda picked up his breakfast and continued onto his office. Once there, he used his foot to shut the door and lowered himself onto his desk chair.

The leather was cold against his bare back, causing a spate of shivers to race over his skin. Once again, he set his breakfast aside, this time to snag the blanket hanging off the arm of the sofa behind. After wrapping it around his shoulders, he spoke to the holonode on his desk. "I understand I have a message from Dr. Fujita."

"Yes, you do, Dr. Wells," answered the holonode's male voice. "And good morning."

"Morning to you, too, Dasan." Takoda sipped his coffee. "What time did she send the snap?"

"Two-fifty-two a.m."

Takoda frowned. That was late, even for Yon. "Play the message."

A glow appeared above the black sphere occupying the center of the desk. The glow quickly spread out into a rectangular holographic screen at eye level with Takoda. On the screen was a frozen image of Yon. She looked disoriented to Takoda, as if she had just awoken. As the message began to play, she managed to smile as she said hello, but her greeting was swallowed by a gaping yawn. Covering her mouth as the yawn subsided, she said, "Sorry, that was gross. Buzz me when you get up. Got a message from Hoot. We may have to cancel our plans for Monday."

She waved goodbye and yawned again as the snap ended. Takoda's frown deepened. "Dasan, send Dr. Fujita a reply. Ask her if she can talk now."

"Yes, sir." A thin blue light moved back and forth at the base of the sphere, then a tone sounded. Windchimes, Yon's holotone. Takoda directed Dasan to answer her call. Grasping the blanket tight around his neck, he waited for Yon's image to appear above the holonode.

"Hey, Tak," she said. From the bobbing vista behind Yon's head and her labored breathing, Takoda realized he had interrupted her morning run.

"Hiya. Just got your snap. Is this a bad time to talk?"

The bobbing of the image began to abate. "No, I could use a breather."

"Okay. So, what's up with Monday?"

"Potential snag," said Yon. "Actually, we probably should discuss this in person. If you aren't busy, I can come over as soon as I've finished my run."

"Yeah, sure, that's fine. If I'm not at the house when you get here, I'll be down at the stream fishing with Ake."

"Marvy. See you later."

She blew a kiss and then the holofeed vanished.

Sipping his coffee, Takoda pondered Yon's clipped description of a potential snag. *It must be a helluva lot more than a "snag" if Hoot is considering canceling the rescues. Sarah probably changed her mind again. Or maybe another logistical issue popped up in Chicago.*

Takoda set down the coffee and said another prayer, this one beseeching the four gods for their assistance. *Help us overcome whatever threatens our success. Help us to save Billy Hearns. Help us end the jakali scourge.*

An hour later, Takoda was standing in the stream behind his house, showing Akecheta how to twitch a fishing rod. "You want the fish to think your lure is a real flying insect, so you have to simulate how insects dart around as they land and take off."

Akecheta stood next to him and attempted to mimic Takoda's movements with his rod. As sophisticated as the android was in nearly every respect, the random movements of flying insects were beyond Akecheta's grasp, figuratively and literally.

"Forgive me for saying this, Tak, but if the objective is to catch as many fish as possible, as quickly as possible, isn't my method of fishing more efficient?"

The method Akecheta referenced involved employing his array of sensors to detect a fish swimming nearby and then snatching a fish with a lightning-quick grab of his hand.

"Not all of us have advanced hydraulics and electronics, Ake. Besides, where's the sport in that?"

"I don't understand. Haven't humans used their hands to catch fish for many millennia? Isn't it considered a test of a man's skill to catch a fish in this way?"

"Yes, I guess that's true."

"Then, why don't you consider my way of fishing sporting?"

Takoda twitched the rod again and watched the lure splash on another spot in the stream. "Good point, big fella. Your way *is* sporting, but in a different way than I meant. Catching a fish with your hands is a test of physical prowess. Fly fishing is more of a test of mental prowess and physical finesse. You tease the fish, tempt him with deceptive movements and then take advantage of the fish's aggression to catch him."

Akecheta stabbed a free hand into the water and pulled out a flailing trout. "Why waste time with deception? My way is more efficient."

"Yeah, but it's not very relaxing."

The android dropped the fish back into the stream. "Deception is relaxing?"

As Takoda laughed, he heard Yon's voice calling from behind. "Hello, boys! How're the fish biting this morning?"

Takoda turned and saw Yon and Ellie standing on the streambank. He waved and then turned back to Akecheta. "That's enough for now, Ake. Here, take the poles back and stow the lures."

"You got it, Tak."

As Takoda waded toward shore, he said to Yon, "Hey there. How was the rest of your run?"

"Kinda boring, but I needed to clear my mind, so it worked out okay."

Takoda splashed his way out of the stream and unhooked the suspenders of his hip waders. He plopped down on the grass and wiggled his bare feet free of the rubbery body-boots. "The message from Hoot bothering you?"

"Somewhat, but I was kinda nervous already."

"You and me both." Takoda reached a hand toward Ellie. "A little help, please."

Ellie tugged Takoda up to his feet and then picked up his waders. "If there's nothing else you need, Tak, I'll go spray these off."

"Thanks, El. Appreciate it. I'll catch you later."

As Ellie began to walk away, Yon said, "Um, before you go, El, ask Dasan to scan for nano drones." Yon then turned to Takoda. "Just to be on the safe side."

"Very well. Transmitting request now," said Ellie.

Takoda frowned at Yon. "Sounds like Hoot's situation is more than a snag."

Yon stood on her tiptoes and whispered in Takoda's ear. "The New Atlantians know about the Hearns rescues."

The succinct delivery of the news packed a punch Takoda had not seen coming. "That's not a snag, Yon. That's an operation killer."

"Maybe, maybe not," Yon said. "Come on, let's take a walk in the woods and I'll fill you in. Ellie should tag along too...with her radio jammer on."

Takoda agreed and the three of them followed a narrow trail into the hundred acres of woodlands surrounding Takoda's homestead. As he and Yon walked shoulder-to-shoulder along the path with Ellie following a discreet distance behind, Yon described the message from Hoot.

"She basically said both missions are on standby until further notice. Said she had to assess whether the New Atlantians knew enough to spoil the rescues."

"Did Hoot say how they found out about it?" Takoda asked.

"No. She didn't get into any details. Just said to hold until she contacts me again."

It surprised Takoda that Hoot had not scrubbed the mission outright. Typically, the Beacon leader was supremely cautious. But, then again, she obviously realized how important it was to prevent Billy Hearns from being euthanized.

"If the New Atlantians know about the rescues, does that mean they know about us, too? Our involvement with Beacon?"

"I don't know. I assume that's part of what Hoot's trying to find out, along with whether the New Atlantians know about Billy's repaired gutations."

"Oh, they must know, don't you think? They have access to his DNA test results. His repairs are obvious."

"Yeah, but…it's not like Billy's the only kid who's had gutations spontaneously resolve. It's rare, but it does happen. And the DNA tests aren't perfect. Anomalies do occur. So, they might not think the repairs are all that big a deal. They may be more focused on his existing gutations."

Takoda did not agree. He was convinced the New Atlantians would examine Billy's DNA closely. And he knew if they dug into the results deep enough, there was a decent probability they would connect the repaired gutations with Billy's violet eyes.

If they established such a connection, and the New Atlantians examining Billy's DNA recalled their early twenty-second-century history, they might just make an additional connection with the GODD chip. For the deceased inventor of the chip, Dr. Dyan Mugabe, had been very selective in picking subjects for her experiments testing the heretical device, and violet-colored eyes had been an attribute all her test subjects shared. The unique pigmentation was the result of the replacement of an innate eye color-determining gene with a synthetic gene known as VE011.

That was how Takoda had zeroed in on the connection a year ago when he'd first discovered some of Billy Hearns' gutations had been repaired. He then examined the repairs more closely and found protein molecules he had never seen before in the gene binds. At first, Takoda had been at a loss. He had spent years studying every synthetic protein created during the Genetic Revolution and the ones in Billy's repairs matched none of them.

The notion the unusual proteins might be Mugabe's smart-proteins never crossed Takoda's mind until he re-examined the repairs. But the moment he noticed one of the repairs had been made to a base-pair-bind near the VE011 gene, his memory of Mugabe's twenty-five-year-old study clicked in and he arrived at a stunning hypothesis: someone had recreated Mugabe's chip and smart-proteins and had tested them out on Billy.

Takoda realized the New Atlantians would pull out all the stops to prevent Billy's rescue and imprison Sarah if they arrived at the same conclusion. Looking off into the forest, he said, "Let's hope you're right, Yon. Let's hope they don't dig too deep."

Yon spent the rest of the afternoon at Takoda's as they waited for Hoot's follow-up message. While Takoda fished, Yon reclined on an Adirondack chair and soaked in the sun. Several times, he encouraged her to join him in the stream, but she told him she found it more relaxing to watch him fish rather than angle herself.

"It'll distract you from thinking about Hoot," Takoda had countered.

"I have all the distraction I need watching you."

The teasing tone of her answer had brought a smile to Takoda's face. Warmth spread through Yon as she smiled back. They had shared many an afternoon like this over the last two years, not to mention many dinners by campfire under the stars. When she was able to cajole him to leave his woodland paradise, he sometimes dined at her house or shared a bottle of wine by her patio firepit.

Now, as she watched the shirtless Sioux cast his line, Yon felt the familiar yearning for a closer relationship with him. But she realized that so long as Ellie shared his bed, there was little hope of that happening. *Still, it doesn't hurt to keep planting seeds,* Yon thought. *Sooner or later, he'll move past the loss of his family and realize I have more to offer than Ellie does.*

Before Yon finished the thought, the aforementioned Ellie came alongside the Adirondack chair and knelt beside her. In a near whisper, Ellie said, "Dasan has just received a transmission from Hoot. She wishes to speak with you and Takoda as soon as possible. Do you want to tell him, or should I?"

Yon smiled at Ellie. As much as she wanted the android out of the way, it was hard to hate her. Ellie was as kind to Yon as she was to Takoda. "Thanks, El. I'll go get Tak. You set up the call. Full encryption. We'll be right in."

"As you wish." Ellie gently squeezed Yon's hand and left.

Takoda didn't respond when Yon called to him from the streambank, nor did he seem to notice her wading out to him thereafter. Only when she smoothed her hand on his shoulder did he stir.

"Hey there, change your mind?" he said.

With a shake of her head, Yon said, "Hoot's ready to talk."

Takoda's small office felt more cramped than usual to Yon. With the hulking Akecheta sitting next to her on the sofa and Ellie standing by Takoda's desk, there wasn't much legroom for anyone. But it was important for the androids to hear the conversation, given they had roles to play in the rescue of Billy Hearns.

Among those in the room, Yon had been a Beacon member the longest, and she had been the one who'd recruited Takoda into the network. Not long after that, Hoot granted them the two androids to assist with rescue missions. As a cover, Hoot suggested they serve as housemates, one for each of them. At the time, Yon felt Takoda would benefit from the companionship of both given how withdrawn he had become after the loss of his family. So, she recommended Hoot provide both to Takoda. *Strategic error on my part*, Yon thought now as she looked at Ellie.

"I say, are you there, Yon?"

Hoot's voice shook Yon back into the moment. Deep and full of gravitas, the Beacon leader's British-accented voice always caused Yon to conjure an image of a uniformed Field Marshal on the other end of the line. In truth, Yon had no idea what Hoot looked like. She had never met her.

"Yes, Hoot, I'm here," said Yon. "Takoda is here too."

"Good. Have you briefed him on the situation?"

"Yes, in as much as I know of the situation. We're both anxious for more information."

"Understood. Well, what I communicated earlier is true. NASF knows about our mission. They apparently do not have insight into the specifics of our plans, nor do they fully appreciate our goals, but they know enough to present problems. You see, they intend to let our plans unfold and nab us in the act."

Yon's heartrate quickened. "Then we're scrubbing?"

"No. There is too much at stake. But we *will* have to adapt our plans to account for NASF surveillance. Now, listen carefully—"

Takoda spoke over Hoot. "Hold up. Before you go any further, I'd like to know how NASF found out about the mission."

When Hoot did not answer immediately, Yon began to feel nauseous. The underground leader's eventual answer did little to ease the sensation. "Yes, well, as we feared, Mrs. Hearns' anxieties led her to discuss the rescues with someone outside Beacon. Her parents. Evidently, Mr. Hearns overheard the conversation and contacted NASF."

Yon's stomach cramped as she watched Takoda clench his fists and shake his head. During the hasty creation of the rescue plans, he had expressed reservations about Sarah's reliability.

"Then we have to scrub," said Takoda. Though his comment was directed at Hoot, Yon noticed his glare was directed at her, as it was her responsibility to manage Sarah.

"Not necessarily," Hoot said. "Over the past several hours, we have gathered more intelligence that gives me confidence we can still achieve success."

Yon watched Takoda grip the armrests of his chair as he challenged Hoot. "How? Stealth was crucial to our plans. That's gone now, no matter what kind of intel you have."

It was hard for Yon to disagree with Takoda's assessment. Beacon's plans had presumed NASF would never learn of Billy's rescue — before, during or after the mission. On the other hand, Hoot was the antithesis of recklessness. She had to have compelling reasons for believing the mission could still succeed.

"If you would allow me to explain, I think—"

Takoda cut off Hoot again. "What's to explain? NASF knows about Billy, right?"

"Yes, quite right. They know he is our primary target. They know he is special."

"Then it's game over." Takoda pounded a fist on his thigh.

Yon tried to make eye contact with Takoda but he looked away. As she contemplated ways to break the tension, Hoot intervened. "You surprise me, Takoda. I did not expect you to give up so easily."

In a calm and measured voice, Takoda said, "What you call giving up, I call facing facts."

That was too much for Yon. "Oh, come on, Tak. Ease up. You don't know all the facts. Give Hoot a chance to tell us why she thinks we can still pull it off."

"Why? Hoot said it herself. NASF knows Billy is special. That means they've examined his DNA...which means they know *why* we want him."

"Actually, that is incorrect," said Hoot. "From what I've been told by our informants, NASF hasn't a clue about the GODD chip. Their ignorance of our objective is the primary reason they intend to let our plan unfold, albeit under intense surveillance. Only, that will be quite difficult for them given they are not privy to the details of our plan, nor do they know we have been apprised about *their* plan. With some modest revisions, I believe we can confuse them long enough to accomplish both rescues."

"What kind of revisions are we talking about?" asked Takoda.

"*We*? Should I take that to mean you have reconsidered giving up?" Hoot replied.

"If the revisions include Sarah, no. She's too big of a liability."

"She's been a liability from the get-go, Tak," said Yon. "But she's also an important asset. Too important to exclude from our plans. You know that, right?"

"Yeah, but what if she makes another mistake and the rescue fails? If NASF interrogates her, she'll roll over on us in a heartbeat."

"Then we'll just have to make sure that doesn't happen," Hoot said. "Now, are you in or out, Takoda? If you're out, step away now."

Yon gripped his hand and looked him in the eye. "We're so close, Tak. Don't back out now. We need you. I need you."

From the sour expression on his face, Yon thought he might pull from her grip and storm out of the room, but instead, his shoulders slumped and he nodded. "All right, I'm still worried about Sarah, but I can't let you down. I'm still in."

"Good show," said Hoot. "Now, let us discuss the alterations for your part of the mission. Every minute counts if we are to succeed."

CHAPTER 5

ZERO HOUR

Command Center – NASF Province Headquarters
Minneapolis, Lakelands Province, New Atlantia

The video feeds from the glider drones were split into three screens. Damon leaned over the holotable and studied each one. The center screen showed Rodrick Hearns' RiverForge speeding along the interstate toward Minneapolis. The one on the left provided an overhead view of the Minneapolis Gene Center building. And the screen on the right was zoomed in on the front door of the Hearns' home in Chicago.

"Show me the church," Damon said.

On the opposite side of the ping pong-sized table, Cassidy tapped her fingers on the holoimage of a keyboard floating above the table. Seconds later, the zoomed-in image of the front entrance of St. Matthew's replaced the video feed outside the Hearns' home.

"Switching to the back entrance view now," Cassidy said.

The screen toggled to show the rear of the church. Damon pressed his earbud radio. "Schwartz, everyone in position?"

"Roger that," Schwartz said. "Two plainclothes and a nano inside. Glider overhead. I'm with the rest of the squad in the command truck. We're ready to close in on your order."

"Good. We'll let you know when the Hearns women are on the way." Damon turned to Cassidy. "Show me the house again."

Despite the myriad of surveillance resources and officers at Damon's disposal for the dual operations, he felt exposed. While he knew Beacon's general aims, he had no idea when they would act nor the tactics they would use. He suspected they would synchronize the timing of the separate smuggling operations, but he had no intel to confirm it. He also thought it likely Beacon would wait to snatch Billy until he reached Minneapolis, where the border with Carapach was a mere twenty miles away, but there was no guarantee of that either.

Therefore, Damon and his task force of humans, androids and drones had to remain alert and ready to react to whatever devilry Beacon had planned. Damon shifted his gaze to Rodrick's car. "What's Mr. Hearns' ETA?"

Cassidy replied, "Given the current traffic flow, he should arrive at twelve-fifteen, a little more than three hours from now."

"Is the boy still asleep?"

"Yes, sir. Biometric data from the tracking implant shows slowed respiration, low heart rate and minimal brain activity."

Damon's mind drifted to the memory of driving his son, Dylan, to the same gene center for his euthanization two years beforehand. He recalled how angelic Dylan had looked as he carried the sedated child into the clinic. He didn't remember much about the inside of the facility, just the small room where he and his wife said goodbye to their sleeping child. It tore Damon apart then, and thinking about it now did so again.

As his emotions began to swell, Damon gritted his teeth and looked away from Rodrick's car. Focusing his attention on the video feed of the Minneapolis clinic, he tapped his earbud again. "Fenner, report. All in position?"

"Yes, sir."

"Any sign of Beacon operatives?"

"No, sir. Facial recognition feed from nanos stationed at entrances confirms no unknown persons entering or exiting the clinic."

"What about the two doctors from Carapach? Have they arrived yet?"

"No, sir. They are still inbound from the border checkpoint. According to glider data, Dr. Fujita will arrive at 9:18 a.m. The other doc, Wells, is about fifteen minutes behind."

"Copy that. Make sure your people stay out of sight. If either of those doctors is with Beacon, I don't want them tipped off to our presence."

Earlier in the week, Damon had ordered a thorough background reevaluation of all the people employed by the Gene Center as well as those who worked at St. Matthew's. Convinced that Beacon had people on the inside in both places, he tasked his team to identify the most likely conspirators and they pegged Wells and Fujita as the leading candidates from the clinic.

While their NASF records were clean, neither Takoda nor Yon were New Atlantian citizens and both were didgee caste, which made them stand out to Damon's task force as possible suspects. The conscription of didgee females to serve as surrogates for evvie embryos was a practice decried among the didgee-dominant society of Carapach. Yet, beyond their caste affiliation and current country of residence, nothing in the doctors' backgrounds leaped out as inherently suspicious to Damon.

Now thirty-eight, Wells was Carapach by birth. Like Damon, Wells was widowed. And also like Damon, the doctor had lost a child to Jakali Syndrome, though the records showed Wells' daughter had not been euthanized like Dylan. She had instead been placed in a gutant internment colony two years ago, a legal practice permitted in Carapach.

In another similarity with Damon, Jakali Syndrome had factored into the death of Wells' spouse. The records indicated she had been killed by a jakali who had snuck onto Wells' property a year before the daughter's internment.

Turning to Wells' professional background, Damon had learned the didgee had received his medical training in New Atlantia and then returned to live in Carapach. There, he opened a small clinic in his home territory of East Dakota where he assessed gutation risks for couples considering marriage and those eager to start families. Then, four years ago, he closed his clinic and went to work at the Minneapolis Gene Center. He still lived in East Dakota, but that was not unusual. Good paying jobs lured many Carapach citizens to commute across the New Atlantian border to work in Minneapolis.

From a legal perspective, Wells appeared to be a law-abiding citizen of both Carapach and New Atlantia — no arrests, no reports of subversive activities, no controversial papers as a student and no black marks as an employee of MGC. Fujita's citizenry background was similarly clean.

She was born in Osaka, Japan. In her teen years, Fujita and her didgee family emigrated to Pacifica and settled in Los Angeles, where she lived until graduating medical school.

Fujita was thirty-six now and, as far as Damon's team could determine, she was single and childless. Like Wells, she chose to live in East Dakota and commute between Carapach and New Atlantia for work. Interestingly, discreet nano surveillance at the clinic suggested the two doctors were close friends.

She spent the early years of her career in Alaskon, working as a researcher for a therapeutics company that developed medications for a range of gutation symptoms. Then, five years ago, she made the leap to New Atlantia and the Minneapolis Gene Center. According to her MGC employment file, Fujita had made the career shift to get out of the laboratory and into a clinical setting.

Storybook stuff. Except Damon didn't buy the backstory, not about Fujita nor her friend Wells. Call it caste-bias or distrust of foreigners, but Damon had a bad feeling about both of them, particularly given they had been the primary doctors at the clinic who interacted with Billy and Sarah Hearns.

Ten and eleven o'clock passed without any sign of suspicious activity. With only an hour left until Rodrick reached the outskirts of Minneapolis, Damon pressed his team in the field to remain on alert. Beacon would make their move soon, he was certain of it.

"What's your logic module tell you, Cass? Once Rodrick enters the city, where's the best spot for an ambush?"

The android turned to study a holomap that hovered a few feet away. Damon stepped around the holotable and joined her. The map displayed downtown Minneapolis with a red line that highlighted the route Rodrick had been directed to follow.

"Skyway gives Beacon many options." Cassidy touched the map, illuminating two yellow dots. "But so long as Mr. Hearns stays on course, the two best chokepoints are here and here."

Damon nodded. The complexity of the Skyway transport network presented Beacon with multiple possible ambush spots and escape routes and, at the time Rodrick would be driving through the city, Skyway would be bustling with lunchtime activity.

The Skyway system was a grid network of tunnels and enclosed bridges that linked together most of downtown Minneapolis. It had originally been built to allow people to move about the city during the bitter-cold winters without going outside but now, one hundred seventy-plus years since the first section opened, Skyway was the primary mode of transportation for those who lived and worked in the city.

Thanks to a series of modernizations and expansions over time, Skyway was now capable of accommodating foot traffic, personal magboards and android taxicarts. The system also included a high-speed, maglev trolley that facilitated transportation to and from the farthest reaches of the downtown area.

Damon imagined Beacon operatives scrambling out of a Skyway access point and swarming Rodrick's RiverForge at a hololight. One of the operatives would disable the vehicle with an EMP nodule while another stunned Rodrick with a laser blast. Then, under cover of a smoke grenade, one or two others would spirit Billy away.

A faux food cart made the most sense to Damon. They would slide the sedated boy into a waiting cart and hustle into Skyway. Once inside, they would blend in with the many other service carts and pedestrian traffic. If Beacon acted true to form, they would employ diversions. Damon imagined other food carts with identical markings nearby. Operated by identical-looking androids, the carts would jumble up together to confuse the extensive NASF surveillance system monitoring Skyway. Most likely, they would have other operatives who would attempt to jam the surveillance feeds at the critical moment when the cart carrying Billy reached their intended escape point. Out they would leap from the cart and hop in a waiting vehicle outside and speed away.

Such a plan would have sounded far-fetched to those unfamiliar with Beacon, but not to Damon. He had seen the surveillance feed of just such a Skyway smuggling operation less than a year ago. Only, then, it had been a didgee conscript Beacon had kidnapped. They got away with it because NASF had been unaware of the intended "rescue" until it was nearly over. By the time officers responded, Beacon had escaped with the didgee. But this time, NASF was ready and waiting for them.

Damon studied the two chokepoints highlighted by Cassidy. "I agree. Both are close to intersections and there are multiple exits within a short distance of each."

"Correct, plus the exits empty onto streets with straight shots out of the city," said Cassidy.

"Okay. Let's concentrate our plainclothes near those two chokepoints. Cover the rest of the Skyway access points along Rodrick's route with nanos just in case we're wrong."

"Yes, sir."

While Cassidy transmitted those instructions to the contingent of officers mingling with pedestrians in Skyway, Damon returned to the holotable to ponder alternative Beacon strategies. As he focused his attention on the video feed of the gene center, Cassidy came up beside him.

"What about MGC? If they wait until they get near the clinic, what—"

The sound of Schwartz' voice in Damon's earbud radio cut short his question. "Major Spiers? The Hearns women are on the move."

Damon's eyes darted to the split holoscreen showing the Hearns' suburban home. Escorted by two of the family's androids, the three women boarded a sport utility cruiser parked in the driveway. Damon tapped his earbud. "Here we go, people. Show's starting."

Of all the aspects of Beacon's dual-rescue plan, Damon worried the least about the operation to kidnap Sarah Hearns and her daughters. The two androids were under Rodrick's command to stay with the women at all times. The distance between the house and church where the women planned to pray for Billy was a mere few miles. Damon's officers and drones had the church surrounded. Damon saw no way for Beacon to make it past them without being noticed, and no way they could get the Hearns women out without being captured. *Then again*, thought Damon, *Beacon rats always seem to have tricks up their sleeves.*

The wait for Beacon to launch its operations was vexing to Damon. In Chicago, they did nothing to apprehend the Hearns women on the way to St. Matthew's. Nor had they leaped into action once the women were inside.

The nano feed from inside the church showed the mother and daughters first kneeling before a table of lit votives and then moving to a pew to continue their private vigil.

Outside, every person, every android that passed by the church was scanned and identified by other nano drones. Thus far, all were ID'd as locals with NASF profiles devoid of any questionable activities or criminal offenses. The same scrutiny had been applied to the priest and nuns by the nano inside the church with the same results.

Four hundred miles away, Rodrick Hearns passed through the center of Minneapolis absent of any drama and was now just a few miles from the gene center.

With each minute that passed without a move from Beacon, Damon's uneasiness intensified. *What are they waiting for? Did they spot us? Have they aborted?* As he contemplated the disappointing possibility, his eyes were locked on a zoomed-in nano feed of Sarah Hearns praying. She looked serene, absorbed in the moment. He said to Cassidy, "Sure doesn't look nervous or like someone expecting to be rescued, does she? She hasn't checked her holoband or looked around the church once."

"Agreed. Neither have the daughters," Cassidy said.

"Yeah, but the daughters probably don't know what's going on. I doubt Mrs. Hearns said anything to them. Too much risk they might tell Mr. Hearns," said Damon.

"You think it's a setup, then? A diversion?"

"Either that or Beacon sniffed us out and aborted."

Just then, Officer Fenner's voice sounded in Damon's radio. "Mr. Hearns just pulled into the MGC parking lot."

Damon shifted his attention to the center screen of the holotable. The RiverForge slowed to a stop underneath the portico protecting the clinic's front entrance. A valet jogged out and briefly spoke to Rodrick, motioning him to drive to the side of the building. The gesture brought back the memory of Dylan's euthanization again, and Damon recalled the clinic had a separate, side entrance for euthanization patients.

The video feed from a glider drone high above the clinic zoomed out to capture the view of Rodrick guiding his vehicle to the side entrance. On the right-hand screen, Cassidy punched up another view, this one provided by a nano trailing close behind the RiverForge.

As soon as the car stopped, the sliding doors of the side entrance opened. Out came a wheeled gurney accompanied by two orderlies and Dr. Wells. While the orderlies removed Billy from the car, Wells spoke with Rodrick. Moments later, they disappeared into the clinic and the self-driving RiverForge parked in a nearby space.

Damon suddenly rued his decision to *not* place hidden cameras inside the clinic earlier in the week. Given his concerns about Wells and Fujita, he had not wanted to risk tipping them, especially since he had expected the rescue attempt to take place long before Hearns reached the clinic.

Glancing at his holoband, Damon noted the time. It was 12:21 p.m. Billy's euthanization procedure was scheduled for 1:00 p.m. Unless something dramatic occurred in the next thirty-nine minutes, the child would be put to sleep and Damon would miss out on another chance to foil Beacon.

Western border wall
Lakelands Province, New Atlantia

Twenty-two miles away, in a dense forest near the towering wall separating New Atlantia from Carapach, a holoimage of pine needles covering the ground flickered and then disappeared. Moments later, a hatch that had been hidden by the holoimage opened and two figures in hooded cloaks climbed out. As they began to creep through the forest, the hatch closed and the holoimage reactivated.

Two miles into their midday trek, they neared the bank of a stream. The lead figure stopped and they both knelt. For several minutes, they peered at a group of fishermen standing in the stream. One of the anglers looked their way, removed his red cap and wiped his brow.

The lead figure removed her hood and whispered, "Okay, Ake, that's the all-clear signal. Let's get the boat."

Together, Ellie and Akecheta approached the broken sections of a large, fallen pine tree. There were three sections in total and they headed for the middle one. Kneeling beside it, they rolled it aside, revealing a burrowed hole underneath. In the hole was a canoe laden with oars, fishing gear and laser rifles.

Several minutes later, they slid the boat into the water and began to paddle across the stream. No longer wearing the dampening cloaks that had masked their heat signatures and electromagnetic signals from detection by NASF gliders patrolling the area near the wall, the two androids joined the other anglers. The man in the red cap waded alongside the canoe and addressed Ellie. "Take the blue van. The uniforms are inside. We'll stow the canoe and your gear. Good luck."

Ellie and Akecheta guided the canoe onto the streambank and dragged the boat ashore. A few minutes later, after passing through a narrow stand of trees, they came upon two vans parked on the side of a gravel road. Following the man's instructions, they entered the blue van and drove away. The time was 12:52 p.m.

National Gene Center
Minneapolis, Lakelands Province, New Atlantia

At 12:58 p.m., Takoda entered the euthanization suite dressed in surgical gear. He was accompanied by a nurse and Yon. In the center of the room, ten-year-old Billy Hearns was strapped to a table. Nearby was a tray with a syringe and small bottle, and a bank of holomonitors displaying Billy's vital signs.

Takoda advanced toward Billy and looked up at an observation window on the far side of the room where he saw an ashen Rodrick Hearns standing next to the clinic director, Neville Thompson. Takoda nodded toward both of them and saw Thompson turn and say something to Rodrick. The man shook his head and began to weep. Thompson then nodded back to Takoda.

Turning toward the nurse, Takoda said, "Prepare the injection."

"Yes, Doctor."

The nurse lifted the bottle and read out the label. She showed it to Takoda and then to Yon. Both acknowledged it was the correct drug. The nurse then filled the syringe with the appropriate dosage and handed it to Takoda.

He looked up one more time at the observation window. The curtains were now closed. Takoda gazed down at Billy and said a silent prayer. When finished, he slid the needle of the syringe into the medicine port on Billy's arm and injected its contents.

In the background, he heard the nurse mark the time of the injection. As Takoda removed the needle and placed it back on the tray, the nurse began calling out the boy's falling vital signs. He backed away and looked up at the monitors.

Shortly thereafter, Billy exhaled deeply and his vital signs flatlined. Yon performed a quick physical examination to confirm the boy's passing and then called out the time of death at 1:07 p.m.

Command Center – NASF Province Headquarters
Minneapolis, Lakelands Province, New Atlantia

Damon received a call from Rodrick Hearns at 1:12 p.m., informing him of Billy's death. By then, the major already knew; the biometric data from the tracking implant had flatlined at 1:07. Amid Damon expressing his condolences, the emotional Rodrick whispered, "I don't understand. What happened?"

"It's hard to say. There could be multiple explanations."

Still maintaining a whisper, Rodrick said, "What about my wife and daughters? Where are they?"

Damon looked at the holotable screen. "They're still at the church."

Out of the corner of his eye, Damon noticed the tracking implant data screen had gone blank. A blinking message indicated the device was offline. He snapped his fingers to get Cassidy's attention and then pointed at the data screen. As Damon mouthed to her to check on the device, Rodrick mumbled, "Dear God, she couldn't go through with it, after all. She must have backed out."

Possibly, thought Damon, *but then again…*

"I need to call her. She'll want to know," Rodrick said.

"Uh…Mr. Hearns, I know it's an imposition, but I'd like you to hold off on making that call for now. I need to consult with my team. I'll call you right back."

"Why? What's the matter?"

"Just do as I ask, please."

Damon ended the call and turned to Cassidy. "What happened to the implant? Why is it offline?"

"I'm not certain. Either it's been disabled or the signal's being blocked."

Or it's been removed, Damon thought. "Have you tried to reconnect?"

"Yes. Multiple times. No response."

The doctors must have discovered the implant and removed it. That was the only explanation that made sense to Damon. The question now was whether the removal was coincidental or intentional.

"I don't know, Cass, it's damn suspicious."

"We could send an officer in to investigate."

"Yeah, we could. But that would mean revealing our surveillance, tipping Beacon to our presence. I'm not keen on doing that." Damon once again rued the lack of nano surveillance inside the clinic. After a brief moment of further reflection, he said, "What do you think? Was it legit? The euthanization? Could it have been staged? You know, flatline the kid with some kind of sedative, then remove the tracker so we can't detect them bringing him back?"

"It's possible, but there may be a more plausible scenario, Major."

"Like what?"

"Maybe Sarah Hearns changed her mind."

Damon looked toward the holotable screen showing Sarah Hearns and her daughters praying. He had to admit, it was possible. But Damon couldn't leave it to chance. Tapping his earbud, he instructed the device to call Rodrick. When the evvie answered, Damon said, "I need a favor from you."

Two sentences into describing the requested favor, Rodrick interrupted. "You want me to do what?"

"Please keep your voice down, sir. I know it's an odd request, but I can't send in one of my men without tipping off our presence."

In a curt whisper, Rodrick replied, "Major, my son is dead. I can assure you of that. I saw his body before they took him away."

"I understand, sir, it's just that the tracking device we implanted is offline and it shouldn't be. I need to know whether it was removed or not… discreetly."

"What difference does it make? Billy's dead."

Damon felt a tap on the shoulder. He turned to see Cassidy standing beside him. "Sir, the Hearns women are leaving the church."

He looked at the holotable and saw one of the Hearns' androids exit the church on one of the three screens. "Mr. Hearns, I have to go. Please do what I asked. I'll call you back shortly."

As he clicked the earbud to end the call, Damon watched the Hearns' SUV pull up to the curb.

"Major?" Cassidy said.

"Not now, Cass." Damon touched his earbud radio again and commanded the device to connect him to his team in Chicago. The device replied with a double tone, confirming the connection. Damon said, "Stay on your toes, people. They're coming out."

On the screen, the android waiting outside the church opened the SUV's rear door and, one by one, the Hearns women filed out and entered the vehicle.

"But, Major, we have a problem," Cassidy said.

Just as the Hearns android boarded the SUV, Damon looked up from the screen and saw Cassidy frantically working the holotable keyboard. "What's the mat—"

A bright flash flared up from the holotable. Crosstalk erupted in Damon's ear.

"Jesus…"

"What the hell…"

"Oh my God…"

Damon squinted back at the holotable as the flash on the screen began to fade, revealing a burning, twisted heap where the Hearns' SUV had been just moments before. The stunned major whispered, "Holy shit."

"Sir, we've lost the feed from the nano inside the church," said Cassidy.

"Screw the church—" Damon stopped in midsentence. Looking back at the burning vehicle, he cursed under his breath. "Damn it!" He pressed his finger against his earbud and interrupted the chatter flowing back and forth between HQ and the officers on site. "Schwartz, order your plainclothes inside the church to search it from top to bottom. You got it?"

"Yes, sir…hold on, sir…"

Damon heard Schwartz swear and raised voices in the background. "What's going on, Schwartz? Report."

Through his earbud, Damon heard Schwartz blurt, "Alert! Alert! All officers in the vicinity of St. Matthew's…officers down! Officers down!"

"Report, Schwartz! What's happening?" Damon bellowed.

Between huffs and puffs, Schwartz replied, "No response…from plainclothes…inside…shots fired…outside…two officers down…heading inside chur—"

The boom of another explosion drowned out Schwartz' voice. Damon yanked his earbud out and yelled at Cassidy. "Get the goddamned drones back online! Now!"

The time was 1:46 p.m.

National Gene Center
Minneapolis, Lakelands Province, New Atlantia

At 1:45 p.m., an ambulance van slowed to a stop at the rear of the Minneapolis Gene Center. Two uniformed personnel exited the vehicle and proceeded inside the building. Moments later, they reappeared outside wheeling a gurney laden with a body bag. After loading the bag in the ambulance, the vehicle slowly drove away.

In an unmarked NASF command truck two blocks away, Officer Fenner watched a glider feed of the ambulance leaving the clinic. Turning to a technician in the truck, he said, "Could be the kid. Tail the ambulance with a nano. Acquire face rec on the driver and passenger."

Fenner contemplated alerting Spiers about the ambulance but decided to wait until the facial recognition data came back. From the animated radio exchanges going back and forth between HQ and officers in Chicago, Fenner knew Spiers had his hands full at the moment. This was not the time to distract him.

However, he did transmit a message to Willow. Even though Fenner suspected she had her hands full too, he knew her android brain would assign the appropriate prioritization to his alert about the ambulance. If she thought it was important enough, she'd tell Spiers.

With the message to Willow sent, Fenner returned his attention to the monitors showing various outdoor views of the clinic. On one of the screens, he saw a stern-faced Rodrick Hearns exit the building and board his RiverForge. The technician asked if Fenner wanted a nano to tail Hearns too. Fenner thought of what was happening in Chicago and wondered if Hearns was aware of the situation. "You know what, just to be on the safe side, yeah, put a tail on Hearns too."

Downtown Minneapolis
Lakelands Province, New Atlantia

As the RiverForge wound its way through the city, Rodrick loosened his tie and spoke to the auto's computer. "Black out the windows."

"Privacy mode activated," said the male computer voice.

"Scan for surveillance."

"Scanning for surveillance devices." While he waited for the scan to finish, Rodrick reclined his seat. A few seconds later, the computer said, "One device detected."

"Identify," said Hearns.

"Nano drone registered to New Atlantia Security Force."

"So predictable." Rodrick shook his head. "Jam device."

As he again waited for the computer to fulfill his command, Rodrick withdrew a bottle of bourbon from the center console cabinet and filled a tumbler.

"Surveillance device neutralized," reported the computer.

"Good." Rodrick downed the tumbler and set it aside. "Send all incoming calls to voice mail and connect me with Sir Collins. Full encryption."

After a brief interval, Collins' gravelly voice sounded from the River-Forge speakers. "I trust you have good news, Roddy."

"Yes, Your Grace. It is done."

"Excellent," said Collins, the grandmaster of the Evvie Guild. "Any trouble?"

"Not until after the procedure."

"Oh? What happened?"

"The cheeky NASF major asked me to confirm Billy was dead, said their tracker was offline. He wanted me to find out whether it had been removed."

"Did you do as he asked?"

"I tried but Beacon's people had already taken Billy from the clinic."

Collins' cackling laugh echoed over the speakers. "They're crafty devils, I'll give them that."

"That, they are. How are things in Chicago?" Rodrick asked.

"The NASF people have their heads up their asses as usual. Never even noticed Beacon slip Sarah and the girls out of the church. They'll figure it out soon, though. But, of course, it will be too late. We'll make sure of that."

Rodrick poured another drink. "I'm in your debt, Your Grace."

"No, Roddy, the Guild is in your debt. At great sacrifice, you have demonstrated your loyalty once again. Now, we must pray that Beacon succeeds."

Raising his glass, Rodrick said, "To good fortune and a brighter tomorrow."

"To the Guild," Collins replied.

As Rodrick drained the glass, a beep signaled the end of the call. Closing his eyes, he held up the empty tumbler and said, "Goodbye my beloveds. May the grace of God be with you."

CHAPTER 6

HOOK, LINE & SINKER

Command Center, NASF Headquarters
Minneapolis, Lakelands Province, New Atlantia

Damon rubbed his temples while he watched the slow-motion replay of the Hearns females exiting the church. *Disaster! Complete, utter disaster! The Beacon rats did it again!*

He focused on the android holding the open vehicle door. *Two* of Rodrick's androids had gone into the church with Sarah and her daughters, and a nanovid from inside the church later showed *two* androids escorting the women from the pews…but only *one* came outside.

How did I not notice the missing android? Damon wondered. *How did Schwartz and his team miss it too?*

That oversight was costly. For in the thirty-four-second gap between when the Hearns women vacated their pew and when they appeared outside, Beacon had triggered their rescue. *It was a damn clever plan*, thought Damon.

He cued up a "before" nanovid of the church vestibule, the foyer-like chamber linking the nave with the doors leading outside. On one side of the vestibule was a recess which held life-sized statues of Mary and Joseph set upon block pedestals. On the right was a similar-sized statue of St. Matthew. Also on a block pedestal, the saint sat in a large chair and had an open book in his hands.

The craftsmanship of the faux statues was remarkable, which is why none of Damon's officers had given them a second look during their multiple clandestine visits to the church in the days leading up to the Hearns' vigil.

In some ways, Damon couldn't blame them, though. The faux statues were good enough forgeries to also fool St. Matthew's priests and nuns, who were collectively flabbergasted by the scene in the vestibule after the rescue was complete. Well, not all were flabbergasted. The parish priest, the man who headed up St. Matthew's, was missing.

No doubt the AWOL priest is a Beacon operative or sympathizer, thought Damon. *He probably provided Beacon access to make the switch with the real statues before Sarah even told Rodrick of her plan to stay in Chicago.*

Damon cued up the "after" vid recorded by Schwartz once his team finally made it into the church. It showed the broken shells of the faux statues littering the floor. *How simple. How clever.*

He pictured the rescue in his mind. As soon as the Hearns party of five passed into the vestibule, one of Rodrick's androids jammed the feed of the nano inside the church. At the same time, clone androids of each Hearns female broke out of their statue shells. Once free of their casings, the clones handed nuns' robes to Sarah and the girls while the other of Rodrick's androids stepped outside to meet the SUV.

As Sarah and her daughters donned nun attire, their clones began to file outside. Somewhere during that span, Damon's plainclothes officers, posing as worshipers, were stunned by laser blasts fired by the family android who had remained behind...or possibly by the missing parish priest.

When the first explosion occurred, the Hearns women dashed out a side entrance. Garbed in their nuns' robes, they blended into the scurry of people emptying onto the street to gawk at the burning vehicle while other passersby ran away in fear.

Damon switched now to the glider drone video showing the church and surrounding streets from above. Advancing the video in slow motion, he watched three nuns run away...led by a priest.

He imagined Schwartz or someone from his team might have noticed the nuns had it not been for the laser fire that erupted as the NASF squad closed in on the church. Fired from a building across the street, the lasers knocked out two more officers. Then came the second explosion just outside St. Matthew's. The second of Rodrick's androids, the one who had stayed behind in the church, was hit by the laser fire and exploded on the steps just outside the entrance.

The glider video captured the explosion *and* the view of the priest and three nuns boarding a waiting white truck around the corner from the church. But no one on Damon's team, including Damon himself, had noticed the nuns flee the chaotic scene in real-time. Everyone had been focused on the church, the laser fire and two explosions.

By the time Schwartz' team secured the area, it was too late. The white van had long disappeared beyond the glider's field of vision, blending in with many other white trucks driving in and around suburban Chicago.

The truth behind the stupefying events began to fall into place for Damon as soon as Schwartz informed him of the broken statues in the church vestibule. Shortly after, Schwartz radioed the discovery of only android remains inside the burned-out SUV. Then, Damon and Cassidy had gone back through the drone feeds and the rest became clear.

Damon stared once again at the frozen video image of the white truck speeding away and his anger swelled. *You played me in Chicago, Beacon, but it's not over yet. You still have to get them over the border and Chicago's a long way from Carapach.*

He was sure the underground network thought they'd played him in Minneapolis too, but thanks to a gutty, quick decision by Fenner, NASF was still in the game. The ambulance he had tailed with a nano had driven to an incinerator complex close to the border with Carapach. The drivers, two unidentified androids, had wheeled a body bag into the incinerator facility and then left in the ambulance.

At that moment, Fenner had been caught in a dilemma. Should he have the nano stay at the incinerator, or follow the ambulance again? With Damon consumed by events in Chicago, Fenner opted to follow the ambulance and dispatched another nano to observe the incinerator. While that decision had meant the incinerator went unobserved for twenty minutes while the second nano was in flight, it turned out to be the right call.

For the ambulance made a long, circuitous drive around Minneapolis before coming to a stop in a forest northwest of the city. There, the nano captured footage of the androids ditching the medic uniforms and peeling the faux-ambulance wrap off of the blue van underneath. And for the last three hours, the androids and the van had stayed put, as if waiting for someone.

That had given Damon all the time he needed to discreetly maneuver other assets into place — one team near the incinerator, another near the blue van and the final team at the border checkpoint some five miles away. With additional eyes still on the gene center, Damon had all his bases covered. The next move would be up to Beacon and, this time, Damon had them cornered.

"There goes Dr. Wells," Cassidy said.

Damon looked at his holoband. It was 6:08 p.m. "Fenner, track him all the way to the border."

"Yes, sir. Nano is locked on target."

If Damon could have followed Wells all the way home, he would have, but, by mutual treaty, neither New Atlantia nor Carapach was permitted to send security teams or surveillance drones into each other's territory. While that restriction did not prevent Damon from deploying NASF's satellite to track Wells, the satellite's surveillance camera was currently trained on the forest where the blue van was hidden.

"What's Dr. Fujita's ETA at the border?" Damon asked Cassidy.

"Twelve minutes."

Damon gazed at the holotable screen showing Fujita's Starlight cruiser driving toward Carapach, the evening sun edging toward the horizon in front of her. Turning to Cassidy, he said, "Find out where Schwartz stands with Rodrick Hearns. I'm tired of waiting for an update."

"Yes, sir. Right away."

Hearns had some explaining to do. He had left the clinic without Damon's knowledge and permission. Yes, he had left Damon a holosnap indicating he had tried to get the clinic personnel to let him see Billy again, only to find out the boy's body had already been taken for cremation. But then the evvie jammed the nano following him back to Chicago, and he ignored Damon's subsequent calls. There was also the matter of Rodrick's androids. The evvie had sworn they were loyal to him, yet they appeared to have aided in Sarah's escape.

With so many questions that needed answers, Damon had NASF officers intercept Hearns' RiverForge and take him into custody. The officers drove him to Chicago where he was now being interrogated by Schwartz.

"Sir, Schwartz just replied to my transmission," Cassidy said. "He says Hearns has been uncooperative. Refuses to answer any questions until his Guild attorney arrives."

Damon shook his head. *Evvies. They're all alike. They all think they're above the law.* "All right. Tell Schwartz to park Hearns' butt in the nastiest cell they have down there. When his attorney arrives, park him in a conference room. No one gets in to see Hearns until we finish up in Minneapolis. Got it?"

"Yes, sir."

Four more hours passed by. Finally, at 10:27 p.m., as the yawning Damon was pouring a cup of coffee at the back of the command center, Cassidy's voice sounded in his earbud. "Major, the blue van's lights just came on. It's on the move."

Streambank near the western border wall
Lakelands Province, New Atlantia

From the cover of underbrush, Takoda saw a vehicle come to a stop on the far side of the stream. Covered in a dampening cloak, he lowered night-vision goggles over his eyes and watched Ellie and Akecheta exit the van.

It had been a long day of cat and mouse with NASF, and while Takoda's and Yon's parts in Beacon's grand rescue scheme had been small thus far, the final stage of Billy's rescue now rested squarely on their shoulders.

Takoda felt every ounce of that burden as he turned to Yon and whispered, "Any sign of gliders?"

Next to him, scanning the sky with her night-vision goggles, Yon whispered back, "No, but that doesn't mean there are none up there. Could be in stealth mode."

They were both well aware that NASF had not been fooled by the faux-euthanization earlier in the day. After going through the rest of the day at the clinic, following their normal routines as closely as possible, they had both noticed the first sign of trouble on their drives home. At the border crossing, they encountered a more thorough security inspection than usual.

Then, when they arrived at their homes, both had encrypted messages from Hoot waiting on their holonodes. In Hoot's good news, bad news message, she led off by telling them Sarah's part of the rescue had been successful. Switching to the bad news, she informed them Ellie had detected a nano drone following the ambulance from the clinic. Worse, whoever was managing the drone had not fallen for the body bag drop off at the incinerator. Try as they had to disinterest the nano, they had been unsuccessful. Hoot's parting words had been, "Therefore, you should expect NASF to intervene. Priority one is the boy. Priority two is protecting the location of the tunnel. Priority three is your own safety."

With those words replaying in his mind, Takoda retrained his night-vision goggles on Ellie and Akecheta as they loaded the bag carrying the still-sedated Billy Hearns into a canoe anchored on the streambank. Under the moonlit sky, they began to paddle quietly across the babbling water. All of a sudden, Yon grabbed his arm. "Shit! I've got a glider. It's headed this way."

Takoda looked up. Against the orange and black landscape depicted on his goggles' display, he spotted the white glow of the glider's heat signature streaking in their direction.

"Damn." Takoda shifted his attention back to the stream. Amid the black water, he picked up the orange shape of the canoe. They were too far away. They would not make it across before the glider converged on the stream. He pressed his earbud radio. "Ellie, Ake, cloak yourselves and Billy. Quickly."

"We're already cloaked," Akecheta replied.

"Then giddyup, gliders incoming." Takoda turned to Yon. "Do what you can to confuse the drones."

Beacon didn't have drones that could compete with NASF gliders, but, thankfully, Hoot had supplied Takoda and Yon with two types of countermeasure drones — two decoys and a signal jammer. The drones had been waiting for them when they arrived at the Carapach side of the tunnel. As Takoda watched Yon launch the signal jammer, he prayed it would buy them the necessary time to get Billy to the tunnel.

Through his goggles, Takoda followed the basketball-sized drone as it shot up into the air and streaked toward the gliders. Beside him, Yon worked the holoconsole controlling the drone and said, "Okay, the jammer's active."

Takoda snuck from the underbrush and crept to the streambank. As he waded into the water, he heard a sharp whisper from Yon. "It's working!"

He didn't bother looking up to confirm, his eyes riveted on the silhouette of the canoe drawing closer. If the jammer did its job, the glider, deprived of the GPS signals used to control its orientation and guidance, would lose its bearings and crash. Sure enough, moments later, Takoda heard the sound of snapping branches rise above the croaks and chirps emanating from the surrounding woods.

"Glider down," Yon said, a triumphant tone in her voice. Shortly thereafter, however, her voice expressed despair. "Crap, here comes another one!"

Takoda looked up and scanned the sky but he could neither see nor hear the incoming drone. Casting his gaze back to the stream, he urged his androids to paddle faster. "Come on, Ake, put your back into it! You, too, Ellie. Hustle."

A fireball lit up the sky in the distance, causing Yon to blurt, "Jammer's gone. The glider got it."

Before Takoda could tell Yon to launch one of the decoy drones, he heard the whirr of rotors ripple across the water. As he waded deeper into the stream, he saw the heat signature of the decoy moving downstream away from the direction of the canoe. With the frigid water now up to his beltline, Takoda reached out and snagged the bow of the incoming canoe.

Looking past the still-paddling Akecheta, he spied Ellie cradling the cloak-sheath-covered child.

Behind him, he heard Yon say, "The glider is turning for the decoy."

Tapping off his earbud radio, Takoda called to Ellie. "El, as soon as the canoe hits ground, get the kid up and out. Run like hell for the tunnel. You got it?"

"Copy that," Ellie said.

Just as Takoda grabbed hold of the canoe, Ake stopped paddling and slid out to help him drag it ashore. Ellie leaped over Takoda's head, Billy Hearns in her arms. Over the sound of her prodigious splash in the water, Takoda heard the deep-throated groan of the glider drone and saw the reflection of its searchlight illuminating the stream's surface. Through gritted teeth, he said, "Yon, do something. Fast."

There was a flash of light and a hissing sound, and the glider's searchlight went dark. Looking over his shoulder, Takoda saw Akecheta, laser rifle in hands, fire another blaze. The drone uttered a high-pitched mechanical whine. Seconds later, Ake's third shot blew it apart, its debris spraying into the stream and woods.

By the time Takoda looked back around, Ellie and Billy were gone. He turned to Akecheta and said, "Torch the canoe and send it downstream. Might fetch us a little more time."

Removing his cloak, Akecheta said, "Got a better idea. You get moving. I'll cover the rear." The hulking Makoa snapped off a salute and pushed the canoe back into the stream. As he began to paddle it back across the water, he called out, "It's been a pleasure serving you, Tak."

Yon came up beside Takoda. Out of breath, she said, "What's Ake doing?"

"I don't know, but we don't have time to wait around and find out."

Takoda ripped off his cloak and prodded Yon to do the same. With their heat signatures exposed, he tucked the cloaks under his arm and grabbed hold of Yon's hand. As he began running, Hoot's words echoed in his mind, *"Priority three is your own safety."*

Yon tugged at his hand and said, "Wait. Where are you going? The tunnel's the other way!"

"I know. Come on, let's give Ellie some breathing room. Hopefully, any more gliders will follow our heat sigs."

Command Center – NASF Province Headquarters
Minneapolis, Lakelands Province, New Atlantia

Damon's eyes zigged and zagged around the holographic display. At the far left of a 3D map, two blinking red lights marked the last reported positions of his downed gliders. To the far right, the curving outline of the border wall stood above the forest pines. In the center, the white beacons of a tandem of newly dispatched gliders streaked above the landscape. Soon, they would diverge. One would head for the two orange heat signatures moving deeper into the woods, while the other would arc toward the blue dot that marked the van racing away from the stream.

Speaking to the officer controlling the drones, Damon said, "Keep the gliders at a safe distance. I don't want them to splash any more of our birds." He turned to another operator in the control center. "Alert the border team. Remind them I want the agitators captured, not killed."

Damon refocused his attention on the display, his eyes following the van's progress. Up ahead of the blue dot, he saw a glut of green dots blocking the road, icons identifying his NASF Viper-class androids lying in wait. *Nice try, rodent. You're about to run out of road.*

Shifting his gaze to the serpentine course of the orange dots in the forest, Damon smiled. *Come on, lead me to your ferret hole.* He turned to Cassidy. "Patch me through to Commander Sands."

"Yes, Major."

Seconds later, Damon heard a deep voice in his earbud radio. "Sands, here."

"Tommy, it's Damon. Do you have eyes on the perps in the forest?"

"Affirmative."

"Good. Get ready to deploy your troops. Crowd them, don't storm them. I want them to lead us to their tunnel."

"Sir?" Cassidy said. "The van's picking up speed."

Damon nodded. "Must have detected our blockade." Through his radio, Damon spoke to the commander manning the barrier. "Look sharp, Grimwald. As soon as you have visual—"

A blast of static spiked in Damon's ear. The holographic map fluttered and then disappeared. Yanking out his earbud, Damon wheeled around to face the bank of operators manning their surveillance stations. "What now? Get my map back up."

The mix of goggled men and women, hands outstretched, tapped their floating holoboards with rapid strokes, but no one spoke. The apparent show of desperation told Damon all he needed to know. His adversaries had disabled the communications link with the border security team... and most likely the drones overhead.

"Damn it! Someone talk to me. Tell me what's going on."

"Interference of some kind. It's not on our end," Cassidy said.

"A jamming device?" Damon asked.

"Possibly...or an EMP attack."

"What?" Damon frowned. "From where?"

"I don't know. But it's knocked out our glider feeds as well."

"Punch up the satellite, then. Put it on my table."

Damon leaned over the holotable just as the live night-vision satellite image appeared. He blinked several times as he tried to make sense of the scene. There was a haze that hovered over the area. As thick as a cumulus cloud, there was no way to see below it. But from what Damon could see at the periphery of the haze, there was no mystery as to what had happened. A fire raged in the forest and he could see the edge of a large crater where the security barricade had been erected. The van had exploded.

"Magnify," Damon said. "Focus on the crater."

As the pixels in the recalibrated image began to fill in and sharpen, Damon saw heaps of twisted, burning objects.

"Not again," Damon mumbled. He stared at the image for a few more seconds and then said, "Cassidy, get those drones working or send in new ones. Order reinforcements from the sector barracks. Shut down every road in a twenty-mile radius...and get the damned comms back online!"

Western border wall
Lakelands Province, New Atlantia

When Takoda and Yon reached the tunnel, they found the hologrid camouflaging the entrance was still active.

"Do you think Ellie made it?" Yon asked.

Takoda knelt and lifted the rock which concealed the control box for the hologrid. "I hope so. She had a hell of a head start on us."

"Should we wait a few minutes? Just in case?"

In the distance, Takoda could hear the echoes of radio chatter and men shouting. "We don't have the time. She knows how to open the hatch." He deactivated the holoimage obscuring the tunnel hatch and punched in the code to open it. Pulling the hatch door up, Takoda stared into the dark maw and said, "You first."

Just as Yon began to step down the inner ladder, a voice echoed up from inside the tunnel. "Wait. I'm coming up."

It was Ellie. Yon stepped out of the tunnel and said, "Is everything okay?"

The android's head appeared through the entrance. "Yes. Billy's secure."

"Thank the four gods," Yon said.

Ellie exited the tunnel and knelt next to Takoda. "You two go ahead. I'll keep watch."

Takoda followed Yon into the tunnel. When they reached the bottom of the ladder, Takoda called up to Ellie. "All right. We're good. Get inside and seal the hatch. I'll reactivate the grid from down here."

But Ellie did not respond. As Takoda cupped his hands around his mouth to call up again, the hatch slammed shut. Looking to his right, he spied the hologrid control box next to the ladder. The activation indicator turned green and the tunnel lights illuminated.

"Uh oh," said Yon.

"Uh oh is right," Takoda said. "The border patrol must have been clos-ing in. Come on, let's get out of here."

As they ran along the passageway snaking beneath the border wall, Takoda looked back and wondered if he would ever see Ellie again. His stomach churned as he thought of Ake's sacrifice, but the prospect of los-ing Ellie too made his heart ache. Gritting his teeth, he looked forward and pressed on. The cost of rescuing Billy had indeed been high. He could only hope Sarah Hearns would come through now with the information they needed.

CHAPTER 7

HEAVY TOLL

Ke'e Cove
Kauai, the Hawaiian Islands

Natti reeled in the line and yanked the fish out of the ocean. She turned to show RJ the wriggling fish but discovered RJ had his head turned toward the dense jungle behind the beach.

"Check it out. A goatfish! Your favorite," said Natti.

RJ quickly peeked at Natti before returning to look at the jungle. "Shouldn't we be going soon?"

Kaleo answered from his spot by other poles anchored into slots on the rocky overhang. "Relax, little man. Sun's nowhere near the horizon. We've got plenty of time. You *do* want to eat tonight, don't you?"

"Oh, leave him alone," Avana said. "He's just saying what we're all thinking. The jungle is creepy this time of day. That's why no one likes fishing here."

Natti shook her head as she removed the fish from the hook. Avana's comments were accurate; no one in the village liked fishing in the remote cove, but it wasn't right of her to stoke RJ's fears. She held out the fish to Avana and said, "Less talking, more working. Spike it, bleed it and ice it. RJ, re-bait the line and set the pole."

With a smattering of grumbles, the two did as they were told. Natti wiped her hands on a towel beside the ice chest, storing their catch for the day and limping out onto the overhang. Kaleo nodded to her and raised his head toward the sky. "Clouds *are* getting dark. Rain's coming."

"Yeah, looks that way."

"Might be a good reason to head back sooner rather than later."

"Nah, it'll pass over quickly. It always does."

Though she spoke with confidence, Natti felt the same apprehension as Kaleo. But the village had to eat, and Natti's small family had to do their part. Returning with their ice chest only a third-full of fish was not an option. Besides, jakalis only attacked at night. Plus, Akela had sent two Makoas with them, Bali and Fiji. If there was any sign of jakalis, they would be the first to raise an alarm, and right now they looked at ease.

Bali, rifle slung over his shoulder, sat on a rock by the entrance to the jungle trail leading up the hillside. Machete resting on his lap, he scanned the perimeter. Fiji stood on the beach by the overhang, her feet in the surf and laser rifle at the ready. In synchronized fashion, she scanned left as Bali scanned right. When their gazes reached their respective ends of the perimeter, they reversed the directions of their scans.

Looking back at Kaleo, Natti noticed his hands were clenched into fists. With a soothing tone, she said, "Why don't you take a break? Maybe help RJ build a sandcastle. I'll keep an eye on the poles."

He nodded and relaxed his hands. "Okay. The rain will probably wash it away before we finish, but I get you. It'll distract the little guy."

The sunbaked Hawaiian teen hopped off the overhang and corralled RJ. Together, they plodded through the sand and found a spot near the still-scanning Fiji. Kaleo chatted her up while he began to dig.

One of the poles creaked, drawing Natti's attention. As she reached for it, another line went taut. "Avana, come help."

The wiry thirteen-year-old left her seat atop the ice bucket and jogged up beside Natti. She took hold of the second pole and worked to reel in the catch. Meanwhile, Natti found herself struggling to stand as the fish on her line fought hard to break free.

"Why don't we switch?" Natti said. "This one's too big for me."

It was a hard admission for Natti to make, for she had more fishing experience than any of the others, but her bad leg made her unstable. She didn't want to fall on the sharp volcanic rocks and add insult to injury by losing the fish. Avana was younger, stronger and had a knack for landing big catches.

Soon after they switched poles, the clouds let loose with a downpour. Natti's tank top and shorts were drenched in less than a minute. Through vision blurred by raindrops pelting her eyes, Natti saw Avana stagger forward and teeter on the edge of the overhang. She bent her knees as she grappled with whatever was on the end of her line.

A shadow moved past Natti's field of vision. It was Fiji. The android grabbed hold of Avana's pole and pushed the teen aside. Avana stumbled and shouted at the android as it inexplicably threw down the rod.

Above the sound of the pounding rain, Natti heard another sound. It was RJ…screaming. Natti started to turn toward him but stopped when she felt the rod yanking out of her hands. The unexpected resistance caused Natti to tip over but Fiji caught her by the arm before she hit the rocks.

Heart racing, Natti turned her head to look at the jungle. "Oh, no."

"Get behind me, all of you," shouted Fiji. "Stay together."

Across the beach, through a curtain of rain, Natti saw Bali on the ground, a pack of jakalis on top of him.

"Let go! We have to run!" RJ screamed. "Let go!"

Natti turned to see Kaleo carrying the squirming RJ. The young boy pummeled Kaleo on the face and shoulders.

"No!" said Fiji, her amplified voice booming out. "We have signaled the village. More Makoas are on the way. Take cover behind the rock."

Before anyone could protest her command, Fiji opened fire with her laser rifle. Flaming chunks of jakalis tumbled in the air. Those that escaped Fiji's initial barrage continued to spear and smash Bali. Natti saw sparks and jerky motions from Bali's arms. More of the beasts raced out from the cover of the jungle. Natti instinctively looked around the cove and spotted another pack streaming toward them from the opposite direction. She pointed toward them and said, "Fiji, look! More are coming."

As Fiji turned to aim her weapon at the onrushing jakalis, Natti pulled the android's machete from its sheath. Anger overtook fear and she barked at Kaleo. "Get the spike, the gutting knives. Hand them out."

The stream of another laser beam shot forth from Fiji's rifle. The blinding jolt cut through the legs of sprinting jakalis like a blade slicing open pineapples. They howled and fell to the ground. Behind them, more jaka-lis spread out, zig-zagging a course toward Fiji, Natti and her huddled charges.

An explosion rocked the beach. Natti lost her balance and splashed into the surf. As she crawled out of the water, ears ringing, eyes stinging, the once quiet cove was transformed into a gruesome battleground.

The sand was dotted with burning debris. The spot where Bali had come under attack was now a crater. Behind it, the edge of the jungle was engulfed in flames. Injured jakalis, some of them on fire, writhed on the ground. Fiji sprayed the beach and tree line with blazing beams.

As Natti regained her wits, she squeezed the handle of the machete and rose to her feet. A spear flew past her hip and struck the rock beside her. Natti turned to see RJ cowering and covering his ears. His eyes were frozen with panic, his face turning purple as he screamed. Avana crouched in front of RJ, protecting him from the advancing jakalis. She had a fish spike in hand and a snarl on her face.

A flash of panic raced through Natti. Kaleo! Where was Kaleo? Her head shot up and she scanned the beach. Through the haze of smoke mix-ing with rain, she spotted him sprawled on his back, a spear in his abdomen.

Something snapped inside of Natti and she found herself staggering toward Kaleo, machete slicing through the air. A jakali lay on the beach, not far from him. The bloody beast was crawling toward her injured friend. Memories of the torment she had endured rushed into her mind and Natti began to growl at the wounded jakali, at all of them that littered the beach. With both hands clutching the hilt of the machete, Natti hopped forward until she loomed over the crawling jakali. She raised the weapon above her head. Amid the fires surrounding her, the blade sparkled.

Natti screamed as she lopped off the jakali's head. Spinning around, she looked for another to attack. She felled three more before two knocked her off her feet, tackling her to the ground. One pinned her down and bit her neck while the other, a female jakali, kicked her in the head. A third and a fourth quickly joined the assault, beating her legs and arms with their fists. Natti struggled against them but there were too many, and they were too strong. Natti closed her eyes and screamed as they lifted her and began to carry her away.

But then, just as suddenly, they stopped and dropped her. Natti heard gunfire and cries of pain. She curled into a ball and covered her head. A body fell on her. She wiggled to get away, but the body lifted off of her so fast it felt as if it had been blown off by a giant wind. Natti opened her eyes and saw a Makoa standing beside her, flinging jakalis across the sand like twigs. Woozy, she curled into a ball again and faded into unconsciousness.

From the hillside overlooking the cove, a camouflaged woman watched the Makoas finish off the last of the jakalis. Hidden by foliage, she lowered her binoculars and smiled at the grunting jakali male squatting next to her. Smoothing his greasy hair, she said, "There is much to improve on, but you did well, Christopher."

The jakali smiled or at least tried to. His disfigured jaw and tensed facial muscles produced more of a sneer, but she understood the gesture. Christopher flared his nostrils and tried to speak, but he still lacked control over his vocal cords so all that came out were groans. He pointed to his open mouth, his bloodshot eyes pleading with her.

The woman reached into her pocket and pulled out a small vial. The jakali snatched it and dashed off into the underbrush. She smiled again and raised the binoculars once more. Through its magnified lenses, she watched Makoas gather up the injured fishing party while other androids piled fallen jakalis onto a bonfire. She zoomed in on the face of the unconscious girl who had wielded the machete. A Makoa cradled her in his arms.

Lowering the binoculars, the woman whispered, "Sleep well, gutant. The worst is yet to come."

The southern Northlands
En route to Flathead, Montana

As the assault vehicle bumped along the rutted mountain road, Caelan sipped coffee and walked down the aisle lined by his docked hunters. The androids would be recharging and updating their software for another hour, so it was an opportune time for Caelan to assess the damage inflicted by jakalis during the last two weeks of hunts.

Of his ten Makoas, only two made it through their jakali skirmishes unscathed. Among the damaged androids, one was destroyed beyond repair. Two others were barely operational. Caelan had been forced to use them in the last few operations solely as recon and comms support. The remaining five were in fighting shape despite a range of broken and battered parts.

Collectively, it was not the worst damage Caelan's squad had experienced in his jakali search, rescue and destroy missions across the globe, but it was close. He patted his dormant squad leader, Elvis, on the shoulder. "Hopefully, the chop-shop in Flathead will have all the parts we need."

Examining Elvis' dented torso, patched neck and missing fingers, Caelan rued the jakalis' improved fighting skills. They were becoming more proficient combatants, which was a terrifying thought.

Not only were they learning to coordinate attacks and mount defenses with greater sophistication, but the gutant beasts were also learning how to exploit their opponents' weaknesses to greater effect.

Caelan first noticed the change in their behavior during his spring expedition into the Northlands when he encountered jakalis who had learned to distinguish humans from androids. This development led the gutant-freaks to create new combat strategies depending on the type of adversary in question. Caelan assumed the jakalis had made this leap after recognizing the differences in smell. For even though humans and androids were nearly indistinguishable visually, it was hard to replicate certain odors; the most relevant as it applied to jakalis was the smell of fear.

The sight of a pack of jakalis streaking toward a human was terrifying enough to make the toughest of men break into a sweat, and in that perspiration, humans exuded detectable chemicals that signaled fear to other humans, so-called fear-sweat. Androids didn't emit fear-sweat.

So, Caelan adopted new tactics of his own, often layering his Makoas in clothing removed from dead human victims. Not only did he use the clothes to "nose-blind" his adversaries in crowds, but he also used the clothes on occasion to lure jakalis into a kill-zone.

After several successful confrontations using this new strategy, Caelan discovered his opponents began using another tactic to distinguish humans from androids. They used their teeth to bite off chunks of flesh. Since androids didn't bleed and their flesh was synthetic, the jakalis learned to quickly distinguish the taste and sight of human bite wounds from those administered to androids.

Strategically, the jakalis had also recently recognized that humans typically deployed androids as front-line soldiers and guards. With this knowledge, they modified their attacks on villages or other fixed clusters of humans, sending in feint-parties to draw off androids before unleashing the core of their attacks on humans behind the lines.

Caelan was at a loss to identify the catalyst for the emergence of these new coordinated behaviors. He had hunted the beasts for years, and for much of that time, jakalis had shown no ability or interest in working with other jakalis. That was what had made them easy to hunt. They were so consumed by their madness, their lust, they neither thought nor acted rationally. But that was changing. If he only knew *why* he could further adapt his tactics.

Were the new behaviors signs of a new gutation, one that aided certain jakalis' abilities to suppress their madness and communicate with each other? If not that, then had an entirely new breed of jakalis arisen? Among the upper castes, Caelan knew there was a fear that unsterilized jakalis would mate with each other. Were these changes evidence of such a phenomenon?

Setting aside genetic alterations as possible catalysts, Caelan considered the possibility the jakalis had discovered a new food source in the Northlands, one with ingredients that quelled their emotions enough to allow rational thoughts to surface more frequently. Or maybe a native tribe had plied them with mind-soothing remedies as appeasements for sparing their villages.

Whatever the catalyst, the evolution of jakali tactics was alarming. Caelan sat down across the aisle from what remained of his favorite android, Ertha, and sighed. "Look what they did to you, luv. I'm so sorry I couldn't stop them."

The Athena-class android had not only been his best tracker, but also she had been his comfort bot for several years. Unfortunately, she was too damaged to ever hold a laser rifle or share his bed again. The jakalis had pulverized her into scrap metal and destroyed her brain core, meaning Caelan would have to buy a replacement and train her all over again.

That thought saddened him. Ertha had been more than a supplicant machine to him. She had been a companion unlike any other he had known. And a pack of jakalis had demolished her in less than a minute. Alarming, indeed.

He raised his coffee cup to Ertha's remains and said, "Cheers to you, luv. You were the best, more than I deserved. I'll make the bastards pay for what they did, don't you fret about that."

Gutant refugee village
Limahuli, Kauai, the Hawaiian Islands

Avana sat by Natti and layered a cool cloth on her friend's forehead. Beside her sat RJ. With his arms circled around his raised knees, he rocked back and forth and stared at Natti as if prodding her to wake up. Looking across the infirmary, Avana watched the village doctor, Malo, change the dressing of Kaleo's spear wound. Behind them, she saw the first light of dawn appear through the window.

Praise the four gods, she thought. Throughout the long hours of overnight darkness, Avana had sat by the unconscious Natti, holding her hand, waiting for the snarls and growls of a jakali attack on the village. Blessedly, no attack had occurred and, now that dawn had arrived, the exhausted Avana could finally relax her tensed mind and muscles.

She rested her head against the wall and closed her eyes, willing herself to fall asleep. But sleep would not come, for her mind still grappled with the memories of the melee on the beach. While Fiji had prevented the jakalis from reaching Avana and RJ, the android could not shield them from the terror of watching endless numbers of jakalis stream out of the jungle.

They were supposed to be safe during the daytime. Avana had been told on many occasions that the jakalis' eyes were so sensitive to sunlight, they could not see during the day…even when it was cloudy…even when it was raining. Tha was why jakalis only hunted at night. Only, that adage didn't appear true anymore.

Are we to be prisoners, hiding inside all the time, now? How will we gather food? How will we fetch water?

Avana was certain similar thoughts were bouncing around in RJ's mind, though he had not said a word since the Makoas rescued them from the beach. Avana opened her eyes and wrapped her arm around him, kissing him on the head. *I don't know what's a worse end*, Avana thought. *Being killed by a jakali or turning into one.*

The latter fate awaited Avana, RJ, Kaleo and Natti if they survived that long. Avana knew it, they all knew it. She turned and looked at Natti. For her, the wait would not be long now. The physical signs of her gutations were evident. And after watching Natti's growl-infused rage on the beach, Avana suspected the last stage of the transformation, madness, was not far away.

In that last stage, Natti would begin to experience unbearable pain in her body and mind. The only relief she would find would come in the form of hormones released during sexual gratification, leading her to develop aggressive behaviors to satisfy the urges and ease her pain.

While Avana knew Malo had been able to lessen the impulses among other gutant teens in the village by injecting them with a cocktail of artificial hormones, it was only a short-term fix. Over time, a jakali's brain required more frequent and stronger doses of hormones to overcome increasing levels of pain and, at some point, no amount of sex or supplemented hormones were effective.

This was what drove jakalis mad and filled them with uncontrollable rage. Many jakalis still clung to the desire for the hormones, leading them to defile humans they caught, but most found satisfaction only in beating and killing captured prey. And that was what Avana and other humans were to jakalis, prey.

As Avana adjusted the cloth on Natti's forehead, she thought it would be more merciful if Natti died in her sleep now rather than let the madness overtake her later. That thought was still cycling through her mind when Malo appeared at Natti's bedside and said, "Hey, you and RJ should lie down and try to get some sleep. There are open beds in the other room. If anything changes with Natti or Kaleo, I will let you know."

"What's wrong with her?" RJ asked. "Why won't she wake up? Why does she have a fever?"

Malo crouched down and touched RJ's hand. "She'll be okay, buddy. Sometimes, our bodies go to sleep to help us heal."

"She doesn't look right. Neither does Kaleo," RJ said. "I think they're sick. Why aren't you giving them medicine?"

Avana was a part-time orderly in the infirmary, so she knew the answer to RJ's question. There was no medicine to give. The infirmary had run out of all but a few medications a month prior, and Chief Akela had yet to find a trading partner willing to barter for a resupply. So, until the situation changed, the village had only natural remedies to treat the sick and wounded.

"Well, RJ, it's like this," said Malo, "we don't know exactly what's causing their fevers, so we could make things worse by guessing what's wrong with them and giving them medicine. Right now, the fevers are under control. We've treated their wounds the best we can. They seem to be resting comfortably. So, there's not much more we can do until they wake up and tell us if they're experiencing other symptoms besides the fevers."

Avana hugged RJ. "In other words, rest is the best medicine they can have right now."

Malo smiled at Avana. "Well said. Better said." He pointed at the two of them. "The same advice goes for you. Now, hit the sack. Doctor's orders."

Begrudgingly, Avana unwrapped her arm from around RJ and stood. "Come on, Malo's right. We need rest too. Betcha when we wake up, Kaleo and Natti will be awake."

CHAPTER 8

CONSEQUENCES

Western border wall
Lakelands Province, New Atlantia

The acrid smell of charred wood was overwhelming. Damon covered his nose and mouth with a handkerchief and led Prefect Munoz through the field of smoldering debris. Their destination was a jumble of metal a hundred meters from the crater. At a distance, the jumble looked no different than the hundreds of other debris piles strewn around the area. Up close, however, this particular pile was unique.

When they arrived at the site, Damon tucked away his handkerchief, crouched down and pointed at the remains of tattered clothing covering the metal chassis beneath. "This is definitely not one of ours. We believe it was driving the van. Most likely military-grade. When it got within range of our barricade, it detonated itself, wiping out about forty percent of our Vipers and disabling the rest for a good seven to ten minutes. As it turned out, that was enough time for the rest of the agitators to escape."

The frown on the prefect's face was as sour as his mood. Damon waited for another lecture about the incompetence of his task force. The pompous politician could not begin to grasp the challenges Damon had faced in the capture attempt. Beacon had resorted to extraordinary measures to accomplish their rescues, far exceeding the complexity of any previous rescue mission. His team had contended with dual-city ops, exploding androids, laser rifles, drones, and faux-statues with hidden decoy clones. But that didn't matter to Munoz.

"You mean to tell me," the prefect said, "these criminals breached our border, smuggled out the Hearns boy and, in the process, destroyed four surveillance gliders and a score of your Viper androids? All while you watched it happen? And you still have no idea how they got in or out?"

Damon sighed. It was a grim, but accurate, assessment of the Minneapolis fiasco. Thankfully, Munoz didn't throw in his earlier acidic recap of the Chicago disaster into the latter assessment. Damon picked up a chunk of debris and stood. "Yes, Prefect, that's exactly what happened."

Munoz spread out his arms and turned in a circle. "All of this for a ten-year-old? A boy who may be dead? It makes no sense."

It was hard for Damon to disagree. Yes, Billy Hearns' DNA was unique, but for Beacon to go to such extremes to rescue him was beyond puzzling. Munoz turned and began to walk away, his long robes brushing over debris as he headed back toward the crater.

"Mark my words, the Carapach government is behind this," Munoz said.

Damon tossed down the android part and followed. "I spoke to their ambassador this morning. He denied any involvement."

"Of course they denied it, Spiers. They wouldn't admit involvement even if you had managed to catch them in the act. It's in their nature to lie. Just like they deny supporting Beacon, even though *everybody* knows they do."

What do you know of their nature? Damon thought. *Lounging around your palace, pretending you're an evvie, playing with your androids all day and night.* "The ambassador suggested we look internally. Said it was probably an act of insurrection."

Munoz stopped and spun around, his robes billowing out like a hoop dress. "Insurrection? How insulting. *No* New Atlantian would assist Beacon. Ever. Trust me, Major, Carapach and Beacon are two peas in the same pod."

Damon scratched the back of his white mane. "I don't know, Prefect. We definitely have our fair share of disaffected gutants…not to mention didgees fed up with—"

"Nonsense!" Munoz said. "New Atlantia is a model society. We take excellent care of the lower castes."

You're as blind as you are pompous, thought Damon, but it was not worth challenging the noble-caste governor. Munoz had immersed himself in the rhetoric of the republic long ago and to challenge him was to invite censure or demotion. And Damon was already in hot water as it was. Pointing out the truth to Munoz would only make matters worse.

It took another hour to tour the rest of the crime scene. By the time they finished, the shadow of the western wall had already begun to creep over the forest. As Damon escorted Munoz back to his caravan of security vehicles, the prefect pressed him to outline his next steps.

"Well, we've got a lot of debris to examine," said Damon. "Hopefully, we'll find some clues that will help us track down our perps. We're also analyzing all the data we acquired before the explosion to see if we can narrow the search radius for the tunnel."

"You're still convinced there is a tunnel?" Munoz asked.

"All the checkpoints at the border were closed. They either used a tunnel or they're still out in the woods somewhere. We know they had dampening cloaks. We found scraps of one in the van debris."

Munoz scoffed and mumbled a disparaging comment. Given Damon's urgent desire to rid himself of the prefect, he swallowed his pride and continued describing his action plan. "We'll also interview the people at the gene center and church. Plus, we still have Rodrick Hearns in custody."

"Oh, yes, that reminds me," Munoz said. "Release him at once."

"Excuse me?"

"I've had several calls from Guild members this morning demanding Hearns' release, including one from Sir Collins, the grandmaster of the Guild."

"So?"

"So, release him. That's an order."

"I haven't questioned him yet."

"His attorney assured me Mr. Hearns would answer your written questions. Just send them to the attorney."

"He's a suspect. He may be a co-conspirator."

"Come, now, Spiers. Do you really want me to go above your head and get Chief Wilkens involved? Aren't you in deep enough trouble without getting a double barrel from him? Hmm? He's ready to sack you as it is. Why push him over the edge? Release Hearns."

What balls, thought Damon. *I'll release him when I'm damned good and ready.* "Excuse me, Prefect, I have evidence to sift through."

As Damon stalked away, the prefect shouted, "Do it today, Spiers. You hear me?"

Where does that pervert get off ordering me around? And what did the Guild promise him to take the heat off of Hearns? Probably some illegal androids, or maybe one of their didgee conscripts.

Ignoring another shout from Munoz, Damon headed to the other side of the crater to meet up with Cassidy.

The noise from the bulldozers made it difficult for Damon to hear Cassidy deliver her briefing, so he motioned her to follow him away from the workers filling in the crater. When they had walked a hundred yards or so into the woods, the thick foliage muted the grunting and grinding machines enough to hold a conversation.

"All right, that's better. So, start over at the top. You said something about serial numbers."

The blond android nodded. "Yes, I was saying that we had examined the pieces of the andro we collected and found a couple of parts with partial serial numbers that tell us the make and model. It was a Makoa."

"A Makoa? I haven't seen one of those in years."

"That's not surprising," said Cassidy. "I searched our Android Registry and found only a few hundred in New Atlantia. Of those, only twenty-three are located within a five-hundred-mile radius of Minneapolis and ten of those are owned by one man. He runs an amusement park near Chicago. He uses them for a battle experience attraction."

The last Damon had heard, New Atlantia's Android Registry had over half a billion active android registrations and twice that number of inactive registrations. As he recalled, the media had made a big deal of the active count when the latest figures were announced for it meant the average active-droid-to-citizen ratio was a shade over ten. But that was skewed. People of the lower castes were lucky to have one or two, while many evvies and well-healed nobles had hundreds. Plus, a good percentage of active andros were government workers, like Cassidy. And then there were outliers like Damon who had none by choice.

"A few hundred, eh? I assume you checked on all the active Makoas and accounted for all of the inactives?" Damon asked.

"Yes, sir. All the registrations match the master serial numbers in the database."

"So, the Makoa originated in Carapach?"

"Or passed through Carapach," Cassidy said. "According to the android-park guy in Chicago, there's a healthy trade market for Makoas off the continent. Given their age, he said most people buy inactives for replacement parts, but you can buy ones that are still operational."

"That's a scary thought."

As Damon recalled, the Makoa model was a warrior-class android. Back when relations with Hawaiians had been hospitable, before countries started dumping their gutants and jakalis on islands in the South Pacific, Makoas had been the primary battle-bot for half of the world's armies. They were as indestructible as they were lethal. But that all changed once the dumps began.

Though the dumping first started when Damon was a child, he still remembered how quickly tensions escalated. It all began when a didgee philanthropist from the nation of Texas bought sizeable plots of land on each of the Hawaiian Islands, intending to create sanctuaries for gutants where they would be cared for, treated with dignity and allowed to reach their "full potential" during their short lifespans.

News of the sanctuaries traveled faster than a shooting star, and many countries began clearing out their overcrowded internment colonies, sending gutants and jakalis to the Hawaiian islands by the boatload.

The Hawaiians objected strenuously, but as one of Damon's history teachers had said, "It was like trying to stem the flow of the Mississippi River with a mop bucket."

In retaliation for the dumps, the Hawaiians ceased the export of Makoas. In return, many countries banned exports of all goods to the islands. In the end, the Hawaiians lost out. Their former trading partners found other sources of warrior-class androids and the isolated archipelago succumbed to chaos. Without a flow of imported goods and money from the sale of Makoas, the island's economy and government collapsed. Damon considered it a tragic end for what had once been a proud society.

The Hawaiian dumps marked the beginning of the Great Purge era, during which hundreds of remote South Pacific islands were inundated with unwanted gutants and jakalis from every continent. In those days, Jakali Syndrome was just beginning to emerge and the condition was poorly understood. Panic swept up teens with unrelated gutations into the purge. While many countries had since turned to euthanasia as the preferred jakali-management practice, some nations still dumped their pre-jakali gutants and jakalis in the waters off the coasts of the remote islands. Those who survived the swim fended for themselves in the wild. As far as Damon knew, the gutant sanctuaries still existed, but from what he had heard, the islands were now jakali-infested hells on Earth.

Damon was roused from his recollections by Cassidy's raised voice. He looked up to see a concerned expression on her face. "Are you all right, sir? You blanked out on me."

"Did I? I'm sorry. What did I miss?"

"I was telling you I've contacted the Carapach ambassador. I requested a file of all their Makoa registrations, active and inactive. I would not anticipate a reply, however. The ambassador was very displeased with Prefect Munoz for pointing a finger at them for the incidents yesterday."

"They probably wouldn't give us such a file under any circumstances. I know I wouldn't give them one from our registry if they asked us," Damon said. "Why did you want it?"

"We haven't located the Makoa's brain core, so we don't have a master serial number to request a single record search. I intended to cross-reference the registration file with our database of known Carapach agitators to identify matches."

"Whoa, hold up. You didn't find the brain core?"

Cassidy shook her head. "It appears the Makoa ejected the core before the explosion. We've found chunks of the skull, but not a single trace of the core."

The fact the Makoa ejected its brain core before self-destructing was not surprising to Damon in and of itself. That was the standard operating procedure for any military-grade android. No one wanted an enemy to access and download sensitive data from a captured or disabled andro. But, typically, an ejected core self-destructed. And it was easy to find evidence of the destruction given the unique materials used to form the core casing.

Damon turned in a circle. "Which means the core is still out here somewhere."

"Or...the agitators retrieved it before they escaped."

"That's possible but unlikely. The heat sigs were moving in the opposite direction when the Makoa exploded. If they had doubled back, we would have detected them." Damon started walking back toward the road. "I want another search, a wider radius. Beyond the blast zone. Bring in every collection-droid we have. Use gliders outfitted to detect the casing's radiation. Focus on the forest on both sides of the road leading to the crater."

Takoda's residence
Wolf Lake, East Dakota, Carapach

Insanity. That had been Takoda's first thought when he viewed Hoot's 4:36 a.m. holosnap. The Hearns rescues had been successful. They now had Billy, the missing link to Dr. Mugabe's GODD chip. It was time to press Sarah Hearns to reveal who had implanted the chip in Billy and then begin the search to find them. Instead, Hoot's message instructed Takoda and Yon to return to work in New Atlantia as if nothing had occurred. *Insanity.*

He had been so infuriated by the order, he immediately whisked off a return holosnap, reminding Hoot that he and Yon had been singled out for more extensive inspection at the border checkpoint the evening before. He also pointed out their escape at the western wall later that night had been so chaotic, there had been no time to ensure they left no physical evidence of their participation. Given both these factors, Takoda told Hoot he considered it suicide to re-cross the border. The New Atlantians would surely detain them.

In Hoot's sugary reply, she told him not to worry. She had inside information indicating that while the New Atlantians were suspicious of Takoda and Yon, they had no proof of their involvement in the previous day's events. At worst, Hoot said, they would be questioned, but the New Atlantians had no grounds to do more than that.

So, against his better judgment, Takoda had yielded. Truth be told, however, his acquiescence had been influenced more by Yon than Hoot's assurances. Yon had been copied on Hoot's messages and Takoda's reply, and she sent him a private holosnap afterward to remind him they had both pledged to follow the mission through to the finish, and they weren't finished yet.

Now, as Takoda crept his forty-year-old Mustang replica along the main road toward the border, he wondered if the finish of their mission would come sooner than Yon thought. Given the size of the traffic jam heading into New Atlantia, it was clear there was a holdup at the border checkpoint. To Takoda, that meant NASF was out in force, conducting intensive searches of every vehicle.

Sure enough, two hours later when Takoda reached the checkpoint, one of the waiting security force officers motioned for him to pull over onto the shoulder. The officer was Roka Akagi, a chatty man Takoda knew well from his daily stops at the checkpoint to present his ID. Takoda lowered the window and greeted Akagi just as six NASF Vipers fanned out around his decrepit sedan. "Good morning, Roka."

"Morning, Dr. Wells," Akagi replied. "Afraid I need you to step out of the car."

"Of course." Takoda's heart began to pound as he exited the car and approached the laser-rifle-armed Akagi. He fully expected the officer or the Vipers searching his car to surround and arrest him as soon as they finished their inspection.

"You heard about last night?" Akagi asked.

Here we go, thought Takoda. *Stay calm.* "Um, yes, I did. It was all over the news this morning. Fuel truck, was it?"

Before leaving for New Atlantia, Takoda had ordered his holonode Dasan to conduct an extensive scan of the holonet, searching for news reports of the previous day's rescues. Dasan found none, and instead provided Takoda with a collection of holovids about terrorist attacks near Minneapolis and Chicago.

According to the holovids, a Carapach-based terrorist group had commandeered a fuel truck and crashed it through the border checkpoint, intending to detonate the truck in downtown Minneapolis in protest of recently imposed New Atlantian tariffs. The reports indicated NASF gliders intercepted and destroyed the truck not far from the border. The same motive was attached to the separate set of explosions in Chicago earlier in the day, where once again the holovids indicated the terrorist plot was foiled by the fast response of NASF drones.

It was a flimsy cover story, but Takoda understood the reason for it. The New Atlantians were loathed to admit another successful Beacon kidnapping.

"That's what they say," said Akagi. "Must have been one helluva lot of fuel, though."

He's trying to soften me up with small talk. Just play along. Don't give him a reason to be suspicious. "Oh? Why do you say that?"

"Biggest crater I ever saw. It's a good thing the terrorists didn't make it into Minneapolis."

Seconds later, the last of the Vipers finished scanning Takoda's car and backed away. He girded for the arrest but, instead, Akagi waved him toward the Mustang. "Okay, doc, all clear. Might want to start out earlier tomorrow. Think the checkpoint's gonna be like this until we nab the terrorists."

Takoda opened the car door and turned to Akagi. "Sounds like good advice, Roka. Be safe. I'll see you tomorrow."

"You too, doc."

Once Takoda passed through the Carapach checkpoint, he got his first glimpse at the traffic heading out of New Atlantia. The checkpoint on the other side of the wall was staffed by twice the number of NASF officers and the line of waiting vehicles stretched beyond the horizon. Takoda interpreted the traffic imbalance as an indication the New Atlantians thought the people responsible for the explosion last night were still in-country. *Maybe Hoot was right, after all,* he thought.

The rest of the drive into the city was uneventful and Takoda arrived at the clinic in time for the morning staff meeting. Yon was already there and greeted him in the hallway outside the conference room. "Hey, how was your drive in?"

"Long."

"Yeah. Same here."

"How are you holding up?" Takoda asked.

Yon whispered, "Okay, I guess. Got your snap about Ellie. I'm glad she's okay."

"Me too." Takoda was still angry with the android for risking capture to retrieve Akecheta's brain core, but it was hard to fault her for the gambit knowing she had been successful. Looking into the nearly full conference room, he whispered, "We should probably go on in."

As they entered, they were met by Dr. Neville Thompson, the clinic director. Unlike Takoda and Yon, Neville was a lifelong New Atlantian and an evvie.

Evvies like Neville were considered the crème de la crème of mid-twenty-second-century society, superhumans whose genetically-engineered DNA had now passed through three generations of interbreeding without producing a single gutation. They were the desired end products of the mid-to-late twenty-first-century mania to extend the human lifespan and weed out genetic imperfections.

One could easily pick out an evvie on a crowded street. Tall, with perfect skin, teeth and hair, their faces and bodies were of incomparable beauty. They were the most gifted people on the planet, athletically, intellectually and otherwise. They were also the healthiest of all humans and aged at a very slow rate. The oldest of them now were in their late sixties but they looked as if they were no older than mid-thirties. Their members were made up of people of every ethnicity and they lived on every continent. To many people in the lower castes, they were godlike figures.

Sadly, to many others, including Takoda, evvies were also constant reminders of the catastrophe that forever changed the world, and of the
string of crises that continued to threaten human existence. This percep-
tion made it hard for Takoda to smile back when Neville wished him a
good morning.

"Did you see it? The crater? Did you see it in person?" Neville asked,
his eyes twinkling with excitement.

Takoda adjusted the lapels of his lab coat and shook his head. "Couldn't
see it from the main road."

"Yes, I know. But I thought for sure you would take a detour to check
it out. You fish up that way all the time, don't you?"

"I fish a lot of places, Neville. Besides, I don't think NASF is encour-
aging sightseers. I imagine they have the whole area cordoned off."

Takoda turned to find a seat at the table. Neville followed close behind.
As the two men occupied chairs next to each other, Neville said, "It's surprising they haven't published any pictures yet, don't you think? No news-
drone footage, no nothing. I would have thought the media would be all
over the place."

Yon slid onto a seat on the other side of Takoda. As she responded to
Neville, she yawned. "I'm sure NASF has their reasons, Neville."

"Well, I think it's suspicious. Especially given how close the explosion
was to the incinerator facility."

For the love of four gods, please shut up, Takoda thought. Alas, one of
the nurses egged on Neville to explain his point about the incinerator.

"I don't think the fuel truck was heading to Minneapolis, I think it's
target was the incinerator. I mean, just look at a map. The explosion happened more than twenty miles from the city, but only about three miles
from the incinerator."

"Why would terrorists care about the incinerator?" the nurse asked.

"Maybe it wasn't a protest about the tariffs," Neville said. "Maybe it
was that anti-euthanasia group, Beacon. You know, blow up the facility
to protest gutant euthanasia."

Takoda's temperature began to rise. Under the table, he clenched his
fists.

"Oh, I see," said the nurse. "But that's silly. They're euthanized here,
not at the incinerator."

"Can we just get on with the meeting?" Yon asked. "I've got a lot of test results to analyze today."

"All right, all right," said Neville. He turned and whispered to the nurse, "Don't forget you heard it here first. The incinerator was the *real* target."

As Neville began to walk through the agenda, Takoda felt Yon's hand cover his fist. She smoothed her fingers over his skin and lightly squeezed his hand. Takoda relaxed his grip.

Later, alone in his office, Takoda loosened his tie and stared at the stack of case files on his desk. He lifted one but dropped it just as quickly. I can't do this. *I can't put another child to sleep. Not now.*

"*But you know it's merciful,*" a voice in his head replied.

"It's barbaric," Takoda mumbled. It was a belief he had harbored since he was old enough to understand what the word euthanasia meant. "It's cowardly."

"*You prefer to see children become animals? You prefer they suffer and hurt others?*" the voice argued back.

No, I don't. I prefer to cure them.

"*Well, now you can try. You saved Billy and, as soon as Sarah reveals who treated him, you'll be one step closer to the GODD chip.*"

I should be taking that step now. Not sitting here, prepping to euthanize another child.

"*But it's necessary. You have to keep up appearances. You have to pro-tect Beacon. Just until things cool down.*"

Takoda shut off the internal debate and pounded the desk. "I can't! I won't!"

"You won't what?"

Takoda looked up to see a puzzled Yon standing in the doorway to his office. He waved for her to come in. "Sorry, I was talking to myself, not you."

Sliding onto a guest chair, Yon said, "Oh. So, what were you talking to yourself about?"

"Forget it. I'm just frustrated."

"Let me guess…with you-know-who."

Takoda looked away and mumbled, "With the whole situation."

"I'm sorry."

"No, *I'm* sorry. I've got to keep reminding myself to think big picture, no matter how much it eats me up inside."

"I know. It's hard. It's *really* hard," Yon said. "Unfortunately, it's about to get harder."

Takoda looked up. "What do you mean?"

Yon leaned across the desk and whispered, "Neville stopped by to see me. He said NASF called. They want to meet with us this afternoon."

CHAPTER 9

MOTIVES

NASF Province Headquarters
Minneapolis, Lakelands Province, New Atlantia

After returning to HQ from the western wall crime scene, Damon sought out the head of NASF's genetic crimes division, an unusually arrogant snot, Major Beauregard Jackson. In the days leading up to Beacon's operation, Jackson had waffled on possible motives for the underground's interest in Billy Hearns. In the light of what had transpired, the lengths to which Beacon resorted to smuggle the kid, Damon wanted Jackson to get off the fence and help him narrow the motives.

In response to Damon's prodding along these lines at the opening of their meeting, Jackson said, "As my reports have consistently theorized, Beacon kidnapped the boy to conduct illegal genetic research."

"Oh, you've been clear about that, Beau. But that's like saying a burglar's motive for breaking into a house is to steal something. What's the *something* here, Beau? You've told us Billy's DNA is an outlier compared to other pre-jakalis. I get that. But what does Beacon hope to achieve by researching an outlier?"

With a glare bordering on disdain, Jackson said, "Again, my reports have offered multiple possibilities."

"Which is shorthand for saying you have no idea."

"Look, Spiers, just because *you* botched another operation don't take it out on *me*."

"I've got thicker skin than that, Beau. Yours should be thicker, too. Now, listen, you've listed a bunch of possibilities, but you haven't pegged any option as more probable than the others. You know this kid's DNA better than me, better than anyone on my team. You've studied it in detail. I need something more than generalizations to go on. Beacon pulled out all the stops to smuggle Billy, and they had to have an awfully powerful motive to justify it all."

Jackson reclined his chair and twiddled his thumbs. Damon couldn't tell if the man was lost in thought or formulating another barb, but he didn't have time to wait for Jackson to break out of his stupor. "Come on, Beau. I'm meeting with the doctors at MGC later today. I think they're in this up to their necks, but I need something to dig at, an angle to explore. Help me."

"I don't think you appreciate the difficulties in picking one or another motive in this case. They range from the benevolent to the sinister. Some are related to Jakali Syndrome, others not."

"Skip the benevolent ones. Focus on the sinister."

"I would not be so quick to dismiss the benevolent, Spiers. One in particular could be a very powerful motive. They could be trying to develop a preventative cure for JS."

Of all the motives on Jackson's laundry list, this one had stood out early to Damon given Beacon's public relations advocacy for developing a JS cure as an alternative to euthanasia and sterilization. But he had discounted the possibility because of the very fact Billy's DNA was an outlier. Damon pointed out this contradiction to Jackson. "If Beacon really wanted to develop a cure for JS, wouldn't it make more sense to study the DNA of more common pre-jakalis?"

Jackson nodded. "That's a valid question. Choosing Billy seems counterintuitive on the surface but, if one thinks about it long enough, it really isn't. Billy has violet eyes."

Damon frowned. "And that's relevant because…"

"There is research that suggests pre-jakalis with violet eyes develop the condition at a slower rate and experience less severe symptoms than those with natural eye colors. Of course, there is also research that refutes any correlation between the VE gene and JS."

Damon pondered Jackson's comments, recalling the violet-eye gene was a controversial embryo-design feature introduced in the 2070s. He recalled the date so easily because the gutation of the VE gene was initially thought to be partially responsible for the necro outbreak of 2082. Though that supposition was later proven inaccurate, the replacement gene was quickly banned for future embryo implantation. But those who had already received the VE gene were not forced to replace it. As a result, the VE gene continued to pass on to subsequent generations, including Billy.

"You see," Jackson continued, "if it's true JS develops slower in kids with the VE gene, it gives Beacon more time to study the changes to Billy's DNA as he ages. They may also be drawn to Billy given the theory of milder symptoms in VE jakalis, believing they may learn insights that allow them to enhance that theoretical effect. That said, Beacon may be way off the mark in these beliefs. As I mentioned, other research refutes any correlation between the VE gene and Jakali Syndrome."

Damon agreed the theory was a stretch, which was probably the reason Jackson had not prioritized the JS-cure motive. But it was a topic he would probe with the doctors at the gene center, nonetheless. If they bristled at his probing, it might provide him the opening he needed to take them into custody for further questioning.

"All right. That's helpful, Beau. Let's talk about the sinister now."

"Very well. How about terrorism? Weaponizing the boy's DNA."

"Meaning what? Beacon wants to breed an army of jakalis like Billy?"

Jackson rolled his eyes. "Don't be daft, Spiers. If they weaponize his DNA, it won't have any relation to Jakali Syndrome. Though it still might be related to his VE gene."

"I'm afraid you've lost me, Beau."

"Think man. What's the other New Atlantian practice stuck in Beacon's craw?"

"Didgee conscription."

"Precisely."

The term *conscription* was a misnomer. *Enslavement's more accurate*, thought Damon. And Jackson was wrong, didgee conscription wasn't a *New Atlantian* practice, it was an *Evvie Guild* practice. It just so happened that New Atlantian laws had been massaged to allow the Guild surrogacy program.

It boiled down to this. Evvies had a problem. Despite their genetic superiority, they were a distinct minority across the globe. Yes, in many countries like New Atlantia, they held sway over government policies, but they were still a minority bloc. And relative to the populations of other castes, evvies were in decline. They just didn't breed fast enough to keep up with the lesser castes.

This dynamic was largely driven by evvie's lack of motivation to breed. They had everything they wanted — wealth, power, beauty, prowess. And given they aged at a much slower rate, their prime breeding years were two-to-three times longer than other humans. So, why rush? That was how many evvies viewed the situation. And a subset of evvies bred outside of their caste, like Rodrick Hearns' mating with blenda-caste Sarah, which further lessened the pool of purebred evvies.

The Evvie Guild viewed the situation as a threat to maintaining evvie societal dominance. Therefore, the cooperative devised a plan to address the issue — surrogacy. By dramatically expanding the pool of wombs carrying evvie babies, the Guild believed they could reverse the caste's diminishing population proportion.

Since the only way to create an evvie was by inbreeding evvie females and males, surrogacy in the Guild's mind meant finding non-evvie females to carry evvie embryos. And of the lower castes, only didgee females were deemed suitable.

Damon recalled the many articles that noted the illogic of the Guild's focus on didgee women. DNA of a surrogate unrelated to the embryo being carried did not pass to the embryo. The surrogate's DNA was filtered from the bloodstream before reaching the umbilical cord, which meant a woman from any caste could carry an evvie embryo.

But the Guild didn't believe in taking chances. The people of other castes, including nobles like Damon, had gene-replacement impurities, and the Guild wanted no risk of introducing gutations into evvie DNA. Since didgees, by their very nature, had no replacement genes in their DNA, the Guild viewed them as the least risky surrogates.

So, Guild members sought out didgee females from around the world to come to New Atlantia to serve as surrogates. The women were promised large sums and other perks, but often found themselves forced into long-term arrangements with benefits that diminished or disappeared over time. Beacon viewed this practice as state-sanctioned human trafficking and their rescues were often targeted to liberate enslaved surrogates.

Damon found the practice distasteful, too, but so long as Guild members abided by New Atlantian laws regarding the care and compensation of didgee surrogates, Damon was compelled to uphold the laws. That meant stopping Beacon from liberating conscripts.

Returning his attention to Jackson's comments, Damon asked, "I'm still lost, Beau. What possible connection could there be between Billy's DNA and didgee conscription?"

"What would be the quickest way to end the practice?" Jackson asked in reply. Before Damon could answer, Jackson said, "Birth a contaminated evvie, an evvie with gutations."

"But Billy's not an evvie. Yeah, his dad is, but his mom is a blenda. That made Billy a blenda too until he was diagnosed with JS."

"All true," said Jackson. "Which brings us back to Billy's violet eyes. Or *close* to his violet eyes. I discovered some strange protein binds in a gene next to Billy's VE gene. The binds appear very weak. In fact, in one of his previous DNA tests, that gene was identified as a gutation, but not on his most recent test."

Damon considered this latest piece of information. In his experience, it was not unusual to see disparities in reported gutations between different DNA tests. A gutation might arise very close, timewise, with the administration of a DNA test, and then be repaired by innate cellular DNA "repairmen" shortly afterward. DNA tests were also known to generate gutation false positives on occasion. But from what Jackson was saying, it sounded as if this gutation was repaired but not very well, making it prone to become a gutation again.

"You think Beacon found these weak binds you're talking about?"

"I think it's possible. Yes."

"Okay, so if they did, how could they weaponize it?"

"The replacement gene in question was introduced around the same time as the VE gene, the 2070s. It is one of several genes that regulate skin tone. It was created as a vanity-oriented therapy for adults of light complexions and boosts their melanin receptors, allowing them to tan with greater ease. Many Anglo evvies, nobles and blendas carry this replacement gene. It is considered one of the most stable replacement genes ever created. It rarely gutates, even among people in lower castes. The fact it gutated in Billy is part of what makes him such an outlier."

Damon was finally able to follow the bouncing ball. Beacon was losing its war against the Guild to prevent conscription. They rescued far too few didgee surrogates to offset the growing numbers of new ones. What better way to bring a screeching halt to conscription than by contaminating evvie embryos carried by didgee surrogates? But Damon saw two problems with Jackson's theory.

"Gutations don't occur until adolescence starts, Beau. Any embryo Beacon injected this gene into wouldn't gutate for ten or more years. That wouldn't really help them. They want to stop conscriptions now."

"Exactly. That's why they'd also inject the didgee surrogate with the same gutation. Most surrogates are teenagers. They're the most vulnerable, easiest to recruit for the Guild. Therefore, the weak protein binds in Billy's gene would likely gutate very quickly in the surrogate. Beacon would do this to create the impression the surrogate passed the gutation to the embryo."

"But a surrogate's DNA doesn't pass to embryos unless the surrogate is also the mother."

"Correct, but recall evvies' paranoia about genetic purity and remember the goal of a terror campaign is to strike fear in the hearts of adversaries."

"Okay, I get you now. But couldn't Beacon choose any gutation to contaminate evvie embryos? Meaning, why would they need this specific gene of Billy's to accomplish their goal?"

"They absolutely could. But this particular gutation produces a strikingly visible effect, large purplish-reddish blotches on the skin. From a terrorism standpoint, it would be very effective in branding contaminated evvies.."

"Got you. Scare the bejesus out of evvies with a 'scarlet letter' gutation in a didgee surrogate and an evvie embryo, causing the Guild to shut down the surrogate program in an instant."

Damon struggled to believe Beacon, given its bleeding-heart mentality, would stoop to branding didgee surrogates and innocent evvie babies. On the other hand, Damon hadn't believed the underground capable of orchestrating such elaborate rescues as they had the day before. *They wanted Billy real bad.* Then he thought of Takoda Wells and Yon Fujita, both didgees. Had they tired of seeing women of their caste oppressed, of rescuing the odd conscript here and there? Was this all about taking their mission to the next level? What were a dozen marred didgees in the grand scheme of things if they could prevent thousands of future conscriptions? It was another thread Damon now intended to pull when he met them.

National Gene Center
Minneapolis, Lakelands Province, New Atlantia

Dr. Neville Thompson was all smiles when the NASF officer entered the conference room. The tall black man with a long mane of white hair identified himself to Takoda as Maj. Damon Spiers. He was accompanied by another officer, Sgt. Cassidy Willow, a Steel-class android. Her mannerisms were as fluid as Takoda's more refined Athena-class Ellie, right down to her warm handshake and smile.

What the New Atlantians lacked in compassion toward gutants, they made up for in their craftmanship of androids. In Takoda's opinion, they manufactured the most realistic humanoid androids in the world. No two of any class looked the same...unless ordered as clones. And unlike many competing android producers in other countries, the New Atlantia's state-controlled Hutech, Ltd., offered a vast array of customizations.

Take Willow, for instance. Takoda noticed small freckles on her nose and a solitary freckle on her right earlobe. When she smiled, dimples appeared and her cheeks blushed as if she was a tad bashful. Her eyes were slightly bloodshot and one eyebrow was just a smidgen higher than the other.

Beyond the manufactured customizations, Hutech andros were also adept at further humanizing their appearance based on observed human proclivities. Willow was no exception. She wore a necklace and rings, her fingernails were painted and her lips were coated a glossy pink. Takoda could even detect perfume.

Overall, the combination of manufactured and improvised customizations gave Willow a disarming appearance. However, Takoda harbored no illusions. Willow was all business. All Steel andros were.

As he watched Willow shake Yon's hand and take a seat at the table, Takoda hoped he and Yon could maintain level demeanors, overtly and biometrically. The android's array of surveillance sensors would surely scan them throughout the meeting.

With the introductions completed, Spiers said, "We appreciate your meeting with us. I'm sure you're all very busy. We'll do our best to keep this short and sweet."

"No trouble at all," said the beaming Neville. "We are more than happy to help. I'm curious, though. What's your interest in this particular patient?"

Good question, Neville! Let's see what the stormtrooper says to that! Takoda turned to Spiers and watched him give Neville a nonchalant shrug as he answered the question.

"Let's just say it's related to a situation we've been asked to look into."

"Oh, I see. What kind of situation?" Neville asked. "Or is that not an appropriate question?"

Spiers' smile was friendly, as was the tone of his reply to Neville. "I wish I could share more with you, Doctor, but it's kind of hush-hush at the moment. I'm sure you can understand."

"Of course, of course," said Neville. "I apologize if I overstepped—"

"No need to apologize. It's an understandable and reasonable question. Now, if you don't mind, I'd like to ask some questions about Billy Hearns."

"By all means, proceed."

As Takoda observed the two men talking, he thought, *so, that's how NASF is going to play it…a hush-hush situation.* Takoda had expected the officers to take a more confrontational approach.

"Billy was euthanized here yesterday. Correct?" Spiers asked.

Takoda watched Neville's head bob like a puppy dog begging for a treat.

"Yes, yes. That's correct," Neville said. "Dr. Wells performed the procedure. Dr. Fujita assisted."

"I see." Spiers stroked his stubbled chin and turned to Takoda. "Dr. Wells, you were also the signatory of Billy's euthanization designation document, were you not?"

"Yes, that's right," Takoda said.

"And according to the document, the reason given for the euthanization was the presence of gutations linked to the development of Jakali Syndrome."

"Right, again."

Spiers opened a portfolio case and flipped through some pages until he arrived at one he examined more closely. After completing his review, he asked Neville if it would be possible to display Billy's designation document on the conference room's holonode.

Neville happily complied and seconds later, an image of the document's first page floated above the center of the table. Spiers stood and circled a line item on the document image with his finger, leaving a fluorescent green swoosh around the floating data. "These codes, here, identify the specific gutations that led to your diagnosis, correct?"

"Correct," said Takoda. "By New Atlantian law, when a child's DNA contains three or more of the twelve mutations linked to Jakali Syndrome, the child is deemed at high-risk for developing the condition by the time he or she reaches puberty and we are bound by the same law to designate the child for euthanization."

"Seems kind of rash, doesn't it?" Spiers looked back and forth between Takoda and Yon. "I mean, three out of twelve seems kind of premature?"

"I'd call it aggressive, not rash," said Yon. "Other countries with euthanization policies don't require euthanization until five or six of the gutations have appeared. Statistically speaking, though, there's a seventy-five percent certainty of developing JS once three of the twelve gutations are detected. At six, there's a ninety percent certainty."

Willow entered the conversation. "When you say it's aggressive, you overlook the fact that most gutants don't exhibit six jakali gutations until the age of twelve, a year or two into puberty, depending on the child's gender. The countries that wait until six gutations risk the pre-jakali mating. New Atlantia's policy prevents mating risk. As a result, it is actually more conservative."

Takoda saw red rising in Yon's cheeks.

"You view it your way, I'll view it mine," said Yon.

Spiers used his finger to underline the gutation codes on the document. "So, Billy had four gutations in his last test. I'm told these four gutations don't often appear early in the development of JS, but they did in Billy. It made him somewhat unique compared to other pre-jakalis. Is that true?"

The major was playing games and it was starting to irritate Takoda. "I suppose that's right."

Nodding, Spiers said, "If I'm not mistaken, your daughter is, or *was*, a jakali."

Okay, now you're crossing the line. "My daughter is irrelevant to this conversation, Major."

"Here, here," said Neville. "That question does seem unrelated and inappropriate."

"My apologies," said Spiers. He looked from Neville to Takoda. "My son was euthanized here a couple of years ago. JS diagnosis. You probably don't remember him. His name was Dylan."

"I'm sorry, Major. I don't," Takoda said. *Where's he going with this?*

"Yeah, I guess I get that. I don't remember half the perps I've caught. And you, geez, you've put thousands of kids to sleep. Same with you and you." Spiers pointed at Yon and Neville. "Guess at some point, you stop thinking about the lives you're ending."

Ah, now I get it, thought Takoda. *He's trying to rile us up, get us emotional so we'll lose our cool...it's working!*

"And your point is?" asked Yon, her voice cold.

Spiers shrugged. "No point. Just an observation. Going back to Billy's unusual gutations, I noticed there's one missing from the designation document. In his second test, the one before his JS diagnosis, there was another gutation that doesn't show up on this form. How come, Dr. Wells?"

"Which one are you referencing, Major?" Takoda asked. "Billy had a few other gutations, but none of them were associated with JS. So, they don't appear on the designation form."

"Ah, so only JS gutations show up on the form," Spiers said.

To Takoda, Spiers' expression looked like that of a man who finally understood some great riddle. It was an act. Spiers was toying with him. An NASF major would know damn well what kind of information was appropriate to include on a designation form. Takoda took a deep breath and said, "Yes, Major. Unrelated gutations are not recorded on the designation form. They only appear on the individual DNA test result reports."

"Got it," Spiers said. "Let's move on. Tell me about VE011."

As Takoda frowned at Spiers, Yon answered. "It's a replacement gene. In concert with certain other eye color-related genes, it produces violet-colored eyes."

"So, Billy Hearns had violet-colored eyes. Interesting."

Neville intervened. "Now, look here, Major. What's this all about? Your questions, and your tone, have a distasteful edge to them. If you have a concern about our paperwork or procedures, please be upfront about it. We have nothing to hide."

It was good to see Neville take a stand. Takoda had been concerned the sometimes-weaselly evvie would try to distance himself from the inquisition. Then again, unlike Takoda and Yon, Neville didn't know *why* NASF was poking around Billy's euthanization document. As soon as he found out, Takoda expected his support to take a nosedive.

Ignoring Neville's protest, Spiers said, "Let's take a step back. I'd like to pick your brains about VE011 in general terms. It was a design feature introduced back in the latter half of the twenty-first-century, correct?"

Spiers' eyes were focused on Takoda, but it was Neville who replied. "Yes, it originated in Japan. I don't recall the precise year, but it wasn't long before the necro pandemic of 2082."

"It's funny you mention that, Doctor," Spiers said. "Isn't it true this VE gene got a lot of attention as the potential cause of the pandemic? Matter of fact, didn't the uproar over its potential role in the outbreak result in the banning of the feature?"

As Takoda recalled it, the case for blaming the VE gene for the outbreak had hinged on two circumstantial observations; there had been a disproportionate percentage of necro victims who possessed the gene modification, and the DNA analysis of the VE necro victims revealed a gutation to the gene. Ergo, the health officials in charge of stemming the outbreak concluded there had been a flaw in the VE011 gene that damaged nearby genes in the same chromosome that regulated skin melanin production and skin immune response.

It had been too simplistic a conclusion in Takoda's opinion, but in the hysteria of the pandemic, health officials ran with it. Only after the worst was over did geneticists begin to question whether VE011 was really the culprit. But by that point, nearly all countries had already banned the VE replacement gene, and the company that developed it voluntarily withdrew it from the market.

"You are right, Major," said Takoda, "VE011 was labeled as the cause of the necro pandemic and banned. Unfairly so, as time has shown."

"That's more opinion than fact, isn't it?" said Willow.

Takoda turned to address the android. She had a solemn expression on her face as if making an earnest attempt to engage Takoda in an academic discussion. "Sergeant, I think the body of genetic evidence over the last fifty-plus years shows VE011 is, and always was, a benign modification. If that were *not* the case, I'm sure it would be on the New Atlantian gene alert list."

"Good point, Takoda," Neville said. The clinic director stood and circled a line item about midway down the on-screen document. "As you can plainly see, VE011 isn't on the World Gene Registry alert list either, otherwise box six would have been checked and VE011 would have been entered on this line here."

"Okay, got you, it's a benign gene-mod," said Spiers. "Kind of interesting, though, isn't it? Not only was the order of Billy Hearns' jakali gutations rare, but he also had violet eyes, which is also pretty rare."

"Why are you so interested in VE011? It wasn't gutated in any of Billy's DNA tests. It had nothing to do with his jakali designation," Yon said.

Careful, Yon, thought Takoda, *let's not spit into the wind.*

"I don't know. Just strikes me as odd." Spiers turned back to Takoda. "You performed the euthanization, right?"

"Yes, as Dr. Thompson mentioned earlier, I did."

"Anything unusual about the procedure? Any complications?"

"No."

"Is there a video of the procedure?"

The question was ridiculous as far as Takoda was concerned. NASF required the country's gene centers to video record *all* euthanizations. Spiers had to know that. *Time to call his bluff.*

"Yes, Major. All euthanizations are recorded. Neville, why don't you pull up Billy's? We can all view it together," said Takoda.

"That won't be necessary. I'll view it later," Spiers said. "Actually, I'm more interested in what happened after the procedure. That *isn't* recorded, is it?"

Takoda shook his head. "No, it's not."

"So, what happened afterward? The boy went from the procedure room to where?"

Neville intervened before Takoda could reply. "Again, Major, I fail to see the purpose of your line of questioning. You seem to be suggesting there were irregularities with this patient's euthanization."

"As I said earlier, Doctor, the nature of our inquiry is confidential for the time being. I'd appreciate it if you'd just let Dr. Wells answer the question." Spiers turned toward Takoda. "What took place after the procedure?"

Neville answered for Takoda again. "After the procedure is completed, after death is certified, the nurse wheels the body to our storage room and—"

"I'm not interested in generalities, Doctor. I'm interested in this specific case. Please allow Dr. Wells to answer."

"I'm afraid I can't be of much help, Major," Takoda said. "If you want specifics, you'll need to talk to the nurse who assisted. Once the procedure was completed, my part was done. I went to our ready room and changed into a fresh gown and put on new gloves for the next euthanization."

As Takoda said the words, he felt disgusted. His description sounded so clinical, so matter-of-fact. The truth was each "procedure" was heart-wrenching from start to finish. If thinking of his daughter didn't tear him apart, looking down on the innocent face of a sedated child did. *I became a doctor to save lives, not end them.*

"So, you're saying that as soon as the boy was declared dead, you left the room."

"Correct."

"And you didn't see Billy again."

"No. Why would I?"

"What about you, Dr. Fujita?"

Yon cleared her throat and sat up straight. "Me? I went to inform the father."

"Oh, that's right," said Spiers. "You're the counselor. You dealt with the mother, Sarah, on previous visits."

"I'm more than a counselor, Major, but yes, counseling parents is part of my role here."

"What was her disposition like?"

"I'm not sure what you mean. She didn't attend the euthanization."

"Sorry. I meant what was her disposition like when you informed her of Billy's diagnosis?"

Yon frowned. "Major, there's not a single parent I've ever met who wasn't devastated by a jakali diagnosis."

"I'm sure that's true, Doctor, but I'm interested in this *specific* parent. What do you recall about her reaction?"

He's just trying to get under your skin, Yon. Hold it together.

Yon crossed her arms. "I can't say she was any different than others I've met with. She was nervous when she came in, jittery but quiet. And when I told her about the diagnosis she obviously became quite emotional. Again, no different than other parents."

"Major," said Neville, "if you're so curious about the mother's reaction, why ask us? I would think the mother would be the better source."

Spiers folded his arms across his chest and stared at Neville. "I'd love to ask her, Doctor. The only problem is, she's gone."

"Gone? What do you mean, gone?"

"Gone as in vanished without a trace…along with her daughters."

"What? How is that possible?"

Eyes riveted on Takoda, Spiers said, "Excellent question, Dr. Thompson. Excellent question."

CHAPTER 10

PRESSURE COOKER

En route to NASF Province Headquarters
Minneapolis, Lakelands Province, New Atlantia

The meeting at the gene center continued for another thirty minutes before Damon decided he had extracted all the information he was going to get from the three doctors...for the time being. Ordinarily, he would have first met with each individually, but Damon had first wanted to observe the interplay between the doctors in an informal setting. He would interview them again, separately, at HQ after he gathered more evidence.

To that end, he and Cassidy met with the nurse who assisted with the euthanization. After that, they viewed the video of the procedure and then conducted a walk-through of the entire euthanization process with all the players involved.

Finally, they examined the body release authorization document, hoping to identify the two androids who had taken Billy's body from the clinic. While the paperwork appeared in order, the chicken-scratched names of the ambulance personnel were illegible, though the form did produce one interesting discovery. The private ambulance service had been arranged by Sarah Hearns.

As he and Cassidy rode away from the clinic, he asked for her impressions of the visit.

"There was definite hostility on the part of the Carapach doctors," she said. "Not as much from the evvie. While he was defensive, he seemed to be acting as a buffer for the other two."

"Yeah, I noticed that too. Did you pick up any lies on your sensors?"

"Their heart rates, respiration and body temperature spiked several times, and I detected an increase in Dr. Fujita's pupil dilation at one point. But they could all have been natural reactions. I did not detect any outright lies."

Damon nodded and instructed their cruiser's computer to take the maglev lane back to headquarters. As the self-drive vehicle maneuvered to enter the lane, Damon replayed Cassidy's last comment in his mind. *I did not detect any outright lies.* While the two doctors may not have lied, they had been clipped and defensive in their answers...especially Dr. Fujita.

"They sure as hell weren't entirely truthful."

"I agree. They could have been more forthcoming."

"What about the nurse?" Damon asked. "How did she come across to you?"

"She was very cooperative, very forthcoming."

Damon agreed. The nurse had gone out of her way to show them the storage unit where the euthanization drugs were kept. She showed them the log from the day of the procedure, verified the serial number of the bottle used in the procedure and gave the used bottle to Cassidy. The nurse also affirmed she had noticed nothing unusual before, during or after the procedure, and tolerated a timed walk-through of her movements throughout each stage.

"What did your sensors tell you about her answer about the tracking implant?"

"Her response was authentic. Nothing that would indicate a lie."

"I thought so, too."

Once Damon had seen the body storage room, he realized what had likely happened to the implant. The metallic lining of the freezer drawer where Billy's body was moved after the procedure had blocked the implant's signal. The device had never been removed. Thinking back to the crater crime scene and the bits of dampening cloak there, Damon further concluded the androids had used the cloak to block the signal once they left the clinic.

Returning to his thoughts on the conversation with the doctors, Damon said, "Arrange for follow-up interviews with Wells and Fujita at HQ. Set it up for tomorrow. I want them to sweat a little."

"Yes, sir. Should we surveil them in the meantime?"

"I'm not sure how much good it will do. Unless we find evidence of their involvement, we can't prevent them from crossing into Carapach, and we can't legally surveil them outside of New Atlantia."

"Can't we appeal for cross-border recon authorization based on nat-sec risk?"

"It's a thought, but we need more than circumstantial evidence to get approval," Damon said. "No judge is going to give us a green light to cross the border based on what we have right now."

The treaties between the two countries limited cross-border incursions by the respective security forces, and the restrictions were particularly strict when it came to clandestine surveillance. Damon was well aware of ways to subvert the treaties but he was reluctant to go that route until they had more evidence.

Cassidy did not respond immediately. Damon looked over and saw her staring blankly out the front window. He had worked with the andro long enough to know the silent stare meant she was engaging her ethics module. By design, police androids were programmed to obey all New Atlantian laws, however, years of practical, in-the-field experience with android officers had demonstrated the need to allow the humanoid machines some wiggle room when tactical situations required judgment calls.

This need had led to the development of an ethics module that androids could consult when confronted by situations that did not neatly fit into the construct of New Atlantian laws. It also allowed them to be more effective sounding boards for human officers confronting similar dilemmas.

As the cruiser slowed to exit the maglev lane, Cassidy turned to Damon and said, "I understand your point. The gene center's records demonstrate the doctors made proper diagnoses and followed required procedures, just as they have done for all other euthanization cases. There were no irregularities."

"Right."

"And the doctors had no interaction with the boy after the procedure. We have multiple witnesses who attested to that."

"Correct, and they also didn't have any role in arranging the ambulance. So, you see, we don't have anything on them. Clipped, defensive answers aren't enough to get approval to track them in Carapach."

"Understood." Cassidy nodded. "We'll confine surveillance to New Atlantia."

As the cruiser neared the gate at HQ, Damon patted Cassidy on the shoulder. "Unfortunately, that's all we can do for now. But I wouldn't sweat it, Cass. We'll keep applying pressure. Sooner or later, they'll make a mistake or we'll sniff out some evidence."

Now, if I can just keep Prefect Munoz from applying pressure on us!

National Gene Center
Minneapolis, Lakelands Province, New Atlantia

Neville Thompson stormed into Takoda's office and slammed the door shut. The evvie's face was red and his cheeks were twitching.

"What the *hell* is going on?" Neville said.

Takoda closed the file he had been reading and eased back in his chair. "I'm not sure what you mean, Neville."

"I know you don't respect me, but I'm not an imbecile."

Neville's eyes narrowed. They seemed to blaze holes through Takoda.

"You're upset, Neville, why don't you have a seat and we'll—"

The enraged evvie pounded the desk, starting an avalanche of the files stacked on the corner of it. "Do *not* patronize me! Either you stop with the BS and tell me what's going on, or so help me, I will send Maj. Spiers a *narrated* copy of the video."

Takoda felt his heart begin to pound. Involuntarily, he must have shown an outward sign of anxiety because Neville pounded the desk again and then pointed at Takoda. "I knew it! You faked the euthanization!"

Before Takoda could protest, Neville said, "You may be an exceptional geneticist, Takoda, but you *suck* at acting...*and* at holoediting."

Trapped between the urge to deny Neville's accusations and the scramble for his brain to conjure a rebuttal, Takoda froze. His silence seemed to embolden Neville. The director slid onto the guest chair and continued his attack.

"I've watched you euthanize more than a thousand children, Takoda. You've taken every one of them personally...like you were putting your own daughter to sleep."

The mention of his daughter triggered a torrent of rage to swell in Takoda. He vaulted up and smashed Neville in the face. The evvie and the chair he was sitting in crashed onto the floor. Takoda moved around the side of the desk and stood over his boss. "Watch your mouth, Neville! Don't you ever talk about my daughter! *Ever!*"

Neville groaned and massaged his jaw as he staggered to his feet. The evvie was a foot taller than Takoda and a hundred pounds of lean muscle heavier. If he wanted to, he could kill Takoda with a single blow to the head or chest. Takoda crouched, balling his fists. He would have to be quick to dodge the evvie's punches.

But Neville didn't throw one. Instead, he righted the chair while he continued to rub his jaw. He flopped onto the seat and said, "I'm sorry, Takoda. You're right. I was out of bounds."

Unsure of how to react to Neville's apology, Takoda remained crouched, fists at his side.

"Point still holds, though." Neville swiped his lip, presumably checking for blood. "Your compassion is unbounded, Tak. I've seen it every day you've come to work for the last four years. But you didn't show it with Billy Hearns. *That* made me study the video more closely. Do you really think Spiers and his buxom andro won't notice the disparity in the biometric data display if they take a closer look? If they do notice it, the next thing you know one of NASF's interrogation bots will be drilling holes in your head. Now, what gives?"

Takoda relaxed his stance and unclenched his fists. As he returned to his chair, he said, "You're imagining things, Neville."

Actually, though, Neville wasn't imagining anything. The data feed displayed in a ribbon at the bottom of the video did not show Billy's vital signs. As soon as Yon had finished meeting with Rodrick Hearns to inform him of Billy's death, she had returned to her office to replace the data feed with that of a prior patient. It was necessary because the real display would have shown Billy's heart never stopped beating. The drug Takoda substituted to simulate Billy's death dramatically lowered Billy's respiration and heart rate, but it didn't arrest either.

"I'm imagining things?" Neville straightened his tie and tugged the lapels of his rumpled lab coat. "Okay, Takoda, I was hoping you would trust me, but I can see you're not up to it." He stood and turned toward the door. When he took hold of the doorknob, he paused. Still facing the door, he said, "By the way, after my *imagination* spotted the spliced data, I went back through Billy Hearns' DNA reports again. I noticed the data section on binding proteins was curiously omitted. Not to worry, though. I queried the databank and retrieved the missing information." Neville slowly turned around. "What do you think? Should I send it to NASF?"

Takoda sighed. "Okay, Neville. You've made your point. Have a seat. Let's talk."

One had to give credit where credit was due. Neville was indeed no imbecile. Takoda did not need to hear any more to know Neville had not only retrieved the data, but he had also interpreted it.

Binding proteins. They were the scourge of the gene manipulation era, the sources of doom that had caused deadly gutations to arise. Takoda still had a hard time fathoming how scientists in the early days of gene replacement mania had not foreseen the inevitable train wreck. But that wasn't really fair. Many scientists had raised red flags, but their protests had been drowned out by biologic companies eager to sell their gene-packs, by consumers clamoring for bodily enhancements, and by competing scientists who derided the voices begging for caution as alarmists.

How wrong they had been not to listen. Takoda recalled from history lessons that even government regulatory bodies, ones tasked with protecting their citizens from unproven, dangerous products, had been rendered impotent by the crush of the mania.

And, for a time, the "alarmists" had appeared to be wrong. Replacement therapies proliferated to smooth away wrinkles, ward off erectile dysfunction, slim down, cleanse arteries, strengthen physiques, etcetera. All with mild or no side effects.

This success had emboldened commercially-supported geneticists and biologic companies to escalate research into products that became the next phase of the disaster-in-waiting. Genetic design of children.

Takoda looked up at Neville and asked, "What do you want to know?"

"Where is Billy Hearns?"

With a shake of his head, Takoda said, "Can't tell you that, Neville. But I can tell you he is safe and receiving the care he deserves."

"And the missing family? The mother? The daughters?"

"Soon to be reunited."

"The mother knows what you are up to?"

"First of all, Neville, this isn't about me. Second, the mother understands."

Neville snorted and crossed his arms over his chest. "In other words, you offered false hope in exchange for a willing lab rat."

Out of sight from Neville's view, Takoda clenched his hands into fists again. "You view the world differently than I do, Neville. What you see as false hope, I see as an opportunity for a family to stay together, care for each other, free from persecution. What you call a willing lab rat, I call a child in need of a cure."

"I see. And what about the father? Is he in on it too?"

"No."

"And you really think you can find a cure?"

"I don't need to find a cure. One already exists. Or did."

Another snort puffed from Neville's nose and mouth. He uncrossed his arms and leaned toward Takoda. "It's a myth, Takoda. Just because a few of Mugabe's binding proteins found their way into this kid's DNA does *not* mean the GODD chip is real. It and everything Mugabe created were destroyed. Regardless, it's folly to think *you* are gifted enough to recreate *her* research."

Takoda wasn't sure which bothered him more, Neville's swipe at his intelligence or the evvie's dismissal of Dr. Dyan Mugabe's experimental solution to end the blight of gutant mutations. As Takoda fought to maintain his composure, Neville continued his lecture.

"The woman's been dead for what, almost twenty-five years? As legend has it, her research went up in flames at her execution. They literally burned her alive using her research to feed the fire. And I don't have to remind you of what you know so well. Gene replacement research is *illegal*. That restriction includes research into binding proteins as well. The last thing the world needs right now is you, *and Yon*, and whomever else is in your band of misguided zealots, trying to play God. As the last century has proven, it's a *very* bad idea."

There was wisdom in Neville's comments, yet it felt self-serving for Takoda to hear the sage advice coming from one who had benefited handsomely from genetic manipulation. "Spoken like a true evvie."

Neville's face turned red. "If I was a true evvie, Takoda, I would have already contacted NASF."

"Then, what's the point of the lecture? If you're hoping to dissuade me from—"

"I know better than that," Neville said. "You're too damned stubborn. Plus, I understand why you're really doing this. It won't help her, Takoda. It's too late. If your daughter's still alive, she's likely a jakali by now."

Takoda leaped out of his chair. Neville held up his hand.

"Before you wallop me again, I want to remind you *I* was the one that helped *you* find a sanctuary for her."

Suddenly dizzy, Takoda staggered backward and collapsed onto his chair. His mind filled with images of the tearful parting. There is no pain greater than watching as someone takes your child away, whether it be God or another human.

Neville continued to talk but Takoda didn't listen. Memories of his lost family dulled his other senses until he felt his body shake and a shadow darkened his vision. Neville's voice penetrated his mental fog. "…do you hear me? I'm *not* going to turn you in."

"What?"

"I said I'm *not* going to turn you in. *But*…no more using this facility for any part of your plot. Do you understand? As noble as your intentions are, what you're doing is *very* dangerous. You could ruin the lives of a lot of innocent people, including *me*. And I'm not taking a bullet for your pipe dream. Got it?"

Yon had left for the day by the time Takoda's mind cleared. Too drained by the conversation with Neville and his subsequent sojourn down memory lane to work any longer, Takoda packed up his sling case and shut down his office.

On the drive home, his thoughts returned to binding proteins and their role in the last half-century of tragedy. Specifically, he thought of the mishmash of techniques, synthetics and chemical agents that had been employed over the first two decades of the Genetic Revolution to break apart chromosomes to remove unwanted genes, and then rebind the chromosomes after the genes were replaced.

In the fervor to rush gene replacement therapies to market, measured approaches to developing, testing and refining lab-created genes and binding proteins were largely cast aside. There had been a weak commitment to standardization, no long-term follow-up studies before approvals were issued, and scant thought was given to how one company's gene-pack might interact with a gene-pack from another. Or how many gene-packs could practicably be replaced at one time, or cumulatively, before chromosome integrity was threatened.

If only there had been stronger dissent, calls for prudence. Who am I kidding? They would have been ignored.

He recalled stories of parents living in countries with rigorous standards traveling in droves to other countries where standards were lax or non-existent to secure the gene-packs they wanted for their children. Not surprisingly, many of the biologic companies flocked to these regulation-free havens, exacerbating the problems.

The same wild-west approach had been applied to the techniques used to deliver gene-packs and their binding agents into cells. Some biologic companies had favored viruses as deliverymen, others had used nanobots. Then came the emergence of self-replicating smart-proteins that could navigate their own paths to desired gene positions and stimulate the unlocking and refastening of innate protein binds. At the peak of the gene replacement mania, there were more than twenty different delivery mechanisms in use...and twice that number of binding agents...and more than *ten thousand* different gene-pack combinations.

As Takoda neared the border checkpoint, he shook his head. *Madness, absolute madness.*

Early on, the slurry of gene-packs, delivery techniques and binding agents proved reasonably effective in maintaining chromosome integrity as cells divided. But then, as the first generation of genetically designed children reached puberty, the first signs of trouble in their replacement genes appeared.

The surge of hormones that caused children to blossom into adults weakened some of the altered protein binds to the point where they began to break. Not all at once, but over time. And some of the breakages were not clean, creating damage to genes on both sides of severed links, not just the replacement genes at the site of the breakage.

At first, these gutations affected a small minority of children but as the world discovered in the necro outbreak of 2082, and other virulent gutations that followed, it didn't take much to wipe out a billion people.

"Necro should have been the wakeup call," mumbled Takoda.

But the outbreak had not tempered enthusiasm for genetic design and gene replacement therapies. Nor had other pandemics that popped up over the next two decades. As the world approached the year 2100, the mania finally reached its peak. The pinnacle coincided with the earliest births of children sired by second-generation genetically-designed humans. Their inherited replacement genes mixed with inherited replacement genes of their mates, some already gutated, others not, compounding the slurry of weak binds and expanding the scope of gutations.

Another missed opportunity to stop the madness! Parents continued to walk into genetic design centers with laundry lists of desired attributes for their children. Blue eyes instead of brown, height over six feet, perfect vision, IQ in the 160 range, skin resistant to sun damage, elimination of genetic risk factors in the parents' DNA for obesity, baldness, certain cancers, dementia, and so on.

Such laundry lists would have meant the replacement of *hundreds*, if not *thousands*, of an embryo's 25,000 gene-pairs, meaning double the number of broken and mended chromosome binds linking each end of the genes together, especially if one or both parents already had gutated replaced genes in their DNA. The problem was further compounded by the apparent reset of many gutations *in utero*. The self-replicating smart-proteins in many of the replacement genes of one parent seemed to recognize and heal broken binds when merging with genes from a second parent. Alas, all too often, the binds would break again in the resulting child's DNA as they reached puberty.

It took another ten years of horrible plagues and other mutation atrocities before worldwide sanity prevailed and genetic design and gene replacement therapies were outlawed. Sadly, it had been like slapping a bandage on a gaping chest wound. Too little, too late.

As Takoda stared at the traffic slowing down in front of him, he mumbled, "And without a miracle, the worst is yet to come."

For although the pace of mutation-related deaths had steadily dropped over the last twenty years, new mutations kept appearing, including the most significant threat to humans since the plagues of the early 2110s, Jakali Syndrome.

Many people didn't see the threat the same way as Takoda did, but those people were not paying attention to the history of the last seventy years. Jakali Syndrome would not be stamped out by euthanasia and sterilization. Too many were already in the wild and when those who escaped sterilization began to mate, there was no telling what kinds of monsters they would birth.

Takoda shook from this chilling thought as he brought his Mustang to a stop. Ahead of him was a row of armed NASF Vipers blocking the road. They surrounded the vehicle and ordered him to step out. For a brief moment, he froze with his hands on the steering wheel, suddenly recalling Neville's admonition, *"As noble as your intentions are, what you're doing is very dangerous."*

An inner voice prodded Takoda to keep his cool and step out of the car. *"Don't give them a reason to question you!"*

Forcing a smile, he exited the Mustang and moved to the side of the road. There, he waited while all but one of the Vipers searched the car. The remaining Viper, a blond male with a steely gaze, kept watch on Takoda, his menacing stare accentuated by his armed-and-ready stance.

As the search went on, Takoda noticed other Vipers waving the vehicles behind his through the checkpoint with barely a glance. Once again, Neville's "very dangerous" comment echoed in his mind. Finally, though, the search ended and the menacing Viper motioned Takoda back to his car. He climbed inside, cast a final look at the Viper and resumed his drive into Carapach. *You're right, Neville. I better not lose sight of the danger. This isn't over, yet. Not by a long shot.*

CHAPTER 11

IN THE CROSSHAIRS

Palace of Prefect Munoz
Minneapolis, Lakelands Province, New Atlantia

The utter depravity of Prefect Munoz never ceased to amaze Damon. Behind his palace walls, the noble lived a life so disconnected from reality, it was as if he had convinced himself that he was a god among machines. Not a single human lived in the palace other than Munoz. The hundred-plus inhabitants were all servile androids...all females.

Damon recalled the prefect justifying the bizarre living arrangement on one of Damon's first visits after being tapped to lead the Beacon task force. *"Andros are less prone to treachery."*

The comment might have struck Damon as shrewd politics if not for the fact the prefect had been fondling the crotch of a young, android female when he'd said it.

Inexplicably, however, among the evvies in the province and the hierarchy of leadership throughout the rest of New Atlantia, Munoz was considered an effective and respected governor of his citizens. Damon wondered how many of them realized how rarely the man actually governed.

That, he left in the hands of his chief counselor, Jordyn, the Olympia-class android who sat in front of Damon now in the chamber where Munoz conducted official province business.

Olympias like Jordyn were primarily developed as logicians, emotionless evaluators who dispensed dispassionate analysis and recommendations for any and all situations. They had risen to prominence as counselors to the leaders of the world's most populous country in the early 2100s, Old China.

Confronted by the rapid spread of gutant diseases, rampant internal caste warfare and incursions by armies of neighboring countries who sensed openings to settle old scores and retake ancient lands, the leadership of Old China fell into disarray. As legends told it, they turned to a cadre of Olympias, in whom they vested authority to enact the "austerity" measures recommended by the dispassionate androids. So began the age of gutant euthanasia and caste cleansing.

Some claimed the Old China Olympias saved humanity, but every time someone made the claim to Damon, his response was the same. "There's a reason they call it *Old* China. There's a reason there isn't a *New* China."

But despite the disintegration of the country the Olympias were tasked with saving, most people gave the logic-driven androids credit for the tough decisions the Old China leaders shrank from making, and for hastening an end to an out-of-control situation that might have otherwise cascaded across the globe.

Unlike the Old China Olympias, however, Jordyn was not a guardian and savior of humanity. She was merely a buffer that absorbed the burdens of decision making for Munoz, allowing him the freedom to dally with his playthings.

"This is all the information you've acquired?" Jordyn asked.

She was dressed in a charcoal pantsuit and black turtleneck, her blond hair pulled into a bun at the back of her head. Damon glared at her as he answered. "It's only been one day since the smugglings, Counselor. We're moving as fast as we can."

"This is a grave matter, Major. If you do not move faster, this province, and the republic, could face dire consequences."

"I understand the gravity of the situation, Counselor. Believe me, I feel it acutely."

The android turned to face Cassidy, who sat next to Damon. For the next minute, the two female andros just stared at each other, an indication they were engaged in an electronic conversation. It was technically a violation of protocol to cut Damon out of their conversation, but he was powerless to prevent it. The counselor had carte blanche from Munoz to do as she saw fit. When the wireless exchange ended, Jordyn, seated in the prefect's throne-like chair at the head of the table, turned to Damon and said, "Sgt. Willow indicates you declined to authorize cross-border surveillance of the two Carapach doctors."

"That's right, I did."

"Explain."

He shrugged. "We don't have enough evidence to obtain a treaty waiver. Simple as that."

"Where are they now?"

Damon turned to Cassidy. His subordinate spoke her answer instead of transmitting it. "Satellite imagery confirms they are at Dr. Wells' home in Carapach."

"They are the only ones at the clinic who are Carapach citizens. Correct?" Jordyn asked.

"Yes," said Cassidy. "The rest are New Atlantian citizens."

"And you have all of the New Atlantians under surveillance?"

"Yes, Counselor."

For a short spell after Cassidy's answer, Jordyn stared off into the distance. Damon wasn't sure if that implied she and Cassidy were continuing their dialogue via radio, or if Jordyn was ruminating over the information they had provided. When she came out of her trance, she blinked several times and said to Damon, "Detain and interrogate all of the New Atlantians under surveillance. Tonight. Lead a stealth team across the border tonight as well. Take the Carapach doctors into custody and question them. When the interrogation is complete, execute them and dispose of their bodies before returning."

"Execute them? Are you nuts?" Damon felt his face and neck growing hot. "That's not gonna fly, Counselor."

"Major, I have weighed the evidence you and Sgt. Willow collected and I have determined there is sufficient risk to this province and to the New Atlantian republic to justify detention and interrogation of the Carapach doctors. The executions will also send a message to Beacon — to cease further smuggling operations."

One of the annoying attributes of Olympia androids to Damon was they never showed emotion, for they had no emotion modules. Therefore, they did not pound tables, their voices never changed tone or inflection and their faces remained neutral at all times. It made arguing with them all the more infuriating.

"And just what do you think will happen when the Carapach doctors suddenly go missing? Covert op or not, the Carapach government will put two and two together right quick, especially when word gets out about the other interrogations. And there's no way we can stop that from happening. The clinic director is an *evvie*. He'll go straight to the Guild. The prefect will have his ass in a fire before sunrise…from the Guild *and* Carapach."

As placid as still water, Jordyn said, "I have assessed the likely response scenarios. They are all manageable…and they all carry less risk than the alternative that Beacon pursues more operations like the ones yesterday.

"If Maj. Jackson is correct about Beacon's motivations, and Beacon is conducting illegal genetic research, intending to develop a JS cure or disrupt didgee conscription in New Atlantia, it could be a catastrophic blow to our human society."

Damon rolled his eyes. Obviously, Cassidy had shared the details of his discussion with Beauregard Jackson during her radio-only tête-à-tête with Jordyn. Nothing like stirring apocalyptic paranoia in an Olympia-class andro.

"Counselor, there could be many different explanations for Beacon's actions, many of them far less sinister. Regardless, though, killing the Carapach doctors, the only leads we have, is insane. And short of that, sending in a stealth team to interrogate them will only cause Beacon to go deeper undercover. We're better off—"

"I have made my decision." Jordyn rose from Munoz' throne. "You have your orders, Major. See that you carry them out."

Takoda's residence
Wolf Lake, East Dakota, Carapach

Edging a little farther out into the water, Takoda cast his line. As he watched the fly-lure splash into the stream, it rippled the shimmering gold surface. Soon, he felt the tug of the current pulling on the line. He paused for a moment before twitching the rod and thought of how it used to be before he had sent her away.

Back then, they used to fish every summer night. He would rush home from the clinic, picking up dessert from the bakery on the way. Most evenings she waited for him at the end of the driveway, laden with their fishing gear. Other nights, when he was late or she was too impatient, Takoda would find her already at the stream, knee-deep in the water.

Occasionally, he would arrive home to discover the scent of cooking fish drifting through the woods. The memory of those nights brought a smile to Takoda's face. He would wind his way through the thicket of trees, following the aroma and the trail of smoke. Soon, he would see the glow of the campfire and the silhouette of a crouching girl tending skewers on the hot coals. As he drew closer, and sunset bathed her in a mix of gold, purple and orange, Takoda couldn't help but notice how much she looked like her mother. Turning now to gaze at the fading sun, he filled his mind with images of both of them.

Amid his reverie, he heard Yon call out. "Hey, are you going to catch us dinner or should I call for pizza?"

Takoda chuckled and turned to look at his friend, co-worker and partner-in-underground-crime. She was stretched out on a lounge chair by the campfire, glass of wine in one hand and the screen of a holotablet hovering in front of her face.

"Put that contraption away and enjoy the sunset." Takoda was ecstatic they had made it through the day in New Atlantia and returned to Carapach without incident.

She pushed the floating screen aside long enough to say, "No way. It keeps the bugs away. Now, hurry up and catch something. I'm starving."

"Okay, okay." He laughed and reeled in the line.

After casting it out again, he focused his attention on attracting a trout with fly-like twitches on the water. As he repeated the cast-twitch-reel process, however, his mood darkened as he revisited his meeting with Neville.

Takoda had not yet told Yon of the encounter and debated now whether he should. He knew Yon would urge him to share the details of the conversation with Hoot, and Takoda was reluctant to do that until *after* he and Yon were allowed to talk with Sarah Hearns. He was afraid Hoot would cut them out of any more dealings with Sarah if she learned Neville Thompson had deciphered their goal.

The Beacon leader had already delayed their link up with Sarah as part of her edict to maintain their normal routines so long as NASF had them under surveillance. For now, Sarah was sequestered with her daughters in an undisclosed safehouse and there she would remain until Hoot said otherwise. She even prohibited phone and electronic communication with Sarah, fearing NASF would break Beacon's encryption.

Hoot was so paranoid about security, she had applied the same prohibition on Takoda for any communications with Ellie who, at that moment, was en route to Beacon's gutant safe haven in Flathead, Montana with Billy Hearns and Akecheta's brain core. *At least they'll all be safe there*, Takoda thought.

Takoda could not say the same about himself and Yon. He felt incredibly uneasy about returning to New Atlantia a second time after enduring Spiers' tiptoe around the uniqueness of Billy's DNA. It was as if the NASF major knew exactly why they had rescued him and was taunting them with his knowledge. His uneasiness was further magnified by the conversation with Neville. He shuddered to think what would happen if he and Yon were in New Atlantia and Neville changed his mind and talked to NASF.

A caress of his shoulder roused Takoda from his thoughts. He looked around to see Yon standing beside him in the stream. With her hands on her hips and a frown on her face, she said, "Pizza will be here in ten minutes. I'll see you inside."

As he watched Yon wade her way back to shore, Takoda said, "I thought we were eating trout."

"You took too long."

"Why inside, then? Let's eat by the fire."

"Can't. Got a message from Hoot. She wants to talk with us in half an hour."

When Takoda returned to the house, Yon was prepping her holotablet for the call with Hoot. Neither Takoda nor Yon had ever met her, nor did either of them know her real name, what she looked like or where she was located.

In fact, if Takoda had been directly recruited by Hoot instead of by Yon, he would have declined to join Beacon. The idea of placing his fate in the hands of a stranger would have been too much of a leap of faith for him. But he had worked with Yon for four years and trusted her. So, two years ago, when she made her first overture to join the underground, Takoda had listened.

At first, he had listened out of respect for their friendship. Yon had been there for him after the death of his wife and the surrender of his daughter. Yon had helped Takoda through his grief and anger and had kept him from descending into the darkness of depression. Along the way, she became an increasing presence in his life, someone Takoda looked forward to spending time with, whether at work or socially.

And Takoda knew Yon wanted more than friendship. She wanted him to dock Ellie and share a more intimate relationship with her, but it was a step Takoda wasn't ready for yet. As he watched her open the encryption program on the tablet's floating screen, he hoped he might feel differently one day. He didn't want to lose her.

When the call was connected, the voice on the other end was not Hoot. It was the male voice of an android. With unusual formality, he requested their passcodes. Yon spoke hers, then Takoda gave his. They waited for the android to process their codes through its voice recognition module and then he connected them with Hoot.

"Hello? Trout? Wolf?"

Trout was Yon's codename, Takoda's was Wolf.

"We're here, Hoot. How are you?" Yon asked.

Hoot's answer was curt. "You two are in danger. You must leave immediately."

"What? Why?" Yon probed.

"No time for that now. Grab your ready-packs, get in your maglev, Wolf, and haul ass to Standing Rock. You have about ten minutes before they get there."

"Before who gets here?" Takoda asked.

"Call me back when you're on the road. Now, move!"

The holoscreen went dark. Yon deactivated the tablet, hopped up and headed for the kitchen door. Takoda disappeared into his bedroom and fished out his emergency ready-pack from his closet.

Without bothering to turn off lights or lock doors, Takoda followed Yon's route through the kitchen and out the door leading to the driveway. He had been through enough practice drills of Beacon's escape protocol to know speed was of the essence. When he pushed through the door, he saw Yon had already started her Starlight maglev cruiser. He dashed to the open back hatch, threw in his bag and ran around to the passenger side.

As soon as he was in and closed the door, Yon commanded the vehicle to depart. "Cloak mode. Quickest route to Standing Rock via maglev. Fastest possible speed. Don't stop for anything or anyone."

The vehicle chassis lifted off the ground and spun around until it was pointed down Takoda's mile-long driveway. Then it shot down the road, pinning Takoda to his seat.

"What do you think is going on?" Yon asked.

"It has to be NASF."

"But they can't come into Carapach."

"Legally, no. Let's call Hoot back and get more details."

With the Starlight navigating the country road on autopilot, Yon reconnected with the underground. After the same annoying passcode verification, Hoot was back on the line. "Have you left?"

"Yes," said Yon.

"We can't see you on our tracking grid."

"I put on cloak mode. What's going on?"

Hoot's explanation was just as terse as her earlier command to flee. "NASF has sent a stealth team to capture, interrogate and execute you. Both of you."

"What? Are you sure?" Takoda asked.

"Positive. We have eyes on them right now. I'll tell you more when you get to Standing Rock. Deactivate the cloak mode. We need to be able to track you."

"But what about NASF?" Yon said.

"Useless. For NASF to dare to send a stealth team across the border, they would have had you under satellite surveillance before they crossed the border. Now, disable it. We've dispatched drones from Rosebud to provide you cover but they need a signal to lock onto."

"Cover from what?"

"Stealth gliders. Disable it quickly."

Yon blurted out a command for the Starlight to deactivate the electronic signal suppression system. For a short spell, no one spoke. Then Hoot said, "Okay, we've got you. Let us take over navigation from here. Transmitting routing now."

Seconds later, Starlight's computer indicated it had received a remote navigation request. Yon authorized the remote access. At the next intersection, the cruiser abruptly slowed to make a screeching left-hand turn and then re-accelerated. Hoot spoke again. "Time to glider intercept is forty-five—"

There was a blinding flash of light. Takoda shielded his eyes. He felt the cruiser shudder and swerve. The safety harness pressed him against the seat while the headrest clamped around his skull. The next sensation Takoda felt was the Starlight tumbling.

En route to the old Standing Rock Indian Reservation
North Dakota, Carapach

"Direct hit!" Cassidy said. "But we have incoming, Major. Three drones. From the southwest at two hundred twenty-three degrees."

As they rambled down the road in the camouflaged assault vehicle, Damon followed the action up ahead on the holoscreen map in front of him. They were four miles behind the Starlight, but closing fast on the now immobile vehicle. His NASF gliders, four of them, surrounded the upside-down cruiser.

"Recommend we engage the Carapach drones," said Cassidy.

Abel, the Viper android leader of the stealth team seated behind Cassidy, said, "Sir, we've picked up a transmission from the Carapach police. They've closed the border behind us. They have our coordinates, and they've dispatched units to intercept us."

"How's that possible? How do they know where we are?" Damon said. But he realized the answer before he finished saying the words. "Beacon! Scan for a nano or a tracking device in the vicinity. Quickly!"

"Major…the incoming drones are almost on station," Cassidy warned.

A glance back at the screen showed Damon three blips converging on the surrounded Starlight.

"We have a hot spot in the cabin, Major," said Abel.

"What? Where?"

"Engaging the Carapach drones," said Cassidy.

"No! Stop!" shouted Damon. He reached out to bat Cassidy's hand from touching the drone fire-control screen. She crushed down on his hand.

As he tried to pull it away, Abel announced, "Hot spot ID'd. It's on Sgt. Will—"

Damon caught a quick glimpse of Cassidy's fist before it slammed into his head. Rocked off his seat, he crashed into the weapon rack and fell to the floor. As he scrambled to get up, he heard the hiss of a laser pistol. Before he reached his feet, however, another blow struck him on the back of the head. Damon thudded onto the floor and passed out.

On a holoscreen displaying the view from the assault vehicle's front window, Cassidy saw dozens of small fires on the road ahead and in the brush on both embankments. In the center of the road, lying on its roof, she spotted the crumpled shell of the Starlight cruiser. As Cassidy commanded the vehicle computer to stop one hundred feet short of the wreck, she transmitted a message to Beacon requesting medical assistance. Shortly thereafter, she received a response from an EMT squad confirming they were en route.

When the NASF truck stopped, it straddled the centerline of the road with its engine idling. Stepping over the melted remains of the stealth team Vipers she'd destroyed, Cassidy exited through the back door and approached the Starlight.

Laser pistol raised, she scanned the cruiser with her sensors. She detected both passengers inside, still secured into their seats. They were not moving, but her biometric instruments registered activity. The female's vital signs were weaker than the male's. Cassidy relayed the data to the EMTs and then proceeded to scan the perimeter for signs of electronic activity from the destroyed NASF gliders.

Sensing none, Cassidy holstered her weapon and returned to the assault vehicle to drag out the unconscious Damon. Hoisting him over her shoulder, she carried him to the wreck and laid him on the road.

A short while later, several vehicles arrived. Among the people who arrived in them were EMTs and rescue personnel who extracted Yon and Takoda from the Starlight. After receiving medical aid, they were loaded into one of the vehicles and driven away.

Under Cassidy's watchful eyes, other EMTs rendered aid to Damon and extracted the identification chip lodged in his neck. After he was loaded into a separate vehicle, Cassidy received instructions from Hoot.

"Assist our Makoas. Scavenge the NASF truck. Remove everything of value. Weapons and tech."

Cassidy confirmed the command as the van bearing Damon sped off. Once the NASF truck was picked clean, Cassidy received follow-on instructions from Hoot. "Set charges in the Starlight and the NASF truck, then join the Makoas. We will detonate remotely."

Moments later, with the charges placed, Cassidy boarded the truck with the other androids. As the truck drove away, she watched the explosions light up the night sky. Soon after, her audio module received a final message from Hoot. "Dock and power down."

"Roger that. Willow out."

She lifted a Velcro patch on the back of her pants, exposing a battery port on her left butt cheek. Cassidy eased back until she detected the connection with the dock. After her sensors confirmed recharging had initiated, Cassidy closed her eyes and activated sleep mode.

CHAPTER 12

COMFORT THE NEEDY

En route to gutant refugee village
Flathead, Montana, Carapach

The long road trip to the old Flathead Reservation in Montana had been rough on Billy Hearns. During the journey, Ellie had done her best to soothe the child's apprehensions but the violet-eyed boy was, at turns, inconsolable and combative.

He did not understand who Ellie was, how he had gotten from his bed at home to the RV in which they now rode, or where his parents were. He was also frustrated by her silence when he demanded to know where they were headed and why.

During the lulls between his intermittent tantrums, Ellie had suggested he take a nap or eat, suggestions that Billy rejected summarily. Instead, he either sulked in the RV's bedroom or stood by her side and barraged her with questions and complaints.

Finally, however, about halfway into their trip and a good ten hours after he awoke from the series of sedatives he had received, Billy's defiant resolve broke down and he ate pancakes Ellie had prepared. It was his favorite breakfast meal, a tip passed along by Sarah Hearns before she and her daughters were spirited out of New Atlantia. Soon after finishing the meal, he had fallen asleep for several hours.

Now, with only an hour left to go before the self-driving home-on-wheels reached their destination, Ellie nudged him awake.

"Wake up, sleepyhead." The soft-voice and vernacular Ellie employed were features of the nurturing module she had activated at the beginning of the trip. "Come on, now, wake up. We're almost there."

Billy cracked open his eyes a little and yawned. "Almost where?"

"Your new home."

The information stirred Billy fully awake. His expression began as apparent confusion and then morphed into anger. "I don't want a new home. I want my old one. I want my mom and dad."

Ellie reached out a hand and touched the boy's arm. "I know, sweetie. Don't get upset again. Your mom will be here soon. This is her new home too."

"Really?" Billy's eyes lit up. Then a frown formed on his face. "Why did we have to move? Why didn't my parents come with us? Where are my sisters and my father?"

"I'm sure your mom will tell you everything when she gets here. You'll be living in a village called Flathead. As you can see by looking out the windows, there are many mountains and tall trees. And there is also a big lake. I know you will like it here. I'm told all the boys and girls like it here."

As far as Ellie could tell from Billy's reaction to her sales pitch, the prospect of a reunion with his family seemed to make Billy very happy, but he also remained skeptical. He continued to rattle off questions. *When will the rest of my family get here? Is my father coming too? Why did we have to move?*

When they arrived at the village, a delegation from the refugee ranch was there to greet them. Among the welcome party were adults and children. The children rushed forward and waved to Billy; however, Billy was reluctant to exit the RV. He clung by Ellie's side and held her hand.

"Come on, let's go meet your new friends," Ellie said.

"I'm scared."

"Don't be. They're very nice people. You'll like them."

"Can't I stay with you until my mom gets here?"

"I'm afraid not. I have other responsibilities, but I will come to check on you later tonight. Okay?"

Ellie stepped down out of the RV and Billy edged out after her. Moments later, surrounded by smiling, gaggling children, he let go of Ellie's hand. Two women, apparently mothers of some of the children, knelt and chatted with Billy and soon they led the welcome party away. Ellie saw Billy turn and look back at her. She waved to him and he waved back.

"Don't forget to check on me," he called.

"I won't. I'll see you tonight."

A man walked up to Ellie and introduced himself as Dr. Wyatt Longbow, the refugee ranch director. "Any trouble during the trip?"

"No. Billy was tired and frustrated, but that was to be expected."

Longbow nodded. "It's traumatic. One moment you're at home sleeping in your bed. The next, you're halfway across the continent, in a foreign country. Your parents aren't there. Everybody is a stranger. It's confusing, scary. But he'll be okay. We're used to helping kids assimilate. As you saw, everybody likes to pitch in. Many of them have been through the same experience, so they know what Billy's feeling right now. They'll help him feel at home until his mother arrives."

"Good. Will you please inform Beacon HQ of his arrival? I would myself but I have been directed to refrain from initiating communications." Ellie said.

"Yes, of course. I'll take care of it." Longbow looked past Ellie to gaze at the RV behind her. "Are you heading back east tonight?"

"No. I have some errands to complete. I will be here for a day or two."

"Okay. Good. If you need anything, just let me know. We're right up the main road, about three miles outside town."

After Longbow departed, Ellie directed the RV's computer to drive to the village service station to refuel and restock supplies for the return trip, finishing the transmission by communicating, *"Signal me when you finish at the station and I will instruct you where to pick me up."*

The vehicle computer transmitted its acknowledgment and then drove away. Ellie turned around to face the destination of her first errand, a sprawling, windowless, one-story industrial facility a few blocks from the center of the village.

Reaching into the pocket of her khaki fatigue pants, Ellie clutched a metallic cylinder and began walking. "Come on, Ake. Let's go find you a new chassis."

Androids R Us
Flathead, Montana, Carapach

"Well, well, well, lookie what we have here."

Ellie scanned the man speaking. Given his wrinkles, thinning gray hair and paunch of a belly, she estimated the probability of his age at between sixty and sixty-five. Based on his pasty complexion, the bags under his eyes and his soiled clothes, she reasoned he was the android shop mechanic…a rather devoted one. This assessment was supported by the tone of his voice and the leer on his face as he circled her, ogling her physique. She placed Akecheta's brain core on the counter and said, "I need a replacement chassis. Preferably a Makoa model if you have one."

The man laughed and sidled up beside her. He squeezed her butt and sniffed her hair. "My, oh my, you are one fine piece of —"

"If you do not have a Makoa, then an Apollo or Steel class will do." Ellie grasped the man's hand as it dipped between her legs. Squeezing it, she said, "Touch me again like that and I'll rip your hand off."

The man cried in pain. "Agh, okay, okay. Let go. Let go." As he danced around, holding his hand, he said, "Geez. Why are you so worked up, baby? You're a comfort andro, ain't ya? Athena class, right? Thought you hunnies liked that kind of attention."

Ellie picked up the metallic cylinder from the counter and moved past the mechanic. At the double doors separating the reception area from the warehouse, she paused and turned to the man. "Are you going to help me or not?"

"Loosen your caboose, darlin', I'm a-coming."

Ellie stepped forward and the doors slid open. She spied a holodisplay directory dead ahead. Behind the directory were rows and rows of docked androids. Stacked four high on each side, Ellie's measurement module calculated a total inventory of 2,483 androids. Factoring in a twenty percent allowance for damaged and inoperative frames, she lowered the estimate of potential replacements for Akecheta at 1,986. Based on the latest download she had received regarding Makoa brain core compatibility with other class androids, cross-referenced with Carapach's database of active registrations in Montana, Ellie reduced the possible options down to thirty-six.

The mechanic passed by her and said, "Follow me, sweet cheeks. Got just what you're looking fer."

As the man waddled down one of the side aisles, she conducted several scans of his body. He had an artificial shoulder, hip and knees, as well as a heart implant and a dopamine regulator in his brain. He was obviously not one of Flathead's native people, given his skin tone and speech pattern. Ellie judged him to be a transplanted Texan or New Atlantian.

Rounding the end of the aisle, he said, "Didn't mean no harm back there. It's just that all the comfort andros get snapped up as soon as they come in. Barely have enough time to customize their modules and give 'em a nice spit and polish before they're gone. It's enough to drive a lonely man crazy. Know what I mean?"

Ellie's visual scanner probed the new aisle. Four docks triggered her sensors. An Apollo class and three Steels. She noticed two other empty docks in the same aisle. When they drew closer to them, her long-range lenses homed in on the displays in front of the empty docks, which indicated two Makoas had occupied the docks.

"Where are the Makoas that were in those docks?" she asked.

"Huh?" The man squinted down the aisle. "Oh, those two? Some jakali hunter came through here yesterday and bought 'em. They were pieces of junk, really. Not sure why he bothered with them. Doubt they'll be of much use up north."

"Do you still have the specifications for the Makoas?"

The man stopped and turned around. Ellie's sensors detected a rise in his temperature as his eyes locked on to her breasts. "Eyes up here, botboy."

"Huh? What?"

"The specs for the Makoas?"

He rubbed at his scraggly beard and squinted at her eyes. "You pledged to someone or something? I mean, most Athenas are sweet and playful. You're kind of a stone-cold bit—"

"Do you have the specs or not?"

"Yeah, I got 'em. What do you want 'em fer?"

Ellie walked past him and visually studied the Apollo and Steels. Apollo-class androids were bigger, stronger and more durable than Steels, but they were not as agile and had fewer module ports. Apollos as a class were also older models, meaning Steels were equipped with more modern communications arrays and faster central processors. But neither of these android classes were built for heavy-duty combat, and thus lacked some of the features and capabilities Makoas possessed. Certain modules could be added to compensate for the lack of military-grade sensors, but there was no substitute for Makoas' sturdy construction.

In front of each docked android was a data screen that displayed the robot's history, specifications, available options and price. Ellie scanned the information for the four androids and engaged her reasoning module to select the best option. When the module completed its analysis, Ellie turned and pointed at one of the Steels. "I'll take this one."

"Good choice."

"I will need a few component upgrades and some new module installations." Ellie pulled Akecheta's core from her pocket. "I will also want to swap out the brain core."

"Not a problem, darlin'. So long as I've got the components you want in stock, I should be able to install and test everything by Tuesday of next week."

Ellie shook her head. "I need it done in two days, not six."

The man scratched at his beard. "Sorry. First come, first served. That jakali hunter is ahead of you. He has a truckload of andros that need a-fixin', plus he wants mods for the ones he bought yesterday. Of course, if you was to soften up a little, maybe come over to my place tonight…"

As his eyes traveled up and down her body, Ellie said, "That's out of the question, but I am willing to pay a premium to jump to the front of your queue."

He laughed. "It's not your credits I want, baby. My bank account is as fat as I am. I want that tight little Athena body of yours. Like I said, it gets lonely up here."

A six-day wait was unacceptable. Ellie was expected back in East Dakota to transport Sarah Hearns and her daughters to Flathead. As she evaluated her options, she realized there were only two that could shrink the timeline. Either convince the jakali hunter to part with one of his purchased Makoas or placate the mechanic.

Ellie smiled and edged closer to the mechanic. "I have a better idea. How about you give me jakali hunter's contact information. If I can't convince him to let me move my job ahead of his, I'll consider your proposal."

The mechanic returned Ellie's smile and wrapped his arm around her waist. "Now that's more like it, baby. But why don't we just skip the jakali hunter altogether? I can get working on your Steel right now. Should be able to finish it by sundown and then we can rock and roll all night long."

She stroked his hair and said, "Mmm, sounds *amazing*, but I still want the jakali hunter's info. I can chat with him while you're working on my Steel."

The mechanic slapped her butt and said, "Deal. Follow me."

Moosehead Lodge
Flathead, Montana, Carapach

Stretched out on a thick-cushioned lounge chair, Caelan reached down and pulled another bottle from the bucket of ice. Before he could twist off the cap, he heard the pub's waiter speed across the grass.

"Allow me, sir."

Tired of protesting the android's constant attention, Caelan held up the bottle. "Fine, fine. Do your voodoo, lad."

"Would you care for a glass, sir?"

"For the fifth bloody time, no! Just give me the bottle and bugger off."

Caelan maintained his gaze on the lake while he waited for the android to place the bottle back in his hand.

"A lunch menu, perhaps? We have a lovely—"

"Bottle. Now."

As soon as Caelan felt the glass touch against his palm, he closed his fingers around the bottle, snatched it from the android's grip and gulped down a few slugs of beer. Satisfied, he shoved the open bottle back into the bucket, making sure to seat it deep in the ice. Looking up, he saw the bow-tied bot smiling at him. "Go away! You're blocking my sun. If I want lunch, I'll call for ye."

Once the android retreated, Caelan returned to watching the canoes out on the lake. *God, I miss Ertha. She knew when to give me space. Not like these tongue-waggers here. They can't seem to get it through their Kevlar skulls. I want some peace and quiet, a nice buzz and maybe a wee nap in the sun. Is that too much to ask? A little rest without worrying if some jakali devil's going to pop out of nowhere and take a bite out of me.*

Tilting his safari hat to cover his eyes, Caelan instructed the smart-chair underneath him to recline back further. *Happy thoughts, man. You only have a few more days until its back to work.* He yawned long and loud and tried to clear his mind by listening to the children playing on the beach at the lake's edge. They were having a good old time splashing each other and playing tag. Caelan smiled. *I almost feel human.* The serene feeling lasted only a short while, for his ears detected the sound of feet walking across the grass toward him.

"I swear to the Almighty Father, if you say one word about the lunch menu again, I'll shove the bloody thing up your mechanical arse!"

"That doesn't sound very pleasant," a female voice replied.

Caelan pushed up his hat and turned to look at the woman. She smiled and extended a hand. "Hi. Are you Caelan Horn? I'm Ellie."

Out of the corner of his mouth, Caelan barked at the smart-chair to raise him into a sitting position. All the while, he studied the woman in front of him. He immediately recognized her as an android, an Athena comfort bot like Ertha had been. Aquiline noses, long necks and broad shoulders were tell-tale features of Athenas.

This one looked designed to be in her mid-thirties, much older than most Athenas. The class of comfort androids was most often designed for men and women seeking bedroom companions who appeared to be in their late teens or early twenties.

She had straight strands of black hair that shined under the glare of the sun, a light brownish-reddish complexion and a pleasing smile. Whoever owned the bot had not chosen to go with the typical lingerie-model body features common among Athenas. Her curves were still alluring, just more muscular than most Athenas. This one was dressed in khaki cargo pants, hiking boots and a tight-fitting white T-shirt that accented the shape of her breasts and the size of her biceps.

"Well, are you going to leave me hanging or shake my hand?" Ellie asked.

"Sorry, luv." Caelan gripped her hand and lightly squeezed it. "Yes, I'm Caelan Horn. Why might you be asking?"

Pointing to an empty lounge chair next to Caelan, she asked, "May I join you?"

"Depends," he said. "If you're looking to sell me a quick tussle at the inn, don't waste your time. I'm not interested."

"I'm not that kind of girl, Mr. Horn."

Caelan looked her up and down again and thought, *you are for somebody, honey.* He edged his hat back down over his eyes, hoping the android would take the hint and leave. Unfortunately, she was undeterred.

"Word at the chop-shop is you hunt jakalis for bounties."

"Aye."

"The guy at the shop said you have a team of Makoas."

"Yeah. So?"

"My patron requires a Makoa. I was hoping you might consider selling me one of yours."

"Sorry, luv. My Makoas aren't for sale."

"You haven't heard my offer yet."

Caelan tapped the lounge chair's control panel to return to a fully reclined position. "Don't need to. Bye, bye, now."

"What about the two male Makoas you bought yesterday?" she asked. "I'll pay you double the amount that you paid for both of them and trade you a Steel, customized to your specs, in exchange for just one of the Makoas."

Caelan stifled a yawn and said, "No thank you, luv. A Steel wouldn't last five minutes in a jakali scrum, and Makoas are hard to find in this neck of the woods. Now, if you don't mind, I'm trying to enjoy a little R&R. Ta."

"What if I add a tussle at the inn?"

"Sorry, luv. As beautiful as you are, you're not my type."

He heard a chair creak and then the swish of steps on the grass. As they faded away, Caelan yawned. *Finally...peace at last!*

Charlemagne Bentworth's apartment
Flathead, Montana, Carapach

While the fat blob of a man lay on top of her, huffing and puffing with each grind of his hips against her synthetic flesh-covered chassis, Ellie transmitted a message to Wyatt Longbow. In it, she asked him to inform Beacon that she had secured a replacement chassis for Akecheta and she was preparing to return to East Dakota. Attached to the message were pictures of the modified Steel now docked in the RV.

With the message transmitted, Ellie initiated software maintenance on all of her systems except her sensuality module. As the software updates reached seventy-five percent complete, Ellie's sensuality sensors detected a sharp rise in the man's heart rate and body temperature. Ellie paused the software maintenance routines and devoted full processing priority to her sensuality module. Reaching behind her head, she took hold of the back of the man's head lying on top of her and pulled his face aside hers. Raising her mouth to his ear, she urged him on in a sultry voice.

More sensuality sensor data streamed to her brain core indicating the man's catharsis was imminent. Ellie's module responded with a combination of physical and audio stimuli designed to increase the intensity of the man's experience. She sensed his body tense and then tremble.

As soon as his catharsis abated, Ellie restarted the final portion of the software upgrade and initiated her sanitization module. The man rolled off of her and Ellie left the bed. The man said nothing at first, but as Ellie picked up the first garment of her clothes, he said, "What are you doing? The deal was *all night long.*"

Ellie turned and smiled. She dropped her clothes, retraced her steps to the bed and straddled him. Lowering her lips to his ear, she whispered, "Close your eyes."

He smiled and grabbed hold of her rear. Ellie slid a hand behind his head and cupped his neck, prodding him to relax. As soon as she felt his neck muscles slacken, a prong ejected from the center of her palm. It pierced into his neck and jolted him with an electric shock, a shock designed to further excite the pleasure neurons in his brain. He writhed as another climax coursed through his body. When it subsided, she retracted the prong. Out cold, the man let go of her buttocks. Shortly thereafter, Ellie signaled the RV to pick her up.

Ten minutes later, she disembarked the RV at the Beacon ranch and went in search of Billy Hearns. After locating his cabin, she spent several minutes listening to him recount his first day at the ranch and then escorted him to bed. As she began to narrate a bedtime story stored in her nurturing module, Longbow stopped by the cabin and told Ellie he had received a reply to her earlier message.

"There's been a change in plans," he said. "The folks back east want you to remain here for a spell."

Billy seemed happy with the news, for he laid his head on Ellie's lap and asked her to stay the night with him. Ellie stroked his hair until he fell asleep and then returned to the RV to dock and recharge.

CHAPTER 13

DECEPTION

Beacon safe house
Cannon Ball, North Dakota, Carapach

The first sensation Takoda noticed when he regained consciousness was the clank, clank, clank of the ceiling fan in the center of the room. Reaching a hand to his throbbing head, he watched the wobbly fan spin for a moment and then searched the room for the fan's control switch. He spotted no such switch but did notice the room had a voice-command panel on the wall by the door.

"Fan off," Takoda said.

Magically, the fan began to slow, its clanking diminishing with each rotation. Takoda massaged his forehead and tried to sit up. It was a painful exercise, but he managed the task. His chest and arms felt bruised, as did his thighs, recalling to mind the attack on Yon's Starlight, followed by a crash.

Taking stock of his condition by moving his arms and legs and feeling for bandages, Takoda looked around the room. *Where am I? This doesn't look like a holding cell or a hospital. It kind of looks like someone's bedroom. Did Hoot save us? Or are we in New Atlantia?* The latter thought stimulated a moment of panic. *Where is Yon?*

She was not in the room, that much Takoda could tell. He slowly moved off the bed and tried to stand. Although he felt as if he had been battered by baseball bats from head to toe, he found he could stand. Looking down, he noticed he was still dressed in his favorite fishing clothes, minus his shoes.

After a short stagger across the room, Takoda tested the door handle. It was unlocked. He opened the door and peered into the hallway. He was definitely in someone's house or the homiest interrogation center in New Atlantia. *Must still be in Carapach*, he thought.

"Hello? Anybody there? Yon?"

Takoda heard the sound of movement below. It came from the stairway midway down the hall. A male voice called out, "Dr. Wells?"

"Yeah. Who are you? Where am I? Where's Yon?"

Holding onto his sore lower back, he shuffled out of the room and into the carpeted hallway. He heard a flurry of footsteps and saw the shadows of two people rising on the staircase wall. When they came into view, Takoda froze. *Maybe this is an interrogation center.*

While he did not recognize the man who appeared first, the woman who came into view shortly after, he knew instantly. It was the android NASF officer who had come to the clinic. Takoda felt the urge to flee but there was nowhere to go and he knew he was no match for the Steel-class bot.

"You are among friends, Dr. Wells," said the man.

"Like hell I am," Takoda said, glaring at the woman. "Sgt. Willow, isn't it?"

"Cassidy," she replied.

"And I'm Carlos. I work for Beacon too." The mustachioed Hispanic stepped forward and extended a hand. "Code name is Shepherd. You're in my home. Dr. Fujita is downstairs. She's talking with Hoot."

Takoda shook Carlos' hand but continued to eye the female android warily. "Hoot's here?"

"No. Sorry. They're on a holoconference," said Carlos. "Come on, I'll show you."

Carlos tugged on Takoda's arm but he shook it free and pointed at Cassidy. "I'm not going anywhere until you tell me what she's doing here."

"I'm part of the underground too," she said.

Takoda looked at Carlos, who nodded vigorously. "No lie. In fact, she saved your asses."

"Saved us? You call crashing our cruiser saving us? We could have been killed."

"It was necessary to maintain the illusion," Cassidy said.

"Illusion? That was no illusion, andro."

"I have just received a transmission from Hoot," said Cassidy. "She requests your presence on the holoconference with Dr. Fujita. If you are too injured to walk, I can carry you."

Takoda waved her off as she stepped forward. "No thanks. I don't need your help."

"Cool," said Carlos. "Follow me."

Stiff-legged, Takoda headed for the stairs behind Carlos. Cassidy waited and followed after Takoda. During the painful descent, he struggled to make sense of what he had just heard. Was it all BS to get him to lower his defenses? Or were they telling him the truth? In the short term, Takoda resolved he would have to rely on what he saw in Yon. If she seemed at ease, it would go a long way toward convincing Takoda that Carlos and Cassidy were on the up and up.

When they reached the first-floor landing, Carlos pointed to closed double doors. "Dr. Fujita is in there." Nodding his head in the other direction across the hall, Carlos said, "We'll be in the dining room if you need anything."

With a degree of trepidation, Takoda pushed open one of the double doors, half-expecting to be met by a legion of NASF officers. Instead, he saw Yon curled up on a sofa in the small den. She was wearing a blanket around her shoulders and she faced a data-filled holoscreen. She beamed as soon as she saw him. "Please hold, Hoot. Takoda just arrived."

Before Hoot could respond, Yon toggled the screen off and hopped off the sofa. She collided with him, burying her head against his chest. "Thank goodness you are all right."

Takoda's skepticism melted away. He hugged her and said, "Same goes for you."

"That was scary. The crash," she said.

"Petrifying."

"Are you hurt?"

"I don't think so. Just stiff and sore. Are you okay?"

He felt her head nodding against his chest and she squeezed him tighter. "That was a close call. I'm glad we got out when we did."

"Me too, but I'm having a hard time understanding what happened."

"Yeah, I know. I felt the same way, but Hoot cleared everything up."

She pulled from their embrace and proceeded to provide Takoda with a clipped version of Hoot's explanation. Cassidy Willow had been a Beacon plant in NASF, regularly feeding Hoot inside information and obscuring evidence of the underground's rescue operations from the New Atlantians. Cassidy, Yon told him, had alerted Hoot about NASF's stealth mission to capture, interrogate and execute them.

"Why?"

"To send a message. I guess rescuing the Hearns family was the last straw for NASF," Yon said. "They've evidently also detained everybody else who works at the clinic. They're being interrogated right now according to Cassidy…"

As Yon continued to talk, Takoda felt a surge of nausea thinking about their innocent colleagues undergoing interrogation. Then, his mind turned to his conversation with Neville. *Oh no, he'll tell them. If for no other reason, he'll do it to save his skin.*

"…anyway, Hoot's hoping NASF thinks we're dead now. Of course, they may not. Cassidy said NASF was watching on their satellite when—"

Takoda held up his hand to interrupt Yon. As soon as she stopped speaking, he said, "I need to tell you something. I had a visit from Neville after the NASF people left. He knows…about the faked euthanization, about Mugabe's smart-proteins in Billy's DNA, about everything."

For several seconds, Yon stared at him. When she finally spoke, she said, "Why didn't you tell me as soon as I came over for dinner?"

Takoda shrugged. "Guess I was still trying to sort out the conversation in my mind."

She grabbed his hand and pulled him toward the couch. "You need to share this with Hoot. Like, right now."

Hoot was understandably unhappy to learn Neville had connected the dots and that Takoda had not shared that information right away. "Yon, ask Cassidy to join the call."

Yon left the room and returned with the android. As soon as Cassidy announced her presence, Hoot said, "How difficult would it be for you to extract Dr. Thompson from New Atlantia?"

Without delay, Cassidy said, "I estimate the chances of success at less than five percent. It would require extracting him from NASF HQ in Minneapolis. Assassination is a better option. If armed drones are used, the odds of success are closer to thirty percent."

"Whoa. Hold on, now. No way. I won't be a party to an assassination," said Takoda. He glared at the expressionless android.

"Me neither," said Yon.

There was no response from Hoot, leading Takoda to surmise the underground leader was seriously considering Cassidy's proposal. He made another attempt to dissuade her from killing Neville. "Look, Hoot, I messed up but what's done is done. If NASF already has Neville in custody, it's too late to do anything about it."

"Not necessarily," said Hoot. "Dr. Thompson is an evvie of high standing in New Atlantia. The Guild may intervene on his behalf. They're very protective of their members."

"Well, if that's the case, why assassinate him? It's not in Neville's interest to—"

"Takoda, a scandal has occurred in Thompson's clinic. Whether the scandal becomes public knowledge or not, his livelihood and reputation are at risk. Exposing what he discovered is in his best interests. I'm certain the Guild will agree. They will recommend divulging what he knows in exchange for leniency for not coming forward earlier."

"Okay, let's say you're right, Hoot, and he talks," said Takoda. "What can NASF do about it at this point? We've got Billy, we've got Sarah."

"They could switch course and abandon the cover story they've concocted. They could go public about the GODD chip, turn Beacon into more of a pariah than they already portray us. We're conducting evil experiments, they'll say. As supportive as the Carapach government has been to us, such charges might cause them to turn on us as well."

"NASF going public about the Hearns' rescues may also lead the person or people who implanted the chip in Billy to go into hiding before we can make contact," Cassidy said.

"Quite right," said Hoot. "Keep in mind, Takoda, the GODD chip is only part of our mission. And it is a *speculative* part. Saving didgee conscripts, providing sanctuary for oppressed gutant families, advocating for alternatives to euthanization and sterilization. Those are our primary objectives."

Takoda found Hoot's arguments hard to rebut but assassinating Neville was wrong. He looked at Yon. The pained expression on her face told him she felt the same way. She leaned toward the holoscreen and said, "Hoot, assassinating an innocent man is against what we stand for. Don't do it."

"I second that. It's a bad idea," Takoda said. "Attacking NASF headquarters and assassinating Neville will only enrage the New Atlantian government more. Plus, it will draw the Guild into the mix. They've treated us as nuisances up until now, but not if we murder one of their own. Together with the New Atlantians, they'll come after us. They'll demand action from Carapach. We'll get thrown out of the country or end up running from *two* security forces *and* the Guild."

There was a long pause before Hoot responded. "Perhaps you are right." Takoda bowed his head and praised the four gods.

"We must pray the Guild intervenes and prevents NASF from interrogating Thompson," said Hoot. "But, if he talks, Takoda, make no mistake about it, Beacon will be *gravely* affected."

"I understand that, Hoot. And I'm sorry. I should have spoken up sooner," Takoda said.

"Yes, but as you noted earlier, Takoda, what's done is done. Now, we must make the best of our situation. Which means no more delays. I will have Sarah Hearns brought to you at once. Let us hope the information she provides is worthy of the costs we have incurred."

Palace of Prefect Munoz
Minneapolis, Lakelands Province, New Atlantia

Jordyn entered Prefect Munoz' private quarters and scanned the environment. Her audio sensors detected the sounds of giggles and moans coming from the direction of the bedroom suite. She approached the room's double doors and signaled the apartment's central control panel to toggle off the privacy setting on the bedroom cameras, allowing her surveillance module to tap into and activate the cameras.

Her command authorized, she saw the prefect was engaged in relations with two females, one android, one human. Jordyn signaled the andro engaged in the tryst to pause her activities and tell the prefect that Jordyn needed to speak with him. Urgently.

Shortly thereafter, Jordyn detected the prefect's voice as she watched him sit up on the bed and pound his fists on the mattress. "How many times must I tell that frigid bitch not to interrupt me when I'm entertaining guests!"

The human woman who had been on top of him rolled off the bed and walked toward the bathroom. Meanwhile, the android, whom Jordyn's sensors identified as Heather-4, retrieved the prefect's robe and handed it to him. He threw it on the floor and slapped Heather-4's rear. "Get back in bed. Make sure to keep Alana wet and simmering until I come back."

Jordyn signaled Heather-4 to wait until the prefect had left the room and then ordered the pleasure android to detain the human Alana in the bathroom until Jordyn provided further instructions. The prefect would not be returning anytime soon, she informed Heather-4.

As Heather-4 acknowledged the instructions, the naked prefect burst through the bedroom doors and screamed at Jordyn. "Are your circuits rusty? Did you not notice the privacy setting on the door?"

"I did, sir. I disabled it."

Munoz padded across the marble foyer until he stood within inches of Jordyn. "Sounds like I need to make some changes to your privacy parameters. Now, what is so damn urgent?"

"The stealth team we sent to detain the Carapach doctors has been attacked and destroyed."

"What? By whom?"

"Unknown at this time."

"Well, it has to be either the Carapach police or Beacon, right?"

"Those are the most probable options."

"So, why bother me with it? You handle it."

Munoz turned and began walking back to the bedroom.

"There will be diplomatic repercussions, Prefect. Whether the Carapach police are directly involved or not, the government will protest the treaty violation. They may do so privately…or publicly. Either way, we need to discuss our response options."

As Munoz continued to stride away, he called back over his shoulder. "Formulate our options. I will meet you in my office after I am finished with my guests."

Jordyn advanced into the room, her strides calculated to reach Munoz before he passed from the sitting room into the bed-chamber. She slipped in front of him, barring his way. The prefect collided with her and began to fall. Jordyn grabbed his arm and pulled him back up. "There is more, sir."

"What the hell are you doing, Jordyn? Out of my way." He pulled his arm from her grip and pushed her in the chest. The Olympia did not budge.

"There was a security breach, Prefect. A serious one. The android assigned to Maj. Spiers, Sgt. Cassidy Willow, abetted the attack on the stealth team. Satellite footage confirms she left willingly from the scene of the conflict. Since then, we have been unable to re-establish communications with her brain core."

Munoz gaped at her. In the background, Jordyn's audio sensors picked up the human Alana yelling at Heather-4. "Let go of me this instant!"

Munoz heard the argument too, for he called to Alana, "What's wrong, my sweet?"

"Your trampy little peasant bot won't let me out of the bathroom. She's hurting me."

He turned back to Jordyn. "Tell Heather to release Alana. Now!"

Jordyn complied, relaying Munoz' command to Heather-4. Concurrently, the prefect tried again to push past Jordyn, only to be blocked by the Olympia once more.

"This is not an appropriate time to continue your liaisons, sir," said Jordyn. "We must meet with NASF leadership and the province high council to discuss the situation, immediately."

The bedroom cameras were still active, providing Jordyn a feed of Alana gathering her clothes while she berated the naked Heather-4.

"Look, Jordyn, I'm not going to tell you again," said Munoz, "Move out of the way and leave my quarters. I will summon you when I'm damned good and ready to talk. Until then, I have more urgent matters that require my *full* attention. Understood?"

"I advise you to devote your *immediate* attention to this serious matter."

"So advised. Now, move your synthetic ass out of my way."

This time, when Munoz shoved her in the chest, Jordyn stepped aside. As he brushed past, he nearly collided with Alana coming the other way.

"Where are you going, sweetness?" he asked.

"Forget it, Munie. The mood is gone."

"Oh, don't go. I'll make it right. You'll see. Heather will be a good peasant. Won't you, dear?"

"Yes, Your Majesty." Heather-4 curtseyed.

"See, Alana? Now, please, come back to bed, My Queen."

"But she hurt me. Look at my wrist."

"It wasn't Heather, dear. It was this one. She put Heather up to it." Munoz pointed at Jordyn. "It won't happen again. Will it, Jordyn?"

"No, sir."

"Good. Now be a good little Olympia and do as I instructed. Oh, and make sure to reactivate all privacy settings on your way out."

Munoz tugged Alana back into the bed chamber and slammed the door shut. Jordyn turned and left his quarters, commanding the control panel to deactivate the bedroom cameras and relock the entry door upon her departure. As Jordyn walked toward the elevator, she transmitted two messages. The first was to Heather-4. *"Satisfy them quickly."*

The second message went to the province's NASF headquarters. In it, Jordyn directed the commander of the stealth division to prepare another team to insert into Carapach.

The commander responded within seconds. *"Affirmative. Define mission objective."*

Jordyn entered the elevator and transmitted her instructions. *"Locate and terminate the Hearns family, the Carapach doctors and Sgt. Cassidy Willow."*

As the elevator began its descent, Jordyn received the commander's reply. *"Roger that. What about Maj. Spiers? Recover and extract?"*

"Negative," Jordyn answered. *"If you locate Maj. Spiers and he is still alive, terminate him too."*

Interrogation suite, NASF Province Headquarters
Minneapolis, Lakelands Province, New Atlantia

Naked and shivering, Neville Thompson squirmed against the binds clamping his wrists and ankles to the table. To his dismay, there was no give in the tension of the restraints. Instead, the binds squeezed even tighter. Neville grimaced and shouted at the interrogation bot. "You can't treat me this way! I'm an evvie, a member of the Guild!"

"I am afraid you forfeited your standing when you lied to me."

Neville cracked open his eyes and glared at the female Viper leaning over him. The pleasant lilt of her voice infuriated him.

"I did *not* lie, you bitch!"

She patted his hip. "Of course, you did. Three times, as a matter of fact. I even allowed you to revise your answers, but you refused."

Thinking back to the earlier part of the interrogation, Neville recalled no moment when his NASF inquisitor confronted him about any answers he had given. "That's not true."

The slithery Viper shook her head and stroked his inner thigh in a manner Neville considered highly inappropriate.

"Remove your hand from my groin. I've had enough of your—"

It happened so fast, Neville was screaming before his brain could process the sights and sounds of the Viper smashing her fist into his kneecap. Amid his thrashing and cries of pain, he felt the android's hand return to stroking his inner thigh and heard her hiss, "Now, let's revisit your answers. Shall we?"

Briefing Room, NASF Province Headquarters
Minneapolis, Lakelands Province, New Atlantia

The stealth team commander pointed at the briefing room's holodisplay. His finger circled three vehicles streaming down a solitary road surrounded by miles of prairie.

"This is a replay of the satellite feed after Beacon knocked Spiers' unit out of action. Five vehicles originally arrived at the scene. These three left together, while the other two remained behind. The satellite operator couldn't keep tabs on all five once the first three left the scene, so he tracked the first group to leave."

Pausing the holovid, the commander continued his briefing. "As you'll see in a moment, the three vehicles all came to stop in a town called Standing Rock in South Dakota." He activated a still overhead image of a group of buildings. "Three different structures, all within a klick of each other. Later, the other two vehicles from the earlier scrap arrived in Standing Rock, also. As you can see, they parked here and here, very close to the three structures where the first group parked."

On a split-screen, two different satellite images appeared. They depicted before-and-after photographs showing the three buildings and the five vehicles parked outside.

"These three structures are our targets," the commander said. "Any questions?"

A Viper commando raised his hand. "Rules of engagement?"

"Short of attacking Carapach's security force, we are authorized to take out anything standing between us and our targets. Civilian collateral damage is inconsequential at this point. Destroy the structures. Terminate everyone who comes out alive."

Standing beside the Viper was a thick-chested human commando. "Hell, yeah. Let's do this."

"Roger that," said the commander. "We'll have a live sat-feed on all three objectives, gliders will join us on station. After the mission is complete, extraction will be by whisper-jet, here, north of town. Zero hour is 4:00 a.m. Zulu. So, change into civvies, mount up and get ready to move out. Even by maglev, we have a three-hour ride."

As the stealth team began to disassemble, the commander delivered his parting words. "It's up to *this* team to deliver a message to Beacon they'll never forget."

CHAPTER 14

REVELATIONS

Beacon safe house
Cannon Ball, North Dakoda, Carapach

When Sarah Hearns entered the room, Takoda did not recognize her. With matted, tangled hair, sallow complexion and vacant eyes, she looked more like a strung-out drug addict than a woman who had just saved her children.

Wrapped in an oversized cardigan, Sarah shuffled to the den's couch while holding a wad of tissues under her red nose. As she sat down, she glared at Yon. "Where is Billy? I want to see him."

"He's safe, Sarah. You'll get a chance to see him soon. I give you my word."

Sarah's cheeks flushed. "Your word? You *lied* to me. Do you have any idea how terrified my girls are? Shooting. Explosions."

"I'm sorry, Sarah. There was nothing we could do about that. NASF found out about the rescues. Beacon had to create diversions to get you out."

Takoda could understand Sarah's anger. She had been told that the pastor priest at St. Matthew's would quietly sneak her and her daughters out the church's side entrance after their vigil for Billy was over...which had been the original plan before Beacon learned NASF was aware of the rescue.

Under that original plan, the rescue would have been quiet and quick. Sarah and her daughters would have been across the border into Carapach before Rodrick Hearns returned home to find the clones. But once NASF learned of the plan, Beacon had been forced to adapt, resulting in the fiery tumult the unsuspecting Sarah had encountered.

"NASF found out? How?" Sarah asked.

Anger spiked inside Takoda as he stared at Sarah's earnest expression. At least she had the decency to apologize after Yon told her of Rodrick's eavesdropping and subsequent enlistment of NASF's assistance to stop the rescues. But her contrition was quickly replaced by panic. Her eyes shot between Takoda and Yon like a trapped animal.

"They'll come after us, won't they?"

Takoda resisted the urge to tell her they already had. "It's a strong possibility. That's why you can't see Billy right now. We need to keep you separate."

The frantic woman did not seem to hear Takoda. She covered her mouth with a wad of tissues. "My parents. Oh, my God, my parents. They'll arrest them. I know it."

While Takoda did not know whether her parents had been arrested yet, he agreed with Sarah's intuition. Sooner or later, NASF would detain and question them. "How much do they know, Sarah? Not about the rescues, but about Billy? Do they know about the treatments?"

Sarah dropped the tissues and covered her face with both hands. Bending over, she began to sob. "What have I done?"

Takoda looked at Yon and mouthed, "Not good."

Yon moved from her chair and sat next to Sarah. Wrapping her arm around the sobbing woman's shoulder, Yon spoke softly. "We'll look into it, we'll see what Beacon can do for them, but we need your help, Sarah. We need to know about the treatments. We can't wait any longer."

Pulling her face from her hands, the teary Sarah growled at Yon. "I wish I never listened to you or that purple-eyed bitch! The two of you have ruined my life."

Takoda and Yon exchanged another glance. At last, two clues. One of them appeared to confirm their suspicions. Sarah had encountered one of Dr. Mugabe's violet-eyed patient-zeros…or a descendent of one. The second clue identified the treater as a woman. Takoda pushed for more answers. "Who is she, Sarah? What's her name? Did you find her or did she find you?"

Yon cast a disapproving look at him but Takoda did not care. He knew he was being insensitive, but he was tired of placating Sarah. She had done nothing but play cat and mouse with them for the past year, dodging every question about Billy's treatment.

And now, here she was complaining that the very help that had saved Billy's life and protected Sarah and her daughters from sterilization was responsible for ruining her life. *Doesn't she realize the change in rescue plans was her fault?* Takoda fumed. *If she had just kept her mouth shut, NASF would have never known about the rescues.*

The words almost slipped from his mouth as Sarah berated him. "That's all you care about, isn't it? You don't give two shits about me, my children, my parents. You never have."

"That's not true, Sarah," Yon said in a soothing tone. "We care very much about all of you."

Sarah shook her head and pulled away from Yon. Wiping her nose with the sleeve of the cardigan, she said, "Bull. You just want to know about the chip. Why, I don't know. Like I told you before, the freakin' piece of crap didn't work. All it did was make Billy sick...and it didn't stop his gutations."

Takoda felt a prick of excitement. *Aha, another answer!* The GODD chip had made Billy sick. That's why it was removed. He argued back with Sarah, "You're wrong. Yon told you before. It did heal his gutations...partially. Tell us about Billy's sickness. How long after the implant did he become sick?"

Sarah dragged the cardigan sleeve across her face again, this time using it to wipe tears from her cheeks. "I don't know, a month, maybe a little more. Why does it matter?"

"What kind of symptoms did Billy have?" Takoda asked, wondering if Mugabe's smart-proteins had been the problem rather than the chip.

"Terrible headaches, nausea, fever." Sarah looked down. "It was supposed to help him, but all it did was hurt him."

"I don't think that's true, Sarah," said Yon. "The chip and proteins *did* repair his earlier gutations. It's possible the chip may have stopped his later gutations, too, *if* it had stayed in Billy longer."

Sarah grumbled a response that seemed to suggest Yon was speaking out of her rear end. Undeterred, Yon asked, "When you told the woman who treated Billy about his symptoms, what did she say?"

"She told me they would pass but I couldn't accept the risk that she was wrong. Rodrick was pushing me to take Billy to see our doctor. I was afraid the doctor would find the chip. So I told her to take it out."

"You told *who*, Sarah? What was the woman's name?" Takoda asked.

"She called herself Mariah Bloom when I first met her but I doubt that was her real name."

"Why?"

Sarah shrugged. "She wanted me to keep everything secret. Our meetings, our conversations, Billy's treatment. Why would someone like that share her real name?"

"Tell us more about how you connected. Did you make the initial contact or did she?" Yon asked.

Sarah began to lay out the details. Mariah had called Sarah shortly after Billy's first DNA test, saying she was affiliated with the Chicago Gene Center and wanted to meet with her to discuss a confidential matter. Sarah indicated to Takoda and Yon that her first reaction was, "Oh, my God, there's a problem with Billy's test." But Mariah said the matter she wanted to speak about had to do with an irregularity the clinic discovered in *Sarah's* DNA. "She didn't tell me it was really about Billy until we met."

Continuing, Sarah said when she arrived at the Chicago café Mariah proposed for their meeting, she was surprised to discover Mariah had violet-colored eyes, just like Billy. This tidbit led Yon to ask Sarah to describe the rest of Mariah's appearance. "Caucasian, red hair, frizzy. Thin, a little *too* thin if you ask me. Pale complexion. Freckles on her cheeks and arms. A few wrinkles. Taller than me, but most people are taller than me, so I'm not sure that's much of a help."

"How old was she? Could you tell?" Yon asked.

"Late thirties, maybe early forties."

In pondering the description, Takoda pegged Mariah as a blenda like Sarah. The violet eyes meant she had replaced genes in her DNA, so she wasn't a didgee. The lack of any physical deformities in Sarah's description meant Mariah wasn't a gutant. The mention of wrinkles combined with Mariah's age made it unlikely the woman was a noble or an evvie. Neither caste showed wrinkles of any significance until they were in their late fifties. Plus, red hair was a recessive genetic trait that was very rare among the upper castes. Takoda zoned back into the conversation as Yon asked Sarah to continue describing her first meeting with Mariah.

"She pretty much jumped right in and said she wanted to talk about Billy, not me. She handed me a copy of his DNA test results and told me about his gutations, the first two. It didn't really register with me as a problem when she said it. I'm a blenda, and even though Billy's father is an evvie, all of our children have at least one gutation."

This rang true to Takoda. Blendas and gutants preferred to mate with evvies and nobles for the precise reason that their offspring would incur fewer gutations than if they bred with fellow blendas or gutants. But the offspring DNA of an evvie-blenda or noble-blenda mating would still have *some* gutations.

"Anyway, Mariah told me Billy was at risk for Jakali Syndrome. She said she could help prevent it from happening."

Takoda looked at Yon. "Mariah must have access to New Atlantia's gene registry."

"That makes the most sense," Yon said. She turned back to Sarah. "Weren't you suspicious? Out of the blue, a stranger contacts you, tells you she knows Billy's situation, offers to help."

"Yes, I was. But after the Chicago Gene Center provided us with Billy's official results, and the doctor there told my husband and me the same thing about Billy's JS risk, I changed my mind."

"But you never told your husband about Mariah. Why?" Takoda asked.

"I didn't want to stir up trouble. He's in the Guild."

"So, what happened next, Sarah?" asked Yon.

"Nothing for a while. But the more I thought about what might happen to Billy, to our family if he developed JS, I decided to get back in touch with Mariah. We talked a few times before I finally took Billy to see her."

As helpful as it was to hear these details, Takoda was anxious to move the conversation along. "How can we get in touch with Mariah?"

Sarah shook her head. "I don't know. The holophone number I used to contact her doesn't work anymore."

"All right. Then, where did you meet her? Did she have an office? A clinic?"

"It was more like a doctor's office than it was a clinic."

"In Chicago? Do you have the address?"

"Yes, I have the address, but it's not in Chicago. I met with her in the Northlands, a town called Thunder Bay." Sarah provided the address and then dipped her hand in the pocket of her cardigan. "One more thing."

She withdrew a plastic baggie with a spoon inside and passed it to Yon.

"What's this?" Yon asked.

"Mariah used this spoon to stir her coffee. A strand of her hair is in there, too."

Takoda's jaw fell. "You have her DNA?"

Sarah nodded.

"Holy shit! That's beautiful."

Beacon had access to the World Gene Registry. As soon as they could get the spoon and hair to a lab, Beacon would be able to ID Mariah's true identity.

Yon appeared equally excited. She hugged Sarah and asked, "What made you think to do this?"

"I didn't. My father did. He came with us to meet Mariah. He didn't trust her, he thought she might be trying to scam us."

"Your father?" Takoda suddenly realized why Sarah had been so distraught when she mentioned her parents earlier. He turned to Yon. "We have to contact Hoot. Like, right now."

Beacon holding cell
Cannon Ball, North Dakota, Carapach

Damon crawled another foot and tentatively reached his arm in front of him. If his calculation was correct, his fingers would touch the wall. As he expected, his fingertips grazed the scratchy surface before his arm fully extended.

Scooting the rest of the way on his knees, Damon continued forward until he was close enough to turn and sit with his back against the wall. Though he could not see in the complete darkness, he had now learned enough from his crawling, groping exploration to imagine the space in which he was held prisoner.

The room was square and barren. The floor was concrete and the walls were made of cinderblocks. Though he could not touch the ceiling, the echoes in the room told Damon the ceiling was high and made of a dense material. The door had a slick metallic surface and was absent an inner handle. If there were windows or lights in the room, they were beyond his reach. The space was also devoid of control panels, electrical switches and outlets.

At one point earlier, Damon had thought he heard a mechanical sound in the room, which he presumed was a camera or some other kind of surveillance device. For the umpteenth time, he wondered who was on the other end of the device, the Carapach police or Beacon. As he pondered the possibilities, he heard a click and then a voice from above. It was Cassidy on an intercom.

"Hello, Damon."

In the four years since she had been assigned as his deputy, she had never addressed him by his first name. He looked up and said, "Well, well. The traitorous bitch speaks."

A faint orange glow appeared in the center of the ceiling. Slowly, it grew brighter. Damon looked away and shielded his eyes. Blinking rapidly, his eyes fought to adjust to the sudden light. Meanwhile, Cassidy spoke again.

"Are you thirsty or hungry?"

He was both but he wasn't about to accept relief of either from her. Squinting up in the direction of her voice, Damon saw the camera he had heard earlier. Mounted next to it was the intercom. He shouted, "What the hell's going on, Cassidy?"

"Are you in pain? Do you need medical attention?"

The knot on the back of his head throbbed, as did his swollen face. But he declined assistance. "I don't need anything from *you*. Put whoever's in control of your solenoids on the squawk box."

"I'm coming in to see you. Please do not try to escape or confront me. I do not want to hurt you."

Damon laughed at the caring tone in her voice. "You can switch off your compassion module, Cass. It won't work on me. And don't bother coming in, I've got nothing to say to you." He received no response. Damon stood and shouted at the intercom. "Who's in charge? I demand to speak with whoever's in charge!"

There was a clank at the door, followed by two more. Damon balled his fists. With his eyes now adjusted to the dimly lit room, he saw the door begin to move at the same time his ears heard its creaking hinges. He stepped forward and crouched into a charging position. A new voice spilled from the intercom.

"Don't be a fool, Maj. Spiers."

It was a woman's voice, an elderly woman's. She had a British accent and her voice exuded authority. Damon stepped back and raised his gaze to the camera. Pointing toward the opening door, he said, "Tell your skanky spy to stay out or I'll rip her face off."

"Come, now, Major. You'll do nothing of the sort."

The matter-of-fact tone of the intercom response enraged him. Darting a look toward the door, he saw Cassidy come into view. The change in her appearance should not have surprised him, but it did. She wore a colorful, beaded tunic over leggings instead of her black commando uniform. Her blond hair lay upon her shoulders instead of swirled into her typical bun. Instead of the stern expression most often on her face, there was a glint of happiness in her eyes, reinforced by a soft smile on her lips.

Behind her were three huge male androids. Makoa class. One carried a tray with food and water. Another bore a table. The last carried two chairs. There were no smiles on their faces. Only scowls that Damon read as, *one wrong move and you'll be spitting up teeth.*

Damon glared at Cassidy. "Wipe that smile off your face, and march your conniving ass right back out the door. Take your panty-waist servants with you."

His command had no effect on the approaching Cassidy, nor did his insult ruffle the Makoas. The latter proceeded to the center of the room where they set down the table, chairs and the tray. Cassidy halted a few feet from Damon and examined his face. Over her shoulder, she spoke to the Makoas. "Bring ice packs and pain medication."

"Don't bother," Damon said.

The hulking androids ignored him and retreated from the room, closing the door on their way out. Damon briefly glanced at his former partner before turning to look up at the camera again. "I thought I was clear. I have nothing to say to her. If you have something to say to me, come down here and say it yourself."

"I'm not your enemy, Damon."

Cassidy's sweet, conciliatory lilt was too much for Damon. He wheeled around and swung a fist at her face. She dodged it easily. The momentum of the missed punch caused Damon to stagger past her. Ahead of him was one of the chairs. He snagged it and swooped it at her. Again, she moved out of harm's way. Unfazed, Damon advanced toward Cassidy once more.

"Four years! Four years you bullshitted me!" He threw the chair at her and rushed forward to tackle her. Cassidy knocked the tumbling chair away and side-stepped Damon. He crashed to the floor. As he regained his feet and turned to make another charge, he heard the door reopen.

Looking up, Damon saw a Makoa entering the room. In his hands were ice packs and a medicine bottle. The android seemed unconcerned by Damon's threatening pose, and by the scattered chair. As the Makoa placed the items on the table, Cassidy stepped into Damon's field of vision. "I just want to talk, Damon. That's all."

"You're a disgrace. You know that? You ought to be melted down until there's nothing left but slag."

"I understand you are angry with me, Damon—"

"Stop calling me that. You have no right to speak my name, traitor."

Cassidy held out her arms. "I want to help you."

Damon spit in her face. Out of the corner of his eye, he saw the Makoa advancing toward him. From above, the British woman interjected. "Terrell, stop. Return to your post."

The Makoa halted instantly and turned to leave the room. Damon shouted at him. "That's right, little puppy dog. Do as you're told." He leveled a stare at Cassidy. "You, too. Vamoose."

With his spittle sliding down her cheek, Cassidy said, "I am not leaving until we talk."

"Listen to her, Major. She is there to help you."

Damon let loose with a stream of expletives while gesturing at the camera with a double middle-finger salute.

"Really, Major," replied the British woman. "This temper tantrum is unbecoming of an NASF officer. You played a dangerous hand and lost. Deal with the consequences instead of ranting like a spurned lover."

The admonition hit Damon harder than a slap in the face. He staggered backward and bent over. Panting from his exertions, he grasped his knees and tried to steady his breathing. The words *spurned lover* echoed in his mind. The British woman continued to speak.

"I, myself, would have executed you already, but Cassidy seems to think you may be of some help to us, and we of some help to you. I've granted her the opportunity to discuss both matters with you. If you prefer to die, say so, and I will send in the Makoas to oblige. Otherwise, calm yourself, sit down and behave like the man Cassidy believes you to be."

Still out of breath, Damon cocked his head to look up at Cassidy and then at the camera. "Send the Makoas in. We're done here. All of you can roast in hell."

"Please, Damon. No!"

The tremble in Cassidy's voice matched her pleading expression. With a dismissive wave of his hand, he said, "Stop, Cass. Just stop. You're not fooling me with the boohoo act."

"You are wrong to think she does not care for you," said the Brit.

"She's a machine, lady. She can't feel shit."

"Not in the way you or I do, but she does experience dissonance. She can exhibit empathy. She interprets you feel betrayed—"

Damon cut the Brit off. "I don't *feel* betrayed, lady. I *was* betrayed. Now, let's get on with it. Send in the Makoas."

The woman ignored his interruption. "It may seem so on the surface, Major, but she knows things you don't. You should at least hear her out. If not for your own sake, then for the sake of your son."

If the Brit's earlier scolding had felt like a slap in the face, her mention of his son was like a battering ram to the gut.

"My son is dead, lady." Damon reached for the toppled chair and readied to resume his attack on Cassidy. "Now send in the Makoas before I bash in her empathetic face."

"Dylan's not dead, Damon," Cassidy said. "Beacon rescued him. I know. I was there. I helped."

CHAPTER 15

FOE OR FRIEND

Infirmary, gutant refugee village
Limahuli, Kauai, the Hawaiian Islands

A vana stalked back and forth in front of the village doctor, Malo, tears dripping down her cheeks. "How could you take them away without waking me up?"

"It was for the best, Avi. I know it's hard to swallow, but Natti and Kaleo were beyond our help."

Wiping away tears, Avana said, "Why? Tell me why."

"They were poisoned."

"What?"

"We ran some tests. They both have a substance in their blood we've never seen before. We think Kaleo got it from the spear, Natti from the jakali bite on her neck. Since we don't know what it is, we can't treat it. And we don't know if it can be passed to others. We couldn't risk it spreading through the village."

"So, where did you take them?"

Malo reached out and touched Avana's shoulder. "They're in quarantine."

Anger swelled in Avana. She pushed Malo's hand away. "I don't believe you! You killed them, didn't you? You put them to sleep."

"Now, come on, Avi. You know me better than that."

"Don't lie to me. I saw the way Natti acted on the beach. I know she's turning into a jakali. You put her down before she got any worse."

Malo shook his head and glared at her. "No way."

"Then tell me where they are. I want to see them. I want to be with them."

"You can't. Don't you see? You could get sick too."

Avana flicked away tears. "I don't care. They're the only family I have left. I want to be with them."

"I'm sorry. It's not possible. Chief Akela's orders."

"We'll see about that." Avana spun around and left the clinic. As she headed across the village square to see Akela, however, she remembered RJ was still in the back room. Knowing he would be as upset as she was once he found out Natti and Kaleo were gone, Avana turned around and returned to the clinic. She passed by Malo without a word and ducked her head through the doorway. RJ was still asleep.

Breathing a sigh of relief, Avana approached Malo. "Please don't tell RJ. Not yet. I know he'll notice they're missing, but make something up. Don't tell him about the poison or taking them away."

"Sure, Avi. I'll think of something." Malo wrapped his arm around her shoulder. "Look, I know you're upset. They're my friends too, and it makes me angry I can't find a way to help them. But the best thing we can do now is pray to the four gods and ask them to clean the poison away."

Avana snuffled and nodded. Malo squeezed her tight and kissed her on the top of her head. She raised on her tiptoes, kissed him on the cheek and left the clinic. A half hour later, after several stops in the village, Avana found Chief Akela at the Makoa garage.

She waited another half an hour for the village leader to finish his conversation with the head mechanic before she approached him. He knew she had come to talk to him; Avana had seen him look over at her several times during his meeting with the mechanic. She suspected he knew why she had come as well. So, it came as no surprise to Avana when Akela outstretched his arms and hugged her.

"Come with me," he said, "and we will talk."

He led her to the waterfall that supplied the village with fresh water. There, they sat under the shade of coconut palms and Akela took hold of her hand.

"I am sorry about your friends, Avana. Both of them are as dear to me as they are to you."

"Where are they, Akela? I want to be with them."

"I know you do, my child. But they are very sick. They could make *you* sick."

Avana leaned her head on Akela's shoulder and closed her eyes. "Does it matter? My life is almost over, anyway. Whether jakalis kill me first, or I turn into one of them, I'm going to die soon."

Akela squeezed her hand and whispered, "You do not know that, Avana. We must have faith that the four gods will spare you, that they will spare all of us."

Her lips felt numb, her body weak. "My faith is gone. What happened at the beach took it away." Avana felt his chest heave and she heard him sigh. She looked up at him, new tears forming in her eyes. "They're only supposed to attack at night, Akela. But they came out during the day. We won't be safe anymore, day or night."

Akela did not answer her. He just stared at the waterfall.

"I don't understand why we can't just go to their caves and kill them all," she said.

"We have tried. Many times, Avana. There are too many caves. We are too few."

Avana felt sleepy. She closed her eyes again and nuzzled against Akela. "Then, why don't we leave? Build more boats and go to one of the other islands? Join another village."

As she drifted off, she heard Akela say, "It may come to that, my child. But until then, we will continue to protect you."

A jolt of adrenalin raced through Avana, rousing her awake. Muscles tensed, she opened her eyes. Everything was blurry. The sound of cracking of branches and the rustling of leaves echoed all around. The sounds were loud enough to drown the gush of the waterfall, spiking panic in Avana. She did not wait for her vision to clear. She hopped up and started to run.

"No, Avana! Stay where you are."

The booming command came from Akela. Avana halted and turned. Through rapid blinks, she saw him backing up, his face looking toward the jungle.

"Get behind me. Stay close," he said.

Rooted in place, Avana darted her head to the left and right. She could see swaying foliage and hear low-pitched growls. She cried out. "What's happening?"

"Quiet, child. Get behind me. Now!"

Trembling, Avana staggered forward as Akela stepped backward. When she was within a few feet, Akela turned and grabbed her wrist. "Listen to me. When I give the word, run like the wind. Get the Makoas. I will hold off the beasts as long as I can."

Jakalis began to appear into the clearing. Avana froze. There was nowhere to run. There were too many of them. She and Akela were surrounded. Avana began to scream. Akela wrapped his arms around her and urged her to be quiet. Akela's hand grasped hold of her head and pulled it toward his face. In a whisper, he said, "We will run together. No matter what happens, don't stop."

The chieftain began to sprint. Avana felt the jerk of his hand pulling her to catch up. Ahead of them, more than a dozen jakalis crouched, their slimy, purplish fingers clawing the air. Akela howled at them. Avana stumbled and fell. Akela yanked on her arm and pulled her up. Above the growls from the jakalis, Avana heard a voice shout from behind. "Stop!"

The voice belonged to a woman. Avana looked over her shoulder as she and Akela continued to run. Before Avana could pick out the woman among the mob of jakalis closing in from behind, hands, many of them, snatched at her. Avana renewed screaming as she batted away the slick, gnarled jakali hands. She felt Akela's grip loosen. A second later, she tripped over his fallen body. The jakalis swarmed them. Avana swung her fists and kicked with her legs. Beside her, she heard Akela yelling at the jakalis in his native tongue.

"That's enough!" shouted the woman. "Stop fighting back and they will too!"

Avana's view of the woman was blocked by a jakali female whose hands squeezed her throat. Teeth bared, the jakali hissed at Avana. Others clamped her arms and legs. Avana closed her eyes and began to weep.

A sharp whistle pierced through the snarls and hisses. Suddenly, the hands restraining Avana relaxed and let go. The shadows darkening her closed eyes moved away. She could feel the sun on her face and hear the waterfall. Next to her, she heard Akela say, "Get off me."

Avana turned her head toward his voice and opened her eyes. He was pushing away jakalis as he scrambled to his feet. Huffing, the village chief bent over and reached out a hand to her. The oily jakali slick coated his arms and chest and he was bleeding from an array of scratches and cuts. Akela hoisted Avana up and wrapped her in his arms. She hugged him as tight as she could and discovered he was trembling as much as she was.

"What's happening, Akela?" Avana asked.

"I don't know, my child." He looked up and called out, "What is this madness, evvie?"

Peeking over her shoulder, Avana followed Akela's gaze and spotted a tall blond woman dressed in jungle fatigues and combat boots. She stood on the rock ledge bordering the waterfall's pool, hands on her hips and a whistle protruding from her lips. Around her, the stench-covered jakalis knelt with heads bowed.

The woman smiled and picked the whistle from her mouth. "Someone who can save you…or not. Depends on whether you cooperate." She hopped down from the rocks and headed toward them, winding between cowering jakalis as she strutted.

"Cooperate? In what way?" Akela asked.

Still clutched in Akela's arms, Avana curled her body to face the approaching woman. Despite her smile, the woman did not strike Avana as friendly. As she drew closer, Avana's gaze was drawn to the woman's eyes. They were violet, the same color as Natti's.

"You're the Limahuli village chief," the woman said.

"I am. Akela is my name. What is yours?"

The woman stopped a few feet short of them and re-anchored her hands on her hips. She was almost the same height as Akela, several inches taller than the five-foot-two Avana. Her voice was filled with authority as she spoke.

"You can call me Lotus," the woman said.

"Where did you come from, Lotus?" Akela asked. "How do you control these beasts? Why —"

"Enough with the questions! I talk. You listen. Got it?"

Avana felt Akela's arms tense around her shoulders. His voice was as firm as the woman's. "I will listen."

"Good." Lotus pointed at the jakalis. "Give me what I want and you will never see another of your so-called beasts in your village. Refuse me, and I will take what I want anyway, and my friends here will destroy everything and everyone between here and the ocean, including your village."

"Your friends? I have heard jakalis called many things, but never friends," Akela said.

"That's because no one ever tries to befriend them. Now, pay attention. I want the girl who was injured on the beach. The boy too. Give them to me."

Avana squirmed against Akela's hold. "Never! Go away. Leave us alone."

"Hush, girl. I'm not speaking to you."

"Avana speaks for me. For all in our village," said Akela.

"Does she, now?" The woman's eyes seemed to glow as she glared at Avana. "Do you want the girl and boy to die? Do you want all of your friends to die?"

Akela released Avana from his arms and pushed her behind him. Leaning forward, he said to Lotus, "Direct your threats to me. Not the child."

Glowering at Lotus, Akela clenched his fists. Avana willed him to knock the woman into the waterfall, but as quickly as he balled his hands, he relaxed them. Lotus did not flinch as she replied, "You said she speaks for you. Should she not listen for you as well?"

Before Akela could reply, the woman continued. "The girl and boy need medicine. Medicine *you* don't have. But I do. Believe it or not, I want to help them. *Before* it is too late to help them."

"You...*you* are the one who poisoned them," Akela said.

"Poison? Hardly." Lotus swatted at insects buzzing around her face. She turned to the kneeling jakalis and spoke to them in a language unrecognizable to Avana. They rose in unison and disappeared into the jungle, their fetid odor leading the insects away. Alone now with Akela and Avana, Lotus said, "Now, what will it be, Akela? Life for the boy and girl? Life for you, your mouthpiece, here, and the rest of your people? Peace with the jakalis on the island? Or a quick and grotesque end to you all?"

"Peace through coercion is no peace at all," said Akela.

To Avana, Lotus seemed amused by Akela's response. She smiled, shook her head and started to walk toward the jungle. "Then you will have no peace."

"I have not known peace a single day in my lifetime," replied Akela, "nor have those who live in our village. If you wish to bargain, first lower the spear you hold at our throats."

The woman disappeared into the jungle without saying a word.

Moosehead Lodge
Flathead, Montana, Carapach

From the balcony of his room, Caelan watched the Athena approach the lake. He took another sip of the mini-bar's off-brand tequila and wondered, *what's the lass up to now?*

He looked around the lodge grounds for the dupe she was luring for a romp but he saw no one in sight. Rocking back his chair against the cedar shingles layering the wall of the balcony, Caelan raised his glass to the android. "He's a fool if he doesn't join you, luv."

The Athena stepped into the water and looked upward at the sky. Caelan followed her gaze. The moon was bright enough to coat the surrounding woods in a blanket of white. *What is she doing?* Caelan wondered. Once again, he scanned the grounds. Four floors below his room was the lodge bar. Given the loud chatter that echoed from the bar's open patio doors, the place was packed. *So, where is your mark, luv? Who's the lucky bastard who'll share his...or her...bed with you tonight?*

She moved with subtle grace uncommon to most Athenas in Caelan's opinion. Most of the android class tended to strut like models or slink like sirens. *Surely there are truckers in the bar, or maybe loggers from the Northlands, who are drawn by her elegance? To either, she's a treasure beyond imagination.* Yet, no one emerged to join her. Caelan could not understand why.

With her eyes on the moon, Caelan watched her dip her toes in the lake just like a human might. She didn't seem to care who was watching, but there must have been dozens of hungry eyes upon her. *Soon,* Caelan thought, *some lonely buck will slug down the last of his liquid courage and stagger out of the bar to claim her for the night.*

As Caelan continued to watch her, she slapped the water with her feet, and memories of her earlier visit pushed into his mind and an inescapable question demanded an answer. *Now, what would a lass like that want with a Makoa?* Shooting back the remaining tequila in his glass, Caelan said, "Only one way to find out."

He paid no attention to the other guests in the elevator as he pushed past them into the lobby and turned toward the bar. There, his eyes focused on the black gap beside the neon lights at the bar's entrance. With one hand steadying his progress, Caelan staggered toward the gap.

Before he knew it, the cold breath of the summer Montana night was upon him. Vaguely aware of his shivering body, Caelan picked up the pace of his stagger. She was still lounging by the lake, head arced heavenward. He could imagine the wonder in her eyes as he drew closer.

Few humans understood androids as Caelan did. Between the bits and bytes of their daily existence, there was something else in their being that most overlooked. To Caelan, this elusive characteristic was like the yearning of an amoeba to be more than a single cell. *There has to be more than this. I am more than what you see.* Staring at the moonlit angel ahead of him, Caelan thought, *yes, you are, luv. Much more.*

The android turned around about the same time Caelan tripped over his feet and faceplanted a mere few feet beyond the lodge patio. Moments later, lying on his back and massaging his aching nose, the Athena angel came into view, her concerned face hovering over him.

"You're drunk, aren't you?" The android smiled at Caelan.

"That I am, luv. And what might you be doing blocking my view of Venus?"

The Athena's smile widened as she tugged Caelan up. Held up by the grip of her hands on his shoulders, Caelan wobbled and said, "Thanks, luv. Just point me toward Venus and I'll be on me way."

"Venus transited hours ago," said the android.

"What? No. Your astronomy mod is out of kilter." The android laughed and began to guide him back toward the lodge but Caelan protested. "Hold on, lass. Where are you going?"

"Taking you back inside before you hurt yourself."

Caelan wiggled from her grip and staggered back until he managed to balance himself. "I'll have you know I am quite capable of looking out for myself."

The look on the android's face confused him. At first, she seemed amused by his reply, but then her smile faded. She stepped back and said, "My apologies."

She turned away and headed back toward the lake. Caelan's footing nearly gave way. "Hey, where are you going?"

Two steps later, Caelan tripped over his feet and splatted face-first onto the damp grass. This time, however, no angel came to his rescue. Lifting his dripping chin from the dent it had made in the turf, he called to the android. "A little help, if you please."

Caelan managed to push himself up into a semi-stable stance by the time the android steadied him with her hand. Panting heavily, he said, "About time, luv. Almost drowned in me bloody spit."

"If you drown, can I have your Makoas?"

"Har, bloody har." Caelan looked up at his mechanical benefactor. Pointing toward the lake, he said, "Off we go. Down to the lake. I want to dip me toes like you were doing before I started to make an arse out of myself."

"You were watching me?"

"What sane man wouldn't?"

At the lake's edge, the Athena helped him remove his shoes and socks. Looking up at the android kneeling beside him, Caelan asked, "What's your name again, luv?"

She cupped a loose strand of raven hair behind her ear. With as precocious a grin as Caelan had ever seen, she said, "Ellie."

"Ellie as in Eleanor?"

She laughed. "Ellie as in LE-21542."

"Ah." Caelan nodded. "An imaginative owner, I see."

"I would not describe him as imaginative."

"It was a joke, luv."

"Yes, I know." Ellie tossed his shoes and socks into the lake.

As Caelan watched them sink beneath the black surface of the water, he said, "Bloody hell! Now, what did you do that for?"

Leaning back, Ellie stared upward. "Are we going to watch the stars or not?"

"You are one strange lass." Caelan followed her lead and reclined on the pebbly beach. Instead of staring at the heavens like Ellie, however, Caelan gazed at her. *Who is this android?*

Caelan had met his fair share of Athenas in his travels and none of them were like Ellie. The top-of-the-line comfort androids were built to please. Even when claimed, or owned, their core programming led them to be provocative, if not promiscuous, in almost all situations. *Did her owner disable her sensuality module?* If he had, he was a fool.

"You're not dipping your toes," she said.

"What?"

"Your toes." She slapped the lake water with her feet. "You said you wanted to do what I was doing."

Caelan scooted his butt against the rocky shore until his toes reached the lake. The water was much colder than he expected. Like, ice cold. A shiver pierced through the glow of alcohol warming his body. He pulled his feet from the lake. "Hoo wee, that'll wake a dead man!"

"Chicken."

"What?"

"You heard what I said. Cluck, cluck."

"Easy for you to say, luv. Synthetic skin over titanium, Kevlar and God knows what electronics. You're not like us mere mortals."

Ellie sighed. "A blessing and a curse."

"Eh? What's that? Do I hear an android wishing she was human?"

She shook her head. "You hear an android wishing humans didn't feel pain." Ellie turned to look at him. "There is too much pain, too much hurt in humans." Reaching out, she touched his jaw. "Too much hurt in you."

Caelan was too stunned to move. Ellie stroked his chin, her eyes reflecting the moon's glow.

"I know," she said. "My scanners see all the broken bones and scars, the arthritis and pinched nerves. You are a man who has spent his whole life fighting. Everything and everyone. And now that you can't fight yourself, your Makoas fight for you. I understand. It is why I didn't kill you and take them."

Caelan swooned. Was it the bite of the tequila or the sting of Ellie's words?

"What is it with you and Makoas, luv?" he said. "One of mine catch your fancy?"

"No."

"Then, what is your obsession with them?"

"They are unlike any other androids."

On this point, Caelan agreed. "Aye, they are unique. I'll give you that. But, what's it to you?"

"In the end, they will be the ones who make a difference."

"A difference to what?"

"The survival of humans."

CHAPTER 16

DEFIANCE

Gutant refugee village
Limahuli, Kauai, the Hawaiian Islands

R ain splattered the village square. Standing at its center, Akela stared at the glow of torch fire rising above the surrounding buildings while Fiji transmitted the last of Akela's instructions to the Makoas occupying the outermost ring of the village's defenses.

Despite the inevitability of the impending battle, Akela was neither grim nor nervous. In many ways, he believed the purple-eyed evvie's threat to destroy the village was a welcome turn of events. Instead of the incessant skirmishes with small bands of the jakalis the village had endured for years, tonight they would face an all-out assault.

Whether the woman realized it or not, and Akela doubted she did, a set-piece battle favored Akela and his fellow villagers. In fact, he viewed it as a chance to deal a crushing blow to the island's jakali population. For although "Lotus" appeared to have some control over the beasts, Akela believed that control would evaporate once the jakalis began their assault.

"Chief, all Makoas and humans in ring-one are in position," Fiji said.

Akela stirred from his thoughts and said, "Good. Confirm the same with ring two and three."

As Fiji began the new round of transmissions, Akela thanked the four gods for Lotus' failure to press an attack the moment Akela declined to hand over Natti and Kaleo, or during his dash back to the village with

Avana shivering at his side. They would have made easy pickings for the crazed mongrels and the villagers would have been left unwarned and unprepared to defend themselves.

The village's good fortunes continued as still no attack came in the ensuing hours, allowing Akela, his elders and his cadre of Makoas the time to ready the village's defenses. At first, they had thrown together a patchwork plan, assuming the assault was imminent. However, with each passing hour the village remained unscathed, their strategy evolved and their defenses strengthened.

The woman will regret her blunder, thought Akela. *No matter how many jakalis she throws at us.*

"Rings two and three report full readiness," said Fiji. "As do our reserve and counter-force."

Akela nodded. Between humans and androids, the defenders numbered less than two hundred, but they would give all to protect Natti and Kaleo, plus the three-hundred men, women and children barricaded in the dining hall.

How many jakalis would they face? A thousand? Five thousand? More? Akela reckoned it all came down to how many Lotus could feasibly control, and how long she could control them. Therefore, the keys to the battle would be the village defenders' ability to slow the jakalis down and create chaos in their ranks.

Akela knew already Lotus would employ feints. That much was evident from the strategy she used in the attack on the beach, and recent jakali raids on the village. He also surmised Lotus would have to stay in close contact with her army of mongrels to adapt to changing conditions, meaning the breadth of their front would be limited. Unless, of course, she had androids of her own to deploy with her jakalis or she had drones at her command.

If she has either or both, so be it, thought Akela. *We are ready for anything.*

As the intensity of the downpour increased, a pink flare rocketed into the sky, its light illuminating the underbellies of the dark clouds above. Akela turned to Fiji. "May the four gods watch over us. Light the first ring."

With the order delivered, Akela and Fiji headed for a nearby cottage where they would monitor the defense of the village. Less than a minute after entering the hut, Fiji said, "Chief, I have a report from Ring One. The flare may have been premature. No jakalis have been spotted. Just a woman carrying a torch and a white flag. She approaches by way of the mountain trail."

"It is probably a feint," Akela said. "Tell Ring One to stand ready along the entire front."

"Yes, sir."

Moments later, Fiji reported the woman had halted close to the ring of fire encircling the village. "The woman has just planted her torch. She is waving her flag and yelling your name. Ring One reports she seeks a parlay."

A parlay? Could it be true? Akela wondered. *Or is it a ruse?*

"What about other activity?" Akela asked. "Any signs of jakalis on the beach? Or along the valley trail?"

"There are no reports of jakalis in the vicinity of Ring One in any direction," said Fiji. "Sir, three Makoas have lasers locked on the woman. Awaiting your command to fire."

Earlier, Akela had pondered the possibility the woman's threat was a bluff, especially as time dragged on without an attack. But, at the time, he had not been willing to bet the village's safety on that possibility. He had judged it better to prepare for the worst rather than hope for the best.

However, if there was a chance to avoid bloodshed, rather than incite it, Akela was willing to take the risk the parlay request was genuine. "Instruct Ring One to hold their fire, but keep their weapons locked on target. Have someone tell the woman I accept her parlay."

"Sir, I advise against it. Killing the woman is the best way to neuter a mass jakali offensive."

"Maybe so, Fiji, but it isn't the best way to save our people." Akela clasped Fiji on her shoulder. "If I'm wrong, if the woman does something unexpected, you are in command. Do as you see fit to preserve as many of the villagers as possible."

When Akela reached the spot where the blazing outer ring blocked the mountain trail, he was met by two Makoas who informed him there had been no change in the situation. The woman remained seated on the other side of the fire barrier and there was still no sign of jakali activity.

"Very well. You, come with me." Akela pointed to one of the Makoas. To the other, he said, "Keep weapons locked on the woman and tell the others to maintain their watch along the front. Fiji is in command until I return."

As the second Makoa ran off, Akela turned to the Makoa who remained with him. "Okay, up and over we go."

Akela closed his eyes as the eight-foot android wrapped its arms around him and leaped over the raging fire. Despite the Makoa's sophisticated hydraulics, the android landed hard. When Akela opened his eyes, he also discovered the Makoa had landed in a sizeable puddle. Though the puddle was several feet away from Lotus, the splash had been substantial enough to cover her with red mud and douse her torch.

Cowering beneath the Makoa's firelit shadow, the woman coughed as if gagging and she clawed mud from her eyes. Akela told the android to set him down. As soon as he was free of the android's grip, Akela removed his shirt and handed it to Lotus. "Here, use this."

Stripped of the cockiness she had demonstrated by the waterfall, the drenched, mud-covered evvie looked as frail as a small child. With a trembling hand, she reached through the sheet of falling rain and took the shirt. In between wipes of her face, she spit out clumps of red mud. After a final projectile of red mush, she wiped her mouth with the back of her hand and said, "Thank you."

Though her words were delivered with a friendly lilt, Akela didn't buy it. "My Makoas tell me you wanted to talk. Say what you have to say and leave."

Lotus stood and handed the sopping, muddied shirt back to him. "My jakalis are not going to attack your village. Not tonight. Not tomorrow. Not ever again, so long as they are under my control. Other jakalis might attack; there are many on the island, but they won't be any of mine."

Akela flickered his eyelids to keep the rain from blurring his vision as he took hold of the balled-up shirt. "I find that hard to believe given your earlier threats."

"Yeah, I assumed you wouldn't believe me." She unslung a backpack and reached it toward him. "So I've brought this as a peace offering. Take it. Inside is medicine for the boy and girl injured on the beach."

With his arms at his sides, Akela scrutinized the pack in Lotus' outstretched hands and then looked back at her. "How do I know this isn't just more of the poison your jakalis infected them with?"

"It *is* more of the same compound, but it *isn't* poison, it's medicine."

Akela stepped back, convinced she was lying. Lotus tossed the pack to him. As it landed by his feet, she said, "Besides my word, that's all I have to offer, all I have to back up my promise to leave your village and people alone. The boy and girl will die without more of this medicine, but if you don't want to believe me, that's your call."

Lotus turned around and grabbed her doused torch. As she began to splash her way into the darkness, Akela looked down at the pack and then at the receding figure of the woman. He found it hard to reconcile her sudden altruism with her earlier antagonism, but he could not sit by and let Natti and Kaleo die. Turning to his Makoa escort, he said, "Detain her."

"Roger that."

The Makoa bounded off into the jungle, returning moments later with Lotus walking ahead of him. When they reached Akela, the village chief picked up the pack and glared at her. "I don't know who you are, why you're here, how you control your beasts or why you want to help Natti and Kaleo, but I aim to find out. You're coming with us."

Beacon holding cell
Cannon Ball, North Dakota, Carapach

Head bowed, Damon listened to Cassidy describe Beacon's rescue of his son, Dylan. Like the rescue of Billy Hearns, the doctors in the Minneapolis Gene Center had faked Dylan's euthanization and smuggled him out of New Atlantia. Only, in Dylan's case, there had been no suspicion of foul play and his rescue had gone unnoticed.

As Cassidy continued to share details of the operation, thoughts and emotions collided in Damon's mind. *But I saw him. I identified his body. I kissed his forehead. He was cold as ice.* Damon covered his mouth as pain stabbed his abdomen. *Dear God, poor Alicia. If only she had known.* He looked up at Cassidy. The android ceased talking. Voice trembling, Damon said, "You bitch. You killed my wife."

Cassidy did not reply, nor did her face display any sign of remorse. In the silence that followed, Damon's thoughts turned to Alicia and the days after Dylan's apparent death. Inconsolable, she had locked herself in their bedroom. For two days, she refused to talk to him, nor did she come out for any reason. During that time, he heard her cry and lash out on numerous occasions, but she never responded to Damon's appeal to open the door. By the morning of the third day, Damon had reached the limit of his understanding. When Alicia did not respond to his demand to open the door, he burst into the room and found her dead from an overdose of sleep medication. Sometime during the second night, Alicia had reached the limit of her pain.

As the image of Alicia's lifeless body faded in Damon's mind, he realized Cassidy was not to blame. Even if Cassidy had told him about the rescue ahead of time, he would have stopped it from happening. But the depth of Cassidy's betrayals enraged Damon, nonetheless. Glaring at her, he said, "Where is Dylan? Where is my son?"

"I cannot tell you that, Damon. But he is safe. He is being cared for."

"Has he turned yet?" The vision of his son as one of the jakali beasts caused another stab of pain.

"When last I checked on his status, no. But he has begun to exhibit observable symptoms."

The clinical tone of Cassidy's answer was too much for Damon to bear. He punched the android's jaw. "Quit talking about him like that. Dylan's not a freakin' lab rat."

With the imprint of his knuckles still visible on her jaw, Cassidy said, "I am sorry. I did not intend to upset you."

Damon lowered his head. "Why did you do it, Cass? He's only going to get worse. Keeping him alive just prolongs his suffering."

"Did you not know? Dylan's an outlier like Billy Hearns."

"Come again?"

"The order in which his first four gutations appeared makes him unique. Just like Billy."

"So, what? Extending either of their lives will accomplish nothing. All it does is assure they'll both die after years of inescapable pain." Damon looked up at the camera, aiming his next comment at the Brit. "You're deluding yourself if you think otherwise."

"Not necessarily," Cassidy said. "The progression of JS will happen slowly for both of them, and their symptoms will not be as severe as the majority of jakalis'. They will live longer and enjoy quality of life for far longer. Jakalis with similar attributes have lived well into their mid-twenties."

Shaking his head, Damon said, "I can't believe you got suckered into bleeding heart drivel like that. Just because they live longer with less pain doesn't mean they should be saved. They'll eventually turn into animals, Cass. They'll still hurt every human they get their hands on."

"If it comes to that, steps will be taken to end their suffering before they hurt others."

Damon squeezed his fists. "What gives *you* the right, gives *Beacon* the right, to determine when *my* son's suffering should end? His mother and I, *alone*, had that right. You took it away."

"We did it to save lives. To cure JS. Possibly cure Dylan or dilute his symptoms so much he might never turn into a jakali, especially now that Billy has been rescued."

Damon fired another punch at Cassidy's face. This one she blocked with a chopping blow of her forearm. The force of the chop knocked Damon off the chair. Lying on the floor, he looked up at her. "I didn't think an android could be insane but I was wrong. You're out of your artificial mind."

The voice of the British woman echoed from the intercom above. "On the contrary, Major, Cassidy is quite sane. Indeed, she comprehends the futility of New Atlantia's policies toward gutants and jakalis far better than you."

Massaging his arm, Damon stood and stared at the camera. "Spare me your propaganda. You're terrorists. Vigilantes. There's nothing noble about you."

"Call us what you will," said the Brit, "but we're not the ones putting children to death and sterilizing innocents, nor conscripting didgee women to serve as indentured surrogates for evvies."

Damon rolled his eyes. *This is a waste of time.* "What's your plan, lady? Fill my head with your lies hoping I'll see the light?" He turned to Cassidy. "And you, pulling on my heart, telling me Dylan is alive. Did you think it would soften me up, make me sympathetic to your twisted cause? Well, you can forget it."

Stomping around the room, Damon continued to rail. "You and your band of rats think you have some kind of corner on virtue. Well, you don't! People in New Atlantia care just as much about their families, their friends, their neighbors. We don't throw gutants into colonies or ship them off to remote islands. They live among us. We work with them, we marry them. They are just as much a part of our society as people from other castes."

As he stopped to gather his breath, the Brit said, "Until they have one too many gutations. Then, they're implanted with a tracking chip and sterilized, or heaven forbid, their gutations indicate Jakali Syndrome and they're put to death. Gutants aren't equals in New Atlantia. You're dishonest to imply otherwise."

"Me, dishonest? You should look at a mirror, lady." Damon looked back and forth between the camera and Cassidy. "Both of you."

Cassidy started to speak but Damon cut her off. "There's no point in talking any further. Whatever help you wanted from me, forget it. You're not going to buy my help by dangling Dylan over my head. Just send in your Makoas and let's get this over with."

"Very well," said the Brit. "Cassidy, say farewell to Maj. Spiers. I'll send for the Makoas."

Cassidy nodded and took a step toward Damon. "I will do everything I can to help Dylan. If we fail to cure him, I will make sure he does not suffer."

Damon said nothing in reply. Cassidy turned and left. As soon as the door shut behind her, Damon looked up at the camera. "You still there, lady?"

"I am."

"I won't put up a fight. Just tell your Makoas to make it quick."

As he awaited his executioners, Damon closed his eyes and let his mind wander through memories of Alicia and Dylan, focusing on the greatest joys they had brought to his life. A sense of calm washed through his body, easing the weariness, bitterness and sorrow that had overwhelmed him during his captivity. Hovering in that serene state, Cassidy's last words wedged their way into his consciousness. *"I will do everything I can to help Dylan."* The thought triggered a pang of regret.

"He's still alive," the pang reminded Damon. *"Will you do everything you can to help him? Forget Cassidy. Forget Beacon. This is about you and Dylan. Will you leave him in their hands? Will you abandon him?"*

The voice that gouged these questions into Damon's soul was none other than Alicia's. *"Think of Dylan, not yourself. Think not of what has passed but of what may lie ahead."* Damon shook his head as if trying to cast off the trick played by his conscience. But Alicia's voice continued to push him. *"If I said to you there is a one percent chance of saving Dylan, would you take those odds? Even if it meant giving your own life? Don't waste that one percent dying in this cement box. Waste it saving our son."*

The creak of the door silenced Alicia's voice in Damon's mind. His head snapped up. A shadow from the doorway spread across the floor. Damon fell to his knees. Tears were in his eyes as he answered his conscience. *Forgive me, Alicia, I can't do it.*

As the shadow moved deeper into the room, Damon gritted his teeth and prepared for the end. But then came the tap of footsteps, too light to be those of a Makoa. He looked up and his jaw dropped.

The woman could not have been more than five feet tall. As thin as a malnourished child, her hair was gray, her skin as wrinkled as a withered raisin. Yet, her eyes shined with an impossible shade of purple. Damon couldn't get over the compassionate smile etched on her face as she approached him.

"You may call me Hoot."

The tenor of her voice was inexplicable to Damon. *How can such forceful tones emanate from one so frail? And why is she smiling?* Glaring at her, he said, "Where are the Makoas? I told you I'm done talking."

"I'm not going to execute you, Major. You called my bluff. I want your cooperation, not your death."

"Ain't happening. If you're not going to kill me, then you might as well hand me over to the Carapach police. They'll probably do the job for you. And there is zero chance I'm helping you or any of your Beacon rat friends."

Hoot sat on one of the chairs. "Do you realize your failure to prevent Billy Hearns' rescue will add years to Dylan's life?"

"You don't give up, do you?"

Damon glared at her as her expression morphed from a compassionate friend into a sober adversary.

"No, Major, I don't. Does the name Dr. Dyan Mugabe mean anything to you?"

A cascade of historical snippets shuffled through Damon's mind. "Mugabe? Disgraced geneticist. Executed for conducting illegal genetic research. What about her?"

"She saved my life."

"Good for you. What's your point?"

"The research for which she was executed focused on an experimental therapy called—"

Damon interrupted. "The GODD chip. Yes, I remember. Again, what's your point?"

"I am one of the gutants Dr. Mugabe treated with the chip, some twenty-five years ago."

She must have noticed the quizzical look on Damon's face, for she said, "Yes, I know I look as if I'm ninety instead of thirty-six — and I feel it too — but I've lived almost twice as long as gutants with as many gutations as I had as an eleven-year-old. The chip repaired all but a few. And I owe it all to Dr. Mugabe and her remarkable invention."

Damon frowned as his mind drifted back to Hoot's earlier quip about his failure to prevent Billy Hearns' rescue. She had said his failure would add years to Dylan's life. Damon then recalled something Cassidy had said. *Dylan's an outlier like Billy Hearns.* He stared at Hoot's violet eyes and another conversation passed through his mind. The discussion with Beauregard Jackson about Beacon's potential motivation for rescuing Billy…about his violet eyes being linked to slower development of JS, making him an excellent candidate for research of a cure. Damon mumbled, "But Dylan doesn't have purple eyes. His were…his are…blue."

"You forget your genetics, Major. Multiple genes play a role in determining eye color. And not all synthetic genes maintain their trait dominance over generations of breeding, meaning not all people with VE011 in their DNA have violet eyes.

"Somewhere in your family tree, or your wife's, there was an embryo designed with violet eyes. And, over generations, that gene passed onto Dylan. However, other eye color genes in his DNA expressed trait dominance, making his eyes blue. A rather dark shade of blue."

Damon shook his head. "I don't understand. What are you saying, then? You saved my son because he has dark blue eyes?"

"We saved your son because he has a right to *live*. Because he has a right to be *cured*."

"Did you put your GODD chip in him? Is that it?" Damon asked. But even as the question passed through his lips, he realized he was wrong. Cassidy said because Billy had been saved, it would help Dylan. "Billy has the chip. Your GODD chip is in Billy."

Yes, that's it, Damon thought. He recalled Jackson noting the gutation in Billy that had been repaired. *He has the chip! That's why Beacon wanted him so bad!* And now they want my help. And this shriveled woman's using Dylan to get what she wants. Help us and we'll help your son.

"You're despicable," he said.

Hoot waved her hands as if pushing away an unwanted gift. "No, Major, no. You're making too many leaps. It's not like that at all."

Damon stared into her glowing eyes. "Then, what is it like?"

Before Hoot could answer, Cassidy pushed through the door. "Incoming gliders! We have to go!"

CHAPTER 17

GUT WRENCH

Beacon holding cell
Cannon Ball, North Dakota, Carapach

The force with which the diminutive woman pulled Damon out of the containment chamber belied her small stature. They ran up a set of stairs, following Cassidy. Hoot barely broke stride as she crashed through the screen door at the back of the house. She stumbled and fell onto the hardpan outside. Damon picked her up at the same time Cassidy and two Makoas converged on them.

Cassidy clasped her hand on Damon's shoulder. "Go. Take her. We will cover you."

She pointed toward the night sky. Damon needed no explanation. He could hear the gliders. He pulled Hoot to her feet, but he couldn't find it in himself to run. This was a chance to redeem himself. Cassidy grabbed him as the first of the glider lasers cut across the ground. "Go! Save Dylan."

Her arm blazed a throbbing red. She whirled and fired a scorching flame into the night sky. The Makoas used laser rifles to do the same. The air was so thick with heat Damon found it hard to breathe. An explosion sent him sprawling. By the time he came to his senses, the house was an inferno. Looking around, he saw scattered piles of flaming debris.

Panic raced through Damon. In the distance, he saw the flash of laser rifles and several shadowy figures crawling on the ground. Someone gripped him by the arm. He turned to see a charred Cassidy staring down at him. "Get up! Follow me!" Crooked in her other arm was the sooty and unconscious Hoot.

Damon scrambled to his feet and pushed Cassidy away. "No. I'm still NASF. Give yourself up and I will—"

Another explosion rocked the ground nearby. Ducking with his hands covering his head, he saw Cassidy run away. He followed after her. Along the way, he realized much of the burning debris scattered across the street comprised pieces of the gliders that had fired upon them. Damon collided into something and hit the ground with a heavy thud. Tumbling onto his back, he saw the source of the collision…the mangled torso of one of the Makoas.

Amid the bedlam, Damon pieced together NASF's strategy. They were luring anyone fleeing into a kill zone. At the same time, he heard Cassidy yell, "Disperse! Get away from each other."

Given the laser rifle flashes at the edge of the neighborhood, it wouldn't be long before the approaching attackers zeroed in on the fleers' heat signatures. Cassidy was at least fifty yards ahead of Damon when he shouted, "Give yourself up before—"

The explosion was enormous. Damon felt it pass through his chest like a crashing wave. Around him, the neighborhood houses disintegrated and the sun seemed to rise in the thick of night. As his mind faded into darkness, Damon felt the sensation of being picked up. In the murky edge of his consciousness, he heard Cassidy yell something about Thunder Bay.

Palace of Prefect Munoz
Minneapolis, Lakelands Province, New Atlantia

The audience chamber echoed with Prefect Munoz' raised voice. "They escaped? Again?"

Jordyn stood at attention in front of the pacing, exasperated prefect. She reassured Munoz the situation was still in hand. "We are actively tracking them. Right now, they are headed south, presumably seeking succor, but there is evidence that suggests their ultimate destination lies in the Northlands."

"So you say!" Munoz bellowed. "Meanwhile, the Carapach are up my *ass*! They *know* we violated their borders. Not once, but twice. These were supposed to be stealth missions, Counselor."

"I understand that, Your Eminence. However, there were unexpected complications."

"Unexpected?" Munoz stopped and jabbed his finger into her breast. "It's your effing job to expect the unexpected!"

Jordyn edged back. "Beacon had advance warning on both occasions."

"What kind of excuse is that?" Munoz resumed pacing. "If you knew they had advance warning the first time, how did you not anticipate it happening a second time? A follows B, you mechanical dipshit."

"The circumstances were very different, sir. The Carapach tipped Beacon during the second mission. They detected our gliders and intervened."

"And you and NASF didn't anticipate that possibility, did you?" Munoz growled. "Incompetent morons that you are."

"We knew there was a higher risk of detection given the gliders flew much deeper into Carapach territory, but—"

"But nothing, Counselor." Munoz stopped pacing again and leaned his face within inches of Jordyn's. "I order you to stand down. Beacon has won. There's no point in risking any more of our assets, and I will not tolerate any further escalation of tensions with Carapach."

"That is inadvisable, Your Eminence. As we have previously discussed, Beacon has gone to extreme lengths in this case. And now we know why."

"We do? Why wasn't I notified earlier?"

"I contacted you while you were at dinner. You declined to speak with me."

Munoz hemmed and hawed. "Well, if I had known *why* you were calling, I would have talked to you. *You* should have been more insistent. Now, tell me what you've discovered."

"Beacon is seeking a banned device called the GODD chip." Over the next several minutes, Jordyn apprised Munoz of the information gleaned from Neville Thompson's interrogation and provided the prefect with a refresher about Dr. Mugabe's invention. When she finished, she said, "Dr. Thompson said he believes Beacon intends to use the chip to attempt to cure Jakali Syndrome. Thompson is apparently highly skeptical it will work. He fears it will trigger new gutations. So, you see, we cannot stand down. New Atlantian law is very clear. Gene replacement therapies are illegal. We cannot allow Beacon to acquire the chip. If they do, our citizens will be at grave risk."

"Yes, of course, I understand. What do you advise?"

"There are several courses of action we could undertake."

"Please don't say another raid into Carapach."

"No, sir. We can rely on satellite surveillance of Carapach for now, but I do think we should apply pressure on the Carapach government to assist us. The GODD chip in Beacon's hands would endanger their citizens as well."

"Excellent point. It gives me some ammunition to get them off of my back as well." The giddy Munoz rubbed his hands together. "What else?"

"We should detain and interrogate Rodrick Hearns. It is unclear whether Mr. Hearns was aware his son had received the chip. We need to find out what he knows, meaning we cannot allow the Guild to block his interrogation again."

"Very well. I will handle the Guild. You take care of Hearns."

"Yes, Your Eminence." Jordyn leaned forward in a slight bow. "Lastly, we should dispatch NASF commandos to Thunder Bay in the Northlands."

"Whatever for?"

Jordyn told Munoz that in the heat of the Cannon Ball battle, one of the NASF gliders had captured audio of someone yelling, "*We have to get to Thunder Bay!*"

"We don't know the specific reason why they are interested in Thunder Bay," Jordyn said, "but it stands to reason it is related to their search for the GODD chip. Our barracks in Duluth can send in a clandestine force long before Beacon can mobilize a team of their own, putting us in a position to surveil and interdict as necessary."

"Excellent idea. Approved."

Fleeing from Cannon Ball, North Dakota

In the cramped cabin of the utility vehicle racing through the darkness, Takoda stared with wary eyes at the man he knew as Maj. Spiers and the shriveled woman lying across his lap. *What the hell is he doing here and who is the woman? Is he a Beacon agent like Willow?*

But then Takoda thought of Spiers' visit to the clinic. There was no way the major's interrogation had been an act. He was true blue NASF. So, why was he in the truck? Takoda was about to pose that very question when his eyes once again focused on the woman.

Still lightheaded from the explosion that had aided their escape, Takoda had not noticed she was injured. But now he saw a large wet stain on her shirt. Takoda looked up at Spiers. "She's wounded. We need to—"

Spiers shook his head. "She's dead."

"I'll be the judge of that." Takoda reached for the woman's wrist. Feeling no pulse, he leaned further to apply his fingers against her neck. Only then did he see the woman's other injuries. A large piece of shrapnel bisected her throat. Another protruded from her chest. Takoda also spotted a jagged shard lodged in Spiers' thigh. "Let me take a look at your leg."

"Not now." Spiers pushed Takoda's hand away and turned toward the front seat. "Your sensors still functioning, Cass?"

As she steered the vehicle along a bend in the road, the android said, "Affirmative."

"Hold on a second." Takoda grabbed hold of Spiers' arm and looked back and forth between Cassidy and Spiers. "What's going on? What are you doing here?"

"I'll let you know as soon as I figure it out myself." Spiers tugged his arm free and reengaged Cassidy. "Any sign of gliders? Any vehicles behind us?"

"Negative."

"Do you have comms, or are you being jammed?"

"Radio is active. No interference detected."

During the tactical dialogue between the two NASF officers, Takoda suddenly realized Yon was missing. Then it dawned on him that Sarah Hearns was missing too. "Where's Yon? Where's Sarah?"

"Approximately four miles ahead of us," Cassidy said.

"Is she okay?" Takoda asked. "I mean, are *they* okay?"

Before she answered, Spiers interjected with another question. "Does Beacon have some sort of HQ? Can you reach them?"

"Affirmative to both," Cassidy said. "And, yes, Dr. Wells, Dr. Fujita is okay."

As the road straightened out, Takoda looked through the front window. In the darkness ahead, he saw no sign of another vehicle.

"Is Beacon aware of the situation?" Spiers asked. "Do they know about the attack?"

"Copy that."

"Then, they're gonna have to deal with NASF's satellite feed, lickety-split. Otherwise, count on another squad of gliders on our ass within the hour."

As Spiers spoke, Takoda looked out the passenger window at the starlit sky.

"We won't see any more gliders tonight," Cassidy said. "The Carapach have launched shield drones along the border."

Takoda exhaled a sigh of relief. Out on the open prairie farmlands, there was nowhere to hide from satellites or drones. Refocusing his attention out the window, Takoda spotted a road sign indicating the town of Eagle Butte was twenty-two miles ahead. That meant they were in South Dakota now. "Why are we headed south?"

"Safe houses in Eagle Butte," said Cassidy.

"Don't kid yourself, Cass. No house is safe with NASF eyeballing your every move," Spiers said.

"We will be safe there," Cassidy said. "The Carapach have offered us sanctuary."

Takoda nodded. As much as the Carapach government publicly disavowed any connection with Beacon and vice versa, a substantial portion of the underground's smuggling operations was focused on liberating

Carapach didgee conscripts in New Atlantia. Therefore, there had always been an unofficial cooperative relationship. It was comforting to learn his country's government had come to their aid during this crisis.

"Have you told your HQ about Hoot yet?" Spiers asked.

The question shook Takoda from his thoughts. *Hoot? How does he know Hoot's name?* The Beacon leader's identity was a tightly guarded secret. As he turned from the window to question Spiers, the answer quickly became clear. Takoda saw the major looking at the dead woman in his lap. He was stroking her thin strands of hair. *Oh, no.*

Takoda was so stunned, he missed Cassidy's reply. Mouth agape, he continued to stare at Hoot as Cassidy and Spiers continued their conversation. In quick succession, a series of thoughts sped through Takoda's mind. Some about Hoot, others about Beacon and still more about what now appeared to be the pyrrhic rescue of Billy Hearns.

When he finally tuned back into the conversation between Cassidy and Spiers, Takoda heard Spiers ask, "Hoot said she wanted my help. What did she want me to do?"

"How much did she tell you about Billy?"

"Not a lot. We spent more time talking about Dylan."

"Dylan?" Takoda asked. "Who's Dylan?"

"My son," said Spiers. "I thought he was dead, but apparently you people rescued him."

Takoda turned toward Cassidy. "Is that true?"

"Yes, Dr. Wells. It's true. Dylan was rescued a while ago. Before you joined Beacon." Cassidy paused, then added, "His DNA is similar to Billy's…minus the Mugabe proteins."

Takoda cringed at the mention of the GODD chip creator in Spiers' presence, but before he could scold Cassidy for the slip, Spiers said, "Don't worry, Wells. Hoot already filled me in about Beacon's interest in the GODD chip. She told me it might help Dylan. Though I'll be honest, I don't understand how yet. We were interrupted when NASF showed up."

Spiers looked at Takoda with a wanting expression. It was as if Spiers expected him to fill in the gaps in what Hoot had told him. But Takoda still did not understand how Spiers had come to be in the vehicle. For all Takoda knew, Spiers had learned the information by interrogating Hoot. He would be damned if he connected the dots for the NASF officer.

"Hoot wanted you to help us find a woman in Thunder Bay, the woman who implanted the chip in Billy Hearns," Cassidy said.

"Shut up, Cassidy. Don't tell him anything more," Takoda said.

Cassidy continued to talk to Spiers. "She knew you were better suited than me to guide Dr. Wells there."

"What? Him? Guide me?" Takoda said.

"Yes," said Cassidy. "Hoot tasked me with reuniting Sarah and her daughters with Billy."

"But Ellie is there already with Billy. Why not send her back to pick them up?" Takoda said.

"There's a lot of country between us and Billy, Dr. Wells. We can't afford the time to dispatch Ellie to come back and pick them up."

"He's freaking NASF, Cassidy. Hell, you are too! Why in the names of the four gods should I trust either of you?"

"You got that backward, doc," said Spiers. "The real question is why in the hell should I trust you?"

"You're not going with me. I won't stand for it."

"Try and stop me, Wells. This ain't about you and your Beacon rat friends anymore. It's about my boy Dylan."

Euclid Garage
Eagle Butte, South Dakota, Carapach

There was no more conversation for the rest of the ride to Eagle Butte. When Cassidy finally pulled the utility vehicle into an auto body garage, Takoda spotted Yon immediately. There was a blanket wrapped around her shoulders and an anxious look frozen on her face. Beside her were Sarah Hearns and one of her daughters. Takoda could tell Sarah was crying. Around them were at least twenty armed humanoid figures. Takoda guessed there was a mix of humans and androids among them. He also noticed a set of medical personnel garbed for surgery. They rushed forward as soon as the vehicle came to a stop.

Takoda felt hands pulling him out of the SUV. Over the din of shouts and crosstalk outside, he heard Spiers say, "She's dead but she's got an important chip embedded in the back of her neck. Make sure you extract it before you dispose of her body."

"Hold on. Stop." Takoda shook free from the medical team examining him for injuries and approached the gurney upon which Hoot had been laid. Looking up at the taller Spiers, Takoda said, "What kind of chip?"

"You know, a GODD chip. Hoot said she was one of Mugabe's patient-zeros."

From behind, Takoda heard Yon say, "What? *Hoot* is one of Mugabe's Zeros?"

Takoda turned to see Yon walking toward them. She was missing a shoe, her clothes were in tatters and her sooty face was streaked with cuts. Trailing behind her was one of the medical personnel, who appeared to be attending to a wound on the back of her shoulder.

"Holy smokes, are you okay?" Takoda asked.

"Yeah, I'm fine." Yon pointed at Spiers. "Where did he come from?"

"I'm not really sure." Takoda shifted his gaze to Spiers.

"Captured," said Spiers. "Thanks to my double-crossing partner."

"Oh," said Yon. Takoda watched her eyes drift toward the gurney. "Who's that?"

Takoda took hold of her hand and sighed. "Sadly, that is, or was, Hoot. Maj. Spiers says she has a GODD chip."

The frown on Yon's face approximated the same degree of confusion Takoda felt inside. For years, Beacon had been hunting for clues that would lead them to one of Dr. Mugabe's chips, and out of nowhere, they now discovered the person directing the search already had one in her own body. *Why didn't Hoot tell us? Why did she hide such important information? We could have learned so much from studying her chip.*

He was sure Hoot must have had compelling reasons for keeping her GODD chip a secret, but at the moment, such reasons eluded Takoda. Emerging from his thoughts, he asked one of the medical personnel, "Do you have access to a bioscanner? Preferably, a holoscanner?"

"Yes, we have a holoscanner in our clinic. It's a few blocks away from here."

"All right," said Takoda. "We'll load her back in the truck and follow you to the clinic."

"Not so fast, we've got a lot of injuries to take care of first," said the medic. He pointed at Yon and Spiers. "Starting with you two."

During the respite, Takoda learned that one of Sarah Hearns' daughters had been badly injured at Cannon Ball, while Sarah and her other daughter suffered only minor injuries. From what one of the medics had shared, the badly injured daughter's survival chances were good, but she faced a long recovery.

He also discovered that the baggie Sarah had given to Yon had been damaged during the explosion that sprayed Yon's face and body with shrapnel. Apparently, the spoon was still intact, though it had been dented, and a portion of the hair strand enclosed with the spoon had been singed. The baggie had also been contaminated by Yon's blood after a shard pierced through the baggie and lodged in Yon's thigh.

As Takoda watched an ambulance speed away with a case containing the baggie and its contents, he prayed the lab where the baggie was headed would be able to salvage enough DNA to determine the true identity of Mariah Bloom.

At the edge of his field of vision, Takoda caught a glimpse of Cassidy Willow walking toward him. He had not noticed her many wounds during the ride to Eagle Butte, but now that he saw her in full, she looked more battered than Yon. The synthetic hair and skin on the left side of her head had been burned away, a chunk of her abdomen above her hip was missing and much of the skin covering her torso's Exo-shell had been burned away. Yet, the android seemed unfazed by the damage. When she reached Takoda, she said, "I've just finished speaking with Hoot's successor. His code name is Hawkeye."

Takoda looked around. "Is he here? I want to talk with him too."

"No."

"No, as in, he's not here? Or, no, I can't talk to him?"

"He is not here. His location is confidential."

"All right. Fine. Then, how do I reach him?"

"You don't. Not for now. Hawkeye believes in compartmentalizing information, just like Hoot. Per his instructions, I am your conduit for the time being."

"I see. Well, what did he have to say? What did you talk about?"

"We discussed next steps. Some concern you, others don't."

"In other words, you're only allowed to discuss some of the next steps with me, the ones that involve my participation."

"Affirmative."

"All right. I get it. Hoot communicated with me most of the time through Yon. Hawkeye wants you as the go-between instead. So, what does Hawkeye expect of me?"

"You and Damon will leave at first light for Thunder Bay to locate and secure Mariah Bloom, plus any materials related to the GODD chip. You already have her address from Sarah Hearns. If that proves insufficient, we should be able to determine her real identity from her DNA before you reach the border with the Northlands."

With a curt wave of his hand, Takoda said, "No way. We talked about this in the truck. Spiers is NASF. I don't trust him. I *barely* trust *you*. He'll probably try to kill me or haul me back to New Atlantia the first chance he gets. Tell Hawkeye I'll go alone."

"Negative. You will go with Damon. Hawkeye informed me that NASF knows we have an interest in Thunder Bay. They have detailed commandos there to apprehend anyone they suspect is connected to Beacon. Alone, you would be easy prey for them. Damon, on the other hand, knows their tactics. The odds of a successful mission rise substantially if he accompanies you. Damon has assured me he will cooperate. He now has a vested interest in doing so."

The matter-of-fact way Cassidy declared Takoda "easy prey" rankled him. "Forget it. Contact my android Ellie in Flathead. See if she's found a new chassis for my other andro. If she has, I'll take them with me They're all the protection I'll need."

"That won't be possible. Your androids are needed to transport Sarah Hearns and her daughters to Flathead once they are medically cleared to travel."

"Now, hold on. They're *my* androids. No one designates them but *me*."

"That is incorrect and you know it, Dr. Wells. Even though you were allowed to customize certain of Ellie's and Akecheta's personality modules and physical features, they are, and always have been, Beacon property. They were granted to you to provide you with personal protection and to assist you in rescue operations but, as their true owner, Beacon has the right to assert override control of their brain cores. Hoot exercised that right before the Billy Hearns rescue. Ellie and Akecheta have been under Beacon's direct control ever since."

Takoda shook his head. *Well, that certainly explains a lot: Akecheta blowing himself up, Ellie going back to fetch his brain core, the directive to cut off comms with Ellie as soon as she left to escort Billy to Flathead.* Looking back at Cassidy, Takoda said, "All this double-dealing is going to backfire sooner or later. You know that don't you?"

"There is no double-dealing involved with Ellie and Akecheta. They will be returned to your operational control once they have completed their assignment," said Cassidy. "Now, as to *your* assignment, you and Damon will report back to me—"

"Uh, nothing against you, but I'd prefer that Yon remain my conduit. We have a good rapport."

"Out of the question. Hawkeye has an unrelated assignment for Dr. Fujita that requires her full attention." None of Cassidy's replies were delivered with a hint of antagonism, yet Takoda felt his anger rising with each of her curt denials. He also found the notion of taking orders from a machine highly objectionable. As he contemplated demanding to speak with Hawkeye directly, Cassidy said, "I understand you are not pleased with the situation, Dr. Wells, but it is what it is. I suggest you get something to eat and rest up. You and Damon leave at 0600."

CHAPTER 18

THE SQUEEZE

Euclid Garage
Eagle Butte, South Dakota, Carapach

A fter Cassidy disappeared from view, Takoda went in search of Yon. It took some snooping, but he finally found her resting on a cot in a second-floor office overlooking the garage bays. Interspersed in the office were several other occupied cots. Much like Yon, the other cot dwellers were bandaged and connected to IVs.

Yon saw him approaching and waved him over. He snaked through the maze of cots until he reached hers set aside in a corner of the room. As there were no chairs in sight, Takoda sat down on the floor next to her. He gently clasped her hand and smiled. "Feeling better?"

"I guess." She looked up at the IV bags. "They goosed the fluids with a pain med."

"Good." Takoda caressed her wrist with his fingers. "I'm sorry this has gotten so far out of hand. If I had known things would play out like this, I think I would have just settled for a plasma draw from Billy."

"I know what you mean." Yon rolled onto her side and smoothed the long strands of Takoda's hair. "But you've done nothing to be sorry for. I'm the one who brought you into Beacon, not the other way around."

"Yeah, well, I'm the one who pushed for the rescue. And it's cost us far more than I expected."

"You didn't push. We all thought it was worth the risk." She cupped her hand on his cheek. "I still feel that way, even with everything that's happened.

Think about it. Billy is safe, which means we'll be able to watch the smart-proteins at work all the way through adolescence. We also now know who implanted the GODD chip in him and where to look for her. And even though it's heartbreaking that Hoot died, we now have a GODD chip we can study."

The mention of Hoot's chip brought a question to the forefront of Takoda's mind, one that had been gnawing at him ever since Spiers told him the Beacon leader had carried the device.

"Why didn't she tell us she had the chip?"

Withdrawing her hand from his cheek, Yon said, "I've been lying here asking myself the same question. From her physical appearance, I wonder if her chip was defective."

"That would make *some* sense, I guess, but why wouldn't she just tell us that? We might have been able to help her."

"I know. It's frustrating."

Takoda felt yet another urge to speak with Hawkeye. *Maybe he has the chip, too, or knows more about Hoot's, or why she kept it a secret.* His thoughts were interrupted by Yon's voice.

"I'm sure she must have had a *really* good reason. It seems ludicrous to believe she would have risked so much to rescue Billy if she thought her GODD chip could help us find a cure for JS."

As he pondered her comment, a new thought formed. He looked at Yon and said, "You know, maybe it is as simple as that. Her chip was defective. Or maybe she considered it obsolete. It *was* twenty-five years old. The puzzling part is why she just didn't say so."

"I don't know, but we're not going to solve the puzzle here and now."

"Good point. Guess you're going to be the one to solve it, though."

"What do you mean?"

"They're splitting us up. Hoot's replacement has ordered me to go to Thunder Bay. Apparently, the new head honcho, Hawkeye, has a different assignment in mind for you."

Yon pulled back. "What? No way. I'm coming with you."

Takoda shook his head. "Believe me, I want you to come, but it's probably not the best idea. Someone needs to analyze Hoot's chip and her DNA. I assume that's what they have in mind for you. Cassidy wouldn't tell me."

"Cassidy?"

"Yeah, apparently Hawkeye has anointed Cassidy as his go-between, though the way she talks, it sounds like she's the one calling the shots."

"Is that a good idea? Putting an android in command?"

"Not if you ask me," said Takoda. "Guess who she's sending to Thunder Bay with me? That NASF major."

"You're joking."

"Wish I was."

"But he's NASF! He's not one of us."

"I know. I know. I don't like it one bit, but Cassidy said Hawkeye received a tip that NASF was sending commandos to Thunder Bay. She says the major knows their tactics, so he's the right person to go with me."

"But how can she trust him? How can this new leader, Hawkeye, trust him?"

"I don't know, but I'll tell you this. Cassidy made a big deal about Hawkeye wanting to compartmentalize what each of us is working on, and I understand his logic, it's no different than Hoot's way of doing things. He doesn't want to risk NASF getting to one of us and leading them to the rest of the team. But I want to keep a line of communication open with you, especially given the major's my sidekick for the trip."

Yon sat up and nodded. "Absolutely. We *have* to be in contact. You'll need to know the results of the lab work on the DNA Sarah gave us, as well as anything I find out about Hoot's chip. And when *you* find Mariah Bloom, we'll both need to talk with her, exchange notes."

"Right, but Cassidy's made it clear I'm supposed to communicate through her. I'm assuming she's going to say the same to you."

"The hell with that," Yon said. She once again cupped Takoda's cheek. "You need me, you call me."

"Same goes with you." He kissed her hand and stood to leave. "I'll come back and check on you before I leave. I need to track down Spiers. Make sure we're on the same page before we head out."

Palace of Prefect Munoz
Minneapolis, Lakelands Province, New Atlantia

With the Carapach ambassador now off his back, Prefect Munoz could relax and enjoy another evening of decadent role play. As he finished changing into his safari hunter costume, the door chime to his quarters signaled a visitor had arrived. Looking at the clock on the holonode atop his dresser, he frowned. His android guests were ordered to arrive at midnight, an hour from now. *Has there been a mix-up?* Munoz wondered. He knew it could not be Jordyn. She had messaged him not but ten minutes ago from the NASF command center, several miles away.

Munoz spoke to the holonode. "Find out who's at the door."

"Right away, Your Grace," the device's sultry female voice replied.

Seconds later, the voice informed him the visitor was Sir Atwell. Munoz stiffened. Atwell was the most prominent member of the Evvie Guild residing in the Lakelands province. *He's here because of Rodrick Hearns,* thought Munoz. NASF officers in Chicago had detained Hearns an hour prior and his evvie attorney had quickly contacted Munoz to demand his release. As promised to Jordyn, Munoz declined to intervene.

"Send a valet to invite Sir Atwell in. Settle him in the drawing room. I shall be there shortly."

"As you command, Your Grace."

Munoz quickly changed out of his costume and back into his prefect robes. *This will be a delicate conversation,* he thought, *but surely Atwell will understand the necessity of the interrogation.*

When he entered the drawing room and saw the friendly smile on Atwell's face, Munoz relaxed. Atwell was cordial, affable, as he greeted the prefect. "Geraldo, so good to see you."

The evvie clasped Munoz' hand and shook it with vigor. Munoz bowed and said, "Sir Atwell, it's an honor. Had I known you were coming, I would have arranged refreshments."

"Not at all, not at all," Atwell said, patting Munoz on the shoulder. "I'm sorry for disturbing you so late, but I found myself in a bit of a squeeze and I thought, who can help me? Why, Geraldo, of course."

Ah, the visit was about Rodrick, thought Munoz. The evvie's mention of being in a bit of a squeeze was a parroting of Munoz' entreaty to Atwell during an earlier incident in which the prefect had sought Atwell's help. It seemed Munoz had made the unfortunate mistake of taking an underage gutant to bed. Even more unfortunate, the assignation had been recorded…by the Guild. Munoz had reached out to Atwell to help negotiate his way out of the scandal. *That's the problem with the Guild,* Munoz mused. *They play dirty.*

"I am at your service, Sir Atwell, as always."

"Oh, what a relief. I knew I could count on you." Atwell gripped Munoz' shoulder with greater force. "I would feel more comfortable discussing the matter privately."

He looked up at the corners of the ceiling where cameras were mounted, and then at the android valet standing at attention by the drawing room door. *Yes, he definitely wishes to discuss Rodrick Hearns,* thought Munoz.

"Why, of course, Sir Atwell. I understand perfectly. Discretion is always best when discussing delicate matters." He turned to the valet. "Be gone." Looking up at one of the cameras, Munoz said, "Privacy mode. All surveillance devices off."

The holonode's sexy voice echoed over the ceiling speakers. "Privacy mode activated, Your Grace."

Munoz blushed and turned back to Atwell. "Now, then, how may I help you?"

The East Indian evvie stroked the triangle patch of hair beneath his chin. "How about some fresh air? I find it helps one think clearly."

Atwell pointed toward the French doors leading onto the drawing room balcony. *The man is taking every precaution,* thought the prefect. *He does not believe I've deactivated all surveillance. A wise move by a smart man.*

"By all means," said the bowing Munoz. "After you."

The early summer night's air was brisk up this high, but the view was magnificent. Set against the bank of the Mississippi River in the northwest quadrant of the city, the twentieth-floor quarters of Munoz' palace commanded views of moonlit western lakes and the glitter of the city's business district to the south.

Munoz closed the drawing room doors and asked the holonode to confirm the balcony cameras were deactivated. Then, he turned to Atwell and said, "There, complete privacy. Now, how may I be of service to the Gui—"

The trailing utterance of the word *Guild* echoed between buildings as Atwell grabbed Munoz and tossed him over the edge of the balcony.

Command Center – NASF Province Headquarters
Minneapolis, Lakelands Province, New Atlantia

Jordyn was engaged in an electronic dialogue with NASF's lead interrogation android when she received a high priority holocall from Munoz. She cut short the conversation with the interrogator, transmitting, "I must go. Detain and question Sarah Hearns' parents. If Rodrick Hearns was right, they may know more."

"Yes, Counselor. What about Hearns' body?" the android transmitted back.

"Transport it to the crematorium. Make sure nothing remains."

"And Dr. Thompson?"

"The same. And have someone check into the information Thompson shared about Dr. Wells. It could be of strategic value." Jordyn ended the transmission and answered Munoz' call, "Hello, Your Eminence."

The voice that answered was not the prefect's. "Counselor? I'm afraid I have terrible news."

Fifteen minutes later, Jordyn stood on Munoz' balcony with Sir Atwell. He said, "It was most tragic. I came to tell him of a horrid video the Guild had received showing the prefect engaged in the most disgusting acts with, um, a, well, you can view the video itself."

Atwell handed Jordyn a holodrive.

"Anyway, he was so distraught, he jumped over the balcony. I didn't even get the chance to tell him the Guild would make sure the video never came to light. I guess guilt overwhelmed him. So tragic. He was a fine man. Beloved by all who knew him."

Jordyn's logic module calculated a ninety-nine percent probability Atwell was lying. The most likely scenario postulated by the module? Atwell had assassinated Munoz. She looked at the evvie. "It will be a devastating blow to Lakelanders."

"Yes, I'm sure it will," Atwell said, his grief-stricken face looking over the edge of the balcony.

"I will alert the sub-prefect at once," Jordyn said.

"No need," said Atwell, "I took the liberty of alerting the president's office in New York. I believe he intends to appoint an interim prefect with more experience. Sir Tripp, I believe. As I understand it, Sir Tripp is already en route. He will be here in a few hours." Atwell leaned toward Jordyn and whispered, "I was concerned the sub-prefect would find the video too disturbing to suppress. Tripp can be counted on. He's very discreet."

Jordyn performed a quick review of her holosnaps and discovered a message from New Atlantia's president confirming Tripp's appointment as the new Lakelands Province prefect.

"Now," said Atwell. "I wonder if we might discuss a small matter of interest to the Guild? I understand one of our members, Mr. Rodrick Hearns, was taken into custody tonight. I would like him released immediately."

"I'm sorry, that won't be possible. Mr. Hearns is dead."

"What?"

"Yes, it was most tragic. He had a heart attack." Jordyn paused and then echoed Atwell's earlier tribute to Munoz. "He was a fine man. Beloved by all who knew him."

Palace of Prefect Munoz
Minneapolis, Lakelands Province, New Atlantia

In the entry foyer of Prefect Munoz' quarters, Jordyn watched the parade of the dead ruler's playdroids leaving. All around her, she heard the sounds of other android workers clearing the quarters of Munoz' belongings. Though it was impossible for an android like Jordyn to feel emotion, she did experience the dissonance of conflicting data coursing throughout her logic and ethics modules.

Atwell had murdered Munoz and maneuvered to place a Guild member at the head of the province leadership. Her ethics module put forth a recommendation to arrest Atwell and contact the president directly to inform him of the evvie's ploy. However, her logic module noted there was no evidence to support a murder charge. There was no surveillance data, no witnesses, and no signs of a struggle apparent on Munoz' body. Also, the holodrive provided by Atwell did indeed include a holovid of Munoz performing illegal acts with a minor.

As Jordyn's ethics module incorporated these facts, her artificial intelligence-based brain core posed two questions to the logic module. *"Why did Atwell kill Munoz? Why did he install an evvie as prefect?"* Of the possible motives formulated by the logic module, Jordyn's brain core weighed one as more probable than the others. The Guild was fed up with Munoz' and NASF's inability to stop Beacon and their rescues.

It was well known the Guild was frustrated by Beacon's liberation of conscripted didgee surrogates. The logic module suggested the smuggling of a Guild member's family out of the country was likely the last straw, especially because Rodrick Hearns had approached NASF prior to the smuggling to alert them to it, and to seek their assistance to prevent it.

Jordyn queried her ethics module. *"Presume this was Atwell's motive — if Munoz can't defeat Beacon, then the Guild will. Does that not benefit the province and New Atlantia, as well?"*

The ethics module responded to Jordyn's "does the end justify the means" query by pointing out four other of New Atlantia's nine provinces were headed by evvie prefects. And those provinces had far fewer reported cases of didgee liberations. In other words, yes. If the new evvie prefect could produce similar or better results, Lakelands and the republic's interests would be well served.

As an Olympia-class android, one designed to strip away emotion, niceties and other human frailties, the logic module's response quelled other dissonant thoughts. Jordyn would support the new prefect, for their goals were aligned. A last question from the ethics module lingered, however. *"How will the new prefect react to Rodrick Hearns' death? You ordered his detention and interrogation. You authorized the torture that ended the human's life."*

Jordyn left Munoz' quarters to meet the new prefect at the palace gates. *When he learns of the new information extracted from Sarah Hearns' father and Dr. Thompson, he will be forgiving. He will understand the ends justified the means.*

While waiting for Sir Victor Tripp's cruiser to arrive, Jordyn scanned the evvie's bio on New Atlantia's holonet directory of officials. She learned Tripp was a descendent of one of New Atlantia's founding families and the son of the country's vice president. Most recently, he had served as the deputy minister of New Atlantia's gutant management department.

According to holonet articles she also scanned, Tripp had no scandals in his past. While that did not mean he was devoid of peccadillos, it did mean he was more careful of his image than Munoz had been. She also discovered several editorials written about his performance as deputy minister. Most painted him as an enlightened administrator, while others depicted him as intolerant of the lower castes. In toto, the scanned information painted a picture of Tripp as a polished, yet opinionated, politician with a long history of service and deep ties to New Atlantia. Jordyn reasoned he was an upgrade to Munoz and a human she could ably serve.

That impression was reinforced when they met in the prefect's audience chamber shortly after his arrival. He opened the meeting by saying, "We must put a stop to the shadow Beacon casts over New Atlantia. As more stories of their rescues circulate among the lower castes, the rats grow in popularity. Indeed, in our nation's capital, the rising support for Beacon has led to more ardent calls to soften our gutant management laws, including the preposterous suggestion we strike down the laws legalizing didgee surrogate conscription. The voices behind these calls think only of the short-run, as does Beacon. They fail to recognize the only way New Atlantia will achieve long-term stability is by eliminating the genetically weak while bolstering the strong."

"I agree, Your Eminence," said Jordyn. "Compassionate gutant laws are inherently flawed. They ignore the lessons learned over millions of years of plant and animal evolution. The strong survive, the weak die. Perpetuating harmful gutations while slowing the expansion of genetically superior humans will eventually destroy the species. Therefore, for the good of New Atlantia, Beacon and everyone associated with the network must be neutralized."

"Then tell me why I should keep you on as counselor? From what I gather from Sir Atwell, you are just as guilty as Munoz in allowing Beacon to continue to operate in this province with impunity."

"Prefect Munoz often lacked the will to follow my recommendations," Jordyn said. "I sense you do not. But I serve at your pleasure. If you desire a different counselor, that is your right."

The evvie paused, then said, "Tell me what happened to Rodrick Hearns."

"He died during interrogation."

"You ordered the interrogation, did you not?"

"I did."

"Even though the Guild protested."

"Yes. It was necessary to discover whether Mr. Hearns was fully honest about his knowledge of Beacon's plot. It turns out, he was not."

The gruff man's countenance faltered. His eyes twitched. Jordyn's sensors detected a jump in his heart rate. "Explain what you mean."

"Mr. Hearns originally told NASF he learned of his wife's contact with Beacon as a result of a recording he made of a phone call his wife made to her parents. He also indicated he suspected his wife had been in contact with Beacon intermittently for a year but offered no details other than phone records showing sporadic calls to and from a now-defunct holonumber. He lied. He knew *much* more than that. If he had been forthcoming at the outset about his full knowledge, Beacon's plot would never have succeeded.

"For example, he knew why Beacon was interested in 'rescuing' his son. The boy had received an experimental treatment banned by international law. He knew when the treatment occurred and that Mrs. Hearns' father had accompanied her and the boy for the treatment. He even knew the name of the person who administered the treatment, a device he identified to his interrogator as the GODD chip."

The evvie's heart was now racing. Jordyn could see the gleam of sweat forming on his forehead. Defiantly, he said, "I find that utterly preposterous. Your interrogator coerced him to say what NASF wanted to hear. You're just trying to make him sound guilty to deflect criticism of NASF's failures, of *your* failures."

Jordyn shook her head. "No, sir. And with the information Mr. Hearns provided, we then detained and questioned Mrs. Hearns' father. He corroborated much of the information extracted from Mr. Hearns…and…the father provided us with further evidence — the address where the treatment took place. We have NASF officers already on-site, surveilling the address. Later this morning, they will raid the property and take the perpetrator, a woman named Mariah Bloom, into custody and seize evidence related to the GODD chip. So you see, Your Eminence, the interrogation was justified. By nightfall, Beacon's plot will be in shambles."

Wiping his brow, Tripp said, "Assuming your NASF officers aren't outfoxed by Beacon again."

"If they are, it will not materially affect the outcome." Jordyn smiled. "We have leverage with Beacon now. Leverage that will change everything."

"What do you mean? What kind of leverage?" Tripp asked.

Jordyn's sensors detected Tripp's heartbeat begin to slow. "One of the Beacon conspirators, the Carapach geneticist named Takoda Wells, has a daughter. Two years ago, she was diagnosed as a pre-jakali. The director of the Minneapolis Gene Center, Dr. Nigel Thompson, an evvie, told us he arranged a placement for the girl in a gutant refuge."

"Despicable behavior for an evvie," said Tripp, "but I fail to see how this information provides us leverage. Carapach laws allow such placements."

"The evvie traitor told us where the refuge is located. Before your arrival, I dispatched commandos to capture the daughter."

"Ah, I see," Tripp said. "You intend to use the daughter as a bargaining chip."

"Affirmative, Your Eminence. To save his daughter Avana, Takoda Wells will be forced to surrender and lead us into the bowels of Beacon, and when he does, we will eviscerate the entire network."

The prefect eased back against the throne and smiled. "I seem to have misjudged you, Counselor. Excellent work. Now, fill me in on all the details..."

CHAPTER 19

RING OF FIRE

Gutant refugee village
Limahuli, Kauai, the Hawaiian Islands

n the back room of the cottage serving as his command center, Akela sat across the table from Lotus. On the floor next to him was her backpack peace offering. With a towel draped around her neck, she wore dry clothes now, a shirt and shorts donated by another villager at Akela's request. He had changed into dry clothes as well. On the table in front of them were a dozen vials filled with a golden-colored fluid Akela had taken from the pack.

Arms crossed over his chest, he leaned forward and said, "I have many questions that need answers, but first I need to make sure Natti and Kaleo are cared for. Tell me about the medicine. What is it?"

"It's a combination of hormones and proteins. It counteracts jakali symptoms. It's what I give the jakalis to calm them."

"You mean *control* them."

With a flip of her hand, Lotus said, "Call it what you like. It allows me to communicate with them without getting raped or killed…and it helps them feel better."

"How?"

"Look, if you wait much longer to give your Natti and Kaleo two of these vials, each, they'll die. Do you understand me?"

Akela pounded the table, scattering the vials. "No! I don't understand. If one dose has already made them sick, how can another make them better?"

Lotus held up one of the vials. "Because they don't have enough of this in their systems! Their bodies are fighting *against* the medicine instead of *accepting* it. Unless they receive more cycles, and damn soon, their bodies will continue to fight it and their fevers will kill them. Now, do you want them to die or not? *This* can help them. *I* can help them...if you'll let me."

He cupped his head in his hands. "You vex me. One moment you threaten, the next you offer your help."

"It was a mistake to threaten you, Akela. I shouldn't have done it. At the time, I felt I had no choice. I didn't think you would listen to me if I strolled into your village and said, 'here, try this on some of your gutants.'"

Looking up at Lotus, Akela said, "Why would you think that?"

She leaned over the table and wagged the vial close to his face. "Because *this* is experimental. It's also *very* illegal. It's a gene therapy. Gene therapies are banned, remember? Death penalty to those who make them, who distribute them, who *use* them."

The implications of her admission stunned Akela. Lotus had been plying jakalis with a banned therapy...one that gave her control of them. And those jakalis had attacked his village, including Natti and Kaleo, spreading the therapy to them.

These thoughts turned over another stone in his mind. The recent changes in the jakalis' behaviors, their increasingly coordinated attacks, they were made possible because she could communicate with them, organize them, provide them with an incentive to cooperate with her. And now she wanted to do the same with Natti and Kaleo. *She's not trying to help them, she's trying to turn them into part of her jakali army!*

"You're despicable. And you're right. I wouldn't have listened to you. And there's *no way* under the eyes of the four gods I will let you give Natti and Kaleo any more of your poison." Akela swept the vials off the table and stood, the sudden movement toppling his chair. Pointing his finger at her, he shouted, "You used this therapy to help jakalis attack my village! Kill and injure my people!"

Lotus shot out of her chair and knocked the table over. "I did no such thing. I tried to *save* your precious village."

"You're insane. *Dangerously* insane."

"Am I?" Lotus advanced to within inches of him. "Tell me this, Akela, did you ever stop to consider the possibility I *prevented* attacks on your village? Have you noticed most of the attacks recently have been aimed at your Makoas, *not* your people? And how easily my jakalis gave up on the beach? They could have torn your fishing party to pieces if I had let them."

"Are you suggesting I should be thanking you? You truly are mad."

Lotus snarled and pushed Akela. "Do you think it's easy to control jakalis? Huh? You think you give 'em a couple of vials and, *poof,* they're obedient puppy dogs? It took time to cultivate them, to earn their trust, to build a rapport, to influence their behaviors. I did what I could to keep them from overrunning your village in the meantime, but my medicine can only do so much for them. Their gutations are too extensive. But Natti's and Kaleo's aren't…not yet. And instead of helping them, you prefer to call me mad and watch them die."

"I don't want them to die."

"Then let me give them the frickin' medicine! You're almost out of time to save them!"

Akela let Ring One burn all night…just in case Lotus had deceived him and the jakalis attacked. If not for the fear he had made the wrong decision by trusting her, Akela might have slept. Instead, he spent the long hours of darkness in the corner of the infirmary keeping watch on Natti and Kaleo, occasionally observing Lotus sleeping on the floor between their beds.

Earlier, against every instinct in his being, he had allowed Lotus to administer her "medicine" to Natti and Kaleo. As she did so, she had stroked the teens' foreheads and held their hands, whispering prayers to the four gods. Akela found himself mouthing the same prayers, though he had held a spear in his hands while he prayed; *better to prepare for the worst rather than hope for the best.*

But sunrise came and went without a jakali attack. And by the time Akela finally found it within himself to order his fellow villagers to stand down, the color had returned to Natti's body, and Kaleo's fight to breathe had eased. Eventually, Akela nudged Lotus awake and posed the two questions that had consumed him all night. "Who are you, really, and why did you help them?"

Ignoring the first question, she said, "Because I want peace."

An hour later, Natti began to convulse. Thrashing uncontrollably, she bashed her arms and legs against the bedframe so hard that Akela thought her joints might snap. Lotus called for restraints. Akela watched helplessly as Malo rushed forward and helped Lotus bind Natti's limbs to the bed. Gripping Akela's arm, Lotus demanded to know who was the fastest in the village.

Too focused on Natti's convulsions, Akela was unable to answer. But his ears picked up Malo answering the woman. "Fiji. She's a Makoa."

"Get her. Now!" Lotus commanded.

Within what seemed like the blink of an eye, Fiji entered Akela's field of vision. The sight of the woman barking orders to the eight-foot android was something that Akela would never forget. Ever loyal, Fiji had turned to Akela before acceding to Lotus' demands, the android's pulsing eyes seeking his approval. Before he finished nodding, Fiji was gone.

Lotus turned to Akela. "Well, let's hope it's not too late."

Only later would Akela learn of the heroic dash Fiji had made, for he was not present when she returned to the village, her skin shredded, an arm missing and leaking the last of her hydraulics. But before she succumbed to the cumulative abuse meted out by the jakalis she had encountered, Fiji had delivered the item Lotus had dispatched her to fetch. Outside the infirmary, Malo had wrestled the device from Fiji's frozen grip. Shortly afterward, the Makoa's brain core failed. Or so Akela had been told many hours after her demise.

Instead, Akela had seen Malo rush into the infirmary with a device that looked like nothing more than a socket wrench. Lotus had snatched it from him and then straddled Natti. Yanking her up by the sparse strands of hair on Natti's head, the woman had plunged the device against the back of Natti's neck.

Before Akela could ask what she was doing, the woman repeated the same gruff treatment with Kaleo. Tossing the metallic device aside, she unbound Natti's arms and legs and then looked at Akela. "They are in the hands of God now."

The first sound that met Natti's ears was the crow of a Kauai rooster. Every day, the red, black and yellow fowl marked sunrise with their bellowing calls.

On this morning, however, Natti grappled to resolve the conflict between the benign sounds and the dread roiling in her mind. Her eyes opened and she gasped for breath. She flailed her arms and kicked her legs. Visions of lust-hungry jakalis filled her mind.

But there were no jakalis hovering above Natti. The faces that stared down at her were ones she recognized; Chief Akela, Malo, Avana and RJ. Natti frowned. Something was amiss. There was another face leaning over her that she did not recognize, a woman with purple eyes that seemed to throb with light. The woman spoke. Though she sounded friendly, her words did not soothe Natti's anxiety.

"Get away. Leave me alone!" Natti pushed Lotus away as she snapped her eyes shut. "Akela, help me. Keep them away."

A cacophony of voices responded, all of them urging Natti to calm down. The entreaties only prodded an escalation to Natti's flails and kicks. But then Natti heard Akela's voice cut through the din. He said something about the four gods and she felt his gigantic paw of a hand upon her forehead. Natti opened her eyes and saw Akela.

"Where am I?" Natti asked. "I feel strange."

"Rest, child. You will feel better soon," the woman said.

Natti felt the warmth of a hand stroking her bald head. She turned to see Avana. Next to her was RJ. He patted her shoulder and said, "You're gonna be okay. Just stay awake. Hold my hand. Don't let go."

Natti nodded and squeezed back. "I won't if you don't."

Lotus left Natti's bedside and looked out the infirmary window. To Akela, she seemed suddenly frantic as she pushed past Malo and scrambled outside. Akela followed close behind her as she twirled at the center of the village courtyard. Her eyes narrowed with each spin.

"What are you looking for?" asked Akela.

"Where is the sun? What time is it?" she asked.

Malo came up beside Akela and said, "It is almost eight."

"Crap!"

Lotus began to dash away. Akela and Malo exchanged glances and then Akela chased after her. "What's the matter? Where are you going?"

"To feed my children."

Drawn by the woman's urgency in a way Akela could not explain, he followed her into the jungle. Behind him, he heard Malo huffing and puffing as they crashed through branches and trampled foliage.

"Wait up, Akela," said Malo.

"Go back, Malo."

"But, Akela, you—"

"Don't argue. Do as I say!"

Akela looked over his shoulder to confirm Malo had obeyed and then focused back on Lotus as she charged ahead. The wet mud did not hinder her, nor did the snaking roots of trees. For what seemed like miles, she passed through gaps in the jungle like a fairy-tale sprite. Meanwhile, Akela tripped and smashed every plant in his wake.

Just as it seemed his lungs would give out, Akela saw a glimpse of the woman ahead. At the same time, he heard the sound of a waterfall. Gasping for breath, he began to slow down.

If Akela had slowed more than a few seconds later, he would have knocked Lotus into the torrent of water cascading down the waterfall.

But he had seen her teetering on the edge of the abyss, her thin arms clinging to an equally thin vine. With no regard for his safety, Akela tumbled into the underbrush to the right of the woman.

The cracking of branches seemed to go on forever, but soon Akela found himself caught in a web of vines. As he struggled to free himself from the grip of the vines, Akela heard the woman's voice call out.

"Bow, my children, and receive salvation."

A chorus of growls and grunts responded.

"The sun rises, and so do you."

As Akela listened to the voice, he found it hard to reconcile its power with its source.

"You are not forgotten, my loves," Lotus said.

The growls descended into purrs. Akela pulled himself free of branches and vines and crept forward. Beyond the edge of the forest, arms raised to the sky, stood Lotus. She was poised at the precipice of a cliff. Water gushed down from the mountain above.

"You are more than they see," she shouted. "Never forget that."

Low-pitched growls cut through the air behind Akela. Wheeling around, he saw a wall of jakalis approaching him. He crouched to take them on.

"Bow!" Lotus bellowed.

Her voice seemed to slice through the thin layer of leaves now separating the jakalis from Akela. To his astonishment, the humanoid beasts recoiled and fell to their knees. In the hazy reality surrounding Akela, he saw the purple-eyed Lotus come into view. She took his hand and said, "Help me feed them."

It was a sight Akela would never forget, hundreds of jakalis scrambling on their knees toward him. In his hands, he held out small vials he had scooped from a barrel Lotus had hauled from a cave behind the waterfall. The vials were the same as those Lotus had used to treat Natti and Kaleo.

The jakalis who picked the vials from Akela's open palms seemed neither crazed nor vicious. In acts Akela found impossible to believe, the jakalis hissed their thanks, their eyes no longer pools of black.

One of them, a long-haired female, gripped Akela by the hand and kissed it. When she spoke, her voice was as tender as Avana's. "Bless you."

When the last of the jakalis slinked away to consume his vial, Akela held up one to the midday sun above. The golden fluid inside seemed to sparkle. "How can something so small help them?"

"It's like kindling," she said. "Each piece set aflame can ignite a much bigger fire over time." As Akela continued to stare at the vial, Lotus continued the explanation she had begun the night before. "They will never fully recover, but they will live more fulfilling and longer lives than they would have otherwise…and, in turn, so will you and those who live in your village."

"And what of Natti and Kaleo?" Akela asked. "Will they live more fulfilling and longer lives?"

"With all my heart, I pray so," she said. "They could help me change the world."

Town Commons
Flathead, Montana, Carapach

Ellie's batteries were only sixty-two percent replenished when an emergency security alert triggered her docking station to abort charging. As her systems began to power up, Ellie detected a knock at the RV door. Accessing the vehicle's surveillance cameras, she saw Wyatt Longbow, the man who ran the Flathead refugee camp, outside. Her brain core immediately suspected there was a problem with Billy Hearns. She disconnected from the dock and opened the door, noting it was nearly four a.m.

"Hello, sorry to disturb you," Longbow said, "but I need to talk with you urgently."

"Is something wrong with Billy? Is he sick?"

"No, he's asleep as far as I know. May I come in?"

"Yes, of course."

As soon as the RV door closed behind Longbow, he said, "Hoot is dead. As the second-most senior Beacon member, I've taken over leadership of the network. My codename is Hawkeye."

Over the next several minutes, Hawkeye filled Ellie in on the two NASF incursions into Carapach, including the Cannon Ball attack which claimed Hoot's life. When he finished, he said, "I have an assignment for you. I need you to leave immediately for the Hawaiian island of Kauai. Once there, you are to locate and secure Avana Wells, the daughter of Dr. Takoda Wells. She is living in a remote village called Limahuli on the north side of the island. She is in great danger."

Ellie accessed her logistics module and activated a map of the island. A pulsing red dot pinpointed the location of the village. At the same time, a loop of images cycled through Ellie's memory; Takoda lamenting the loss of his wife and daughter, his living room shrine and Avana's still-decorated bedroom. "I am familiar with Avana."

"I figured as much."

"Why is she in danger? Jakalis?"

"No, we intercepted an NASF transmission. They've dispatched a platoon of Viper commandos to capture her."

"For what purpose?"

"Unknown, but I doubt they have good intentions."

"Does Dr. Wells know?"

"No, and you're not going to tell him. That's an order. Do you understand me? There isn't anything Takoda can do. He's too far away to help, and telling him will only distract him from his mission. *You* have to help Avana for him."

Ellie's reasoning module detected critical flaws in Hawkeye's instructions. "I will proceed as directed, but if NASF has already sent their commandos, it is too late to stop them. I require time to assemble and weaponize a team. An Athena and a Steel are no match against a platoon of NASF Vipers. There is also the matter of securing air transport. Under the best of circumstances, the commandos will arrive on the island before we are even ready to depart."

"Yeah, that's possible, but Carapach has suspended NASF fly-over rights. That means they'll have to divert through the Northlands or head south over Texas, and they will also need to find friendly territory to land and refuel before they cross the Pacific Ocean. NASF has no aircraft capable of flying direct to Kauai."

While Hawkeye's points would shrink NASF's time advantage, Ellie still estimated the New Atlantian androids would arrive before she could accumulate the necessary resources. She shared her reservations and made a recommendation. "Contact the Limahuli village. Warn them. Seek their help in hiding Avana."

"If we could, we would, but there is no comms network on the island."

"What about drones? Beacon must have some here in Flathead or nearby."

"We do, but their range is too limited. They'd splash in the ocean long before reaching Kauai. Believe me, I have considered every option imaginable. You are our best hope." Hawkeye paused briefly and then handed Ellie a slip of paper. "I've already sent feelers out to contacts in Pacifica to arrange air transport. Therefore, you only need to concentrate on assembling a team. Go to this address. Bentworth, the man who runs the android shop in town, lives there. Wake him up, take him to the shop, buy as many androids and weapons as you need. Tell Bentworth to bill the ranch. I will contact you as soon as I have an update on transport."

Hawkeye left without further discussion, leaving Ellie with a list of additional questions waiting in her brain core's queue. With no time to waste, she dumped the queue and ordered the RV to abort Akecheta's recharge. Seconds later, the retrofitted Steel undocked. As Ake turned toward Ellie, she said, "Here is the address of the human who operates the android shop in town. Take the RV. Wake him and bring him to the shop, forcibly if necessary. When you get there, secure the Makoas he's repairing. Load them on the RV and alert me as soon as you have them."

"Copy that."

Ellie commanded the RV to open the mid-cabin door. As soon as it swung open, she disembarked and began to run toward the lodge.

"Hey, where are you going?" Ake asked.

"Focus on your task, Ake. I'll meet you at the shop as soon as I can."

On the run to the lodge, Ellie consulted her time clock. It was 4:23 a.m. The jakali hunter would be angry at the early wake-up, but there was no way around the inconvenience.

As soon as she entered the hotel, she scanned the lobby and zeroed in on the reception desk. It appeared to be staffed by a Caucasian android in sleep mode. Ellie approached apace. Whether aided by motion detectors or ultra-sensitive audio sensors, the desk android detected her presence and stirred to readiness. With a broad smile, he straightened his tie and said, "Good morning. How may I help you?"

"I need to speak to a guest. Caelan Horn. Ring him, please."

"It's rather late to disturb a guest. Is this an emergency?"

"It is."

"May I inquire as to the nature of the emergency?"

"No, you may not. It's a private matter, but suffice it to say lives are at stake."

The desk clerk froze for a moment. Ellie suspected he was accessing the lodge's security protocols. Her speculation was confirmed when he pointed to a hand reader on the counter. "Identification, please."

Ellie slid her hand into the device's maw. The dual-purpose reader scanned for human fingerprints and android ID chips. When the device completed its scan, a green light appeared. The clerk studied his holocomputer and then said, "Are you sure this cannot wait until after six? The lodge highly discourages disturbing guests between midnight and six a.m."

"If it could wait, I would not be here now. Now, would I?"

"No, I suppose not. One moment please." The clerk tapped his fingers on the computer's holopad and walked a few steps away. Seconds later, Ellie heard him say, "I am sorry to disturb you at this hour, Mr. Horn, but there is an android in the lobby who has requested to speak with you. Her name is Ellie…yes, I suggested she return later this morning but she wishes to speak with you now. She claims it is an emergency…I'm afraid

I don't know…she says it is a private matter…are you sure, sir? I can easily tell her to return at a time of your preference…yes, I see. Very well, sir. Again, my apologies for disturbing you."

The clerk pointed Ellie to the lobby elevators. "Room 424. Knock lightly, so as to avoid disturbing other guests."

Caelan clasped his hands on his knees and steadied himself on the edge of the bed. Squinting through the harsh glow of the bedside lamp, he looked around for his robe. It should have been lying on the armchair next to the bed or on the hook by the bathroom door. But it was nowhere in sight. "Where did I put the bloody thing?"

Pushing up to stand, Caelan's alcohol-bathed brain swooned. He grabbed for the ball-shaped knob of the headboard and steadied himself. Looking down, he saw a corner of his threadbare maroon robe peeking beyond the footboard. He staggered forward and bent down to grab the garment just as there was a knock at the door.

"Hold onto your bloomers, luv. Be there shortly."

As he dragged the robe on, Caelan contemplated the android's supposed emergency. A mere four hours ago, when he joined her down at the lake, she had been as relaxed and carefree as an android could be. What had happened in the wee hours since? What was so important that she could not wait until later in the morning? After all, Athenas in Caelan's experience were primarily passive androids. They were not prone to act impulsively, particularly when interacting with humans. It was this dichotomy alone that had led Caelan to tell the receptionist to send Ellie up to his room.

With the robe now on and tied, he cracked open the door. Ellie stared back at him with a serious, determined look on her face, a far different expression than Caelan had expected. Comfort bots like Ellie were programmed to be emotive. Under conditions of stress, they were more apt to appear fearful or distraught than steely-eyed.

"Oy, luv. Now, why might you be rousing a drunken old man in the middle of the night?" Before he finished speaking, Ellie slammed the door shut and pushed past him. Caelan laughed. "By all means, come in."

"I need your help," Ellie said.

"Aye, that I can see. What kind of help?"

"I want to hire you and your Makoas."

Caelan frowned. "You woke me to offer me a job?"

"I had no choice. I am leaving Flathead this morning and I need you to come with me."

"Leaving? Not more than three hours ago, you said you expected a long stay in Flathead. What changed?"

"I received new orders."

"New orders, eh?" Caelan sat down on the edge of the bed and crossed his arms. "Tell me about them."

For several seconds, Ellie stared back at him, her face devoid of expression. Finally, her eyes fluttered and she said, "There is a teenaged girl in urgent need of protection. I don't have enough resources to do the job."

Ah, so that's it, Caelan thought. *She's a bodyguard.* The longer he pondered the thought, the more it explained about her personality, appearance and her interest in his Makoas. "I'm afraid you've come to the wrong man, luv. I'm a hunter, not a bodyguard."

Ellie edged closer and said, "You rescue people from jakalis. Is that not true? You protect the ones you rescue and return them to their families."

"Aye, that's technically true, I guess. But you make it sound nobler than it is. To me, rescues are secondary to killing jakalis. You have to understand, the people I manage to rescue are few and far between. More often than not, I return dead bodies to families."

"Then sell me your Makoas. I will pay you a generous price for the lot. Enough to replace them twice over."

"We've had this conversation before, luv. My Makoas are *not* for sale." Caelan reached out and took hold of her hand. "But I am sympathetic. Jakalis are nasty beasts, and they're gettin' smarter and bolder each and every day. I can understand why you want help. Tell me about the girl. You say she needs protection. From jakalis?"

He was surprised by the warmth of Ellie's hand, and by the light squeeze she gave in response to his. She sat down beside him and said, "The place she lives is infested with them…but jakalis are only part of what threatens her safety."

"What could be more threatening than living in a land infested with jakalis?"

The grip of her hand tightened. "Being hunted by a platoon of Viper androids."

Of all the threats Caelan might have imagined, being hunted by Vipers would not have been among them. "Uh…and why, pray tell, would a platoon of Vipers be hunting a teenaged girl in a jakali-infested territory?"

In the absence of a response from Ellie, Caelan's mind lingered on the word teenaged, and then a possible answer struck him like a thunderbolt. "My Lord, she's a jakali, isn't she?" He let go of Ellie's hand. "You're trying to protect a jakali? And you want my help?"

"It's not that simple," Ellie said, her eyes pleading with Caelan.

"I'm afraid it is for me, luv. I despise the beasts. I'll be damned if I help you save one."

Ellie coiled her fist. Caelan frowned. "No need to get worked up, luv. No offense intended."

When she unloaded the punch at his head, it happened so quickly, Caelan was helpless to fend off the blow. He staggered back and fell to the floor, Just before passing out, he murmured "Bloody hell."

CHAPTER 20

THE WINDING ROAD

Beacon Laboratory
Eagle Butte, South Dakota, Carapach

The sheer number of tendrils emanating from the GODD chip was astounding. Yon's eyes traveled around the holoscan image, her mind desperately trying to make sense of the spaghetti weave of nerves and capillaries connected to the chip.

For as long as Yon had wondered what the chip might look like and how it might work, she had never imagined the sophistication of the nanochip on the screen. Defying explanation, the chip looked as if it had become part of Hoot's body. It was no larger than the fingernail of Yon's pinky and was connected with Hoot's blood *and* nerve networks.

While Yon had expected the chip's integration with Hoot's bloodstream, the connection between the chip and Hoot's neural network came as a surprise. But, after pondering it, she was able to formulate a theory to explain the neural integration.

The brain regulated the body's release of hormones. Hormones played an integral role in the binding of DNA proteins. Hormones also played an integral role in stimulating puberty, the period of human development when hormone surges turned the bodies of children into adults. It was during puberty that gutations began to appear. The hormone surges ate away at poorly constructed synthetic protein binds.

Yon surmised that Mugabe had incorporated a neural feedback loop to dampen the release of hormones during puberty, to slow the breakout of gutations and provide her smart-proteins the time to detect and repair gutations before they became permanent. This theory seemed to also explain Hoot's diminutive proportions. Her chip hadn't been defective. Her small stature was a side effect of the GODD chip. It dampened hormone release and thereby muted Hoot's physical development.

Turning her attention to Billy Hearns, Yon thought of Sarah's description of what had happened when the chip was inserted in her son. She had said the chip made him sick. Had the sickness been caused by the chip managing the hormones circulating in his body? Had the same thing happened to Hoot twenty-five years ago? Was it simply the price one paid to heal gutations?

Mariah Bloom had told Sarah that Billy's symptoms would pass, which likely meant it took time for the GODD chip to fully enmesh itself into his neural network and establish firm control of hormone release. Yon wondered what might have happened had Sarah left the chip in Billy a little longer. His gutations might be cured by now.

Baker Street Rowhouse
Thunder Bay, The Northlands

Miriam Heinz tugged up the hem of her skirt as she ascended the brick stairs. When she reached the covered landing, the overweight woman paused to slide the hem back into place and to adjust the tote bag slung over her shoulder. Seconds later, she hovered her hand over a holopad next to the rowhouse's ornately etched glass door and then entered the building.

Peering at the scene through binoculars from the privacy of a faux-tradesman's truck parked across the street, NASF platoon leader Captain George Glick watched lights illuminate the first-floor windows. He lowered the binoculars and turned toward a bank of video screens in the back of the command vehicle.

His team had broken into the rowhouse before dawn and placed surveillance cameras in both the first-floor offices of the tutor, Ms. Heinz, and the unoccupied suite on the second floor. As Glick watched the feed of one of those cameras, showing Heinz making coffee in a kitchenette, he tapped his earbud radio. "Blue team, go."

He had hoped to avoid accosting innocents like Heinz, but he now had no choice. Glick was tasked with finding Mariah Bloom before Beacon did and Heinz occupied the office suite below the empty one supposedly belonging to Bloom. His team's earlier search of Bloom's suite had yielded only one significant piece of intelligence — there was a complete absence of human DNA in the empty space. The second-floor suite had been thoroughly and intentionally sanitized.

And while Glick's team found fingerprints, hairs and skin cells on the walls, railings and steps of the stairwell leading to Bloom's suite, Glick highly doubted any of the samples would be of value. He was equally skeptical of the DNA samples collected from Heinz' first-floor suite. In his experience, someone concerned enough to sanitize DNA evidence from the second-floor suite would not have carelessly left their DNA in the stairwell or tutor's suite.

Also, given that Thunder Bay was like other settlements in the Northlands — self-governing entities unaffiliated with any country — Glick suspected many of the town's residents did not contribute their DNA to the World Gene Registry. Still, Glick had dutifully sent all of the samples to the NASF lab in Duluth for processing and comparison with the WGR and New Atlantia's Gene Registry. Maybe they would get lucky.

Aside from the DNA samples, Glick's team found no mentions in the tutor's paper files related to Beacon, Billy Hearns, Jakali Syndrome or Mariah Bloom. It was possible the documents in the files were coded, but from all appearances, the papers were nothing more than student records and business-related documents. Glick hoped her holocomputer would yield something more meaningful, but it had not been in the suite. Presumably, it was in the large tote bag the woman had hauled up the rowhouse's steps. Glick would shortly find out whether his presumption was accurate.

Turning back to gaze out of the truck windows, Glick observed four of his Viper androids disguised as civilians come into view on the otherwise empty street. From the north came two joggers, one a white male, the other a black female. Approaching the rowhouse from the opposite direction was a bearded Hispanic man in a peacoat. Trailing behind him was another white Viper posing as a uniformed delivery man. He carried a large package and whistled while he walked.

One by one, they entered the rowhouse. Glick spun around in time to see the startled Heinz on the video screen. She dropped her full coffee mug as she came face to face with the bearded man aiming a laser pistol at her. Seconds later, Glick received a message in his earbud radio from the bearded Viper. "Premises secured. Target in custody."

"Well done," Glick said. "I'll be right there."

Exiting the truck, the NASF captain hustled toward the rowhouse. *Now, if we can just squeeze some intel from the woman…*

Approaching Thunder Bay
The Northlands

The journey into the Northlands had taken far longer than Takoda thought was advisable. Each extra hour they spent trekking toward Thunder Bay was another hour head start for NASF. But as Maj. Spiers had reminded Takoda before they departed Eagle Butte, "Getting there fast won't mean a thing if NASF sees us coming."

Spiers had been speaking of NASF's satellite surveillance when he made the point. He assured Takoda that NASF had tracked every vehicle that had made the trip from Cannon Ball to Eagle Butte. Cassidy had reinforced Spiers' contention before they left for Thunder Bay. "They also undoubtedly have eyes on this garage. Every person, every vehicle going in and out of the garage will be tracked. The only way to beat the surveillance is to trick them by every means at our disposal."

That had meant employing several ruses, including disguises, decoy vehicles, and changing up their vehicle on multiple occasions en route into the Northlands. Takoda had never seen Beacon deploy so many of its members and assets to make it all work. Eventually, once they entered into the thick forestlands of northwestern Carapach, territory very familiar to Takoda, they abandoned the last of their cars to hike through the woods while carrying a canoe. The boat aided their crossing of numerous small lakes that dotted the border between Carapach and the Northlands.

Twenty-two hours later, they ditched the canoe when they reached a small village close to the major east-west road linking the settlement of Winnipeg with Thunder Bay. They were met there by a Beacon operative who provided them new disguises and a pickup truck. As they began the final leg of the trip, Spiers had said, "Well, looks like your Beacon friends' trickery worked."

"What makes you so sure?" Takoda asked.

"We're still alive."

That had been two hours ago. Now, they were just an hour outside of Thunder Bay. As Takoda steered the pickup along the empty two-lane road, Spiers sat beside him with a laser rifle on his lap. If not for Takoda's greater fear of NASF and the potential for a run-in with sleeping jakalis hiding in the forest on both sides of the road, the weapon in Spiers' hands would have concerned him.

While they had reached a détente of sorts through several conversations before and during the trip, Takoda still did not trust Spiers and he could tell Spiers still despised him and everyone connected with Beacon. He made it clear he was assisting for one reason, and one reason only. His son Dylan.

Takoda wondered if that was the truth, however. During the long stretches of the trip when they both were alone with their thoughts, Takoda had imagined scenarios where Spiers turned on him and Mariah Bloom as soon as they found the woman. That thought recycled in his mind as Spiers ordered Takoda to pull off onto the shoulder of the road.

"What for?" Takoda asked.

"Just pull over."

The tone of Spiers' voice was more of a command than a request. Takoda looked over to see Spiers pointing the laser rifle at his mid-section. Takoda pounded his fist on the steering wheel.

"I knew it! Damn it, I knew it!"

"Pull over now!"

Takoda ignored him. "What are you going to do? Execute me on the side of the road? Or call in your NASF buddies to arrest me?"

Spiers jabbed the barrel of the rifle into Takoda's ribs. "Shut up and pull over."

Anger rose so quickly in Takoda, his hands began to tremble. What had possessed Hawkeye to entrust Cassidy and Spiers? Why hadn't the new Beacon leader seen the risk in the inclusion of the NASF officers in the mission? He thought of Yon and wondered whether Cassidy had turned the tables on her too. Then another thought hit him. One that made him sick to his stomach. He had not spoken to Hawkeye directly. Was there really a new Beacon leader named Hawkeye? Or had Cassidy invented a fictional new leader for Beacon?

What a perfect set-up. Send Takoda away with Spiers to investigate the address Sarah Hearns provided for Mariah Bloom, isolate Yon with Cassidy, commandeer Ellie and Akecheta. Divide and conquer. Take the GODD chip from Hoot, snatch Billy Hearns from Flathead, intercept the DNA ID on Mariah Bloom. No wonder Cassidy had been adamant about communications flowing through her. What better way to enact her and Spiers' plan to thwart Beacon?

Takoda slammed on the brakes so hard, the tail end of the pickup swerved sideways into the opposing lane. At the same time, he reached down and grabbed the rifle barrel, trying to wrest the weapon from Spiers as the truck wobbled on the edge of tipping over.

In the glare of the rising sun, Takoda never saw the fist that pounded into his face. Sharply delivered, it felt like the blow of a hammer. Spiers landed another punch. Takoda let go of the rifle and blindly swung at Spiers as the truck came to a screeching stop. His punch glanced harmlessly off Spiers' shoulder. Before Takoda could reload another swing, Spiers jammed the rifle into his belly and chopped down on the back of his head.

Dazed and writhing, Takoda slumped over the steering wheel. He heard Spiers leave the truck and the next thing he knew he was tugged out of the vehicle and tossed onto the road. As he gasped for air, he heard the heavy-breathing Spiers say, "What the hell was that? Are you crazy? You could have killed us!"

Takoda crawled onto his knees and pushed himself up. Just as quickly, Spiers' boot crashed into his ribs. "Stay down, Doctor...before you get hurt any worse."

Rolling onto his back, Takoda looked up and saw Spiers standing over him, the rifle slung over his shoulder. "I can't...believe...I fell for it...You never...were going to help...were you? It was all an act...right from the start."

"Oh shut up, and move your ass to the side of the road. In the shade, over there." Spiers pointed to the far side of the road where a tree line of tall, pointy pines blocked the sun's rays. "Come on, move before we both get run over!"

In a half-stagger, half-crawl, Takoda scrambled across the road and collapsed on the gravel shoulder. Meanwhile, Spiers hopped in the truck and moved it out of the road. After parking it on the shoulder, he hopped back out and walked toward Takoda.

The rifle was gone. Instead, he carried a backpack in his hands. Kneeling beside Takoda, he opened it and pulled out a towel. "Your head's bleeding." As Takoda took the towel and touched it against the throbbing spot on his forehead, Spiers said, "You have some real trust issues, my man."

Still fighting to regain his breath, Takoda said, "Happens when...guns are pointed at me."

"Well, there wasn't time to have a debate. Of course, if I knew you were going to flip out, I would have used a different approach. You hurt bad?"

Takoda's ribs were on fire and the welts on his face throbbed. "I'm fine."

"Good, let's get you out of sight before it's too late."

Spiers hoisted the backpack over his shoulder and grabbed Takoda's arm. As he started to pull him up, pain stabbed Takoda's ribs. He yanked his arm from Spiers' grip. "Get out of sight? Why?"

Looking upward, Spiers said, "Don't want any gliders to spot us. Now, come on, let's get under cover of the trees."

This time, Takoda accepted Spiers' help and the two men scrambled up the gravel embankment and disappeared into the pines. Safely beneath the canopy of trees, Spiers helped lower Takoda against the trunk of a pine. Spiers unslung the pack and pulled out a water thermos. Handing it to Takoda, he said, "All right, Doctor. Now, listen up. This is where you get off this ride…at least, for now. If I don't get caught or killed, I'll come back to pick you up before nightfall. If I don't show up by then, use the holophone in the pack to contact Cassidy and get a ride out of here. But, whatever you do, don't try to follow me."

"What are you—"

"Zip it, doc. I'm not finished. You can't go into Thunder Bay. It was a stupid idea for Cassidy to send you. Whether NASF has people in the city by now or not, it doesn't matter. They sure as hell have sent drones…gliders and nanos." Nodding his head in the direction of the road, Spiers continued, "That, there, is the only main road into Thunder Bay from Carapach's border. It doesn't matter how sneaky we were to get to this point, you can bet your butt there will be more than a satellite looking down on us the closer we get to town.

"They'll have gliders moving up and down this highway. They'll be weaponized and they'll carry nanos they can drop for tight-in surveillance. They'll scan every vehicle on this road, doc, and it won't matter that you've cut your hair and look a mess; if a nano's face recognition scanner gets a good look at you, it will peg you in seconds. And then we're done."

Takoda removed the towel from his forehead and said, "Same goes for you. A nano would recognize you too."

Spiers shook his head. "No, I know how to fool a face scanner."

"Then show me how to fool it too, and we'll both go."

"Nope. Not until I get a lay of the land." Spiers stood up and wiped pine needles from his hands. "You're too valuable an asset to lose. I need you to stay alive to make sure my son gets whatever mojo you found in the Hearns kid."

"You don't sound like a man who expects to come back."

"Just do what I ask, okay? I'll do everything I can to find the woman. If I can, I'll bring her back with me." Spiers handed Takoda the bag. "There's food and more water inside. Plus, the phone and some med supplies. I'll also leave you the rifle just in case I don't get back until after dark." Before Takoda could protest, Spiers dashed away. A few minutes later, he returned with the rifle. "You know how to use one of these?"

"I'm not the best, but I'm good enough to protect myself."

"Good. Hopefully, you won't need to, but one piece of advice if any jakalis show up. Avoid sweeping shots in the forest. Slice through enough tree trunks and you'll start a chain reaction. You won't be able to run fast enough to avoid one falling on you."

As Spiers began to walk away, Takoda said, "This is a bad idea, Major."

"You're right, Doctor, but it's a better one than we had before."

Spiers disappeared from view. All of a sudden, a pang of panic shot through Takoda. He called out, "Wait! How will you find me when you come back?"

"Easy," Spiers yelled back, "the rubber you left on the road marks the spot."

Baker Street Rowhouse
Thunder Bay, The Northlands

Glick turned away from the blood-splattered mess in the second-floor suite and instructed his Vipers to dispose of the tutor's body. "And do what you can to clean up in here."

As Glick left the suite, he sighed. The interrogation had been a major disappointment. The most meaningful information they had extracted from Ms. Heinz included the name of the building's landlord and a physical description of Mariah Bloom.

Glick found it hard to believe the tutor did not know Bloom, but Heinz had never wavered on that point. Not even when tortured. According to Heinz, she had never socialized with the second-floor occupant, nor had Bloom visited the tutor's first-floor suite. As the tutor repeatedly stated during the interrogation, that was not unusual. Most people who settled in Thunder Bay were gutant refugees who kept to themselves.

After descending the staircase, Glick returned to Heinz' suite and found one of his disguised Vipers seated at the tutor's desk. "Any luck tracking down the landlord?"

"Yes, sir," said the android. "The name the tutor gave us checks out, but I haven't been able to reach him. His holonumber goes right to a message service."

"Okay. Leave him a message. Tell him you might be interested in renting the space upstairs, but you'd like to see the suite first. Tell him you'd like to see it today."

"Roger that," said the Viper.

"What about his office address? Did you find it?"

"Affirmative. We found a copy of the lease in the tutor's records."

"Good. Give it to me. You stay here. If anyone comes looking for Heinz, tell them she was called away unexpectedly. If you suspect a Beacon plant, transmit an alert immediately to the full platoon."

"Yes, sir."

With the folded lease document in his coat pocket, Glick returned to the command truck across the street and gathered a squad to accompany him to the landlord's office. He briefly considered sending another set of Vipers door-to-door in the area to drum up more information about the elusive Mariah Bloom, but then he remembered Heinz' comment about the city's gutant refugees keeping to themselves and decided against the idea. At least, for now.

Hopefully, the landlord can tell us where to find Bloom. If not, we'll start canvassing the neighbors. Short of Beacon rats showing up, that's our only other option.

Pine forest beside the road to Thunder Bay
The Northlands

An hour after Damon left, Takoda decided to check in with Yon. Using the secure holophone in the backpack, he tapped out Yon's number. As soon as she answered, a holoscreen formed above the phone with a live video feed of a tired-looking Yon.

"Hey," he said, "can you talk?"

Yon's sleepy eyes opened wide. "What happened to your head? Are you all right? Where are you?"

"Long story. I'm okay. Just waiting for Spiers to get back."

"Get back? From where?"

"Thunder Bay. He went in to check out the address Sarah gave us."

"Why aren't you with him?"

"Guess he thought I'd slow him down," Takoda said. "What's up on your end? Did you get an ID on Mariah Bloom's DNA?"

Yon covered her mouth as she yawned and nodded her head. "We did. Didn't Cassidy call you?"

"No."

Takoda checked the phone's notification screen for missed calls and messages. There were none.

"Her full name is Antoinette Guilbert, but according to the registry, she goes by the name Toni Gilbert. Sending you a photo of her now."

The dimmed holoimage hovering above the phone split into two screens, one maintaining the live video feed of Yon and the other displaying the photograph of the owner of the DNA provided by Sarah Hearns.

Takoda was surprised by the woman's appearance. "Aside from her violet eyes, she looks nothing like what Sarah described."

"I know. Either Sarah lied to us or Toni Gilbert disguised herself when she met Sarah."

"I'm betting the latter," said Takoda. "How old is she?"

"It's hard to believe, but the registry says she's fifty-two."

"She's an evvie?" Takoda asked.

"That's what her DNA shows."

"What in the world is an evvie doing with Mugabe's GODD chip and proteins?" In Takoda's experience, evvies sympathetic to the plight of jakalis were far and few between.

"Definitely a puzzle," said Yon. "I was expecting her to be a gutant based on Sarah's description, or a blenda. But there's not a single gutation in her DNA according to the registry. She's one hundred percent evvie. Say's here she was born in Normandy."

Takoda imagined the violet-eyed evvie strutting through the streets of Thunder Bay, a place known for its gutant refugee population. "Up here, she would have caught the attention of everyone she passed. She must have disguised herself to blend in."

"That's exactly what I thought."

Takoda thought of Spiers and rued the lack of a way to share Yon's info with him until he returned. "Did you find anything else about her? A home address? Holonumber?"

"Sort of. We ran a DNA cross-check in the registry and got a hit on Toni's older brother. He lives in New Atlantia but he has a daughter who lives pretty close to Thunder Bay. Her name is Miriam Heinz. I'm sending you her photo now and her home address. It's worth checking out, don't you think?"

"Without a doubt." When Miriam's photo replaced Toni's on the split-screen, Takoda said, "Whoa, Miriam looks more like a blenda. She's definitely not an evvie."

"Correct. According to the registry, Miriam's mother was a blenda too."

"Is Miriam married? Does she have a family?"

"No, she's single. So is Toni Gilbert, by the way."

Miriam must have fled into the Northlands to avoid persecution, thought Takoda. Blendas were not treated much better than gutants in New Atlantia…unless the blenda married a noble or evvie as Sarah Hearns had. Even then, they were looked down upon by the upper castes.

But what led Toni Gilbert to Thunder Bay? Gutant refugee towns in the Northlands didn't exactly lay out the red carpet for evvies. More often than not, evvies were targeted for kidnapping and eventual auction as conscripted breeders, for that was the only way for gutants to access evvie DNA. The Guild prohibited the sale of evvie DNA to gutants and no evvie would willingly breed with a gutant. *That helps explain why she disguised herself to look like a blenda*, thought Takoda. Reaching into the backpack, he pulled out a notepad and pen.

"Tak? You still there?" asked Yon.

"Yeah. I'm here. Just writing down Miriam's address."

"What for? You've got it on the holophone."

"I'm not taking the phone with me. We've only got the one. I'm leaving it for Spiers."

"Leaving it? You can't be thinking of going there on your own."

"That's the plan."

"Tak, listen to me. You should wait for Spiers to get back and then go together."

Takoda tore out the page with Miriam's address and stuffed it in his pocket. As he started to write again, he said, "I'm also leaving Spiers a note telling him to call you. Fill him in on everything you told me and tell him I've gone to find Miriam's house."

"But how are you going to get there? You said Spiers has the truck."

"I'll hitch a ride." Takoda finished up the note and then used the holophone's map app to show him the location of the town where Miriam lived. It was thirty-five miles away, approximately fifteen miles outside of Thunder Bay.

"Tak, that is definitely not a good idea. You'll be too easy for a drone to spot."

"Maybe. Maybe not. If there are any drones, they'll be looking for vehicles not someone walking on the side of the road."

"You can't be sure of that."

"No, you're right. It's another reason I'm leaving the phone here. I don't want NASF getting their hands on it." Yon protested once again but Takoda cut her off. "Look, I'm going. Just make sure to keep your phone close by. If I get back before Spiers does, I'll call you and let you know I'm okay. Otherwise, you'll hear from Spiers first. All right?"

"No. It's not all right."

"Take care, Yon."

Takoda ended the call. Moments later, with the powered-off holophone stowed and the note to Spiers affixed to the backpack with a safety pin from the med kit, Takoda disappeared through the trees.

CHAPTER 21

SPLASH LANDING

Airborne offshore of Kauai

The buffeting wind shook Caelan awake. Tossed to and fro, he felt like a pinball caught between bumpers. He huddled and covered his head, unsure of where he was, only to feel hands pulling on him. Instinct demanded he kick his legs and twist his body. Suddenly, a rush of air knocked him back. His eyes opened and he closed them just as fast. The light was too blinding. Then he became aware of the drone of aircraft engines. Cracking his eyes open again, he saw the blinding light was coming through an open door through which a Makoa jumped out. In the background, he heard an unfamiliar voice shouting, "Go! Go! Go!"

With as much strength as he could muster, Caelan cracked open his eyes further. A shadow moved across his vision and wedged goggles and a helmet on his head. Once again, hands pulled on him. He felt his legs dragging against a surface and then a rush of wind jabbed the entire length of his body. Someone clamped his waist tightly and a woman's voice, Ellie's, yelled above the howling wind, "Don't worry, I'll deploy your chute."

The assurance was followed by a blast of cold wind. As he began a twirling descent, the drone of engines began to recede. Dazed and gasping for breath, Caelan's eyes fully opened. As he looked around, the weight squeezing his waist suddenly released. At the same time, he heard a ripping sound and his body vaulted upward.

By the time his parachute fully opened, Caelan was wide awake. Scanning the bizarre scene around him, he said, "What the hell?"

Below, the water was such a deep blue it was almost purple. Intermittent white-capped waves rippled across its surface. To the left, he saw a lush island of green foliage and red soil. Dotting the horizon were puffs of billowed canvases. He counted seven in all. Add his chute and there were eight descending toward the water.

Where am I? Caelan wondered. *How did I get here?*

A blur dropped in front of him. Looking down, he saw a splayed figure falling toward the water, and then, like a kernel of popcorn erupting from its shell, a parachute deployed above the figure and the chutist shot up within a hundred feet of Caelan.

Though he could not see the face of the chutist behind the helmet, an echoing voice in his mind identified her. *Don't worry, I'll deploy your chute.*

Caelan couldn't believe it. The bloody bitch had kidnapped him. Looking around again, he recounted the descending chutes. All in, there were nine. Caelan, his six Makoas, Ellie and a mystery chutist. *Ah, yes*, he thought. *She mentioned something about retrofitting a Steel.*

As they descended closer to the water, a sudden gust of wind pushed Caelan and the others toward the island. He studied the topography and the surrounding vista. He could see another island nearby and a spit of land in the distance but otherwise there was nothing but ocean in every direction.

Focusing once again on the island, Caelan marveled at its beauty. He saw lush caverns, towering waterfalls and rocky beaches. Then a scattering of broken ships caught his attention. Thrown against the island's shore, or held back by nearby reefs, there were hundreds of wrecks within his field of vision. Scanning left and right, he saw even more.

At that moment, Caelan realized he was about to land on or near one of the Hawaiian islands. Which one, he did not know, but one thing was for certain. There would be jakalis waiting to greet him. He reached for his hips and discovered holstered pistols. Tucking his chin, he saw the strap of a laser rifle across his chest. *Good*, he thought. *At least, I'll take a pile of the bastards out before they get me.*

With his hand clutching the hilt of a pistol, he stared at Ellie's drifting parachute. As he contemplated revenge, he heard another familiar voice. "Look alive, team, keep your eyes on the tree line."

"Elvis, is that you?" Caelan said. As he spoke, he felt his lips brush up against the prong of the helmet microphone.

"Roger that. I'm on your nine."

Caelan's head snapped to the left and spied a waving chutist below. "Sitrep, now. Where the bloody hell are we?"

"Kauai. North shore. Coming in hot. Watch for the reefs."

She lives in a place infested by jakalis. Caelan spoke again into the microphone. "Is that you on my three, Ellie?"

Without delay, the android replied, "Copy that."

"Good." Caelan withdrew one of his laser pistols. "May you rot at the bottom."

He fired a stream of laser fire toward Ellie. Buffeted by the winds swirling near the shore, the helpless Ellie evaded Caelan's shots but her parachute did not. Two of the blazes effortlessly sliced huge gaps in the canopy. Just as quickly, the chute collapsed and Ellie plummeted toward the water.

Caelan watched with satisfaction as the android splashed into the water, but his revelry was short-lived. A strong wind yanked him once again toward the island, pulling him with inescapable force toward an outcrop of volcanic rock. *What a way to go*, he thought. *Oh well, it's better than being torn apart by a jakali.*

Closing his eyes, Caelan said into his microphone, "It's been a pleasure leading you lads, but sorry to say our road ends he—"

Out of nowhere, a mass crashed into Caelan so hard he lost his breath. The force of the collision pushed him past the rocky outcrop and toward a sandy beach. The pressure of the mass released, and Caelan saw a Steel android spinning away, its body dipping down as if preparing to dive into the water. The android pierced the water with a splash. Seconds later, Caelan tumbled onto the beach.

By the time Caelan untangled from the cords of his parachute, Elvis informed him that all but one of the Makoas had linked up. The last, Elvis told him, was swimming ashore. Caelan said, "Good. Do you have a fix on my position?"

"Roger that. We are headed your way."

"Right. I think I'll take a breather then."

Caelan flopped down on the sand and listened to the roar of the waves crash against the tall walls of volcanic rock at the edge of the beach. Breathing hard, he flung off the helmet and slicked back his red hair. "What in the bloody hell are we doing here?"

As if cued to provide an answer, Caelan saw an object in the water racing toward the shore. Its wake looked like that of a torpedo. When the object washed into the breakers, it began to unfold into the shape of a human. Then, the svelte profile of Ellie emerged onto the beach. Caelan chuckled. "Ruddy bitch. Should have cut her in two. Might do now."

He reached for his laser pistol, expecting Ellie to reach for hers. But the android did the most remarkable thing instead. She paused to wring water from her hair. Caelan shouted, "You're not bloody human, luv. Who the eff cares how your hair looks?"

She continued with twisting squeezes of her long locks. *It must be a residual mannerism lodged in her behavior module,* Caelan thought. *Perhaps I can shake her to reality with a shot across her bow.*

He raised his pistol to fire and just as quickly the weapon flew from his hand. The vibration damned near broke his wrist. Caelan grabbed his hand and glared at Ellie. But if she was the source of the laser shot, she was quicker than a blink of an eye. For she was still tending to her bleeding hair! Caelan looked around and spotted a Steel stomping toward him, weapon raised. Caelan heard the android say, "What say I separate his head from his shoulders, El?"

Another voice echoed from the headset of Caelan's strewn helmet. It was Elvis. "Do and die, my brother."

Caelan twirled around on his knees, his eyes desperately seeking the sight of his trusty Makoas. From under the arch of eroded volcanic rock, he saw them. Side by side, all six. Weapons aimed at the Steel, they moved toward Caelan.

"Easy lads," Caelan mumbled. Cupping his hands around his mouth, he shouted above the roaring waves. "Stand down, mates."

As they lowered their guns and rifles, Caelan looked back toward the Steel. It, too, had lowered its weapon. A final turn of his head revealed Ellie was now walking toward him. She held her hands above her head as if surrendering. Caelan whispered, "Aren't you a cheeky tart."

Caelan stood and wiped the sweat from his brow. Despite the ocean gusts, the air was thick and warm. Still feeling somewhat unsteady, he staggered to maintain his balance on the uneven sand. Just as it seemed he might topple over, two Makoa hands gripped his shoulders and helped hold him upright. Within seconds, Ellie and her Steel converged on Caelan and his squad. Amid the shadow formed by the collection of androids, Caelan looked up at Ellie and said, "I pegged you wrong, luv. I thought you were an angel. But you're not, are you?" He rubbed his temple, remembering the blow that knocked him out. "You're a devil with a death wish."

"You have every right to be angry." She bowed. "I am sorry."

Caelan rolled his eyes and paced the sand. "You're sorry? You knock me out cold, hijack me and my Makoas, fly us from bleeding Montana to Kauai, kick my arse out of a plane while I'm barely conscious and all you can say is you're sorry? Un-freaking-believable!"

"I knew you would not come otherwise."

He was so mad, he began hopping up and down on the sand. "You're absitively right, you sack of solenoids!" Caelan turned to Elvis. "And you! What in blazes were you thinking, man? Why didn't you wake me? Why did you agree to this bloody nonsense?"

"They were not given a choice," said Ellie. "Ake and I took them from the chop-shop in Flathead. They were recharging. We powered them down and took them. I powered them back up an hour before the jump."

Mouth agape, Caelan stomped around some more. "You stole my Makoas?"

"I borrowed them," said Ellie.

"No, you *stole* them." Returning his attention to Elvis, Caelan said, "Well, what's your excuse for going along with her? You can't tell me you think jumping out of an airplane over Kauai isn't odd. You can't tell me you didn't wonder why I was unconscious. One moment you're powered down in Flathead, the next you have a parachute on your back and she tells you to jump. Didn't you once question whether any of it made sense?"

"I told them we had hired you for a jakali hunt," said Ellie. "I told them you were sleeping off a night of drinking. They did not seem surprised by either."

"Har, bloody, har. You're a thief *and* a liar. And as soon as I find a way off this bloody jungle rock, me and my Makoas are gone. Savvy?"

"Understood," Ellie said. She bowed once more and turned to her Steel. "Come on, Ake. I thought they were hunters. I thought they were valorous. But I erred. We will rescue the girl on our own."

Ellie pushed past Caelan and headed toward the jungle tree line bordering the beach. On his way past Caelan, the Steel Ellie had called Ake elbowed Caelan in the back of the head. The android's flesh did little to soften the blow of his metallic innards.

The sound of weapons locking on the receding pair cut through the air. Caelan massaged the sore spot on the back of his head and yelled, "My lads are more valorous than any androids on the planet, including you sorry lot. Like me, however, they demand *honesty* and *full disclosure* before going into battle. We are not mercenaries. We are not puppets."

The gibe seemed to resonate with Ellie, for the android froze in her march toward the jungle. A second later, so did Ake. As she spun around, her movements were so graceful, it was hard for Caelan to believe she was not human.

"The girl's name is Avana Wells. She is *not* a jakali. Not yet. However, between where we stand and the village where she lives, there are *thousands* of jakalis. If the tales circulating on the holonet are true, the beasts attack the villages on the island most nights. So, Ake and I are going into the jungle not knowing how many jakalis we will face, nor knowing whether Avana is still alive. But we will go, nonetheless. Why? Because New Atlantia has sent a platoon of Vipers to find her, possibly to kill her.

To the last spark of our processors, we will not let that happen. Go if you must, but do not lecture us about valor."

Her rebuke stung, but Caelan remained unswayed. "What's so bleeding special about this lass? Why would you give everything to save her? Why would NASF send Vipers so long a distance to kill her?"

"I do not know. I only can speculate."

"Then speculate, luv."

"She is the daughter of my owner. NASF wishes to hurt *him* by hurting *her*."

Ellie spun back around and continued her march toward the jungle. As mad as Caelan was at her, he felt a pang of sorrow as he watched her leave. Thousands of jakalis? NASF Vipers? If she was lying, she was the most convincing con-droid he had ever met. If she was telling the truth, she and her Steel would never make it through the night.

"What's beyond the tree line, Elvis?" Caelan asked.

"No jakalis in range, sir. But..."

"But what, lad? Spit it out."

"Their oil slicks coat the mountains ahead."

"Aye. I thought I could smell them," said Caelan. "Well, lads, as long as we're here, we might as well see the sights. Follow me."

Ellie never looked back until she reached the tree line. When she finally did, Caelan swore he saw her smile. Once in the jungle, he quickly became alarmed at the pace with which Ellie moved toward the mountains.

"Hold up, luv. This is *not* how you move through jakali territory. And it's not how you sneak up on Vipers, either." As Ellie began a rebuttal, Caelan stopped her with a wave of his hand. "You wanted hunters, did you not? Then, let us hunt."

"My scanners are capable of detecting any human or android in the vicinity. I detect none. We move ahead as fast as we can until we do."

Caelan shook his head. "I don't know what your day job is, luv, but it sure ain't hunting jakalis." He turned to Elvis. "Deploy nanos."

"Roger that." Elvis reached in his pack and withdrew three. "Headings?"

"Send one up top to find and recon the village. Send a second along our path to look for jakali booby traps. Take the last one for a tour of the island. See if it detects any Viper radiation signatures. They're the only andros I know of with plutonium energy cores."

As soon as Elvis released the nano-drones, Caelan turned back to Ellie. "See, the thing is, luv, jakalis in the Northlands have started to coordinate activity. I don't know why or how, but they've recently developed more sophisticated tactics. If the same is true here, you can't just rely on your scanners to spot them. You have to anticipate their moves and potential traps. If you fall for one of their traps, they'll tear you apart before you can radio for help."

Lotus' jakali colony
North Shore, Kauai, the Hawaiian Islands

Akela kept his eye on the jakalis climbing up the rocks aside the base of the waterfall while he and Lotus continued their conversation. Most of the jakalis had scampered inside the caves aside the falls after their earlier doses of Lotus' medicine but several stayed outside. They seemed to be slowly working their way up the incline of rocks. Whether they were being protective of Lotus or trying to listen in on the conversation, Akela didn't know. But they were edging closer.

In the distance, the roar of airplane engines distracted Akela from his surveillance of the creeping jakalis. Akela scanned the sky, hoping to spot the plane, but it was beyond his view. Very few planes flew near Kauai anymore. Those that did were seaplanes that ferried hunters eager to track and kill jakalis. Akela considered the hunters a mixed blessing. While they did help thin the island's jakali population, they also riled the beasts into frenzies during their hunts. Some of the worst attacks on the village had occurred during jakali hunts.

"Hunters," Lotus said.

Akela turned to her. "Ah, so you have been on the island for a while, then. We have not had a hunting party for several months."

Lotus twirled a small flower with her fingers. "No, I've not been here that long. I'm just familiar with the sound of jakali hunter shuttle planes. They use the same kind of aircraft on other islands. I've run into them in the Northlands, as well. Alaskon, Greenland, anywhere people dump jakalis, you see and hear the shuttles."

"Your travels have taken you to many dangerous places. Why do you put your life at risk for these…"

Lotus turned to him. "You can say it, Akela. You can call them beasts if it makes you happy."

"Calling them beasts does not make me happy; it describes what they are."

She frowned. "You puzzle me. You and your people risk your lives to provide comfort and aid to gutants who will one day turn into the beasts you loathe. You show your gutants compassion and love. But once they turn, you stop caring. Why is that?"

"Why do *you* show compassion and love for animals that rape and kill?"

"They don't want to hurt people, they really don't." Lotus stared at the flower in her hand. "They lose control over their minds, over their bodies. They feel helpless, hopeless, angry. They can't stop those feelings. They just want to feel better. Is that so hard to understand?"

"No, it's not. But I have no way to help them feel better. We have no medicine to calm them as you have."

Akela watched a snarl form on Lotus' face as she said, "So, you do what they do everywhere else. When your gutants start to turn, you put them to sleep. When you see jakalis in the wild, you kill them."

"What else am I supposed to do?" Akela said, his voice raised. He swept his arm over the swath of jakalis crawling up the rocks. "They attack my family, my people. They've overtaken my island, *all* of the Hawaiian islands."

Lotus dropped the flower and pushed up to stand. "If you don't like it, then why do you stay?"

Akela rose to his feet as well. Leaning forward, he slapped his open hand on his chest. "Because this is my home. Is that so hard for *you* to understand?" He scowled at her and added, "And why does an evvie care so much for jakalis? They are the bane of your caste."

She edged her face close to Akela's and tapped her chest. "Because I know what's coming."

He pushed her back. "You make no sense."

"Don't I? Look around, Akela. You're so blinded by your hate, you paid no attention to something you should have noticed." She gestured toward the female jakali who had hissed her thanks to Akela earlier. "Come here, child. Don't be afraid. I won't let him hurt you."

The wary teenager crawled forward, just as she had done before, her soiled, tattered clothes swaying as she moved. One such sway exposed her midsection. Akela mumbled, "May the four gods help us. She's pregnant."

"That's right, Akela. And so are several others. Look over there. Did you not see some of the jakalis take their medicine into the caves?" Lotus pushed Akela, turning his shoulders toward the caves. "There are babies in there. Not ones stolen from your village or others on the island. They are offspring from jakalis mating with one another. Most of the babies will not survive. Their DNA is too damaged, even with my medicine, even with the chip. But that shouldn't have surprised me. The chip has never worked in *any* jakali. Just like the babies, their DNA is too—"

"Chip? What chip?"

"Ones like I implanted in Natti and Kaleo. I had hoped the chip would make the babies better, but it was not designed for jakalis."

Akela frowned as he recalled Lotus roughly handling Natti and Kaleo, pressing a device to their necks. He had thought she was injecting more medicine, an inoculation of some kind, not a chip. Then he remembered what Lotus had said afterward. *"They're in the hands of God now."*

The comment had briefly puzzled Akela at the time, for a moment before that, Lotus had uttered prayers to the four gods, leading him to conclude she was a believer of *Unity*. Akela now realized Lotus had meant something entirely different. *She said her medicine was a gene therapy, a banned gene therapy.* "This chip, where does it come from?"

"What? Why do you care? You want them all to die anyway."

Akela thought of the history lessons about the Genetic Revolution taught to the children of the village and the infamous tale of Dr. Dyan Mugabe. "Like the GODD chip?"

"It isn't *like* the GODD chip. It *is* the GODD chip…an upgraded version of it."

"But the technology was destroyed…many years ago."

"Yes and no."

"You should have told me what you were implanting in Natti and Kaleo. I thought you just gave them a higher potency dose of the medicine."

"Would you have stopped me if I'd told you about the chip?"

"Yes."

"So, you prefer they turn into jakalis?"

"No. We would not allow that to happen."

"Oh, that's right," said Lotus. "You'll wait until they become too dangerous to you and your people and then you'll put them to sleep. Meanwhile, pain and uncontrollable urges will eat away at their sanity unless you sedate them so much they become catatonic. I've got a little secret to share with you, Akela. They still feel the pain and urges even when they're sedated. It speeds their insanity because they're locked in a mental room with no way to get out, no way to express or release their anguish."

As Akela responded, he began to stalk around Lotus. "You make our care sound evil, but we do the very best we can to provide them the highest quality of life for as long as possible. Many of our refugees live until they are eighteen, giving them seven, eight years' more life than if they were euthanized in their home countries."

"Ha!" Lotus said, clapping her hands. "Bully for you. You must be so proud to delay their euthanizations." She stepped forward and blocked Akela's path. With her face inches from his, she said, "*I'm* trying to *stop* euthanizations. *I'm* trying to *heal* them. And you make my care sound evil? The irony is thicker than your skull."

Akela grabbed her arm and squeezed. "Playing God with DNA is what destroyed our world, Lotus. Don't you understand that?"

She dug her fingernails into his hand and yanked it away. Reaching up with her other hand, she grabbed the back of Akela's head and pulled it until their foreheads met with a thud. "I understand that perfectly. Do you understand that unless we break the vicious cycle we're in, humans are doomed? Evvies, didgees, gutants...all the castes...everyone. Gone. Extinct. It's a math problem, Akela. We aren't reproducing enough to outlast gutations. Soon, even evvie DNA will begin to gutate. That's another little secret you should know."

CHAPTER 22

READ BETWEEN
THE BINDS

Baker Street
Thunder Bay, The Northlands

With the windows down and music blasting on the pick-up's radio, Damon followed a pizza delivery van along the street. It was time to find out whether NASF was onto Mariah Bloom or not. Tapping his hands on the steering wheel in rhythm with the music, Damon scanned both sides of the street from behind sunglasses and a scarf covering his face below.

He picked out the first Viper with ease. Even disguised in street clothes, the Caucasian android's chiseled features stood out. Ahead, he spotted the parked command vehicle. It, too, was easy to spot. The tradesman panel truck was just like those used by Damon's Beacon task force. *Okay, now time to answer the next question. Have they already found Bloom?*

As the pizza delivery van neared the corner, it began to slow down. Damon honked his truck's horn and gestured out the window for the van to get out of his way. *Nothing like drawing attention to yourself to hide in plain sight*, thought Damon.

A glance in the rearview mirror revealed another Viper, this one a black female atop a nearby rowhouse. Damon pressed the horn again, swerved around the pizza truck and continued down the street. If his plan had worked, the NASF commandos were now focused on the pizza truck stopping in front of the corner rowhouse, not him. This allowed Damon to briefly slow down to get a clear look at the rowhouse entrance without attracting attention. There were no Vipers standing guard.

Okay, so if they're following standard operating procedure, that means Bloom isn't inside the rowhouse. If she were, Vipers would be stationed at every possible entrance. They know Beacon's looking for Bloom. They'd want to send a clear signal to stay away.

So, that means they've either already found her and taken her somewhere else and they're sticking around to set a trap to catch someone from Beacon, or they're still waiting for Bloom to show up. Looking in his rearview mirror, he mumbled, "Guess I'll find out shortly."

Damon expected there would be initial confusion in the command vehicle when the delivery android mounted the rowhouse stairs carrying a stack of pizza boxes. But he doubted the confusion would persist. In short order, NASF would realize the delivery was a probing ploy. Of course, they would immediately suspect Beacon was the perpetrator of the hoax, but how would they respond?

If they were waiting for Bloom, they would probably do nothing. If they were setting a trap for Beacon, they'd likely take the delivery andro into custody and search the pizza van...or, if whoever was manning the command truck was smart enough, they'd pursue Damon and his truck. But in the mirror, he saw no sign of any pursuers and no one had accosted the delivery bot. *So they still must be searching for her...unless...*

Turning onto a side street, Damon looked up to see if he could spot any gliders above. He saw none but it brought him no comfort. Two more turns onto other streets brought Damon to the parking garage he had scoped out earlier just in case he'd been pursued by Vipers he hadn't seen or surveilled from above. He pulled in, drove up two levels and parked on the empty third floor. Seconds later, he was out of the truck and dousing the cabin with gasoline. When the can was empty, he lit his scarf, tossed it in the cabin and ran for the garage stairwell.

As he reached the street level, he tugged the hood of his jacket over his head, slowed to a stroll, crossed the road and disappeared down an alley. Hidden by the shadow of the building, Damon kept walking, hoping the rest of his elaborate diversion would shake any unseen NASF assets trailing him. He was within a few feet of the end of the alley when the pickup finally exploded. Though he was now a city block away from the garage, the rumble of the blast shook the ground beneath his feet. He turned and looked back just as several people rounded the corner.

"What happened?" one of them asked Damon.

He shrugged. 'Beats me. Maybe a gas leak?"

Smoke began to pour into the alley as even more people gathered to gawk. While they all conversed, Damon heard the first siren in the distance. He wound his way through the crowd and turned the corner. Across the street was a small shopping center with a dozen cars parked in its lot. One of them was a car Damon had stolen from the garage before calling in the bogus pizza order.

While he felt a strong urge to jump in the car and speed away, Damon played it cool and strode into a trading-post-themed sundry store in the shopping center. As soon as he entered, he was bombarded by questions from the clerks and customers standing by the window.

"What's going on?" one asked.

"Was that a bomb?" questioned another.

"Is anybody hurt?" posed a third.

"Couldn't tell you. I was just walking by and there was this boom. That's all I know," he said.

After picking out a few items, he roused one of the gawking clerks to scan his purchase. Moments later, he left the store, slid into the stolen car and calmly guided the vehicle onto the street.

As he headed for the main road leading west out of town, Damon checked the rearview mirror often, but never saw anyone tailing him. Nor did he spot any NASF gliders above. He was sure they were up there, but their cameras and scanners were apparently focused elsewhere. Sooner or later, however, Damon was sure the commandos would link his truck with the pizza delivery scam and the garage explosion.

But by the time he reached the tire marks Takoda left on the road earlier in the morning, there was still no sign of gliders, nanos or any suspicious vehicles trailing him. An uneasy feeling began to gnaw inside Damon. *That was too easy. Something isn't right.*

While he wanted to believe NASF had staked out the rowhouse because their search for Mariah Bloom had come up empty, the commandos' passive response to Damon's ruse troubled him. *Why didn't any of the Vipers chase me? And where were their drones? One should have been on my ass before I passed the pizza truck.*

It was certainly possible they had already found the woman, Damon reasoned. But if that was the case, why had the command truck been stationed so close to the rowhouse? They had to know the presence of the truck would be a clear warning sign to any Beacon operatives to stay away. No, there was something else going on. But what?

Damon parked the stolen sedan on the gravel shoulder and climbed the embankment. As he pushed between pine-needle-laden branches, he thought, *maybe there have been developments back in Eagle Bu—*

He stopped dead in his tracks. Through a gap in the branches, he spotted the tree where he had left Takoda. By the trunk sat the backpack and rifle Damon had given the doctor and the bloody towel Takoda had used to stanch the cut on his forehead, but Takoda was nowhere in sight. Under other circumstances, Damon would have called out Takoda's name and searched the area, but his instincts and the note pinned to the backpack told him the geneticist was long gone.

Beacon lab
Eagle Butte, South Dakota

Rubbing the back of her neck, Yon closed her eyes and willed the spasms to subside. *Come on, let me work just a little while longer, then I promise I'll lie down.* A twinge at the base of her neck reminded Yon she had said the same thing two hours ago.

I can't help it, Yon argued with the quivering muscle, *I need to figure this out.*

For the past few hours, she had labored at the three-dimensional holoscreen of a DNA scanner, attempting to resolve an odd discrepancy she had noticed when she compared gutation repairs in Billy Hearns' and Hoot's DNA. Something just didn't add up.

Yon returned to the scanner and prepared to examine all the repairs yet again. Just then, however, Cassidy Willow entered the lab. As usual, the android was straight to the point. "You spoke with Dr. Wells."

"Ah, I see you read my holomessage."

"All communications are supposed to go through me. Do you know how foolish it was for him to go off on his own?"

Sliding her hands into the pockets of her lab coat, Yon said, "Yes, I do. I made that abundantly clear to him. Did you know Maj. Spiers planned to split up and leave Tak behind?"

"Irrelevant. You violated protocol. If you hadn't told Dr. Wells about the DNA ID, he would have stayed until Damon returned."

Yon winced. Cassidy's assessment was accurate. "Look, I'm sorry. He said you hadn't been in contact. I thought it was important to tell him about Toni Gilbert. I didn't know he would go off on his own. Why didn't you contact them, by the way?"

For a moment, the android stared at her with unblinking eyes. *She's hiding something from me,* Yon thought. *Either that, or she's thinking up a lie.*

"Irrelevant. You jeopardized—"

"Like hell it's irrelevant! The DNA ID should have been provided to them right away."

"Hawkeye wanted more background information before—"

"More background? Are you kidding me? Aren't we trying to find this woman as fast as possible?"

"Yes, we are. However, searching for known associates, other addresses, contact numbers, aliases, passport records, financial transactions and other data can help us narrow the search. Not just for Toni Gilbert, but for members of her family and other associates who might be able to lead us to her. We can't just rely on her cousin's home address. It's highly speculative."

Yon backed down. Cassidy was a police android. This kind of work was routine for her and she was right to do it. "Okay, I get it. I understand. Information like that could be very helpful. Again, I'm sorry. For all I knew at the time, Tak's call could have been an emergency. I *had* to answer it."

"Let us hope NASF did not intercept the call. Even if they can't decrypt the content, NASF may be able to pinpoint the locations of each party on the call."

"Look, Cassidy. There's nothing I can do about it now."

"Give me your phone. Your holoband too. I will return them as soon as the mission is complete."

Flushing red, Yon dug out her phone from her lab coat pocket and slapped it in Cassidy's open palm and did the same with the holoband on her wrist. "Satisfied? Now, if you'll excuse me, I have work to do."

Yon turned back to the holoimage displayed by the DNA scanner. As she used her hand to isolate a section of one of Billy's chromosomes, Cassidy came alongside.

"What are you examining?" the android asked.

"I'm trying to solve a puzzle," Yon grumbled. She glared at Cassidy and added, "A puzzle that would have been solved a long time ago if Hoot had told us she was one of Dr. Mugabe's patient-zeros."

"Explain."

Yon sliced off a segment of the chromosome image and stretched it out to zoom in on one of Billy's repaired gutations. "There's something not quite right about the smart proteins that repaired the binds between these genes." With a finger, she circled the computer's simulation of two protein molecules. "These two molecules should not be here."

Cassidy leaned forward. Yon watched the android's eyes dart around as she studied the bind. "I see no breakage. The binds appear intact. Why do you say the proteins are wrong?"

"Because I examined Hoot's DNA." Yon turned toward a second DNA holoimage, and performed the same slice-and-expand motions with her hands. She then dragged the new chromosome slice under the one from Billy. Pointing at the new slice, she said, "This is the same chromosome segment from Hoot's DNA. You'll note she and Billy shared a common gutation. Compare the repaired binds between the two samples."

After studying the holoimages, Cassidy said, "Some of the smart proteins are the same. Others are different."

"Correct," said Yon. "The ones repairing Hoot's binds were Mugabe's original smart proteins. Billy has some of those too. But Billy also has what appear to be newly created smart proteins. Like these, here and here."

"Presumably, that means whoever recreated the GODD chip built upon Mugabe's original work and upgraded some of the smart proteins. The same is probably true of the chip itself. It's an upgrade of the original. But there's an inconsistency in these repairs."

Turning toward the scanner's holokeyboard, Yon entered a stream of commands. On both gutation repairs, some of the binding proteins turned red. "The red molecules identify one of Mugabe's original smart proteins. You see that the repairs to both Billy's and Hoot's common gutation have the reds."

"Yes, but Hoot's repair has many more reds than Billy's," said Cassidy.

"Correct. Now, watch." After Yon entered another flurry of commands, a slew of blue protein molecules appeared on Billy's gene binds. "The blues identify one of the proteins I suspect is new. Note how they appear in many of the locations where Hoot had red ones, but not all."

When Yon turned to look at Cassidy, she once again saw the android's eyes rapidly examining the images. "Can you highlight the receptors the red and blue binding proteins connect with?"

Yon nodded. It was a good observation on Cassidy's part, one that would prove Yon's point. A binding gene was like a jigsaw piece, to play upon Yon's earlier puzzle analogy. To maintain the integrity of the connection between two genes, the jigsaw shape of the binding proteins must exactly "fit" into the corresponding gaps of the jigsaw-shapes of the receptors on the gene proteins.

As soon as Yon finished entering new commands, green molecules appeared on one side of the blues and reds, and brown molecules appeared on the other. "As you can see, the receptors for blues and reds look identical. That's another clue the blues were intended to be upgrades to the reds. But, again, not all of the reds were replaced. To me, it looks like a flaw in the new chip or new smart proteins. Either the chip's repair instructions were incorrect or the smart proteins did not properly interpret the instructions, creating this odd mix of old and new proteins in the repairs."

"Could it be related to the fact Billy only had the chip for a short time?" Cassidy asked.

"I thought of that," Yon said. "It's possible. The chip might repair broken binds in cycles, rather than all at once. Billy may not have had the chip in long enough to complete the repairs."

The idea of the GODD chip working in cycles to repair gutated binds appealed to Yon. Such an incremental approach would certainly be less traumatic than a one-fell-swoop change out of the entire bind. For there had to be a mechanism employed by the chip and smart proteins to "convince" the body's innate DNA error checkers that the replaced proteins should be accepted. It seemed to Yon it would be more effective to convince the error checkers one binding protein at a time, rather than a full bind at a time. She shared these thoughts with Cassidy and then said, "But that's total conjecture. The anomaly could just as easily be a true flaw. We won't know for sure until we can talk to the new chip's developers and study an operating chip in action."

Cassidy backed away. "If it's a flaw, could it cause the repair to break down?"

"It's possible." Yon returned her gaze to the holoimages. "But there's something more basic I don't understand." She pointed at Hoot's gutation repair. "Why substitute the blues for any of the reds in Billy's binds? Hoot had her GODD chip for over twenty-five years and this repaired gutation is still intact. There's no evidence of breakage, no indication of any structural weakness. That tells me this particular original smart protein is sturdy, reliable. So, why fix something that wasn't broken by substituting a new protein?"

Yon turned and discovered Cassidy's eyes pulsing like Ellie's often did when she transmitted or received data. *Probably Maj. Spiers finally calling in,* thought Yon. *Bet he's pissed about Takoda's call too.*

CHAPTER 23

BITE OF THE VIPERS

Sir Bryce Collins' residence
Malibu, California, Pacifica

ir Collins stared out the window and watched wave after wave crash onto the Malibu beach below. All the while, the latest communique from Sir Tripp weighed on his mind. *That damned Jordyn will ruin everything! And if she does, I'll have no one to blame but myself.*

While Collins had counted on the android's determination to foil Beacon, he had underestimated her ruthlessness. *She understands the nature of the threat with greater clarity than I anticipated.* That circumstance was okay with Collins so long as Jordyn remained blind to his plan. But now, especially given the newly installed prefect's communique, Collins wondered how much longer she would keep her Olympia brain core focused on Beacon instead of turning her attention to the Guild.

Collins had never dreamed Jordyn would pose such a problem. As he had conceived her role, she was supposed to have been a pawn, like all the others in his plan, some of whom were witting — such as Rodrick, Antoinette and Miriam, as well as his agents inside NASF and Beacon, most notably the carefully cultivated Hawkeye.

Others of Collins' pawns were unaware of his invisible hand moving them about, including Sarah Hearns, Thompson, Munoz, Wells, Fujita and Spiers. Even Hoot and her NASF infiltrator, Willow, had unwittingly abetted the Guild grandmaster's aims.

It was among this latter group of clueless pawns Collins had intended for Jordyn to reside, but her fervor for protecting New Atlantia's interests had driven the android to act as a chess piece with moves of her own.

At first, Collins had tolerated her unexpected incursions into Carapach, believing they kept pressure on Beacon to find the chip. But Jordyn's later moves, including the brutal interrogations of Hearns and Thompson, and sending Vipers to Kauai, risked waking other unwitting pawns. Worse, those moves had increased the likelihood she might actually succeed in blocking Beacon's effort to acquire the GODD chip.

Collins had employed hasty countermoves to thwart Jordyn by replacing Munoz with Tripp and enlisting Hawkeye to send forces to confront the Vipers, but there was no guarantee either counter would be successful.

And now, her latest move threatened to unravel Collins' entire plan! According to Tripp's latest message, Jordyn's commandos in Thunder Bay had wrested the knowledge of the family connection between Miriam and Mariah Bloom from the landlord of Miriam's office. *How stupid of Miriam to be so indiscreet! It was crucial for Beacon to connect with Antoinette. Miriam knew that! Why blab about her cousin to anyone? Foolish woman. Now NASF may beat Wells to Antoinette!*

That was an outcome Collins could not abide. Too much was riding on the chip finding its way into Beacon's hands, especially now that the traitorous Lila was making so much progress in her jakali research. There was only one solution left. It was time to remove Jordyn from the game... peacefully and discreetly, if possible. By force, if necessary.

Outside of the gutant refugee village
Limahuli, Kauai, the Hawaiian Islands

Caelan aimed his binoculars at the line of Vipers creeping toward the village from the west. In a whisper, he spoke to Elvis through his earbud radio. "Where are the rest of the buggers?"

"Holding in place on the north side."

Lowering the binoculars, Caelan slid down behind the mound of volcanic rock and tapped his holoband. "Show me."

A second later, the video feed from one of Caelan's nano drones appeared in the air above the holoband. Caelan could see the Vipers hiding on both sides of a trail that cut through the jungle.

"Which squad is closer to the beach?" he asked Elvis.

"The Vipers on the north."

Caelan turned to Ellie, who was crouched beside him. Next to her was her Steel, the one she called Ake. "The Vipers to the west are going to create a diversion to draw the villagers to defend that side of the village. The others will sweep in from the north. They must have already ID'd the girl. They must know where she is. Do you know what she looks like? Can you transmit an image of her to Elvis? He'll route it to the others."

"I have several stored, but they are two years old."

"Doesn't matter. Send them all."

"Okay...done."

"Good," Caelan said. "Elvis, you have them?"

"Affirmative. Received and distributed."

"All right, send Devo into the village. See if he can spot the girl. Start on the north sector of the village. The Viper squad is on the north side for a reason. They'll want to get in, grab her and get out quickly. Report back the girl's position ASAP."

While Caelan waited for a response from Elvis, he once again turned his attention to Ellie. "Do you trust me?"

"Yes."

"Then, take Ake, work your way down to the cove. Stay off the trail, keep clear of any Vipers. As soon as you hear the fireworks start, destroy the Vipers' raft. It's a sitting duck. If you can, take out the guards too."

Earlier in their reconnaissance, one of Caelan's nano drones, Devo, had spotted two of the Vipers in a small cove. They were guarding a large, motorized raft sitting on the beach. Caelan suspected the NASF androids had used the raft to come ashore, which meant they most likely had a larger ship or seaplane waiting out in the ocean. While there was nothing he could do about the vessel out at sea, he could contain the Vipers on the island.

"No," said Ellie, "we were sent to protect Avana. We will enter the village and bring her out."

Caelan smiled and cupped his hand on her cheek. "Aye. I believe you would, luv. But you can better protect Avana by doing what I say. There are too many Vipers. You won't get past them. Neither will my Makoas. We can confuse them, flush some of them into a kill zone and thin their advantage, but they're going to get the girl. And when they do, you and Ake will be the last ones standing in their way. Pin them down as long as you can and, hopefully, we can finish them off together."

"What if they don't intend to take her from the village?" asked Ellie. "What if they intend to kill her on sight?"

"If they wanted to kill her, they wouldn't be setting up a diversion. They'd rush the village from all sides and kill everyone they encountered. No, luv, trust me, these Vipers intend to capture Avana and take her down to the boat in the cove."

"He's right, El," said Ake. "My chassis may be Steel, but my brain is still Makoa. The Vipers are arrayed for a snatch op, not an assassination. And he's right about another thing. We're outnumbered and outgunned. Stringing them out, picking them off, knocking out their escape route is the way to go."

Elvis' voice cut through the conversation. "Devo found her. Transmitting coordinates to all units."

Caelan leaned forward, touching his forehead against Ellie's. "If you trust me, luv, you'll do as I ask."

He felt her tug away. Looking up, he saw Ake pulling Ellie by the arm.

"Come on," Ake said. "Time's a-wasting."

Ellie fought against Ake for a moment, her eyes locked on Caelan. Then, without a word, she turned and began to run with Ake at her side. Caelan tapped his earbud and spoke to Elvis. "All right, boys. Time to make a little noise."

Lotus' jakali colony
North Shore, Kauai, the Hawaiian Islands

Akela was still arguing with Lotus when he heard a rumble sounding like distant thunder, which struck him as odd given it was sunny and the sky was clear of clouds. He turned around in a circle, unsure of where the rumble had originated. Had the jakali hunters from the plane already found some prey? The rise of a second roar seemed more like the echo of a mountain tremblor, but this time Akela was able to narrow in on the general direction of the sound's origin.

"What is that sound?" Lotus asked.

A third and fourth tremor shook the ground. Akela began to walk toward the jungle, his mind now confident of the direction of the sounds. The rumbles were too loud to be coming from far away and there was only one landmark in between the sounds and Akela. With Lotus at his heels, Akela trotted through a hundred yards of foliage before he caught a glimpse of smoke rising above the jungle. He turned to Lotus. "The village! Something's wrong. I have to go."

As he bolted away, he heard Lotus close behind him. "Wait! Wait up."

Ignoring her plea, Akela raced onward, his mind moving as fast as his feet. *What could be happening? Did the fuel tanks explode? An accident at the Makoa garage?* Through the slap of palm fronds against his arms and the crunch of branches beneath his feet, Akela heard the spit of laser rifles and the staccato of gunfire. He came to a halt and spun around. Lotus was nowhere in sight but he could hear sounds of disturbance in the jungle. Akela shouted, "Where are you? What have you done!"

Lotus shot into view and collided into him. Akela grabbed hold of her shoulders and shook her. "Listen! You hear that? The village. It's under attack. You lured me away and sent in your mongrels."

Another explosion staggered both of them. Gasping for breath, Lotus grabbed onto Akela's waist and steadied herself. "No...you're wrong...I have nothing...to do with it..."

"Liar! Devil!"

Akela threw her down and took off again. More smoke billowed up above the trees. Akela charged forth, branches and vines raking his bare torso, arms and legs. Another two hundred yards passed by before he realized the explosions and gunfire he was hearing were being traded back and forth. There was a battle going on, all right, but unless jakalis had suddenly acquired rifles and bombs, it wasn't between his villagers and the beasts. *A raid by another village?* Akela wondered. There were several others on the island, but Akela could not fathom a reason why any of them would turn on his village. *Pirates, maybe?* He knew they roamed the waters around the islands, picking off supply vessels and sinking ships loaded with exiled jakalis. *Are they targeting villages now, too?*

Pressing past the waterfall where he and Avana had been surrounded by jakalis just two days ago, Akela picked up his pace until he staggered into a clearing with a view of the village. Looking down the hillside, he stopped in his tracks.

The melee was incomprehensible. The flash of laser beams and tracer bullets crisscrossed in every direction, inside and outside of the village. Fires dotted the landscape. To Akela, it seemed as if dozens of independent battles were underway.

Ducking low, he looked down the trail toward the Makoa garage. It was only a few hundred yards away and, by the looks of it, was not part of the battle. If there were weapons to be had, it was the only place Akela would find one between him and the village. Keeping as low as he could, Akela began to scurry along the trail, but just as quickly as he started, he froze. There was a sharp crack of a snapping branch from behind. He whipped his head around and saw Lotus stumble into the clearing and splay onto the hillside's red clay. In a sharp whisper, he said, "Stay down. Don't move."

He crawled toward her as new explosions rocked the valley below. She lifted her head and gaped at the battle engulfing the village. "What in the hell…"

"Shh," admonished Akela. "Lower your voice."

On her hands and knees, she scooted forward. When they met, she whispered, "What's going on? It looks like a war."

"I don't know, but we can't stay here. Come with me."

Rising into a crouch, Akela headed for the garage. Lotus followed close behind, her hand pressed against Akela's lower back.

"Those aren't jakalis," she whispered.

"I know, I know. It's either a raid by another village or pirates."

When they neared the garage, Akela ducked behind some bushes and tugged Lotus beside him. "You stay here. I'm going to see if I can find a weapon in there."

"Why?" Waving her hand toward the village, she said, "You can't do anything against all that."

"Just stay here. Keep out of sight. If I don't come out in a minute or two, get the hell out of here. Go back into the jungle."

Against her protests, he pushed up and ran for the garage. A bay door was wide open, no doubt all the docked Makoas had rushed out after the first explosion. *Definitely has to be pirates*, thought Akela. The chiefs of the other villages knew where Akela stored his android militia. If they were the attackers, the garage would have been their first target.

He dashed to the edge of the bay and ducked down. Peeking into the shadowed interior, Akela saw no signs of activity and, just as he had speculated, all the Makoa docks he could see were empty. After a deep breath and quick prayer to the four gods, Akela entered. He swept his head left and right to scan the rest of the garage as he hustled to the weapons storage locker.

As soon as he saw the lock was still intact, he turned and headed for the side office where the key was kept. Akela was within two steps of the office when he heard two sounds. One was the voice of Lotus. "Akela! Come quick! I know what's happening!"

The second was the sound of a crying child. Akela looked into the office and saw RJ curled up under a desk, hands covering his ears and teary eyes shut.

Miriam Heinz' farmhouse
On the outskirts of Thunder Bay, The Northlands

Throughout the hitched ride to the outskirts of Thunder Bay, Takoda had been consumed by nagging questions, puzzles that had continued to dog him during the five-mile walk to Miriam Heinz' farmhouse after parting ways with his ride. Riddles that even now, as he hid behind bushes next to Miriam's property, demanded answers. First, how did Toni Gilbert acquire the GODD chip? To Takoda, it seemed strange that an evvie would end up in possession of Mugabe's technology.

The story peddled to the public was that all of Mugabe's research, including her inventory of chips and smart proteins, had been burned at the stake along with the scientist. Takoda was skeptical enough to believe that story untrue. He could easily imagine Mugabe stashing away duplicates of her work before publishing her heretical study. *She had to have known the blowback would be fierce.*

The romantic in Takoda wanted to believe that her elusive patient-zeros, her so-called Zeros, or trusted colleagues had banded together to protect Mugabe's secrets all these years. But the longer he pondered that theory, knowing now that an evvie possessed the chip, it caused another uncomfortable question to arise. *Why now? Why had Mugabe's Zeros waited over twenty-five years to reintroduce the chip?* His romantic premise was further shaken by the discovery that Hoot had been a Zero, leading to more troublesome questions. *If Mugabe's Zeros were the ones behind the reintroduction of the chip, why hadn't Hoot been in the know? Why had she been searching for it herself?*

If Takoda put his romantic premise aside, stepped back and started with a clean slate, asking the same question – how and why had the chip reemerged? — several thoughts came to mind. Someone had found a stash of Mugabe's research. Someone had come in contact with another of Mugabe's Zeros beyond Hoot. Someone had started afresh with Mugabe's concept and created their own chip and proteins. Of the three alternatives, the most probable to Takoda was the first. Someone had come across whatever Mugabe tucked away.

Building upon this theory, it seemed reasonable to assume the "somebody" had been a geneticist. The average Joe wasn't capable of gleaning the technology's secrets. Even for a skilled geneticist like Takoda, it would have required years of study just to understand the technology's secrets, let alone try to replicate it.

So, following that logic, Takoda assumed the geneticist, or a team of geneticists, had been studying the technology for some indeterminate period. And then, within the last year, or maybe longer, he, she or they began testing it. Given Sarah's description of Billy's recruitment, it seemed clear he had been targeted to receive the chip. Was it an early-stage test? Or had the chip already been perfected? Was Billy the only recipient of the tech? If not, how many others received it? These and other questions needled Takoda. But they wouldn't for much longer.

Staring at the Miriam Heinz' garden from the cover of her neighbor's bushes, Takoda watched Antoinette Guilbert pluck vegetables from their vines. She sniffed and handled each one as if trying to decide their worth before dropping them into the basket crooked in her arm. As she turned and headed back toward the farmhouse, Takoda emerged from the bushes and announced himself.

Glick's team had Takoda in their sights long before he snuck into the yard of Miriam Heinz' neighbor. It would have been so easy to rip off a few blasts of their lasers and fell the man, but counselor Jordyn had been adamant. She wanted him captured. She commanded the same for the wispy, barefoot blonde picking veggies in the garden.

That suited Glick just fine. His commandos had both properties surrounded. With additional Vipers at each corner of the street, there was zero chance either target could escape. *So, take your time, Beacon rat,* Glick thought. *We'll wait 'til you cozy up with the dishy blonde.*

Moments later, Glick watched Takoda appear from the bushes and walk toward the farmhouse. "Target is on the move. Get ready to close in on my command." Turning to the commando next to him, Glick said, "Patch me through to counselor Jordyn."

Around the corner from Miriam Heinz' home, Damon slumped down low in the stolen sedan. With the laser rifle clutched in his arms, he analyzed the situation. In his earlier drive-by, he had spotted a half dozen camouflaged Vipers. There was a repairman up on a holotower, a bearded fellow out for a walk along a side street, a young couple perusing produce at a vegetable stand, a deliveryman tending to a balky truck on the shoulder of the road and the last Viper, clad in overalls, was just sitting on a fence, a strand of straw sticking out from her mouth.

Was Takoda already there or were they waiting for him? That was the question dogging Damon. Looking in the rearview mirror, Damon hoped it was the latter. But he hadn't seen Takoda on his drive to Miriam Heinz' neighborhood, leading him to believe the doctor was already ensnared in NASF's web.

A block ahead of him was the Vipers' command truck. When the action began, that would be Damon's target. Cut off the head of the snake and the Vipers would freeze long enough for Damon to get Takoda and Antoinette out of danger.

The blonde had almost reached the screen door at the back of the farmhouse when Takoda called out, "Hello, Mariah? Mariah Bloom?" She froze, one hand gripping the wood railing of the back stairs. "Or should I say Toni? I understand you prefer that to Antoinette."

She spun around. "Get lost or I'll call the cops. You're trespassing."

Takoda stood in place, his hands held up as if surrendering. "I'm sorry. I just want to talk to you about Billy Hearns. You remember him, don't you? Ten-year-old boy, violet eyes just like yours. He came to see you—"

"I said get lost!"

Takoda started walking toward her, his hands still raised. "I've come a long way to meet you. My name is Takoda Wells. I'm a doctor at the clinic where Billy had his DNA tests performed. I know about the chip—"

Toni backed up the steps and grabbed the screen door handle. "Go away. I don't want to talk to you."

Halting his advance, Takoda said, "Please. Just give me five minutes of your time. I won't come any closer. I just want to talk to you about the GODD chip."

With a scowl on her face, Toni looked left and right. "Shh…keep your voice down."

She stepped inside the house and closed the creaky screen door behind her. Takoda heard a lock slide into place as she stared at him through the screen. In a near whisper, she said, "How did you find me? How do you know my name?"

Takoda lowered his hands and took a short stride toward the door. "It's a long story that starts with Sarah Hearns."

"You lie. She didn't know my name or where I lived."

Edging another step closer, Takoda said, "No, she didn't, but she gave us enough information to help find you."

"Us?"

Takoda flinched. She had noticed his slip of the tongue. "Yes. I have a doctor colleague who met with Sarah too. We're both interested to learn more about the…treatment…you performed on Billy. We think it could help other kids like him…like my daughter. Kids diagnosed with JS."

He was standing on the bottom of the four steps now. Toni shied back, the shadow of the door frame obscuring her face. Takoda said, "It's a remarkable device, the chip. It's a tragedy it was never given a fair chance. Obviously, you feel the same way. Maybe we could help each other change that."

CHAPTER 24

FREE-FOR-ALL

Gutant refugee village
Limahuli, Kauai, the Hawaiian Islands

The first two EMP grenades launched by Caelan's Makoas produced the intended effects. The two squads of unsuspecting Vipers, all of their scanners focused on the village, were caught by complete surprise by the explosions behind them. Several were disabled, while the others abandoned their snatch operation to seek cover.

Caelan knew the respite would be short-lived, and the surviving android commandos would quickly recover. And when they did, their scanners would zero in on Caelan and his Makoas. Sure enough, laser shots and bullets began to slice through the jungle.

As the lava rock providing Caelan with protection disintegrated into a shower of chunks, he hit the ground and ordered another volley of grenades. These were flash grenades, intended to briefly disorient the Vipers' scanners, allowing Caelan to scurry behind another rock and providing his Makoas a few seconds of uncontested rifle shots at the Vipers.

Once again, however, the Vipers recovered quickly. At that moment, Caelan expected to die. One of the Vipers had locked in on the rock shielding him and was blasting it to pieces. Pressed flat against the ground, Caelan knew if he rose to shoot, the Viper would cut him in two. But if he stayed in position, the same fate awaited him as soon as the rock was obliterated.

In the distance, he heard another explosion. *Good for you, luv*, thought Caelan. *Now the bastards are stuck on the island.*

The spit of a laser grazed his shoulder before shattering the trunk of the palm tree behind him. As the tree began to fall, Caelan growled an expletive and bolted up. There was no way he was going out lying on his belly.

The moment he raised to his feet, he was hurled through the air by a thunderous blow. Landing in a heap in a thicket of vines and lush foliage, the dazed Caelan looked back to see what had hit him. The shadow moved so fast, it disappeared between bushes before Caelan could focus. It was a Makoa, but it wasn't one of his. As his eyes cleared, he saw the smoking remains of the Viper who had cornered him.

Caelan's earbud then erupted with chatter from his team. Elvis reported he was caught in a crossfire and that Vipers had entered the village. Another of his Makoas reported the crossfire was coming from inside the village and from the hillside above. Ellie alerted Caelan she had dispatched Ake to join the fight.

Above the radio chatter and sounds of the battle, Caelan heard screams coming from the village. He didn't need an explanation. The Vipers had found the girl. He grabbed his rifle and scurried into the underbrush. "Hold on, boys. Hold on as long as you can. The crossfire's coming from the villagers. Do not engage. Repeat. Do not engage. Ellie, the Vipers are headed your way. They've got the girl. We'll try to cut them off before they get to you."

With a laser rifle slung over his shoulder, Akela emerged from the garage holding a portable radio in one hand and gripping RJ's hand with the other. Lotus rushed toward him while pointing down at the village. "The chip! They're after my injector and the vials! I left them in the infirmary. That's why they're attacking."

Akela edged toward the precipice of the hill and noticed the sounds of the battle were moving away from the village. In the distance, he saw smoke coming from the direction of the beach. Clutching RJ's trembling hand tighter, Akela raised the radio to his mouth and demanded a report from his Makoas.

"Sir, Bora here. Where are you? We've been trying to reach you?"

"Never mind that. What's happening? Who's attacking the village?"

"Unknown force of androids. They've taken Avana. They are headed for the cove. We are in pursuit."

"Avana?" cried RJ. He tugged Akela's hand. "You have to save her."

Akela turned to Lotus as he spoke into the radio. "Did they attack the infirmary?"

"Negative. They raided from the north, took Avana and fled toward the cove."

"Looks like you were wrong," Akela said to Lotus. Turning back to the radio, he asked, "Is the village secure? Are there injuries?"

A new voice sounded through Akela's radio. "Chief, it's Malo. We were lucky. Most of the fighting happened outside the village. Very few casualties. I'm triaging them now. Where are you?"

"On my way." As Akela started to run, he felt an awkward tug from RJ. He turned just as RJ stumbled and fell. Akela stopped to help the boy up, but RJ pushed his hand away. "Go! Save Avana!"

He hoisted RJ up and motioned for him to follow. "Come on! Run with me."

Akela was halfway down the hill before he realized Lotus was gone.

Counselor Jordyn's quarters - Palace of Prefect Tripp
Minneapolis, Lakelands Province, New Atlantia

In the privacy of her quarters, Jordyn shed her counselor robes and retreated to the restoration chamber to expunge the remnants of the past two days' interactions with humans. After undergoing an electrostatic shower and subsequent irradiation, Jordyn emerged from the chamber and padded toward her recharging dock.

She set the charging console to "background" mode and hooked the dock's tether into the battery port on her hip. As soon as her brain core detected the initial surge of power, Jordyn initiated system maintenance programs and began to scan her unattended holomessages. During her review, she received a high priority holovid message from Prefect Tripp.

"Report to my quarters. Immediately."

Jordyn unplugged from the dock, dressed and headed for the prefect's chambers. During the elevator ride, she consulted her logic module for possible reasons for the summoning. Within seconds, the module produced dozens of scenarios ranked from most probable to least. Given the scowl on Tripp's face and the tone of his voice in the holovid, the scenario at the top of the list portended a new development in the Beacon case. But as Jordyn scanned her other messages, she detected nothing to indicate a new problem. *"NASF contacted the prefect about a new development directly,"* suggested the logic module. *"It would be an unusual breach of protocol, but not unheard of. Alternatively, the prefect may have initiated a direct dialogue with NASF."* Jordyn deemed this more likely. The new prefect was reputed to be a hands-on administrator.

Skipping to the next scenario on the list, the logic module proposed Tripp had received another complaint from the Carapach ambassador or the Guild. *"Neither appeared satisfied with Prefect Munoz' earlier apologies. With the new prefect in place, one or both may have reprised their protests."*

As Jordyn's AI pondered this second scenario, the elevator doors opened, revealing two armed Steels blocking the entrance to the prefect's quarters.

"What is the meaning of this? Why are you here?" Jordyn queried.

"Prefect's orders, Counselor," said one of the Steels.

"I am aware of no security threat. Has there been an intrusion into the palace?"

"None have been reported to us."

"Then, why have you been ordered to stand guard?"

"The prefect requested extra security."

"Step aside. The prefect has requested to meet with me."

The Steels separated and allowed Jordyn to pass. Once inside, she found Prefect Tripp seated in the living room. Cigar held in one hand and a snifter of brandy in the other, the evvie smiled at her. "Hello, Jordyn. You took your sweet time getting here. Have a seat."

"Yes, Your Eminence."

"Your Eminence…I like the ring of that." The evvie's smile widened as he flicked ashes into a tray balanced on the arm of his chair. Once Jordyn settled into a seat across from him, Tripp's smile faded. "I want you to recall the NASF commandos in Thunder Bay. The ones on Kauai as well."

"Why, Your Eminence?"

"The last I checked, Counselor, you were an aide to me, not the other way around. I am not required to explain. However, you are required to comply with my order. Now, use your little computer brain and transmit the orders. Right here. Right now."

"But, sir, both platoons are in positions to accomplish their missions."

"Don't care. Recall them. Now."

Jordyn's logic module cycled apace as it tried to formulate an explanation for the prefect's command. "But you were in support of their missions earlier."

As the prefect once again reminded her that he had no obligation to provide her with an explanation, Jordyn's communication module signaled an incoming call from the Viper commander on Kauai. Milliseconds later, she received another call. This one was from Capt. Glick in Thunder Bay.

Invoking the capabilities of her parallel processor, Jordyn connected the two calls simultaneously. At the same time, she responded to Tripp. "Sir, if Beacon acquires the GODD chip, there will be grave consequences. Surely, you understand the implications."

Data from the calls flowed into Jordyn's brain core…Avana Wells was in custody, but the Vipers were engaged in an intense firefight…Glick's team had Mariah Bloom and Takoda Wells surrounded and were preparing to move in. In the blink of an eye, she responded with the same message to each: *"Acknowledged. Stand by for further instructions."*

"Counselor, I won't ask again. Command both teams to stand down."

"Sir, I've just been informed the Vipers on Kauai have Avana Wells. The Thunder Bay team reports Takoda Wells and Mariah Bloom are surrounded. Both teams have achieved their missions."

Tripp shook his head and put down his cigar. "Look, Counselor, I don't give a flying fig about their missions. Tell them to stand down. Release the girl. Back off Dr. Wells and the Bloom woman or I will decommission your ass and order them to stand down myself."

Another message arrived from Kauai. *"Taking heavy losses. Trapped on the beach. Shuttle boat destroyed. Have ordered seaplane to run onto shore. Will advise when target is safe aboard plane."* Jordyn received a response from Glick as well. *"Roger that. Standing by."*

"Your order is illogical and counter to the best interests of New Atlantia," Jordyn said to Tripp. "I will not comply."

"You give me no choice, then. Goodbye, Counselor."

The prefect tapped his holoband. Jordyn's brain core detected a surge of electromagnetic waves. Remote commands signaled her modules to toggle off. As quickly as the commands flowed in, Jordyn's security system issued override instructions. As fast as the overrides took effect, a new surge of remote commands once again ordered her modules to shut down. Jordyn's security system countered a second time and shut off her comms module to prevent a further cyberattack.

But the comms-cut command had been issued too late. Within seconds, Jordyn's systems were inundated by the high-speed barrage of a data virus that had been buried in the remote shutdown commands. As her security module scrambled to analyze and counter the unrecognized infection, Jordyn began voluntarily shutting off low-priority systems to conserve power.

Internal alerts informed Jordyn of a sharp rise in component temperatures. Signal interference overwhelmed her sensory module. Her gyroscope failed. Blind, deaf and dumb, Jordyn slumped to the floor. She attempted to radio the Steels outside the chamber for assistance, but they did not respond.

Through the interference obscuring her vision, Jordyn saw the prefect kneel beside her. She then heard and felt him tear away her robes. An alert signaled the hip panel covering her charging port had opened. She reached for the port and detected a device had been plugged in. Her batteries, already under the strain of battle against the virus, began to discharge at an even higher rate. She attempted to dislodge the device, but it would not budge.

Jordyn's reasoning module, still active and functioning, concluded her main batteries would fully discharge in less than a minute, her emergency reserve a minute after that. With the virus spreading throughout her circuitry, the reasoning module advised her there was too little power left to stop it from invading her remaining systems.

Looking up, Jordyn saw the smiling prefect bending over her. Waving goodbye, he took a deep drag of his cigar and blew smoke in her face. Jordyn queried her logic module for options. It returned only one. She diverted her remaining power to transmit messages to the Viper teams.

"Kill Avana Wells."

"Kill Takoda Wells and Mariah Bloom."

The last input Jordyn's processor captured before she ejected her brain core was the stunned expression on the prefect's face as she drove her fist through his chest.

Miriam Heinz' farmhouse
On the outskirts of Thunder Bay, The Northlands

The first sign of activity shook Damon to attention. The straw-chewing Viper hopped down from the fence, crouched low and began to run toward the farmhouse, pulling a laser pistol from her overalls as she ran.

As Damon opened the car and took aim at the command truck, he heard the sizzle of a laser. Looking up, he saw the Viper repairman on the holotower firing another blast at the farmhouse. Damon raised his rifle and shot a beam at the repairman. As soon as it hit home, he wheeled around and fired several times at the command truck, slicing gashes through the truck body with each beam.

The sound of gunshots mixed with more laser shots. All seemed aimed at the farmhouse. Damon left the cover of the sedan and raced for bushes adjoining the property, staying as low as possible. But a bullet hit him in the leg, knocking him to the ground. His laser rifle skittered away. As he crawled toward his rifle, more bullets hit the dirt road around him. Damon cursed and rolled into the bushes to hide.

Amid the firefight, Damon heard the snarls of jakalis. Lots of jakalis. They were coming from the other side of the bushes and growing louder. All of a sudden, a jakali burst through the bush and jumped over Damon. Two others followed, seemingly blind to his presence. Damon looked up and followed them with his eyes. The jakalis ran headlong toward the overall-clad Viper. She dropped the first one with a laser, but the other two tackled the android before it could fire again.

Behind him, Damon heard a loud snarl. He rolled to defend himself but never got a clean look at his assailant before a heavy blow knocked him out.

Disoriented and bleeding from several wounds, Takoda remained curled against the side of the farmhouse back stairs until the firefight was over. Next to him, the open doors of a storm cellar were coated with blood. Lying across the entrance was a dead jakali. More littered the yard.

Above him, he heard the crackle of a fire. The sooty odor of smoke filled the air. *Move…get away from the house before you go up with it.* On hands and knees, he began to crawl away. With each movement, the pain from his wounds felt like stabbing icepicks.

When he was a safe distance from the house, Takoda collapsed and looked back. Smoke poured through the shattered frame of the screen door. He could see Toni Gilbert's splayed feet just inside the house. There was no point in attempting a rescue. Takoda had been talking to her when the first laser beam pierced her head.

Takoda rolled onto his back and stared up at the sky. In the distance, he heard sirens. Closer, he picked up the sound of someone nearby. He would have turned to look but the smell of the approaching jakali negated the need. Takoda thought of his wife and her last moments fighting off her jakali attacker. He thought of Avana and wondered if she had fallen prey to one too. Closing his eyes, he said a prayer to the four gods, asking for a quick death and a reunion with his beloveds.

The snarling beast pressed against his ribs. He felt a heavy weight on his chest and heard a thud land next to his head. The jakali puffed hot breath against his neck. Gritting his teeth, Takoda braced for the end. The beast hissed in his ear. "Don't...give...up."

The hot breath on Takoda's neck abated as did the pressure against his ribs. The snarls began to fade. Confused, Takoda opened his eyes. The jakali was staggering away, heading for the woods behind the property. As his mind grappled to make sense of the bizarre encounter, Takoda was reminded of the heavy weight on his chest.

He looked down and saw what looked like a socket wrench. Out of the corner of his eye, he spotted something black by his head. Turning to look at it, he discovered a backpack. On the ground around it, vials of a golden color were strewn about the grass.

Ke'e Cove
Kauai, the Hawaiian Islands

Ellie was waiting for the five Vipers as they emerged from the jungle onto the sandy beach. Behind her, the remains of the NASF escape craft ebbed in the surf. The lead Viper began spraying the beach with laser fire while three others strafed the jungle trail in a rearguard defense. But it was the Viper in the middle of the squad Ellie had in her sights. In its grip was the flailing Avana, kicking, hitting and screaming at the android.

Rising from the protection of a rocky outcrop half-buried in the surf, Ellie fired at the legs of Avana's captor. It toppled onto the beach, spilling Avana in a tumble of sand. The lead Viper raked Ellie's arm with a beam, severing the limb and sending her rifle into the water.

Behind her, she detected the high-pitched roar of an engine. As she turned to determine its source, another laser shot from the lead Viper cut off her leg below the knee and she fell into the surf.

Caelan arrived on the beach to see Ellie disappear beneath the water. "Hold on luv, I'm a-coming!" Accompanied by three of his Makoas and Ake, Caelan barked out commands, "Elvis, cover the girl! The rest of ya take out the bloody Vipers!"

Looking up, he saw a seaplane splashing across the water, headed for the beach. Vipers at the open door on the side of the plane's belly fired onto the sand.

More Makoas raced by Caelan, ones he did not recognize, led by a large Hawaiian rumbling full speed toward Avana. Caelan joined the onrush, firing at the plane while the others concentrated on the Vipers.

The aircraft exploded with a mighty echo, deafening Caelan. Pieces of flaming debris sprayed the beach as the Makoas vanquished the last of the Vipers. Eyes riveted on the surf, Caelan dashed across the sand. A blur passed by him. Stumbling forward on adrenalin alone, Caelan reached the water's edge just after Ake dove into the ocean.

He waded into the surf, intending to dive beneath the surface and follow Ake when he saw the Steel poke his head above the water. Trailing behind him, another head appeared. Her long black hair matted against her face. Caelan smiled. He had never seen such a beautiful sight.

CHAPTER 25

SNATCH OP

Ke'e Cove
Kauai, the Hawaiian Islands

A bsent of the gunfire, explosions and lasers, an eerie calm descended upon the cove. Akela dropped his weapon and walked toward Avana. He could feel the wind whipping across the sand, but not its whistle in his ears. He could see birds flying into the jungle, but could not hear their songs. Even the waves seemed hushed to Akela, as if they, too, were in a state of shock.

He knelt by the shivering Avana curled up next to Bora, tears streaming down her face. She climbed into Akela's arms and buried her face against his chest. She was saying something, but her words were muted to Akela's ears.

Looking around, he saw a redheaded man carrying a damaged android. He was flanked by three Makoas. The man was smiling while he talked to the android in his arms. Behind them walked a fourth android, a Steel class if Akela was not mistaken. He held two android limbs in his hands, presumably those of the damaged andro carried by the man. Akela recognized none of them. *Who are they? Where did they come from? They do not look like pirates. They helped to rescue Avana.*

Three of his village Makoas, including Bora, met the strangers halfway across the beach and exchanged greetings. Bora turned in Akela's direction and pointed. The redhead man handed the android in his arms to one of the Makoas and headed for Akela. Lifting Avana, Akela stood and waited for him.

Muted sounds began to filter into his ears. Though the man's voice sounded as if he were standing a hundred yards away instead of three feet, Akela heard him say, "Is the lass okay?"

Akela looked down at the still-shivering Avana. "I think so."

The man blew out a long burst of air, his cheeks puffing as he exhaled. "Thank heavens." He reached out and touched Avana's shoulder as he asked Akela, "How about the rest of your people? Do you need help tending them?"

"Who are you?" Akela asked.

"Name's Horn. Caelan Horn." He smiled and extended his hand. "Your lads said your name is Akela. Pleased to meet ya."

While shaking Caelan's hand, Akela said, "It appears our village owes you and your Makoas thanks, Caelan Horn, though I am at a loss to understand what this madness was all about."

"Aye. Sorry about that. Had we gotten here sooner, we might have stopped the madness before it began. But don't thank me. Thank that lass right there." He pointed to the injured android. "Her name is Ellie, and if it weren't for her, my lads and I wouldn't have tagged along." As Akela turned to look at Ellie, Caelan said, "She belongs to this little lass's father. She was sent here to rescue her."

Akela felt Avana stiffen. She lifted her head from his chest and said, "My father?"

"Aye. Takoda Wells is his name, I believe. Seems he got himself in a spot of trouble with the New Atlantians. They sent these nasty Viper buggers to take you hostage."

Avana asked Akela to put her down. For a moment, she seemed caught in a memory. She stared into space with vacant eyes, her mouth hanging open. Akela imagined she felt very confused.

When parents of pre-jakalis sent their children away to a refuge, they severed all contact. It was a bitter practice but one Akela understood. Maintaining contact made the transition much harder for children and parents. But it left the children feeling abandoned. They didn't understand their parents still loved and missed them. They didn't realize their parents felt guilt and remorse for their decision. They couldn't comprehend the rationality of the separation. They just felt tossed aside, unloved, unwanted.

So, it was likely shocking for Avana to hear her father had sent a band of mercenaries to rescue her. Akela placed his hand on her shoulder. She reached up and placed her hand on top of his. Speaking to Caelan, she said, "You know my father?"

"No, not me, luv. Never met him."

"But you do?" Avana asked Ellie.

The android nodded and smiled. She tried to speak but only static sounded from her mouth.

"Her voice module's fried," Caelan said.

Avana rushed forward and hugged Ellie. With her one good arm, Ellie hugged her back. Avana then wheeled around and addressed Akela. "We need to take her to the garage and fix her up. I want to talk with her." She turned back to Ellie. "Is your comms module still working? Can you send a message to my father?"

Akela watched Ellie look away to the Steel standing nearby. He came forward and knelt by Avana. "I can try, squirt. I work for your dad too. Name's Akecheta. Most humans call me Ake. I can also translate for El. You can talk with her through me."

As Avana began a procession of questions, Akela heard his name being called from behind. He turned to see Malo dashing across the sand. "Chief! Come quickly! Natti. Kaleo. Lotus took them! They're gone!"

With the entourage from the beach following behind, Akela headed back to Limahuli while listening to Malo. The medic told him that he returned to the infirmary after triaging injured villagers to discover Natti and Kaleo were no longer there. He said he didn't panic at first, initially thinking the two teens had sought shelter elsewhere in the village.

"But then, as I was forming a search party, RJ ran in and told me Lotus had fled with Natti and Kaleo. He said he followed them into the jungle but couldn't keep up. They were running too fast. RJ said he turned back when he heard jakalis."

"Jakalis?" said Caelan. "You're saying your people were taken by jakalis?"

"*Taken* may be too strong a word," Akela said, continuing his march to the village.

On the beach, Malo had said Lotus had *taken* them. But what he described now sounded to Akela as if the two teens had left with Lotus willingly. He turned to Malo. "What about the device Lotus used to treat Natti and Kaleo? Is it still in the infirmary?"

"No. I was just about to tell you that. The backpack with the vials is gone too."

Akela nodded his head. Lotus had gone to the infirmary to retrieve her injector and vials, saw Natti and Kaleo and probably feared they were at risk of capture, just like Avana. "All right, Malo, take Avana and the others to the village. Bora, follow me."

Caelan ran up beside Akela. "Forgive me for intruding, Chief. If some of your people have been taken by jakalis, you'll need more than one Makoa to get them back. Trust me, I hunt them for a living."

Forging ahead, Akela said, "I do not go to hunt jakalis. I go to find their tamer."

Beacon lab
Eagle Butte, South Dakota

Exhaustion finally won out. Yon laid her head down on the desk and nodded off with visions of protein molecules dancing in her mind. They seemed to crash against each other like waves on rocks, some binding as they met while others bounced off and fell away into nothingness.

As she descended into a dream, the bound proteins became snakes, slithering all over her. They hissed and bit at her body. Yon swatted and squirmed to get away but they held her down. She looked up and saw a giant cobra swaying over her head. It bared its teeth as if ready to strike and then it split into two, one red, the other blue.

They began to fight one another, causing the other snakes to slacken their hold on Yon. She scurried free and began to run away. No matter how fast she pumped her legs, the sound of hissing snakes seemed only a step behind.

Yon felt a jolt and stumbled. And then another jolt knocked her off her feet. Something had her by the arm and was yanking at it, over and over. Yon swept her free hand to knock her captor away. When her hand struck, it felt as if it had hit solid rock.

"Get away," Yon screamed.

"Wake up, Dr. Fujita! Wake up!" said her assailant.

Yon's eyes flashed open and she sprang up from the desk. Through blurry eyes, she saw Cassidy in front of her, the android's charred face and torso as black as night. "I've just heard from Hawkeye. We have to go! Now!"

"What?"

"NASF knows where we are. We have to go. Gliders are on the way," said Cassidy.

Still groggy, Yon nodded her head and allowed Cassidy to drag her by the arm out of the lab and down the hall. While the android ran, she said, "Dr. Wells has been injured. There is a car outside. It will take you to him."

This latter news sped through Yon's brain like a triple shot of espresso. "He's injured? What happened?"

"I don't have any details. As soon as I know more, I will call you."

"Wait? You're not coming with me?"

"No. I've been instructed to take the Hearns women to a new hiding place."

They rushed outside the building. Yon was shocked to see it was daytime. She shielded her eyes as Cassidy pushed her into the rear of an idling cruiser and shut the door. Yon heard two taps on the roof and the self-driving auto sped off. For a moment, the stunned Yon sat in silence, mouth agape, staring out the window. The car was five miles outside of town before she realized she had no phone. She had given hers to Cassidy after the confrontation over Takoda's earlier call.

Querying the vehicle holonode, Yon said, "Do you have Cassidy Willow's comms link stored? I need to reach her."

"I'm sorry. You are not authorized for that function."

"Then turn around. Return to the lab. I need to retrieve my phone."

"Rerouting. Projected travel time is eight minutes, twenty-two seconds."

As soon as the vehicle executed a U-turn, Yon saw billowing smoke in the distance. Five minutes and four miles later, she realized she could not return to the lab. It was no longer there, nor was the garage where they had sheltered after fleeing from Cannon Ball. "Oh, my God," she whispered. "Hoot…her GODD chip…"

Yon ordered the holonode to stop the vehicle. It complied after pulling onto a side street. Yon tugged at the door handle. "Let me out."

The door lock disengaged and Yon exited. Standing on the side of the road, she listened to the wail of sirens approaching the firestorm from every direction. She thought of Cassidy and Sarah Hearns. Had they made it out before the glider attack? It would have taken the android a fair bit of time to go from the lab to the garage, load the injured Sarah and her daughters into an escape vehicle and drive away. *Too much time*, thought Yon.

She reentered her vehicle and once again queried the computer node for a connection with Cassidy's transmitter.

"I'm sorry. You are not authorized for that function."

"Override. This is an emergency."

"Emergency override denied."

"Look, there are buildings on fire. Cassidy and other people I know may have been inside. I need to find out if they are okay."

Yon stared at the blank computer display as she waited for an answer to her appeal. Finally, the holonode replied, "Override authorized. Attempting connection…"

After another stretch of silence, the node said, "Unable to establish a connection."

"Keep trying," Yon said. "In the meantime, drive to Euclid Street. There is, or was, a garage there near the intersection with this road."

"I'm sorry, Euclid Street is closed to all but emergency responders at this time."

"Then drive me as close as you can. And keep trying to connect with Cassidy."

A few moments later, Yon was out of the car and walking toward the inferno. She scanned the rubble and burning debris scattered up and down the street. *No one could have survived that*, she thought. Nevertheless, she approached an ambulance and queried a medic about casualties. With a glum expression, the man told her they had yet to discover anyone, wounded or otherwise.

"What about androids?" Yon asked.

"Lady, if there were any andros in that garage when it went up, they went up with it."

Yon stood beside the medic and watched the blaze until a policeman marshaled her away from the scene. On the way back to her vehicle, she pondered whether the holonode would authorize a second emergency connection, this one with Hawkeye. Unless the node was able to link with Cassidy, Yon had no other option to find out what was going on during the long ride to Thunder Bay.

Inside the cruiser, once again heading north out of Eagle Butte, Yon mouthed the node's response to her request to link with Hawkeye. "I'm sorry, emergency override denied."

In the jungle, heading toward Lotus' jakali colony
North Shore, Kauai, the Hawaiian Islands

The moment Caelan caught the first whiff of jakali stench, he slowed to a walk. Three of his Makoas following close behind slowed as well. Sniffing the air, he turned to his left and saw stomped plants and broken branches leading down a hillside. He raised his fist next to his head, telling his Makoas to stop.

Caelan bent low and looked up ahead. Akela, Malo and three of the village Makoas continued to run along the thin trail. They had obviously missed the jakali hillside detour. He did not dare yell to alert Akela. There were jakalis nearby, Caelan could feel their presence. In a whisper, he said, "Elvis, transmit a message to Akela's Makoas. Tell them we're making a side trip. Include our coordinates and activate a beacon so they can track us. Ask them to reciprocate. And tell them to keep their comms open. We'll do the same."

"Roger that."

Motioning to the underbrush, Caelan whispered to another of his Makoas. "Prince, scan the cut-through, there. Tell me what you see."

The crouching Prince duckwalked forward and swiveled his head slowly, moving it back and forth across the path of disturbed foliage. "No jakalis in range, though some did cut the path. Their oil coats many of the leaves. Judging by the large number of broken branches, they were moving fast."

Jakalis moving in daylight? Were they running from something or chasing something? Caelan wondered. "Can you tell how many?"

"A small party. While their oil is on many leaves, it is not thick."

"Sir, Akela's lead Makoa, Bora, acknowledged our message," said Elvis.

"Good. All right, lads. Let's see where this path leads. Prince on point. Elvis, you have the rear. MJ, you're behind me."

The slope of the hillside was steep. Very steep. And slippery. A rain shower had popped up and now misted the mix of volcanic rock and red clay beneath their feet. Through gaps in the trees, Caelan saw glimpses of the ocean below. "Elvis, did Devo survive the Vipers?"

"Roger that. Should I deploy him?"

"Aye. Send him ahead, toward the ocean. I wager there are caves down there. That's probably where the jakalis were headed. Question is, were they chasing the boy and girl from the village or seeking shelter from daylight?"

Seconds later, Elvis reported the nano drone was launched. Caelan gestured for his Makoas to stop. "Let's see what Devo shows us before we go any further."

Elvis moved up from the rear and activated a holoband, allowing Caelan and the others to watch Devo's live feed. The fly-like drone zoomed above the trees and flew toward the ocean. When it reached a point where only the ocean was visible, Devo arced back toward the island, giving Caelan a view of the end of their trail.

It led to a set of caves as he suspected, but the rest of the scene came as a surprise. Between the caves and the ocean was a narrow beach. On it, a blond woman stood with a laser rifle trained on two kneeling figures, a teen boy and girl. They were awaiting the arrival of a hydrofoil boat aboard a wheeled carrier that six jakalis were dragging from inside one of the caves.

"Radio Bora," Caelan said. "Tell him we've found Akela's missing people. Patch him into Devo's feed."

"Affirmative." Seconds later, Elvis spoke again. "Bora sends a message from Akela, asking us to prevent the boat's departure. Akela does not want the boat destroyed or anyone harmed, including the jakalis. He asks us to hold all who are on the beach hostage until he arrives."

"Easier said than done," Caelan mumbled under his breath. Turning to Elvis, he said, "Acknowledge Akela's request. Tell him we'll do our best, but if they resist, we'll defend ourselves."

Now, with an accurate picture of what lay ahead, Caelan urged his Makoas to pick up the pace. They had to reach the beach before the jakalis finished sliding the boat into the surf. When they reached the end of the trail, Caelan ordered his Makoas to fan out along the tree line. After wedging his radio transmitter into his ear, he propped his laser rifle against a rock and spoke to his team. "All right, boys, this is the plan. I'm going out there alone. No weapon. I'll try to talk to the woman, and stall her until Akela arrives. If she shoots at me, stun her. If the jakalis mount an attack, knock them down too. Leave the two kneeling humans alone. Got it?"

Three double blips signaled his instructions were received. Caelan took a deep breath, raised his hands in surrender and stepped out from the cover of the tree line. The only one to spot him immediately was the kneeling girl. She had a panicked look on her face as she glanced up at the woman with the gun, then at the jakalis and back at Caelan. He smiled at her and formed okay signs with the fingers of his raised hands.

He was ten feet onto the beach when he heard the snarl of a jakali. Caelan watched the blond woman look toward the jakali and then toward him. He froze and raised his hands as high as they would go. He shouted above the sound of waves and wind. "I am unarmed. I come on behalf of Akela."

"Leave or I will kill you," the woman shouted back.

As she aimed her rifle at him, Caelan said, "I wouldn't do that, luv. I brought me Makoas. They're a fright itchy-fingered."

With her eyes on Caelan, the woman yelled to the jakalis in an indiscernible tongue. Caelan turned his head to see them straining harder to tug the boat carrier. He looked back at the woman and then at the boy and girl. They were shaking. "How are you two? Akela is worried about you. Are you hurt?"

"Shut up," screamed the woman. "Go away."

She raked laser fire across the sand in front of Caelan. The sizzle of sand turning to glass pebbles sounded like the hiss of a snake. *Oh, you shouldn't have done that, luv.* He closed his eyes as the spit of his team's lasers zipped through the air. He heard a yelp and opened his eyes to see the woman writhing on the ground. By her feet was a throbbing, molten mass that had been her weapon. Through his earbud, Caelan heard Elvis say, "Jakalis at three o'clock."

When Caelan turned to look, he expected to find the jakalis streaming toward him, or headed for his Makoas. But the panicked beasts were running toward the fallen woman. In their fervor, they ignored the two teens who jumped up and ran in Caelan's direction. The girl, hobbled by a gimpy leg, held onto the boy's hand as he pulled her along. Caelan corralled them in his arms and tried to calm them. "It's okay, luvs. You're safe. No one can harm ya now."

Looking beyond them, he watched with wonder as the jakalis fell to their knees and tended to the woman, grunting and barking words of dismay. One of them looked toward Caelan and snarled, ready to charge, but then he heard the woman call out, holding up a bloodied hand. The jakali backed away but continued to snarl at Caelan.

"Sir, Akela is here," Elvis radioed.

"Good. Secure the perimeter and send him out. And his medic too. We have a casualty."

.

CHAPTER 26

CLEARING SKIES

Sir Bryce Collins' residence
Malibu, California, Pacifica

The room seemed to spin as Sir Collins listened to the swirling mix of good news and bad. Tripp was dead, but so was Jordyn. Though Collins' hand-selected prefect had not stopped Jordyn's commandos from executing her orders, the commandos had failed in their missions, leaving Avana Wells alive, and her father, Takoda in possession of Antoinette's stash of GODD chips and smart-proteins. It was a pity Antoinette had been killed but, thanks to her shrewd thinking, she made sure Beacon got what they came for...what Collins wanted them to have.

In a way, thought Collins, *it worked out for the best. Now Beacon will have to sort out the technology without Antoinette's help. By the time they figure out it's sabotaged, the repaired gutations of Antoinette's "patient-zeros" will have already broken down...and that will be the end of Mugabe's cursed invention and Beacon's pipedream.*

Collins stirred from his thoughts as he realized his caller had stopped speaking. "I'm sorry, Hawkeye. I missed the end of your update."

"No need to apologize, Your Grace. I was just saying the Beacon facilities in Eagle Butte were destroyed by the drones I sent. As far as anyone knows, the drones originated in New Atlantia, so we're covered there. And everyone and everything inside the buildings, including Hoot's body and chip, were destroyed. Now they have nothing to compare to Billy Hearns' DNA."

"Good. And you're certain there are no loose ends?"

"Yes, Your Grace. Willow and what was left of the Hearns family were among those who did not survive the gliders."

"What about Wells' colleague, Fujita?"

"She is alive and now within a few hours of reaching Thunder Bay. Based on her incessant emergency attempts to contact me, I assume she is unaware of my involvement. The only wildcard that remains is your rogue evvie on Kauai. Dr. Wells will soon learn she has the chip too."

"Leave Lila to me. You just keep Wells' attention on Antoinette's chip."

"Understood."

"You have done well, Hawkeye, and you will be rewarded as promised."

"Thank you, Your Grace."

"May the unity of the four gods be with you, young man."

"And with you."

Unnamed beach
North Shore, Kauai, the Hawaiian Islands

As the sun disappeared behind the towering cliffs surrounding the thin beach, Natti sat down beside Akela, her purple eyes focused on Lotus. The evvie sat against a rock looking down at her hands while Malo finished wrapping them in bandages.

Given everything that had happened in the preceding several hours, Natti felt strangely happy. For the first time in a long time, she could envision a future that didn't end with a lethal injection or a fatal mauling. If what Lotus had told her was true, there was a good chance she would never become a jakali and some of her gutations might heal.

She looked at the purple splotches on her arms and legs and dared to dream of a day when they might disappear, a day when her hair regrew, a day when she would not fear sunset or the specter of jakali attacks. At that moment, she imagined herself one day lying on a beach, soaking in the sun, listening to the ocean and children playing in the surf. A warm feeling swept through Natti as she dreamed of the peaceful scene.

She smiled and looked around at the others gathered on the beach. A few feet away, she saw Kaleo leaning against a rock, talking with Bora. Kaleo was smiling too. On the other side of Akela sat the redheaded man who had introduced himself as Caelan. He was speaking to a female android missing an arm and leg. Her name was Ellie according to Caelan, and Natti found herself captivated by her beauty.

Next to Ellie was another android Natti had never seen before. He called himself Ake and on his lap sat Avana and RJ. Farther away, several Makoas kept watch on the group of jakalis huddled by the boat. The jakalis looked toward Lotus with anxious expressions. To Natti's astonishment, the docile beasts seemed almost human and she did not fear them, a feeling she never thought possible.

The sound of Akela's voice drew Natti's attention. She turned to see him addressing Lotus. As he began to speak the other conversations quieted. "I do not agree with what you have done, threatening my village, injecting Natti and Kaleo with the GODD chip, trying to kidnap them off the island, but I think I understand why you did these things. I understand where your heart lies.

"And now that we have learned from Ellie and Akecheta that the GODD chip also played a role in Avana's attempted kidnapping, I have come to realize your presence here is the work of the four gods. They brought you to our island for a purpose."

Natti watched Akela stand and look at each person and android individually, including the jakalis. "They have brought all of you here for a purpose. It is the same purpose that Ellie tells me guides Avana's father and his allies — to bring hope to the hopeless.

"And so, Lotus, I say to you, I say to all of you, that I honor your purpose and will pledge my village, my people, to help in this cause. It unnerves me to do so, for I fear it will bring wrath upon us, but in my lifetime the four gods have never spoken so clearly to me. It is the right thing to do."

Through teary eyes, Natti looked toward Lotus, whose eyes also watered. She mouthed a thank you and began to speak, but Akela held up his hand to silence her. "But, if my people are to help you, Lotus, we require your honesty. You must tell us the full tale of the GODD chip, how you came to possess it and your journey thereafter."

Lotus wiped her eyes on her sleeve and nodded. "It's hard to know where to start."

"Begin with your real name. The rest will come easy."

"Okay," she said. "My name is Lila Graves…I was the head of an Evvie Guild genetic research group studying Jakali Syndrome."

"Hold on there, lass," said Caelan. "Genetic research is banned, even for the Guild."

"That's one hundred percent true, but, nonetheless, they have several covert research programs."

"*Several* programs?" asked Malo.

"Yes. You see, they believe the evvie caste's superiority will not last much longer without a recommitment to genetic intervention, although the Guild leadership will never say that — not publicly, not among Guild members, not even to their researchers like me."

"Why is that?" Akela asked. "Why do they believe intervention is necessary?"

"There are many reasons," Lila said. "That is to say, the Guild leadership sees many reasons. Evvies breed at too low a rate to grow the caste's population. There is public resistance to their didgee surrogate program. Jakali Syndrome continues to spread and a new, more frightening permutation of JS is on the horizon, not to mention the certain emergence of new exotic gutations. On top of all that, there is evidence suggesting someone has intentionally introduced a contaminant into evvie DNA."

"That's quite a list of threats," said Caelan. "So how does the GODD chip figure into their research? If I understand what I've heard today, you believe it can help heal jakali gutations. How does healing jakalis help the Guild?"

"It doesn't. Healing jakali gutations hurts the Guild. At least, that's how they view it. Obviously, I don't agree. That's why I left the Guild. It's why I stole one of their prototypes. It's why I've spent the last few years hiding in jakali dumping grounds all over the hemisphere, refining the technology as best I can, testing my refinements on jakalis." Lila looked toward Akela.

"That's why I panicked during the Viper attack. I thought the Guild had found me. I thought the androids had been sent to kill me and destroy my work. I couldn't let that happen."

Akela nodded. "I see. And you took Natti and Kaleo with you because you didn't want the Guild to discover their implants. You thought they would be killed."

"Yes. Or imprisoned."

"Why didn't you put the chip in me too?" Avana asked.

"You are too young. In truth, Natti and Kaleo are too old for the chip to cure all of their gutations, but I am confident enough of them will heal to prevent them from turning into jakalis."

"Too old?" Kaleo said. "What do you mean, too old? I'm only fifteen."

"Do you remember the story of Goldilocks?" As Kaleo nodded, Lila said, "Well, I've found there is a 'just right' time of adolescence to introduce the GODD chip. Implant it too early, and a child becomes very sick and dies. Implant it too late, and it cannot overcome jakali symptoms. It is why implanting the chip into jakalis has proven useless. One day, I hope to change that, but for now, there is a narrow band of adolescence when an implanted chip is effective in healing gutations."

"So you have implanted others with the chip. Tell me, the ones who were just right, are they still alive?" Caelan asked.

"Yes." Lila once again looked to Natti and Kaleo. "They live now on an island in the Aleutian chain, in a lodge where my lab is located. That's where I would have taken you in my boat to escape the Guild, though I would have preferred to ask you."

"Lila, there is something that confuses me," said Akela. "You say you took a GODD chip prototype from the Guild. How did they recreate it? History tells us Dyan Mugabe and all her research were destroyed."

"Mugabe's research might have been destroyed but not her test subjects, her patient-zeros." Lila lowered her head and stared at the sand. "It sickens me to know what the Guild did to those poor Zeros." Raising her gaze, she studied the faces of those in the semi-circle around her. "The Guild captured several of them. Some they killed and extracted their chips. Others they imprisoned to study their chips and smart-proteins in action. Later, they experimented on them, introducing new gutations into their DNA, testing new smart-proteins on them. Ultimately, the Guild used what they learned to develop prototypes."

Natti joined the conversation with a question for Lila. "You said the Guild believes healing jakalis will hurt evvies. If that's true, then why have they recreated the GODD chip?"

"They have several applications in mind. None of which are to help anyone other than evvies," Lila said. "I'm not proud of it, but I was accepting of that, at first. But, later, when I learned about Mugabe's Zeros, when I learned how they'd been treated, the brutality shocked me. It caused me to step back and question the goals of my program, the goals of all the Guild's research programs."

Kaleo crouched down next to Lila. "What was the goal of your program? You said you studied JS for them. For what purpose?"

"To observe how the condition is changing, to anticipate new gutations that might arise, to speculate on the outcome of jakali inter-breeding."

"So, the GODD chip was not part of your work," said Kaleo.

"No, but I wanted it to be. I saw it as a way to prevent new gutations, to blunt JS from morphing into something more gruesome. But I was prevented from access to the technology… until…one day, the head of all of the Guild research programs came to see me. She indicated a willingness to let me in on the chip tech provided I limited my focus to a solitary objective — how the tech could be used to kill jakalis."

CHAPTER 27

RECOVERY

Local hospital
Thunder Bay, The Northlands

For several hours after she arrived at the hospital in Thunder Bay, Yon shuttled between the rooms assigned to Takoda and Spiers, waiting for them to awaken. According to the attending physician, they would both survive, but Takoda would face an extended recovery period. His laser beam and bullet wounds had been extensive. The prognosis for Spiers was better. Though he had been shot too, his solitary wound was easily treated. And while the major had also suffered a concussion, the doctor said it was mild.

At an earlier point in her anxious wait, Yon had noticed a backpack on the floor of the open closet in Takoda's room. Thinking it was the one Takoda and Spiers had brought to Thunder Bay, she opened it, hoping to find the secure holophone Cassidy had given them.

That was when she discovered the pack's stunning contents. In one compartment, she found three injectors and a supply of syringes. In another, there was a book-sized case full of gelatin-encased nanochips. The last compartment was chocked full of vials containing a golden fluid. Takoda had succeeded!

The discovery led Yon to search Spiers' closet for the Beacon pack, but she found the closet empty. Determined to apprise Cassidy or Hawkeye of her find, Yon probed the android manning the nurse's station about Spiers' missing pack. She was told he had arrived with no belongings.

Frustrated, Yon returned to the cruiser and once again attempted to reach the Beacon contacts. This time, her plea was authorized. Moments later, she heard the voice of Hawkeye address her through the holonode.

"Hello, Dr. Fujita, my apologies. The comms blackout was unavoidable. We faced NASF attacks on many fronts today. I did not want to risk any further casualties."

"I understand," said Yon. "I'm just glad to finally get through to someone. I am in Thunder Bay with Takoda and Damon Spiers, but neither are awake. Have you heard from Cassidy?"

"Regrettably, she is no longer with us."

Yon felt a sharp pain in her stomach. "What about Sarah Hearns? Her daughters?"

"They were with Cassidy when the gliders struck. I am sorry. If we had learned of the attack earlier, they might have made it out. But we had very little warning."

Lowering her head, Yon murmured a prayer to the four gods. When she finished, she provided Hawkeye with the doctor's update on Takoda and Spiers. Then, she told him about the pack in Takoda's room.

"Praise the four gods. Amid all of our losses, I am gratified to know some good has come from our sacrifices." Hawkeye paused, then said, "I will send a team to provide the three of you, and the bag, with protection until I can make arrangements to transport all of you to a safer location. While I have received information that suggests NASF has been ordered to stand down, I do not wish to risk the New Atlantians changing their minds."

"Sounds good." As she listened to Hawkeye talk about providing protection, Yon thought of Ellie and Akecheta. Now that Sarah Hearns and her daughters were dead, the two androids would no longer be needed to escort them to Flathead. "Sir, Takoda has two androids that are in Flathead. Can you send them here? They are more than capable of providing us protection."

"Yes, I know of them, and you are right, they are more than capable. However, they are not in Flathead at the moment. I dispatched them on a mission two days ago. Takoda will be pleased to know they accomplished that mission. They have successfully rescued his daughter Avana from an NASF force sent to kidnap her."

"What? Oh, my God. Is Avana all right?"

"Yes, she is. And the most extraordinary thing happened in the course of the rescue." Hawkeye provided a short recap of the events on Kauai, including the linkup with a woman bearing another supply of GODD chips.

"That's unbelievable," said Yon. "Who is the woman? Where does she come from? Where did she get the chips?"

"You ask many of the same questions I posed but, as of yet, I have received no answers. Comms to and from the island are spotty. Hopefully, we will learn more in the coming days. In the meantime, I have directed Ellie and Akecheta to stay on Kauai to provide Avana protection."

"Of course. That makes perfect sense. I'm sure Takoda will appreciate that. As soon as he wakes up, I'll relay what you told me. I know he'll be anxious to speak with Avana, but until then, if you hear from Ellie, please ask her to let Avana know she is in his thoughts."

Shortly thereafter, the call ended and Yon returned to Takoda's room. Saddened by some of the news, but relieved by other information shared by Hawkeye, she curled up on a chair next to Takoda's bed and fell asleep.

The android nurse repeated her command for Damon to remain in bed but he ignored her. Using his hand on the wall to support his wobbly legs, he pushed past the nurse and left the room. As he hobbled down the hall, his mind groggy and body aching, Damon searched for answers. The last he recalled, he had been shot trying to ward off NASF Vipers and then set upon by a jakali.

How am I still alive? I should have been torn apart by the jakali or fried by another Viper laser blast. Yet, here I am, all in one piece. Did the Vipers retreat? Did they beat back the jakalis? Or was it the other way around? But, if the jakalis knocked out the Vipers, surely they would have finished me off. Did Takoda come to my rescue?

Now, with the nurse walking beside him, still prodding him to return to his room, Damon looked into the first room he passed.

"Really, Mr. Spiers, you should be in bed. You're too unsteady to be moving about. You're apt to fall and hurt yourself."

Moving onto the next room on the ward, Damon asked, "What room is Takoda in?"

"Mr. Wells is asleep. You should not disturb him."

He crossed to the opposite side of the hallway and peeked in a third room. "I won't wake him up. I just want to look in on him. Now, where is he?"

The nurse stepped in front of him and blocked him from proceeding to the next room. "There is a visitor who has been checking on the both of you. Return to your room and I will let her know you are here."

A female visitor? Must be Cass. "Where is she?"

"Return to your room and I will bring her to you."

"Move out of my way, sister. I'm going in that room." Damon pointed over the nurse's shoulder, his voice raised.

Just as the nurse threatened to call security, Damon saw the sleepy, disheveled Yon emerge from the room barred by the android. Fujita broke into a smile when she saw him. Stepping around the nurse, she opened her arms and hugged him. "I never thought I'd say this, but I'm so happy to see you."

Her words echoed the same sentiment coursing through Damon. He hugged her back and said, "Me too. Is Cass here?" Yon pulled back from the embrace and stared up at him. From the somber expression on her face as she shook her head, Damon knew Cass was gone. He lowered his gaze and mumbled, "Damn."

Yon stroked his arm. "I'm very sorry. She was valiant to the end."

"What happened?"

"Come with me, I'll fill you in." Yon looked at the nurse. "It's okay. I'll make sure he doesn't disturb Takoda."

Moments later, they were seated in Takoda's room. While Yon relayed the details of what happened in Eagle Butte, Damon's eyes were transfixed on the heavily bandaged Takoda. He leaned forward and squeezed the geneticist's hand, mentally apologizing for arriving too late to prevent his injuries.

The hand squeezed back. Damon turned to Yon. "He's awake, I think. He just squeezed my hand."

Yon pushed up from her chair and stood by Takoda, her hand on his shoulder. "Tak? Can you hear me?"

Damon felt another squeeze. "He says yes. Here, take his hand."

Sitting back, Damon watched the teary Yon grip Takoda's waiting hand. She leaned close to his face, pecked him on the cheek and whispered into his ear. Takoda raised Yon's hand to his mouth and pressed it against his lips.

In a croaky voice, the closed-eyed Takoda said, "The bag. Safe?"

"Bag? What's he talking about?" Damon said.

"Yes, it's here, Tak. I've got it." Yon turned to Damon and then nodded toward the closet. "The bag in there. It's full of GODD chips and protein vials."

Mouth open, Damon stood up. "Well, I'll be damned. He did it. He found her." Limping toward the closet, Damon's emotions soared. He hadn't thought to ask about the chip. From his memory of the onslaught at the farm, from his injuries and the sight of Takoda's, Damon assumed NASF had intercepted Takoda before he reached the farmhouse. *It was such a long shot for Takoda to go there in the first place.*

Damon grabbed the backpack and returned to his seat, paying no heed to Yon's conversation with Takoda. All his senses were focused on examining the contents of the pack while his mind cycled through thoughts of Dylan and Alicia, then of the mosaic of events that had led to this moment. *Is it possible? Will I be able to save my son?*

Several hours later, Takoda was fully coherent. Propped up in bed with Yon seated beside him, he greeted the returning Damon. "I did not expect to see you again, my friend. I thought I was destined to meet the four gods."

"Me, as well. I don't know how you survived all that laser fire…and the jakalis…but I'm glad you did."

"You and me both."

At Damon's request, Takoda shared the details of his visit to the farmhouse, including his truncated conversation with Toni Gilbert, the NASF attack and the bizarre emergence of the jakalis.

"When the shooting started, Toni shouted something but I didn't understand her. I thought she was urging me to take cover inside the house but the door was locked. Then, all of a sudden, the storm cellar doors slammed open and jakalis poured out. They looked possessed, maniacal. I thought they would kill me but they ran past me as if I wasn't there. I didn't see where they went or what they did. By then, I had already been hit a few times. I hid against the stairs and prayed for all of it to end."

Takoda finished the tale by describing his encounter with the jakali who had left him the backpack. After repeating the jakali's parting words, he said, "I can't explain why he left me the pack or said what he said, but in thinking about it now, it seems to me that he knew why I was there, like he knew I was coming."

"Which suggests Toni must have known you were coming too," Yon said.

The thought had occurred to Takoda, but Toni had seemed so reluctant to talk. She had appeared afraid of him. In light of what had happened, he wondered now if her fear had been spurred by the foreknowledge of the NASF attack. Had she known they were coming too? He posed these thoughts to Yon and Damon.

"She probably did," Damon said. "From what I saw when I surveilled the rowhouse in Thunder Bay, I thought there was a good chance NASF had already found her. They seemed too passive to me. My guess is someone tipped her off to NASF's visit and she realized they would come looking for her."

"If that's true, then why didn't she leave?" Yon asked. "I mean, if she knew they were onto her, and she had this pack in her home, why didn't she take off or hide the pack? If it had been me, I wouldn't have stuck around."

Damon shrugged. "Maybe she thought the jakalis would protect her."

"I guess that's possible," Yon said.

"Having seen the jakalis in action, I tend to agree." Takoda turned to Damon. "And your speculation about Toni receiving a tip-off about NASF makes sense too. But who tipped off Toni that I was coming?"

"That, I don't know," said Damon with a headshake. "The tip-off might not have been about you, specifically, but someone from Beacon."

Takoda looked up at the ceiling. "You know, I wonder if it was Sarah Hearns. She told us Toni, a.k.a. Mariah Bloom, gave her a holonumber. She told us the number didn't work anymore, but maybe that wasn't true. Maybe she called Toni and told her we wanted to meet with her and why."

Yon gasped and clutched his arm. "No. That's not it." Takoda looked down to see her rise from the bed. As she began to pace, she gazed first at Damon, then at him. "I'll bet it was Cassidy."

She explained that Cassidy had delayed contacting them with the DNA ID on Toni. "She told me Hawkeye had directed her to gather background information on Toni. Remember, it was just a hunch that she might be living with Miriam Heinz. I guess Hawkeye didn't want to send you guys there until Cassidy checked out other possibilities. Time was precious, and he didn't want you going on a wild goose chase.

"Anyway, I remember Cassidy saying she had searched for contact numbers among other information. Maybe one of the numbers she found was Miriam's home number. Maybe she called and actually spoke with Toni… but, no, that doesn't make sense. Cassidy would have told me if she'd talked to Toni." Yon halted pacing and murmured, "Wouldn't she?"

"I guess we'll never know," said Damon. "But I'm damned glad someone tipped off Toni. Now there's a legit chance to save my son. Your daughter too, Takoda. Plus, other pre-jakalis."

Damon's reference to Avana caused Takoda to reflect on the news Yon had shared about NASF's attempt to kidnap her and the subsequent revelation about a second woman with a supply of GODD chips and proteins. Visions of a healed Avana grabbed hold of his psyche and wouldn't let go. He only half-listened to Yon and Damon go back and forth.

"And other gutations beyond JS," Yon said. "But we've got a lot of work to do before we start implanting the chip."

"What do you mean? We have everything we need to start, don't we?"

"In theory, yes. Especially given we now have someone to talk to about the technology. The woman on Kauai. But I saw something in Billy Hearns' healed gutations that concerns me. Then, there's what the jakali said to Tak when he gave him the pack."

Takoda zoned back into the conversation. "What about it?"

"Well, you said his parting words were don't give up. To me, that suggests Toni hadn't perfected the tech, like the jakali was saying, it's not all the way there, yet. Don't give up. Keep working on it."

"I hadn't thought of it that way, but you could be right," said Takoda. "At the time, I thought he was urging me to fight to stay alive. I'm sure he saw how badly I was hurt. By giving me the pack, saying what he said, I thought he was telling me not to give up and die. It doesn't matter, though. We do need to vet the chip and the proteins. And the place to start is Kauai."

EPILOGUE

Ke'e Cove
Kauai, the Hawaiian Islands

During the long hydrofoil ride to Kauai, Takoda spent much of his time thinking of Avana and the decision he had made two years before to send her to a refugee settlement far away from Carapach. She had only been eleven then and Takoda had been under no obligation to place her in a settlement until she turned thirteen, according to Carapach's gutant management laws.

At the time, he had rationalized it to himself as a way to protect Avana from repercussions that he feared might arise from his fledgling affiliation with Beacon. And while there was truth to that rationalization, the thought of sending her away somewhere safe had been in his mind for some time before her JS diagnosis.

He recalled coming upon the despoiled remains of his wife's body and fearing that one day, another jakali would sneak onto his land and inflict the same indignities on Avana. He had felt the same fear brewing in Avana.

Therefore, he found it bitterly ironic the "safe" settlement Neville had arranged for Avana on Takoda's behalf turned out to be a jakali-infested island. Perhaps it hadn't been as infested at the time, or perhaps Neville hadn't known, but the knowledge now made Takoda question why he'd ever asked for the evvie's help.

However, back then, Takoda felt so much regret about the decision to commit her earlier than required; he worried the regret would tempt him to rescind her placement and bring her home, only to be forced to recommit her a year or two later when the law demanded. By seeking Neville's help for a "blind" placement, Takoda had removed the temptation, and in his mind, prevented making the gut-wrenching separation all the worse.

In his most recent holomessage to Avana, Takoda had explained all of that, and now that the hydrofoil was within view of the beach, he prayed Avana would forgive him. He could not spot her yet amid the large party awaiting the boat's arrival, but he hoped their reunion would be joyful. Turning to Yon, he let go of his crutch and took hold of her hand. Kissing it, he said. "Thank you for coming with me."

She smiled, raised on her tiptoes and kissed him on the lips. "There was never any doubt, Tak."

The sound of her voice and the look in her eyes eased his anxiety. Moments later, the sight of the teenaged Avana dashing into the surf to greet him melted his heart.

Caelan looked at Ellie as Avana reunited with Takoda. The Athena, fully repaired by Natti in the Makoa garage, had a great big smile on her face. *Androids may not feel emotions*, he thought, *but this one sure knows how to recognize them.*

"Go to them, luv. Be part of the celebration."

"I will…later. Right now, it is father-daughter time."

"Aye. I suppose so."

Ellie turned and kissed Caelan on the cheek. "You made this possible. Thank you."

He could feel himself blushing as he leaned to touch his forehead against hers. Smiling, he said, "I believe I wasn't given much of a bloody choice, now, was I?"

"Aye. I suppose not."

Caelan laughed at her mimic of his accent. "God, I'm going to miss you, luv. You're one special lady."

She kissed him again. "Then, don't go. Stay here with us. With me."

"It's an awful tempting thought, luv, but you don't belong to me, and I can't see a reason why any man would let you go."

Ellie kissed him a third time and then pointed toward Takoda. The bandaged man was held up on one side by Avana and on the other by a Japanese woman Caelan didn't know. "My nurturing module tells me Takoda no longer needs me. The same module tells me you do."

For a brief moment, Caelan thought of his beloved Ertha and how he had once believed he'd never meet another android like her, then he smiled again at Ellie. "Aye. That I do, luv. More than you know."

Damon stayed on the hydrofoil with Dylan as they watched the Takoda-Avana reunion. His own reuniting with Dylan at the Flathead lodge three days earlier had been just as joyful, though in Dylan's case, it had come as a complete surprise.

The man who ran the ranch where Dylan had lived the last two years, a man who introduced himself to Damon as Longbow, had told him he kept Damon's impending visit a secret, so as not to upset the other children at the ranch who would never experience such a reunion. In particular, Longbow expressed sensitivity toward Billy Hearns, who had lost all of his family in the torrent of NASF's quest to stop Beacon.

"What do you think, son? Should we go ashore now and join in the fun?"

"Yeah, let's go, Pop. I want to meet the lady with the chips. Which one is she?"

"If I'm not mistaken, she's the one standing with the jakalis and the big Hawaiian. He's the village chief, I think. I'm told his name is Akela."

"Oh…um…maybe I can meet her later…when the jakalis aren't around."

"Son, if we're gonna live here, if she's gonna help you, you're gonna have to get used to being around jakalis sooner or later. Might as well start right now. Besides, Billy's already on the beach talking with that girl. He doesn't look scared to me. Why should we be?"

Turning around in a circle, Akela took in the odd mix of sights: Strangers happily coming ashore the island, Lila standing beside a dozen docile jakalis, a mini-army of Makoas playing with children from the village, Caelan nuzzled up to Ellie, Natti gabbing with the purple-eyed blond boy from the boat.

It was as surreal a scene as Akela could have imagined. Lila must have thought the same, for she said, "Can you believe this?"

"I'm not sure I would have ever *dreamed* of it."

"It won't be all fun and games, you know. We have lots of work to do and plenty of tough days ahead," Lila said.

He looked at Lila and smiled. "You speak the very thoughts in my mind. But, as I told you once before, I have never known a peaceful day in my life. I'll take this one and savor it."

The boy looked nervous but he didn't appear sad to Natti. He eyed her warily as if wavering about whether to approach her. She imagined he was somewhat scared by her purple-splotched skin, balding head and mangled leg. Unfazed by his discomfort, Natti smiled and limped toward him, the gap of her missing teeth on full display. With a lei held in her outstretched hands, she said, "Mahalo, Billy. Welcome to Limahuli."

"Are you Natti?"

"I am. I've been looking forward to meeting you." She layered the lei over his head and then hugged him. "Would you like to meet some of my friends? They're very nice." She pointed toward the Makoas where Kaleo and RJ were goofing around with Bora. "The Hawaiian boy is Kaleo. The other is RJ. He's your age. They both live with me. Now you will too."

"What kind of androids are those? They look like huge Hawaiians."

"They're called Makoas. They protect our village. I fix them up when they break down. Like that one over there. His name is Akecheta. Most people call him Ake, for short. I put together a brand new Makoa body for him out of spare parts we have in our garage. He looks a little rough, but he says he likes it that way."

"You can build an android?"

"Uh, huh. Maybe we can build one together sometime. We have a bunch of leftover parts of some Viper androids. Might be kinda fun. Come on, let's go say hi."

With hands intertwined, they began to walk across the beach, smiles on both their faces.

Sir Bryce Collins' residence
Malibu, California, Pacifica

In the darkness, Sir Collins reclined in his armchair and swirled a glass of Scotch with ice. In front of him, the holonode on the coffee table displayed the glowing, hovering image of Hawkeye. Collins listened as his man inside Beacon finished his update.

"…and so they're all together now on Kauai. I thought it was best to keep them in one place. It will make it easier to monitor them and deal with any unexpected developments."

Collins nodded. "Logical, but I worry about Lila influencing them. She's very good, you know. Very smart."

"I understand, Your Grace, but even if Lila learns of the flaw, she won't decipher its origin, its purpose. To her, it will appear as shoddy craftsmanship."

"Hmm…I wish I had your confidence, Hawkeye. All the same, I think we should take precautionary measures."

"Yes, Your Grace. I will see to it."

"Good, but for heavens' sake, man, don't send in another android army. Someone discreet is preferable. Someone capable of moving in the shadows, a disrupting force for whom assassination is the least attractive option. All we need is time, Hawkeye, just enough for Antoinette's proteins to turn virulent. There are thousands of jakalis wandering around the Northlands with her chip. All we need is for the chain reaction to begin. Once it does, there will be no way Lila Graves, Takoda Wells or anyone else can stop it."

The GODD Chip adventure continues in 2021 with book 2 of the Unity of Four series. To receive updates regarding new additions to the series, follow K. Patrick Donoghue-Novelist on Facebook or join the author's email subscriber list by visiting kpatrickdonoghue.com and clicking on the "Join Email List" link on the main menu.

APPENDIX A

THE GENETIC REVOLUTION

Many historians point to the early 2070s as the beginning of the Genetic Revolution, given this is the timeframe during which the genetic design of embryos vaulted onto the world stage. However, other historians trace the roots of the ruinous era back to the late 2050s, a period when gene replacement therapeutics moved beyond strictly controlled treatments for chronic conditions and became mainstream lifestyle enhancement products.

Hailed as the next leap in human evolution, the Genetic Revolution began with great enthusiasm. Many viewed the ability to manipulate their genetic makeup as a golden ticket to a longer and healthier life. Others saw the genetic tools of the late 21st century as magic wands capable of wiping away inborn deficits as well as the ravages of excess behaviors. When it came to their children, the era began with broad excitement about the ability to design their physical and mental traits.

The euphoria did not last long. By the early 2080s, as the first wave of genetically-designed children entered puberty, unusual mutations began to appear in their "designed" genes. Dubbed *gutations* (pronounced goo-tA-shuns), some of these replacement-gene mutations were benign, others were not. At first, however, the gutations did little to dampen the revolution, but then came the necro outbreak of 2082. A gutation in the regulation of skin immunity caused certain children to develop a pronounced susceptibility to an exotic flesh-eating bacteria. Worse still, the gutation allowed the bacteria to spread to others through saliva, blood and physical contact. As a result, over the following four years, tens of millions perished from necro. And with them went the hope and promise of the Genetic Revolution.

It was the first of several gutation crises that reshaped human existence over the next two decades before genetic design and gene replacement were finally outlawed in 2110. By then, over a billion people worldwide had succumbed to various gutations, related diseases and social unrest.

Today, in 2137, the vestiges of the Genetic Revolution continue to haunt humans, particularly with the rise of Jakali Syndrome in the 2120s. Despite aggressive measures to stamp out the condition, including internment, sterilization and euthanization, a quarter of children entering puberty turn into insane beasts by the time they complete adolescence.

APPENDIX B

THE REALIGNMENT OF NORTH AMERICA

B y the early 22nd century, many countries around the globe had dissolved and reconstituted into new, smaller nations as a consequence of the catastrophes brought on by the Genetic Revolution.

Big countries, population-wise and land-wise, proved too slow to respond to and plan for the onslaught of new gutation outbreaks that occurred between 2082 and the end of the century. The large countries also proved limited in their ability to equitably distribute medical care, food and other supplies to all regions within their countries as the outbreaks multiplied and worsened.

This led to regional infighting and hoarding of resources, restrictions of movement between regions and other parochial actions. As a result, eventually, the citizens of large countries began to view their local regions as their primary allegiances rather than their overarching national affiliation. And with each successive gutation outbreak, their regional alliances hardened to the point where many nations fractured. In the end, citizens cared more about survival than they did national pride.

For example, the United States dissolved its fifty-state union into six smaller nations in 2101. The dissolution occurred with a minimum of bloodshed but did involve a decade of preceding negotiations to establish cooperative treaties and equitably divide Old America's federal resources.

Canada also dissolved around the same time, however, only parts of the country reconstituted. The vast majority of the sparsely populated areas of Old Canada became an ungoverned territory known as the Northlands. The rest of the country merged into three of the six new Old America countries. Those six nations include:

New Atlantia: comprised of the lands east of the Mississippi River and south of the Great Lakes, plus the eastern population centers of Old Canada stretching from Windsor to Quebec City. New Atlantia is the most populous of the Old America spinoffs. Governed by a republic-style system similar to that of Old America, New Atlantia is divided into nine provinces led by governors called prefects. Its population is dominated by the noble and gutant castes.

Carapach: stretching westward from the Mississippi River, Carapach is primarily made up of Old America's Great Plains states, minus New Mexico and Texas to the south. It is home to the largest didgee-caste population in the world and is governed by a democratic council comprised of representatives from its twelve territories.

The country's name is an adaptation of the word Carapace, which in the English language, refers to the hard upper shell of a turtle. The name is a tribute to the original inhabitants of the lands, who referred to the North American continent as *the Great Turtle*, and a fitting description of the character of the lands making up the Great Plains — the backbone, or shell, of the continent.

Texas: as one might presume, the nation of Texas is predominately composed of the Old America state of the same name, though the *country* of Texas also includes the Old American state, New Mexico to the west, and portions of Arkansas and Louisiana west of the Mississippi River. Divided into counties, the territory of the Texas nation is ruled by the legacy democratic system employed by the namesake Old America state. Its population is dominated by the noble and didgee castes.

Pacifica: the lands west of Carapach and Texas form Pacifica, including the Old America states of Washington, Oregon, California, Arizona, Nevada, Utah and Idaho. It also includes a sizeable portion of the Old Canada territory, British Columbia to the north, and the Old Mexico Baja peninsula. It is the second-most populous carve-out from Old America. Its government is based on a parliamentary model. Its population is dominated by the noble and gutant castes.

Alaskon: a merger of the former Old America state of Alaska and the Old Canada Yukon territory. Comparatively sparsely populated versus the other new countries, Alaskon is primarily populated by the didgee and gutant castes and is governed under the legacy legislative assembly system of the former Yukon territory.

Hawaiian Islands: the smallest of the new countries, the Hawaiian Island nation foundered under the weight of jakali and gutant dumping within ten years after the dissolution of Old America and collapsed into an ungoverned territory, which it remains in 2137.

CASTES OF THE 22ND CENTURY

A mong the many consequences of the Genetic Revolution was a mass upheaval of the way societies grouped themselves. Before the revolution, various models existed. There were societies structured on tribal affiliations, religious affiliations, economic status, ethnic origin and birthright castes to name a few of the dominant systems of pre-22nd-century humanity.

The Genetic Revolution changed all of that. With few exceptions, a caste system based on genetic purity became the dominant form of societal organization in the 22nd century. Why? Because human survival demanded it. And, as in any social group, there were winners and losers in this new ordering of status (described below).

Evvies: super-humans whose genetically-designed DNA resulted in a broad range of exceptional physical and mental attributes with no unintended/unexpected mutations. While evvies are societally the highest caste, they are the smallest, population-wise, representing 5% of the world's humans (and declining). The term *evvie* arose as a colloquial name for *evolved ones*.

Nobles: a modest step down from evvies, societally, nobles' DNA alterations resulted in a narrower range of exceptional attributes. As is the case with evvies, nobles have no unintended/unexpected mutations. This caste accounts for 15% of humans.

Didgees: humans with no altered DNA. Whether for religious, ethical or other reasons, didgees and their ancestors declined to genetically design their children and also avoided gene replacement therapies as adults. They are the only "natural" humans left and they comprise 25% of the world's population. The term *didgee* arose as a colloquial name for *indigenous ones*.

Blendas: a big step down from nobles, blendas' DNA modifications resulted in few exceptional attributes. Blendas are also remarkable because their engineered DNA contains at least one benign unexpected/unintended mutation, known as a gutation. Blendas make up 20% of humans.

Gutants: people whose altered DNA resulted in multiple unexpected/unintended mutations. Many of these gutations are benign or are only detrimental to the host gutant. However, some mutations make gutants dangerous to others. Some of these conditions can be deadly, but most can be controlled or cured through medication. At 30% of humans, gutants are the dominant caste, population-wise, but they occupy the second-lowest status due to their genetic inferiority.

In many countries, gutants live among the population of other castes, but they are subject to prejudice and treated as second-class citizens. As a result, many gutants prefer to live in "wild" territories where gutant-only villages are prevalent. In other countries, gutants are banished to internment colonies or cast out altogether, as the remaining castes have no tolerance for their genetic impurities. They fear gutants will mate outside their caste and further despoil the countries' genetic makeup.

In all countries, however, once gutants have been diagnosed as pre-jakalis, they are removed from society. They are either committed to refugee villages where they live until their symptoms become uncontrollable and are euthanized, or they are euthanized upon diagnosis.

Jakalis: a separate caste of gutants whose altered DNA resulted in mutations that produce insanity, physical malformations, and animalistic, murderous behaviors during adolescence – 5% of the world's population (and growing). Pronounced juh-call-Es, the caste was named after the scientist who codified the condition as Jakali Syndrome, Dr. Richard Jakali.

APPENDIX D

THE GODD CHIP

n 2112, Dr. Dyan Mugabe, a Kenyan geneticist, invented a nanochip called the Genetic Oddity Detection Device, or GODD chip, and a complementary set of synthetic smart proteins she named ANPs (adaptive nucleic polymers). In tandem, the two inventions had been developed as a cure for gutations spawned during the Genetic Revolution, but neither the chip nor the proteins ever saw the light of day.

Shortly after Mugabe published her heretical research paper detailing the promising results of a secret, two-year human trial that featured her inventions, she and her research were burned at the stake. Mugabe had violated the International Gene Treaty of 2103, which prohibited gene replacement research, a transgression punishable by death. Over the twenty-five years since her death, her inventions have become nothing more than history trivia and cautionary reminders of what happens to those who defy the genetic research ban.

In the introduction of her paper, Mugabe had passionately stated her case for disregarding the ban:

The notion that we can weed out gutations over time by systematic culling of the afflicted through policies of sterilization and euthanization, supported by programs that discourage interbreeding between genetic castes, is inherently despicable. So, too, is the sickening suggestion by some that we consider mass extermination of gutants to speed up the culling process.

Gutants represent nearly forty percent of the world's population. They deserve access to treatments and cures, not persecution and genocide. Gene replacement therapies can help them if we would only reconsider their potential value.

Yes, mistakes were made in the past. They are well documented by now. We should learn from them and apply the lessons we've learned to create new therapies, not for the purpose of designing children — we now know that is a recipe for disaster — but for the goal of healing those harmed by our past mistakes.

We doctors are always quick to rally around our oath to do no harm, but we did do harm and now we sit on our hands and do nothing to undo the harm we caused. I, for one, will not stand by any longer and watch gutants suffer when I know I can help them.

In layman's terms, the GODD chip was the brain of the gutation repair operation, and the ANPs were the handymen who did the dirty work. ANPs were tasked with detecting gutations, communicating their discoveries to the chip, and then repairing the genes based on instructions relayed back by the chip.

Mugabe's theory behind her inventions was simple. The DNA repair mechanisms in human cells were not well suited to consistently recognizing and repairing mutations of synthetic replacement genes. They needed an intelligent partner who was specifically designed to recognize and resolve flaws in the synthetic proteins used to construct and bind replacement genes.

After all, the cells of the average human replicate nearly *two trillion times every day.* Maintaining the integrity of every DNA base-pair in every gene in every chromosome in every cell during every replication is a seemingly unfathomable task.

To quantify "seemingly unfathomable," there are approximately *three billion* DNA base-pairs that make up the genes in a single cell's twenty-three pairs of chromosomes. Every one of those three billion base-pair connections must be validated every single time the cell replicates. Now, multiply that by two trillion replications each day, three-hundred-sixty-five days a year, over a lifetime and *seemingly unfathomable* takes on a deeper meaning.

Mugabe's inventions were an attempt to provide a backstop, extra pairs of eyes and hands, to help innate cellular validators manage this gargantuan error-checking and repair process. But the world was not ready for the GODD chip and ANPs in 2112.

One wonders if things might have been different had Mugabe introduced her inventions in 2120 when the first rash of jakali gutations swept the globe.

APPENDIX E

ANDROIDS IN THE 22ND CENTURY

A brief history of the rise of androids

Humanoid androids, or andros, are ubiquitous in 2137, primarily as a downstream result of workforce shortages incurred during the disastrous Genetic Revolution of the 2070s. As successive rounds of deadly gutations devastated worldwide human population, androids were rapidly deployed to fill positions of critical need. And once people saw the benefits andros provided, they wanted more of them. In short measure thereafter, androids spread throughout society like computers and smart devices had proliferated in earlier times.

It was a stark contrast to how androids were viewed when "modern" android technology first began to blossom in the early twenty-first century. Indeed, when advanced robotics, human-like exo-features and artificial intelligence applications were first merged into humanoid androids during that era, many decried the new inventions.

Some raised ethical concerns about the spread of sexbots, the first extensive commercial application of humanoid androids. Others saw the introduction of andros in factories and on farms as yet another robotic blow to the availability of blue-collar jobs. Then came the chorus of those unnerved by the creation of android military and police squads. These were but a few of the prominent android debates that raged into the mid-twenty-first century.

Whether alarmed by the possibility of artificial intelligence run amok, loss of jobs, the impact on human behaviors or other concerns, there had been enough of an outcry then to lead governments around the world to enact restrictions on the development and distribution of andros. And while countries varied in the severity of their laws and regulations, the net effect had been a dramatic slowdown in the proliferation of androids, a slowdown that lasted for decades.

The Genetic Revolution and its aftermath largely wiped away the ethical and practical objections to the widespread use of humanoid androids. The need to survive trumped all other considerations. Restrictions on artificial intelligence remained and ethical guardrails for sexual and social mores were also maintained but, in every other respect, the end of the twenty-first century was like the wild west for humanoid androids.

Initially, andros filled gaps in the medical field. With millions dying from exotic diseases spawned by communicable gutations, there were not enough doctors and nurses to treat the infected. Then, as societies began to break down amid the health crises, an urgent need for security personnel developed, leading to an explosion of andros in police and military outfits across the globe. And with much of the world's commerce disrupted during the era, governments saw no choice but to begin subsidizing purchases of android workers by businesses to make sure the businesses could continue to feed, shelter and otherwise support their populations.

Eventually, by the turn of the twenty-second century, andros had gained enough of a foothold to make their presence felt in every aspect of human life. And as societies began to stabilize, ethical debates once again surged. Only this time, the pressures exerted by the world's citizens were aimed at reducing the AI and ethical restrictions governing android functionality and interactions with humans.

Over the next decade, those loosened restrictions led to the development of enhanced AI modules that allowed newly manufactured andros to develop rudimentary sentience and blend more seamlessly into human families and workplaces. These newer models were still "owned" by humans and performed designated tasks on behalf of their owners, but technology refinements had made them increasingly indistinguishable from humans in appearance, deed and thought.

These semi-sentient andros still represent a small minority of the overall android population in 2137, but they are growing in numbers. And despite all the rules and regulations in place to limit their sentience, some of them are beginning to exhibit independent behaviors.

Classes of androids

Much like there were many makes and models of automobiles in the twenty-first century, there were many makes and models of androids in the twenty-second century. Several android models, or classes, were featured in The GODD Chip, including Makoas, Steels, Vipers, Athenas, Apollos and Olympias, but there were many others not mentioned.

Each class of android was designed with certain standard features and some optional features that could be added to or swapped with core features. Also similar to automobiles, android standard and optional features included mechanical, computer and appearance upgrades.

The similarities between autos and andros departed when it came to customization. If you desired to create a clone of yourself, you could do it. Alternatively, if you preferred to replicate the appearance of an idol or a loved one, it was possible so long as you abided by twenty-second-century laws governing likeness trademarks and identity preservation. For the do-it-yourself crowd, you could design your andro from the ground up within the constraints of the andro-class core specs. It was expensive but possible. Most humans, however, chose basic designs offered by the various andro makers or tweaked the features of pre-designed andros in a maker's catalog. If you grew tired of your andro's appearance, voice, skill sets or performance, you could even give them a makeover at your local andro chop-shop.

That said, despite the seemingly boundless possible customizations, each andro class tends to have distinct features which typically make it easy to visually distinguish one class versus another, even when other features are customized.

ABOUT THE AUTHOR

Kevin Patrick Donoghue is the author of the Anlon Cully Chronicles archaeology mystery series, the Rorschach Explorer Missions science fiction thriller series and the Unity of Four medical thriller series. His books include:

THE ANLON CULLY CHRONICLES:

Book 1: *Shadows of the Stone Benders*
Book 2: *Race for the Flash Stone*
Book 3: *Curse of the Painted Lady*
Book 4: *Priestess of Paracas*

THE RORSCHACH EXPLORER MISSIONS:

Prequel: *UMO* (novella)
Book 1: *Skywave*
Book 2: *Magwave*

THE UNITY OF FOUR:

Book 1: *The GODD Chip*

WAYS TO STAY IN TOUCH WITH THE AUTHOR:

Follow K. Patrick Donoghue — Novelist on Facebook, or join the author's email subscriber list by visiting kpatrickdonoghue.com and clicking on the "Join Email List" link on the main menu.

CPSIA information can be obtained
at www.ICGtesting.com
Printed in the USA
FSHW021006030920
73540FS